Gods of the Void

The Empire Marathon: Book 3

By Andrew Valenza

Valenza Publishing

Valenza Publishing LLC.

Schroon Lake, NY 12870

Published 2026

ISBN: 979-8-9919345-6-5

More from Valenza Publishing

<u>Novels</u>

<u>Andrew Valenza</u>

Empire of the Void
Lost World of the Void

Three Short Horror Stories

<u>Ella M. Hayes</u>

Bookends
Witch's Brew

<u>J.T. McGee</u>

Thrall
Enthralled

<u>Jamie Norton</u>

The Second Act Comeback

Children's Books

<u>William Valenza</u>

Bath Time with Teddy
Bubbly
Teddy Bubble and the
Bubble Mops

Comics

<u>Alex Portal</u>

Stories of the American
Revolution: Henry Knox's
Noble Train

Praise for
"The Empire Marathon"

"Truly never read anything like this.."
-Goodreads review for "Empire of the Void"

"Reminded me of the 50's science fiction movies on TV Friday nights when I was a Kid."
-Amazon review for "Empire of the Void"

"Amazing romance, really fun space adventure..."
-Goodreads review for "Empire of the Void"

"Whether you are a science fiction fan or not, this book is a great adventure. I enjoyed every minute reading it.. ready for the next adventure!"
-Amazon review for "Empire of the Void"

"...has all the flavor of early Asimov stories with a little more romance, but all the same intrigue and plot twists."
-Goodreads review for "Lost World of the Void"

"If you're a sci-fi reader, or just want a fun adventurous read that's out of your normal genre, I HIGHLY recommend this!"
-Goodreads review for "Lost World of the Void"

Industry Reviews for "The Empire Marathon"

Dedication

While this series will always be dedicated to my Dad, this book is dedicated to my Mom, my Aunt Patsy, and all the incredible mothers in my life.

When Elizabeth heard Mary's greeting, the baby leaped in her womb, and Elizabeth was filled with the Holy Spirit.

-The Gospel of Luke 1:41

33. Royal Void Outpost-79

A pair of Zar-Meck starfighters, black as the emptiness between stars, escorted the *Silent Horizon* to the moon outpost orbiting above the Great Break, the planetary divide of the jungle world Taranok. As soon as the starfighters were within range, Royal Void Outpost-79's tractor beams locked onto the Earth ship and guided it into the cloaked hangar bay. The Zar-Meck starfighters remained close behind and at the sides, hyper-alert for any sudden actions.

As they passed into the hangar bay, the thin mirage of the bay's cloak wrapped around the *Silent Horizon*, briefly illuminating the cabin and its occupants with its neon blue light.

The three ships touched down in an oddly lifeless hangar. There were two of the larger transport ships on the far side of the hangar, and over a dozen starfighters closer to them, but no imperial officers or the black-armor-clad Zar-Meck foot soldiers anywhere to be found.

When the *Silent Horizon* and its escorts touched down and powered down, a horrible silence ensnared the hangar. It was far from the welcoming party they had expected to be greeted by.

"I have a bad feeling about this, Dex." The words fell delicately from Lieutenant Lacy Prullen's lips.

Dex, her husband and the Captain of the *Silent Horizon*, acknowledged the concern by placing his hand on hers. For the sake of morale, he wouldn't admit he felt the same. "This doesn't change the plan."

He looked from the eerie sight of the seemingly

abandoned hangar to the imperial data tablet docked atop the ship's central console, and input a command.

"Maybe they just didn't expect us so soon," Dex said, trying to comfort his wife-slash-crewmate. He didn't wait for a rebuttal before leaning into the microphone on the command console he'd used often before to record his logs. But this time, the imperial data tablet Lacy had confiscated patched them through directly to the outpost and its speaker system.

He took a deep breath, then spoke boldly for all of the hidden imperials to hear, "This is Captain Dex Prullen of Earth. I have received the Emperor's invitation to return to his planet." He glanced from the left to the right at the Zar-Meck starfighters on either side of him. The preceding skirmish was hard fought, and destined to have brought them here regardless of who ended up winning in the end. Ramps descended from beneath the shining black undercurve of the ships.

"While we are flattered by his interest in us, we must deny his request and instead ask that the Empire leave this planet to the Mok Tau, and all other Mok tribes of Taranok. Please come out into the hangar, unarmed, and with your hands up."

As Dex relayed the message to the outpost's hidden occupants, Lacy tensed in her seat. She could feel anxiety-stricken hearts all around them. There wasn't a single soul in this solar system that had been in their position before. The Mok Tau people had only just learned of other intelligent alien life and the larger Empire only a few months ago. And before the Earthlings came along, none had dared stand up to the Army of the Empire of the Void.

And for her own part, the passenger Lacy had yet to tell Dex about was doing its best to make each morning more and more uncomfortable.

As a platoon, they waited a moment for signs of life; a timid officer poking a head out from behind a doorway, or a squad of Zar-Mecks coming late to the party. But there was nothing.

"Let's try knocking a little louder." Dex shot Lacy a playful side-eye, then glanced down at the already open music library tab on the ship's computer.

Lacy's dimples sank deep as a devilish smile spread across her face. There was still something off about the atmosphere in the hangar, but Dex knew her well, and the request did a little to lift her spirits.

The Empire of the Void got a taste of Earth's jazz music then, as the "Charleston" blasted through all of the speakers of the outpost.

The first blare of the trumpets was accompanied by blasts from the cannons of the Zar-Meck escort ships, firing hot balls of energy down the halls that branched deeper into the outpost. With guns stolen from what was left of the Empire's ground base, Torro-Kaal, Dex, Lacy, and the rest of their squad charged out of the rear of the *Silent Horizon*. The other two Mok Tau squads charged with them from the other Zar-Meck starfighters, in a wide, three-pronged formation, quickly spreading out to the left, center, and right of the hangar bay.

Each group rushed to the nearest cover they could find, anticipating a counter defense of Zar-Mecks and surprised imperial officers. The echo of heavy and rapid footfalls was quickly replaced by the sounds of metal blaster barrels and spears with leaves tied around the top of the staff, dropping onto crates and makeshift barricades. In the midst of the rush, far to the left side of the line, one of the Mok Tau soldiers crashed a few miles an hour too fast into the crates he'd meant to kneel behind, and with the clattering of crates came the distinctive vibrato of a blaster round firing.

Before Dex could issue a command, another soldier from the line, who donned a repurposed Zar-Meck helmet with a red cross painted on the front, rushed over to the clumsy Mok Tau. Dex watched him attend the frog-man in need, and waited for the medic to give back a thumbs up.

After a moment of nothing but the music blaring overhead, Dex rose from his cover, and ran crouching over to the medic and clumsy soldier. "How we lookin', Doc?" he asked.

"Bad burn," the medic said, wrapping the clumsy soldier's leg. "Should wait on ship. Will take care of at village."

Dex nodded, then said to the clumsy soldier, "Well done, private. You earned the first Purple Heart of this war." Then, to the next closest frog-man, "You wait with him on the ship. Go on, move. Help him walk."

As the two walked back to the Zar-Meck starfighter, Dex gave the medic a disbelieving smile and shake of the head. "Boots, huh?"

The medic nodded his agreement, even though he didn't understand the common Earth military term Dex was using to describe new, and oftentimes over-eager, recruits.

Returning to his place in the center of the line, Dex took charge again of the small company. Turning left, he signaled Second Squad's Staff Sergeant Gurg to hold and cover the ships, then turned to Third Squad on the right, led by Staff Sergeant Toork, and signaled to follow behind him with First Squad as they pushed forward.

Both he and Lacy noticed the awkward way the Mok Tau carried their blasters, weapons that were thousands of years ahead of their race but were becoming a necessity for survival far too quickly. Many of the frog-like aliens still carried their traditional tribal spears or daggers, either as a primary weapon or on their persons in some capacity, but Dex insisted they all learn how to use the advanced weaponry. The imperials would make no consideration for a less evolved fighting force. The Mok Tau, along with all the other tribes of Taranok, had to jump headfirst into a new era of warfare.

With just one step into the large hallway that led them away from the hanger, what was already an odd situation felt immediately worse with the hopping music almost teasing the lack of action. It was the cherry on top of their plan, a little extra flair at Lacy's direction. But if that was for nothing, what else was waiting around the corner to mess with their plans for a clean and concise operation?

Dex slashed a hand in front of his throat and said to Lacy, "Kill it. Doesn't work this time, darling."

Lacy feigned a pout and grabbed the data tablet from her belt to silence the song. And once all was quiet again, the dread more easily crept into the air of the perfectly white hallway.

First Squad took another few steps forward down the hall. Without the music, the one bit of personality they'd brought with them, the hallway was totally indistinguishable from the last space outpost Dex and Lacy had been in, Royal Void Outpost-19. The illuminated, slightly curved-at-the-edges hallways lacking markers could have been any part of the entire complex. A quick glance back and forth between where you'd just been and where you're going, the total emptiness and endless uniformity of it, was enough to make one go mad.

"Anything?" Dex whispered to Lacy.

She concentrated deeply, inwardly and outwardly simultaneously. Using a mental awareness of all the organic energy around her, a gift accidentally cast upon her by the Emperor, she searched for hints of hidden imperials.

"Nothing," she said after a moment, unconcerned with her volume. "I don't think there's anyone here."

If it were anyone else, Dex would have shot back with something condemning her assumption. But not when that anyone was Lacy. For one, he knew better than to talk to his wife like that. And for another, her intuition on the subject had been better than most lately.

Lacy continued walking down the hall, running her hand against the wall. Her blaster strapped tightly at her hip, a contrast to Dex's gunslinger-like low hang of his holster.

Somewhere along that wall, she would find a hidden door. Without a Zar-Meck visor or the knowledge of an imperial officer assigned to the outpost, navigation of the place would be nigh impossible, and maybe that was the point.

It was a shame, for the Empire's sake, that the imperials had not planned for someone like the Earth girl who now roamed their halls. Through her fingertips, her flesh connecting with the world around her, her eyes could open to the things unseen. They had previously discovered this phenomenon weeks ago as she tried to understand the data tablet. All of its other users needed special contact lenses to see its hidden screen, but not Lacy. It was convenient, too, with only one set of data tablet lenses.

Dex and the rest of First Squad followed a few paces behind her, with Third Squad a few meters behind them. Even if Lacy had dropped her guard and her weapon, Dex wasn't willing to take risks. Trigger discipline was a foreign concept; his finger remained firm on his blaster's trigger, waiting, hoping someone would pop out from one of the hidden rooms or hallways so he could take a shot at them. There was coldness in his blood; he couldn't deny that, but for what they'd endured at the hands of the Empire? Throughout the planning phase of the mission, he'd convinced himself he could live with it.

"Here." Lacy halted suddenly and pressed her palm against the wall. In her eyes only, a blue seam outlined one of the hidden doors.

Her voice and exclamation of her find caught everyone off guard. How long had they been walking? Searching?

Dex turned to look back toward the hangar bay. At some point in their marching, their path had curved out of the way of a clear line of sight. Now they would be reliant only on comms devices unless the imperials thought better and jammed them. Perhaps that was their plan all along; make the insurgents think they'd fled, then break them up into smaller teams for an ambush. Dex turned back to Lacy and joined her as she opened the hidden door with the data tablet.

The door slid upward with a *hiss* and revealed what looked like an open bay barracks. Bunk beds lined the side walls, with lockers separating each set. Against the back wall was a dining area, and in the center of the room was a simplistic but cozy sitting area.

Dex entered first, checking his immediate right as he crossed through the doorway, looking for hostiles. First Squad's team leader, Sergeant Wrobo, followed nut-to-butt behind him, with his blaster awkwardly held high. He swept to the left and cleared that corner of the room.

Nothing.

Lacy followed after him and swept the far side of the room, then ordered the rest of First Squad to wait outside while Toork led Third Squad on their patrol of the hall.

"Notice anything out of place?" Dex asked when Lacy joined him in the investigation of the bay.

She took her time inspecting the room. Nothing immediately felt off about it. In fact, it wasn't too dissimilar from the barracks she'd stayed in at the Grand Central Space Station, except this bay was slightly tidier. She approached a set of lockers on the right side of the room and opened one.

No lock, she thought.

Again, there was nothing out of the ordinary.

"Maybe they all packed up and left?" she offered. "Planet was a lost cause, and the Emperor was already recalling his forces."

Dex clucked his tongue in thought. "No... No, I don't think so. At least, they didn't pack." He crossed the room to join her. "Look at this. All the uniforms are still here except one," he said, nicking an unoccupied metal hanger. "I'm sure if they were allowed personal items, we'd find those left here, too. No, they weren't recalled. Either they're still here somewhere, or we're surrounded by ghosts."

The last word hit hard, the image of the Emperor's court of phantasms forced itself into her mind.

Ghosts. That was the last thing she wanted to think about now, and ever more.

"Personal items," she said, not sure herself if it was meant to be a question or not, then nodded toward the sitting area. "If no personal items, nothing to occupy themselves, why the pleasure of a living area? Where's the fun in sitting and staring at each other in your downtime?"

Dex inspected the area; four long, short mattresses, and a coffee table with a circular silver centerpiece on top.

"See, I don't think this is for downtime." He knelt beside the table and noticed a button on the side of the centerpiece.

Lacy saw where his eyes were drawn. Her lips parted to warn him not to touch it, but she was a moment too late.

Dex pushed the button, and the room went dark.

She jumped forward a half step, then stopped when the centerpiece showed off its purpose in a horrible scarlet display.

An image of the Emperor loomed over them in the center of the room. Lacy's heart froze seeing that featureless golden face again. As if knowing where its viewer was, the Emperor was facing Lacy. The eyes that weren't there glared at her, condemning her for her escape from his clutches. And though she knew it wasn't really happening, her mind told her that the Emperor's arm was beginning to rise so as to reach out and take her by the throat. Lacy had to stifle a sudden coughing fit from breathing in too fast, and nearly fell back a step.

Dex stepped around the short table. As he did, the Emperor followed him like the eyes of an old painting in a haunted house. But from Lacy's perspective, the image never moved away from her.

"So, this is what they do when they're not on duty?" Dex paced around the Emperor, never breaking contact from the face that seemed to harden the longer they stared at each other. "Eat, sleep, and pray." He waited in vain for Lacy to add a comment. When she didn't, he said, "But I'm sure if we wander around long enough, we'll find a gym, too."

Still nothing from the woman pressed tightly against the wall locker.

Dex didn't need her to tell him what was going on

in her mind, out loud or through their mental connection. He swiped at the projector, casting it from the table. The Emperor fled the room in the blink of an eye, and the lights returned to normal.

Dex then closed the distance between himself and Lacy in three long strides and slowed his movements just before taking her arms so as not to completely overwhelm her.

"Hey," Dex whispered. "You still with me?"

Lacy's eyes were still where the Emperor's hadn't been. It took her a moment, and a quick shake from Dex to bring her back into the room.

"I... Yes. *Yes*. Sorry, I-"

"Don't," Dex offered with a faint smile and brushed her cheek with the backs of his fingers. "Never tell me you're sorry. Not when you've done nothing wrong. It's okay... We're okay."

Lacy shot a glance at where the Emperor had been, then back to Dex. "I'm okay," she agreed.

"You still my girl?" he asked.

Lacy nodded. "Still your girl."

"Guppy kiss." Dex puffed his cheeks up for their special kiss.

"Not now, Dex." Lacy tried to hold back a giggle and rolled her eyes.

But Dex pressed, leaning in and acting like he was about to suffocate.

She put her hands on his chest, pushing him away an inch, and dropped her head toward the open doorway. Sergeant Wrobo and another of the frog soldiers were looking in on them. She almost cut off the moment entirely, but felt Dex's fingers just next to her chin, turning her face back toward him, cheeks still puffed.

There was no point in fighting it. The attempt alone was enough to bring her spirits back, and that was worth a reward.

Lacy puffed her cheeks to match him, and they both

blew out as their lips met.

"Guppy kisses," they whispered together.

"Now, come on, girly. What say we get back to the mission?"

She nodded, blushing. A little added resolve reemerged in her spirit.

After taking that brief moment for themselves, Dex stepped away, exiting the barracks, and tapped Wrobo on the shoulder. Lacy stayed behind for a moment to search for a terminal to which she could hook up her data tablet. Dragging her hands across the wall and inspecting every individual room on the outpost was far too time-consuming. If they could get a map, though, they might all earn weekend leave.

Soon enough, she found a slot in the side of the table in the center of the room and slid the data tablet into it. The information Lacy searched for transferred from the station's network to the tablet and moments later, with a map downloaded, Lacy rejoined the rest of the squad outside the barracks and led the way again down the hall. This time with a solid sense of direction.

"There's an elevator just over here," she announced to the squad.

"Any activity?" Dex asked.

"It's only a map, darling. But if there's any radio chatter, I'm getting nothing."

Dex harrumphed, then called through his communication device to Toork. "Frog Man 3, this is Frog Leader. Report. Any sign of hostiles?"

He could feel Lacy's stern, accusing side-eye. *We are NOT using that as a code name*, she had told him during the planning of the mission.

Why not? It's not like they care. They don't even know what a frog is.

Well, I do, and I think it's mean.

The Mok Tau didn't argue it. Dex had gotten to them first and told them it was a compliment where they came from before Lacy could tell them the truth.

A scratch of static was received by Dex's comm device, then Toork's gravelly, broken English, "No HAH-stills. We find split paths. Team split. Cover more ground. Sar-gant Jurrnup lead other team."

"*No.*" Dex cut in. "Stop, do not split up. I say again, do not split up. Regroup with First Squad. We've acquired a map. We'll reconvene and figure out a new plan from here."

As he gave the last order, Lacy held up a hand and gave a soft, "Shhhhhh..." Then, through her mind, warned him, *this could still be a trap.*

"If it were a trap, they missed their best chance to spring it," Dex rebutted.

The Mok Tau of First Squad tried to hide their confusion toward Dex's sudden response to, as far as they could all hear, nothing. They all understood there was something about Lacy, some sort of mystical power that connected her with the other human, and that she could affect them with a touch of her hand on their bare flesh, but the extent of her powers and how they came to be were far beyond their comprehension. As such, they would not speak of it out loud. These two were aliens who had overpowered their god and had now brought them to the stars. It was not their place to question Dex, and especially not Lacy with her extraordinary powers.

A moment later, Toork and Third Squad joined them in the hall by the elevator. They cleared the next closest room, the mess hall by the looks of it, then the leaders studied the map while First Squad pulled security, and Third looked for supplies they could take back to the village. On one of the walls on the right side of the room was a monitor that stood as tall as the room itself, and next to it was a terminal. As it was, only Lacy and Dex could see her data pad's screen. Not ideal for planning with a team.

Using the mess hall's terminal and monitor, they were able to display the map to their team without the need for the tablet's contact lenses. The map itself revealed the entire outpost's floor plan, a complex much denser than the simple repetitive nature of the endless halls let on. One step down the wrong avenue, and it could be impossible to navigate out.

At the moment the map appeared, Dex straightened and asked no one in particular, "What the hell is all this?"

The text on Lacy's data pad had always been readable, a wonder of the universe that characters in the Empire's part of the universe were the same as the English alphabet, but not something they dwelt on. Call it luck. But the characters on the map had been far from English, somewhere between traditional characters and hieroglyphics.

Lacy felt the same confusion as Dex. "Where's Robbie when you need him?"

Dex restrained himself from pointing out that it was her idea to leave him behind. *For his safety*, she had rationalized.

As he studied the text, Lacy offered, "Encryption?"

He shot her a glance as if to say, 'Go on.'

A faint smile, a *thank you for the confidence*, and then "Special lenses are needed for the data tablets. If I were in charge of security measures around here, this is what I would do to protect information when meant to be viewed by wider audiences. That is, wider audiences with the right clearance."

Dex eyed Toork and Jurrnup. "You guys understand this?" He jerked his head toward the screen, and they both shook their heads. *Primitive*, he told himself, not acknowledging that he didn't have a leg up on them either way.

"I don't think they would, or most people in the Empire," Lacy said. "That'd defeat the point of encryption."

Dex started believing he was picking up what she was putting down. "A secret language, then?"

"Something only the officers and Zar-Mecks understand."

Harrumph "They don't make it easy, do they?" Dex nudged Toork.

The Mok Tau squad leader surveyed Dex, then Lacy, looking for the right response to the earthman's strange question. "They are… what is it… rat bass-tard. Yes?"

Lacy chucked, and Dex outright laughed. "That's right, Sergeant. That's right. An empire full of rat bastards."

You're teaching them profanity now? Lacy sent the thought to Dex.

Irrelevant. Back to the mission?

Roger, sir. Changing gears and tone, Lacy began again, "Elevators are too small for more than a team to ride at a time and can only be accessed with one of these." She tapped the tablet. "And without it, most rooms will be impossible to see and hard to access."

Dex rubbed his chin in thought. How long had it been since he shaved? A month now? He hadn't felt that much hair on his face since… well, since ever, come to think of it. He physically couldn't grow a beard as a teenager (a decent one anyway), and once he turned seventeen, the Army wouldn't even let him try.

Under his breath, he said, "We're supposed to be doing science out here." Then, before anyone could take in what he meant, he announced, "We'll break up into our teams. Lieutenant, you with First Squad, Team Two; myself with Team One. Sergeants Toork and Jurrnup, you take your teams." The teams Dex had established with the Mok Tau tribesmen were meant to resemble a similar structure to the formations he and Lacy were familiar with back on Earth. With only their Mok Tau contingency, not joint forces from the other tribes, there was barely even a full platoon element, yet Dex still regarded himself as the Platoon Leader. Calling himself the Company Commander would be a step too far. Having only two officers and three Staff Sergeants in their platoon, they had the leadership capabilities for four squads, but only the manpower to fill three. Then within those three, there should have been two five-man teams in each squad, each with a medic, but with only three medics, they had to pull overtime for each of their respective squads' teams. And now, with an already understaffed platoon element, they were further down two soldiers. Dex took solace in the fact that, at the very least, he had reliable non-commissioned officers in Staff Sergeants Toork, Gurg, and (at times) Jurrnup. One day, he often told himself, they might have enough soldiers to warrant a Sergeant Major of the Taranok army.

"Lieutenant," Dex went on, "you'll take the elevator and head straight for the command deck. Find that manifest and get back to the ship. Toork, I want your team to hit this floor." He pointed to another section of the map, and then another as he addressed Jurrnup. "Your team takes this one. Three rooms, maximum, then return to the ship."

"Hold on, Dex. What are these?"

"It's a guess, but by the size and shapes of these rooms, Toork's team will hopefully find an armory. Look at this. At the end of the day, the Empire's not far off from Earth. These two rooms look strikingly similar to the indoor range and armory on Grand Central. This section with these tiny rooms should be familiar with how long we were both stuck in them. Don't think we need to revisit them. And down here," he shot a look from Lacy to Jurrnup, letting him know this was Jurrnup's target they were discussing, "I've been in this room before. Looks about the right size, and there's an antechamber for viewing surgeries. This is their medical area."

"That's a lotta guesswork," Lacy challenged.

Dex shrugged. "Any thoughts?"

"Where will you be?"

"I wanna find out what happened to this ghost ship. I'll take my squad on patrol."

Lacy slumped on the table they surrounded, staring down at the tablet, then looked back up at Dex and around the small ring of the leader's meeting. "We've only got one of these toys. How do you expect to get in anywhere?"

Another sigh from Dex. "This is why I kinda wish there was a fight. I thought we'd have a dozen of these little boxes by now." He crossed his arms across his chest and slowly flexed, wondering if Lacy would notice the subtle way he tried to show off. All that time in the jungle was starting to pay off, he hoped. "Brute force," he offered. "If we keep an accurate pace, count our steps, the doors should be easy to find. Once we're there, I'm sure we can find a way to knock them down." He shot a look at Toork.

In the Squad Leader's bag were homemade hand grenades, made from the volatile yellow gelatins that occupied the jungle.

A playful smile cracked the edge of Lacy's lips.

"Empire sure won't be able to hide any longer once those go off," Lacy warned.

"That is the hope," Toork chimed in. "Defeat Torro-Kaal not enough for Mok Tau. 'Mpire make my people suffer too long. Mok Tau want to fight. They run away, not good for us."

"This isn't about revenge, Toork," Lacy tried to gently remind him, but Dex interjected his own thoughts.

"You think they ran away?" He asked with genuine curiosity, not a challenge.

Toork looked around their circle. All eyes were on him, including those of some soldiers from the other squads.

"They not here," he said. "They do not ambush. Gone." He waved his entire arm to emphasize his stance. "We show strength at battle of Torro-Kaal. They fear us then, but we catch'd them by the surprise. They attack us back, but still we take them, and their sky ships. Now they true fear us. We go back to Torro-Kaal on raid, but they not put up fight. 'Mpire know better now. 'Mpire know not mess with Mok Tau."

Dex nodded in partial agreement. "Maybe, Sergeant. Maybe. You're right about one thing; I also don't think they're here. But I'm worried it's not because we scared them off. The battles have been fierce, I won't take that away from you, but the Empire is much stronger than you think. Our strength and our resilience continues to catch them off guard and we got lucky. It's something the lovely Lieutenant and I have made a habit of. But there's no more of that. Luck's gonna start running out fast, and they'll be more alert now. If they left, it's not for any reason I'm on the edge of my seat to figure out."

"Recalled, then." Lacy eyes were locked downward, staring into space. The idea had been dismissed in their conversation prior, but the more they discussed explanations, the more it felt like the only possibility.

Dex leaned back, this time more willing to hear her out. "Go on..."

"Maybe it was that we *did* scare them. Him. The Emperor. We showed him that there is a world that could slip through his fingers. That won't do when you demand total submission..." She paused and swallowed hard.

For a brief moment, Lacy appeared as if her mind was somewhere else entirely. Her starry eyes shimmered ever so slightly before she returned to her thoughts.

"He'd want to wipe the slate clean. Erase all evidence of his working here. Any witnesses, too."

"But why the recall? If troops are already here, send them in as a strike force. Seems like a waste of resources, all that transport back and forth," Dex said with a hint of levity in his voice, as if it were easy to doubt the Emperor's ability to destroy.

"I wish I had an answer for that one, darling."

"Well, he wouldn't have just up and left. There's gotta be something going on." Dex studied Lacy's face, considering the flash that had been in her eyes, then turned to the others. "What do you two think? Does Taranok have a book of revelations you can share with us?"

Blank stares gazed back at him from Toork and Jurrnup.

"End of days stuff, you know. God's wrath coming down on you from the skies."

Toork and Jurrnup exchanged something in their native tongue, then Jurrnup answered, "There..." he struggled to find the right word, then shook his head and said, "No end. But some fear we bring dead to home. Mok Tau turn from god."

Toork cut in. "Mok Tau told to wait for the Red God. Red God save us from Torro-Kaal, or Black Fire punish." He paused, letting Dex and Lacy dwell on what he'd said, then continued, "But Toork not worried. We see what the Red God is. We fight his warriors and crush them!" His words had riled up some of the other Mok Tau in the room, the ones that had broken out of Torro-Kaal and fought off the Zar-Mecks dressed in black and their laser guns.

A small contingency, including Jurrnup, did not share the enthusiasm. There was only a look of mild discomfort on Jurrnup's wide face.

The comparison of mythical imagery and the real-life foe was simple enough for Dex to connect, but Lacy saw something else.

Her mind reeled at the man in Zar-Meck armor who had absorbed the flames of the exploded generators and been enwrapped by them. A picture invaded her mind of him on the Great Break, as they destroyed the planetary roots. The explosion felt large enough to shake the planet, but it was only more flame, more energy, more feed for the Emperor's warrior. She could see him emerging from the Great Break, the flames still radiating from him. A black flame. God's wrath. The Emperor's Wrath.

"Lacy," Dex's voice interrupted her thinking. "Are you still with us?"

She felt unnerved at her mind's wandering thoughts, but once he spoke up, she felt queasy. "I'm sorry... I think I just need a drink."

Dex turned his head up toward the back of the mess hall, the kitchen, and whistled, garnering the attention of the warriors there. "Someone find some water. The Lieutenant needs a drink." He too wished he could have a drink. Although, he wanted something stronger than water, but not as strong as the ceremonial Mok Tau wine that was quite literally powerful enough to fuel the *Silent Horizon*.

Toork continued as if nothing had happened. "There will be no end day for Mok Tau and Taranok. Black flames myth, Mok Tau trust nothing Red God say. Red God weak, and we strong."

The look on Jurrnup's face said he didn't necessarily agree.

"Something to add?" Dex asked the wary team leader.

A quick look from Toork to Dex, then, "No, Captain. Sar-gan Toork right. They are gone. But I do not know if for good. I say we get back to missun."

Dex nodded, but it was Lacy who spoke. "I agree. We need to get moving."

Within the next few minutes, Dex, Toork, and Jurrnup mapped out their targets, determining accurate pace counts to the hidden doors they would be bursting through. At the same time, two of the warriors from Toork's team were sent back to the ships with supplies raided from the mess hall. There was sure to be a very fine banquet that night, and possibly for many more nights to come.

Before long, the teams were split up and moving with purpose toward their targets.

Lacy led her small team of five to the nearest elevator. Their task would be the easy one.

There were no buttons in the elevator, and she didn't have the same access to it as the Zar-Mecks did. By her recollection, the Zar-Mecks could tap the wall itself and be brought exactly where they wanted to go.

The data tablet, though, solved that problem.

One press of a button and they dropped down deep into the outpost, to the core of the moon, and fell into the central orb that rotated in their direction before shooting them back up another elevator shaft.

The Mok Tau pressed against the glass walls of the elevator, amazed by their speed and the inner workings of the Empire's outpost.

Lacy had less interest than the rest of her team. She'd been on this ride before, and this time, her focus was on the speed-distance of the elevator.

Eight seconds to the core. Three to rotate.

When the elevator door opened again, it looked like they hadn't gone anywhere. The hallway was exactly the same as all of the others, just this time without any sign of Dex or the others. And in this part of the outpost, that wasn't a mess hall on the other side of the hall.

The command deck was nearly identical here to the one inside Torro-Kaal. It was a domed, two-story room with a large, pitch-black operations table in the center, with the second story twenty feet above. Surrounding the walls of the first level was a ring of computers, desks, and display screens. The second floor had another smaller ring of workstations. Light poured in from the ceiling, a display of the Taranok's face from the outpost's surface (Lacy knew they weren't on a high enough floor within the outpost for it to be a real window), giving the second floor a look that conveyed its intended purpose was traffic control.

And that's our target.

If their predictions — hers and Dex's — were right, a key step in loosening the Empire's grip on the universe was waiting on one of those computers.

"You three, please stay down here. Grup, would you mind accompanying me up there?"

Private Grup ribbited his acknowledgment. They crossed the room together, passing by the black table. Drawing closer it resembled the data tablet in Lacy's hand. She slowed down as she walked along it and noticed a series of notches in its edges, just big enough to slide the tablet in.

"Hold on," she said to Grup. "I wanna check this out."

She slid the tablet into the notch, and a green grid appeared on the tabletop. The base and sides of the grid were labeled with more characters in the Empire's text. Lacy's data tablet showed an image of the moon, with hangars and ground entrances marked. She tapped the hangar they had landed in, and on the grid appeared a map of the area. Within the grid coordinates that included the hangar were ten small yellow dots, one large yellow square, and over a dozen blue squares. Lacy recognized them as the squad of Mok Tau, the *Silent Horizon*, and the commandeered Zar-Meck starfighters, respectively.

Intrigue guided her finger to a different section of the outpost. Dex's location. Had his team found their target yet? Lacy pulled up the map on her data tablet and rotated through areas she expected Dex to be within the outpost.

The table grid adjusted, showing her selected chunks like blueprints. Each one was blank save for the digital green lines that made up the walls of the outpost.

"Where are you, Dex?" she breathed.

"Loo-tent. The Cap-tain says we move fast." Grup whispered the insistence, much to Lacy's appreciation. She still was no fan of overplaying the Army roles like Dex was, but she appreciated the respect of not being called out loudly in front of the others for getting distracted.

"Of course," she said with a soft smile. "We're here for a reason."

Lacy tapped on one last area before giving up and said a quick prayer of terrified gratitude when the bright blue display appeared on the table. She nearly threw herself away from the table and reached for her comms device.

"Dex! Come in, Dex! Do you read me?"

The ten-second period it took for Dex to respond felt like a lifetime.

"Say again, who is this, and who are you trying to reach? Is this Frog Man 2 calling Frog Leader?"

Lacy's cheeks flushed with annoyance. "Now's not the time. There are hostiles still here. Third level. Well over a hundred."

* * *

"Hey, lock it up back there!" Dex shouted at his team, who were very effectively destroying huge towers of machinery. Their plan of attack: check every room for enemies and destroy anything that looks important to the enemy. It now seemed that Lacy had achieved one of her team's goals. "Are you safe? Lacy, where are you?"

Through the comms, she said, *"My team is fine. We made it to the command room, and I can see everything. I'm looking... here. I see you now. You're one floor above them, about five hundred feet away."*

A hundred hostiles, Dex thought. *Not great odds, but we could set a trap.*

He addressed the Mok Tau. "Everyone on me. We've found the enemy. How many grenades we got left?"

One of the privates checked their pouch. "Three Cap-tan."

It wasn't optimal, but some damage could still be done.

Back into the comms, he asked, "Lacy, can you tell me anything else? Can you see what they're doing?"

"Negative. There's no movement. They're all just gathered together."

"I hear you. We'll check it out."

As soon as his finger was off the call button, Lacy responded with, *"Don't! Please, there's no need. I don't think they know we're here yet. Let's just finish the mission and get out."*

Dex nodded for his team to move toward the hall and mouthed, *Let's move.* "We're going to take a look. We will not engage. Just wanna know what's going on here."

* * *

She watched as the five yellow dots representing Dex's team drifted closer to the blue enemy dots.

"De-... Captain, I say again, do not engage. Please."

"So we're using 'Captain' now?" She heard him laugh through the comms.

"Sir, I'm serious." Lacy's fingers tightened around the small device.

The yellow dots dropped a floor and were only three hundred feet from the room full of enemies.

She pleaded, "Turn back now. We'll meet you at the ship in five minutes."

"They already know we're here," Dex's voice rang through with confidence. Not a hint of fear or caution. She could picture him walking with swagger, hand hovering above the blaster hanging from his hip like a gunslinger, down the hall to face whoever was waiting for them. *"These comm signals aren't exactly secure. Just be glad I haven't said anything reserved for the hut."*

God, I hope *he's walking into a trap.*

"No, ya don't." His voice again on the comm. Lacy was getting better at keeping her thoughts to herself after discovering the events in the Emperor's court had changed some things in her, but at times her more emotionally driven thoughts were picked up by Dex. Presumably, they could have been by other humans, too, if they had been close enough to hear her.

"Dex..." his team's yellow dots hovered just on the other side of the wall from the blue dots.

Before she could resort to begging, Dex came through.

"Holy hell, darling... look at this..."

* * *

Rows upon rows of Zar-Meck soldiers stood in formation. Hundreds of eyes behind the thin purple visors stared Dex and the Mok Tau down, but none of them moved. None of them raised the weapons they held at the low ready.

Lacy's angered and terrified voice blared from the

comm, to which Dex promptly turned the volume down, but not off. Were the Zar-Mecks awake? What was the deal?

Dex and the Mok Tau warriors stepped closer to the formation.

Still no movement from the Zar-Mecks.

A faint purple line from the visor lit up Dex's face as he leaned in to inspect one of the Zar-Mecks. Behind the visor, he could just barely see the eyes of the man behind the mask. They were open and empty as ever. They reminded Dex of photographs of lobotomy patients. Those people were alive, sure, but there wasn't anything resembling life going on in their heads. The skin too, he recalled, though he couldn't quite tell through the thin slit of the visor, was the palest white he'd ever seen.

They surely couldn't be real people. This sleeping formation wouldn't make sense if they were, and why would they be left behind while everyone else was gone? Robots maybe? But then why all the trouble of making them look human — *Or taourun, I suppose,* he thought, considering the near-human alien race that populated the Empire — if they would just be covered with a separate set of armor?

"What are you without the armor?" Dex asked the Zar-Meck. If they could safely remove the armor without waking up the rest of the formation, it'd be one more mystery of the Empire solved, as well as a spare suit of armor for the Mok Tau to don in battle. In fact, they could try to get a dozen suits — if only they had the time here to do so — and have a fully outfitted battalion of armored Mok Tau.

A crash disrupted the near silence in the room from Dex's right. He spun to the sound with his blaster raised.

One of the Mok Tau privates, whose name Dex hadn't locked into memory yet, was crouched over a Zar-Meck, sprawled out on the floor. The private's spear was lodged in its face.

"What the hell are you doing, private?" Dex dropped his blaster to the low ready.

The private shot a weary look at his captain and

yanked the spear from the Zar-Meck's face. The gut-hooked spear tore a greater chunk out of the face than the entry wound had created. If there ever was a face more than eyes under that mask, it'd be impossible to tell now.

"They easy target. We kill them now," the private said.

While that had been the plan from the start, and the Geneva Convention probably didn't apply this far from Earth's solar system, killing the enemy while they weren't even in the fight still felt wrong.

"Get up, private. That one's your bag now. Let's get him back to the ship." He pointed at one of the other privates, instructing him to help carry the body, while the others planted explosive charges around the room. The frog soldier had made a mess of the body, but if Dex were to study the Zar-Mecks, this one was now the least likely to wake up and fight back.

Dex turned his comm device volume back up and was met immediately with Lacy's worried cries.

"Dex! *Dex, what is going on? Can you hear me? Are you okay?*"

"Yes, darling, yes. I read you. We're fine. We're all fine down here, everything's fine. How are you?"

* * *

"What's going on? I saw someone disappear." Lacy almost cracked the comm device, her fingers wrapped so tightly around it.

The nerve of that man to have shut her out like that.

"*Yeah, some of our amphibious friends have a bit of a trigger finger. But we found the enemy. Doesn't seem like they're in the mood to fight today. We're bringing one of them back to the ship.*"

She began to protest, but Dex kept going, anticipating what she was going to say.

"*Don't worry, it's safe. He's missing a bit of his face, so*

I don't think he'll put up much of a fight."

Lacy loosened her grip on the comm. She watched as five yellow dots exited the Zar-Meck room and returned the way they had come.

"Don't do that again, Dex. I can't take that kind of stress right now."

She heard his laugh through the comm. *"I don't think intergalactic warfare is the right career path for you, then."*

She was done, totally done with this back and forth. "I'll see you back at the ship. We'll be there in ten."

As she was about to put the device away on her belt, Dex steadied her hand. *"You still love me, right?"*

Lacy threw her head back and took a deep breath. *He just loves testing my patience, doesn't he?*

"Come ooooon..."

She breathed out. No matter how annoying he could get, they'd never deny their hearts to each other. "From one end of the universe to the next."

A chuckle, then, *"That's what I like to hear. We'll meet you at the ships."*

Lacy dropped the comms device on the table and rubbed her temples. The things she loved about him were, at the same time, his most insufferable attributes.

"Loo-tent oh kay?" Grup nudged Lacy.

"Yes... Yes, Grup. Just dandy."

"Oh kay. We do mission now?"

Lacy perked up. Her eyes shot toward the floor above them. "Yes, let's move." The operations table was merely a display for the inputted tablet, and wouldn't have the information they were looking for. She took one last glance at the grid before removing her data tablet from the table. Dex's team's dots had disappeared completely. The ground shook below her feet, and a quarter of the blue dots disappeared, too. The ones that remained stayed perfectly still.

The computers and workstations of the command

deck's upper level had accumulated a fair level of dust. Whatever happened here, Lacy knew, hadn't been recent. She blew the dust from one of the computer's slots and inserted her data tablet.

The computer screen lit up with encrypted text.

"Damn!" Lacy cursed the Empire. After all they'd been through, they couldn't get just one easy win on the Empire's dollar? One freebie?

As if that was how the universe worked.

She searched around the station for a data tablet port. If her encryption idea was right, everything on the computer should be displayed legibly on her tablet.

If only I could figure out how to download it, too!

Part of her wanted to curse herself out for not studying up on her Empire of the Void military tactics prior to the mission. Having a modern army with a full Information Operations section on par with Earth's would have come in handy for their assault. But there was no turning back now. Earth's coordinates were erased, and the best they could do intelligence-wise for their small army was the first-hand experience of two outsiders and a tiny robot that used to work with the Empire's kitchen staff who didn't even know how to cook, for that matter.

"Loo-tent, is you oh kay?"

Grup's words shocked Lacy into alertness. How long had she been staring at the screen, waiting for an answer to appear?

"Yes! Yes, sorry. I just… trying to figure this out."

"Must be quick. We go back to flyer soon."

"Yes, you're right. Let me just…" She searched the area again, looking for a port for the data tablet and found it above the computer. Once inserted, the solution presented itself. Not to the extent she was hoping for, but she would take what she could get. An unspecified download of recent information.

When the download was complete, Lacy rounded up her squad, placed half of their supply of grenades around the room, and then retreated to the elevator. Coming out on the other side of the outpost, Grup placed the rest of the grenades along the walls, and they sent the elevator back toward the command deck.

Lacy counted eight seconds and then triggered the explosives.

They felt the floor shake beneath their feet, assured that the damage was done. Even if the imperials returned to the outpost, it would take quite a while to be fully operational again.

* * *

Dex and the rest of the squad were waiting for them at the ships. Lacy noticed the vast array of new weapons, tools, and food crates the Mok Tau were loading onto the Zar-Meck starfighters.

"Think we've got enough goodies?" Lacy teased Dex.

Dex glanced over his shoulder at the crates being loaded onto the ships. "Enough to take some stress off of the hunters for a few weeks. And I don't think we'll have any serious kron-kaal or hyper-raptor attacks for a little while."

Lacy gave him a look that questioned if there was more to his thinking.

Under his breath, as he didn't want to give the Mok Tau something to worry about, "...and we'll have an upper hand if there are any holdouts in Torro-Kaal."

Lacy was taken aback at the comment. Not because she disagreed, of course, but to her it sounded "Unlikely there are any left, but that's very optimistic of you."

He shrugged. "I'm working on it." He kissed her cheek and said, "I've got a pretty good reason to keep my chin up."

She blushed and lost the next thought she'd meant to voice.

Dex carried on. "Find everything all right?"

Lacy glanced down at the data tablet hanging on her belt. "Let's hope."

34. Home Away From Home

It only took a few weeks after the battle at Torro-Kaal for the Mok Tau village to be totally unrecognizable from how Dex and Lacy found it when they first arrived on Taranok. The village was fuller with the return of all the lives that had been liberated from the imperial work camp. The hunting parties were both larger and more relaxed, as imperial food reserves were integrated into their diets. The walls of the village were better fortified with the supplies gathered from Torro-Kaal, protected not by spears, but by weapons of pure energy. And, most importantly, the huts were filled with life again as fathers and brothers were welcomed home after years of captivity. Names of the ones previously lost were unburied from memory, and they shared stories of happier days.

The truth of their escape from Torro-Kaal was quickly exaggerated beyond the hit-and-run strategy Dex and Lacy had executed. At nighttime, the veterans of the escape told their families of how Dex had single-handedly taken on a dozen of their captors with naught but his bare hands, and how Lacy walked unscathed through flames as her enemies burned behind her. That part was a little more true, but they still felt the need to embellish. The paintings inside the tribal chief Roak's temple were even painted over, with Dex and Lacy standing over a collapsing Torro-Kaal, and the warriors raised their fists and spears to them in triumph. The reverence they had garnered since first landing only grew with each day. And who could blame the villagers? Dex and Lacy had come from the stars and destroyed both their fears and their god. Something had to replace both.

In the streets they attracted stares of awe and respect. More often than not, the reverent looks were accompanied by praise much stronger than a "thank you for saving my son." The Mok Tau would fall to their knees and attempt to kiss their hands. Lacy had found the right way to dismiss them before they had the chance to turn a brief exchange into a spontaneous public prayer session. Dex, though...

He was still working that part out. His comfort was with his soldiers, whom he was grateful only listened to him as a military leader, and the time alone with Lacy in their hut after long days like this one.

Those were the moments he thought of as the *Silent Horizon* returned from its mission and flew in across the treetops that hid the village. With a quick check-in with the recently established ground control center, a newly erected hut manned by two of the Mok Tau with stolen imperial equipment, a patch of tree coverage was pulled back to reveal a landing zone. The Mok Tau managed to keep the Zar-Meck starfighters in the air, as long as it was only simple maneuvers, but entry and exit from the landing zone had to be done with the help of a slave signal sent out from Lacy's imperial data tablet.

Lacy closed out of the electronic book she was reading on one of the monitors and began the routine of powering down the ship as they touched down. Dex was immediately on his feet to take control of the riled-up Mok Tau in the cabin. The thrill of hurting the Empire and the terror of flying hadn't mixed well with their nerves.

"Quiet. Quiet, guys! Out! Just get out of the ship," he ordered. "Cool down out in the woods. Let off that steam. And hey! Weapons! Never leave your weapons unattended. How many times do I have to tell you? Lacy, can you-"

"On it." She cut him off, opening the airlock in the rear of the ship.

The Mok Tau rushed out and leapt into the trees like an explosion bursting from the ship.

Dex stood at the top of the airlock steps, watching

them scatter, then surveyed the area around the landing zone for another one of their friends.

"You'd think Robbie would be here to greet us, huh?" he mused.

The engine's whir ceased, and Lacy called from the helm, "What was that?"

Dex retreated, closing the airlock behind him to avoid prying eyes. It'd become a hassle as of late to get any sense of privacy. "Robbie," he said again. "He's not here."

Lacy shrugged. "And?"

"Just... odd. D'you think he's mad?"

Lacy spun in her seat with a playful look in her eyes. The look that always told him not a damn thing in the world could bother her. "Robbie? Mad? Don't be silly."

He slowly leaned against the starboard bunk's frame. "He did seem, maybe not mad, but offended when you told him he wasn't allowed on the mission."

Lacy waved away the remark. "I'm sure he's understanding and holds no ill will against us. We got along just fine without him."

"May have been easier with him. Those encryptions weren't exactly a fun surprise."

She rolled her eyes, but her smile never dropped. She then returned to what she was doing at the console and a moment later grunted in modest frustration.

Dex continued, not hearing her quiet exclamation. "Look, I'm not arguing, I think it was the right move to leave him behind. For his sake, at least."

It stole her attention again from the task at hand. A glimmer in her eye told him it was the right thing to say to make sure he stayed on her good side. She cocked her head to the side, nonverbally telling him to continue with his praise of her judgement.

"But you want him to make his own choices. I'm fine with that. That means, though, that if he wants to come, he can come like everyone else on the team, and we're not being overprotective as if he's our kid. 'Cause I'll tell you now," he laughed, "I ain't ready for that. Not on this planet, baby."

His words carried humor that didn't land with Lacy. The corner of her mouth dropped the slightest bit at his words, and her stomach tightened.

Not ready... she thought, keeping the words to herself. "You don't think..." The words almost came out, the admittance of the child growing inside her, but she pivoted, knowing that to tell him now as retaliation would only lead to an argument and guilt for both of them. "...Robbie is a part of this family?"

Dex was taken aback, recognizing that what had come out of her mouth wasn't what she had originally wanted to say. A lump formed in his throat as he stammered out, "N- no. Lacy, no, that's not what I meant at all." He knelt in front of her and took her soft hands in his. Where any other wife would have a beautiful diamond ring on her finger, her's remained bare. There hadn't been time to stop at a jeweler between all of their excursions with the Empire. But the lack of a wedding band had meant nothing to him until her use of that word, 'family,' which felt like she was fortifying a base. "Robbie is as much a part of this family as... well..."

Their eyes challenged each other.

Lacy knew what he was intending to say; she could read where his mind was at, and saw how hard he was fighting to find the right word. She may have been the only person in the universe who could say 'It's the thought that counts' and mean it. To calm his racing thoughts, she kissed his forehead and said, "Don't worry yourself. I know." Then she rose, Dex with her, and offered, "Come on, let's see what he's up to."

She began to walk to the airlock, but Dex still had her hand in his and pulled her back, against his chest.

"Where do you think you're going without a kiss?"

All bad thoughts, all concerns for the future, were gone the instant their lips met.

They found Robbie in the village, lying on a hammock being swung by some of the Mok Tau children. The tails, as they were called for their resemblance to tadpoles, rocked Robbie, who clung to the sides of the hammock for stability. The children laughed, jerking the hammock forward and back, eliciting worried electrical beeps from the robot.

"I do not see how this is relaxing," Robbie said with a slight shake coming from his speakers.

The children responded with more laughter, and one reassured him, "This how we be-like, ha ha," and shook the hammock violently.

Robbie's claws tightened on the edges, almost snapping the rope that held it all together. "If ThAt'S whAt yOu saAaYy. lAcY! You'Re BaCk!"

The children parted as they took notice of Lacy and Dex approaching Robbie. "Getting along with the other kids?" she asked.

The hammock swayed in smaller and smaller arcs as the children moved away, and Robbie attempted to pull himself up. Balance was an impossibility he refused to accept. "Swell, I think. The tails say I am relaxing, except I don't believe them. Maybe I am not meant to relax."

Seeing him struggle to stand, Dex picked the robot up and set him on solid ground.

"Thank you, Dex."

"Don't mention it."

Robbie nodded his half-dome head, then turned to look up at Lacy. "How did the mission go? Did you find new batteries?"

She exchanged a weary look with Dex, one Robbie hadn't quite learned to pick up on yet. They spoke at the same time, a mix a "We-" and "I-"

I didn't see any of his kind, she thought to him. *Did you?*

I didn't really check, but no. Just the Zar-Mecks.

Dex answered Robbie, with his eyes still on Lacy.

"Not yet, buddy." He turned and looked down. "But we're keeping our eyes open."

Robbie's tone remained neutral. "That should be okay. I still have a long life ahead of me. At least a few more weeks."

Lacy's lips parted in alarm, but as before, when they were first told of his power supply, she heard Dex's thoughts and saw his fingers raise in protest. *Don't. Don't freak him out. We'll figure it out.* But when *would* they figure it out? The only other power source nearby was the *Silent Horizon*'s engine, but using that as a substitute would render their spacecraft near-useless. And as far as they'd seen, there was nothing usable on the Zar-Meck starfighters — nothing Lacy knew her way around, at least — and no robots of a similar model back at Torro-Kaal. If an imperial troop transport flew in, they could likely find one, but at the cost of a war-torn Taranok.

As their silence extended, Robbie spoke up again. "Anything can happen in a lifetime. I am not worried."

Dex forced a grin and rubbed the robot's head, saying to Lacy, "Looks like he's stolen all your optimism. Listen to him. He's fine. Come on, I want to lie down for a bit before dinner." He took Lacy's hand and led her past the hammock toward their hut.

Robbie followed close behind, so Lacy whispered, "I *am* optimistic. I know we'll find a new battery even if-"

"Even if we have to pull it from the ship," Dex teased. "I know, I know."

"I just don't want it to get to that."

Dex laughed, garnering a look of interest from Robbie. "You think I do?" he asked Lacy, keeping his voice low. Robbie was sure to hear them, but he wasn't always the most attentive. "This planet doesn't have any beaches. And we're still technically on orders, so I'm entitled to some leave days and I'm not spending them here, I'll tell ya that now." They stepped into their hut, and Dex shut the door behind them that the Mok Tau had installed at his request, leaving Robbie outside.

Solid doors became a game changer for the Mok Tau after they'd arrived, yet many of their biggest admirers didn't respect the privacy that should have come with them.

"Excuse me," Robbie knocked on the door with his little claw. "I cannot reach the knob."

"That's the idea," Dex called through the door, then focused his attention on the immaculate woman in front of him.

She glared back.

He crumbled.

"Think we should have stayed on the ship?" he offered.

"Start taking those leave days?" she stepped closer.

"Little planet, all ocean except for one tiny beach." He put his hands on her waist, pulling her in those final inches.

"Finally pop open that bottle of wine?" Her voice was so light it could float away like a wisp of cloud.

Their lips were only centimeters apart, and it still felt too far.

"We're definitely overdue for a honeymoon…"

Maybe on some atomic level, their lips did meet, but they were torn from the moment by the door creaking open.

"What the *HELL* is it now Robbie?" Dex growled and threw his head back, seeing Roak in the doorway, with one of the priestesses holding his arm for support.

"I… I… wel-come" — *wheeze* — "you back… from…" Roak took a deep breath, sank forward, and a frail, shaking finger pointed up at the sky.

Lacy fell back a step, out of Dex's hands.

The old man, the village's elder and spiritual leader, showed his age more and more with each passing day. It seemed a miracle to Lacy that he'd even been able to get out of bed anymore, much less climb the small hill to their hut. Even his assistant insisted he stay in his temple and let others come to him, but Roak would hear none of it. To him, the gods had already traveled far enough to meet with the tribe;

he could spare a few short steps in their direction.

"Please, Roak, won't you sit?" Lacy crossed the room and gestured to a set of cushions by the wall and a short table where they ate (that is, on the off chance they could escape from group meals with the village).

Dex watched her, wishing she'd taken the selfish route, and asked him to leave. *But she would never, another reason I love her.*

I heard that, and I love you too, her voice practically sang in his mind.

Roak fought against his feeble muscles and paper-thin cheek flaps to smile. He nodded the jerkiest nod his old neck could handle and mouthed a 'thank you.' The priestess, Ronpup was her name, guided him with one hand in his, and the other under his tricep. Thirty steps it took, by Dex's count, to cross ten feet, and sitting down took longer than the crossing.

The old man should have stayed in bed, he thought.

Lacy shot him a warning look before giving her attention to Roak. "Do you need a drink? Either of you?"

A laugh that quickly turned into a coughing fit erupted from Roak. "You'reeee..." A deep breath in, then, "dreenk." Roak pursed his lips. "Too... too hard. M- Mok... Tau..." he tried to shake his head but the movement proved too much for him. Roak took another deep, deep breath in and tried again. "Mok... Tau, s-... s-... stay... with. own. Dreenk."

"Water" was naturally flowing on Taranok, but had a slightly different composition than the good old H_2O Dex and Lacy were used to on Earth. For their enjoyment of it, they had it distilled. The Mok Tau found it repulsive.

Lacy gave Roak a polite smile. She spoke slowly, her attempt not to make him feel rushed. "If you wish. Something to eat then?"

Ronpup spoke up this time. "Please, yes, my Lacy. Roak not eat today."

"I... *wheeze* not... hungry," he said to Ronpup.

Her eyes drooped in Lacy's direction with concern for the elder. "He will eat. If you tell him."

The beauty of being worshiped. Their newest commandment unto these people would be "Thou shalt eat their vegetables."

Lacy didn't need Ronpup's words to move her hand, but she respected the hell out of her for speaking up for Roak's well-being. "Dex, darling, do you mind getting some snacks?"

"As you wish. Let me just rummage through the fridge." Dex mocked an about-face and started for the opposite wall of the tiny hut and the small insulated cabinet they had made with materials from the ship. Most of the village's food was kept in a communal bank, but they were permitted to store some food for themselves, especially now that the village was thriving again.

The "fridge" was by no means on par with what Earth had to offer. Food wasn't kept cold so much as preserved at hut-temperature, but it kept the heavy moisture and bugs out. It was a major development on the planet, but one of the few Dex and Lacy brought that hadn't quite gained popularity yet. Especially when the natives preferred the bugs on their food.

"What'd'ya like, old timer?" Dex asked, opening the fridge, wishing he'd see a cold beer in there. "Fruit or beetle paste?"

Ronpup answered for Roak in her broken English, often complete with mispronounced words. "The *pate*, please. Fruit too hard, he can not..." She searched for the word, but Dex and Lacy both understood she meant chewing and digestion.

Dex grabbed a leaf-wrapped serving of the beetle paste they'd become accustomed to and brought it over to Roak. "I take it you didn't come all this way to say 'hello.'" He took a seat with the others and handed Ronpup the dish to serve Roak.

Roak took a deep breath in. "Guest... tonight."

He took a long pause and bowed his head. The others in the room, including Ronpup, would have thought he was asleep if his eyes hadn't flickered back open. Roak's lips quivered as he tried to force out the words, getting stuck in his throat. He settled, took another breath in, attempted again to speak, then wheezed.

Ronpup rubbed the old frog's back, then pulled a pouch out of her robes. "Please, Roak, dreenk."

His frail hands reached out to grab the water pouch and slowly sipped.

"He say we to have comp'ny to night for bonfire," Ronpup said, to Dex's relief. He didn't think he'd be able to sit patiently through a snail's pace conversation with Roak.

"Won't that be lovely?" Lacy asked in earnest. "It's about time we met our neighbors, isn't it?" She nudged Dex.

"Oh yeah, can't wait. If they're anything like the psychos we met last time, I'm sure it'll be one hell of a party." Their brief run-in with the Mok Rork tribe and their witch leader, Morgup, was still fresh in their minds. Sure, they'd helped the Mok Tau get home after they'd dealt with the witch, but the scars from the rock pits were still tender on Dex's feet.

Ronpup may have read his face, because the next thing she said was, "Mok Rork *wiil* be come. Mok Bubar and Mok Pruba tribes, too."

"What's the occasion?" Lacy asked.

"More people coming to say 'thanks?'" Dex bemused with a joking spirit of entitlement.

Then Roak. "Black... *wheeze*... fire."

They all stared at him, Ronpup included. While Dex and Lacy's faces showed a mix of intrigue and confusion, Ronpup's showed shock and a hint of fear. Clearly, this was her first time hearing of the reason for the meeting as well. And there was that phrase again, the Black Fire.

Dex cleared his throat, swallowing a cynical comment, and instead opted for, "Seems like there's a lot of that talk going around."

Roak eyed Dex, or rather, did his best to raise a single brow. "Mok... Tau... *wheeze*... too?" He then slowly turned his head toward Ronpup for validation.

She swallowed and glanced at Dex and Lacy for an answer, as if she were ashamed of the truth. "There is... talk, Roak. Some may be fear."

A light gleamed in Roak's eye alongside another coughing fit. His best attempt at a laugh. "Pe-... people... will... fear." He took a deep breath. "But... there... no... *wheeze*... need." Roak took another sip of the drink from the pouch, an attempt that took almost a full minute.

Despite Roak's callous dismissal of the tribe's growing anxiety, the room was overcome with a dark cloud. No one wanted to speak. Roak, believing his point was made. Ronpup, afraid to admit she erred on the side of fear. Lacy, not wanting to be disrespectful of the village's superstitions. And Dex, not wanting to outright say how silly he thought it all was. When the silence continued, though, he cared less.

"I feel like these people should already know it was all just a man behind the curtain." As the words came out, he realized the frogs wouldn't understand the Earth reference he'd made. "What I mean is, all your prophecy and tradition, sorry to say, was all a sham. And everyone who came back from the mountain knows it. Sorry, chief, but you got played."

"Dex!" Lacy whisper-shouted with a bump on his arm.

"I don't mean it like that-"

"No," Roak said solidly. "You... right." When he paused then, it was a smooth breath in. His eyelids drifted to closure. There was never so much calm in his face before or after his next statement. "But... who can fool the world to follow... great power they do have. The Red God shape Mok Tau people, Red God can destroy, too..."

Lacy's face hardened. She felt thoughts shooting through Dex's mind, looking for a quick, possibly sarcastic, rebuttal. Before he could, she said, "We won't let that happen. The man who did this to your world is still just a man."

A tangible thought formed in Dex's mind, and Lacy heard, *We both know that's not true.*

Don't give them something new to fear, and I won't say anything about Robbie's battery.

Deal.

"You... *cough*... say. But... R-... Roak..." He tried to push the words out before conceding and tapping his temple to say, 'I know better.'

"Whatever he is," Lacy began, "he's someone we can fight. We've done it before and we'll do it again." She looked to Dex to back her up.

He saw the look in her eyes, the confidence she had in him. "Lacy's right."

That look of gratitude she gave him, he just...

"For all you've done for us." Giving them food, sanctuary from the Empire, kindness, but most importantly, something to fight for, "We won't let anything happen to you, your tribe, or any on Taranok." He squeezed Lacy's hand. *How was that?*

Wonderful, darling.

"Wonder... full." Roak agreed, though he didn't know he did.

Ronpup picked up the role of speaker from him, "This will help make Mok Tau not fear. We need the hope."

Roak's thin lips and saggy cheeks spread in a facsimile of a smile. "That..." he stretched out his arms wide, "all Mok... Tau... need. You... *wheeze* tell... others?" he asked, referring to the other tribal leaders coming for the bonfire.

"We'd be happy to," Lacy said through a sympathetic smile.

* * *

Dusk came to Taranok, and the liveliness of the war

party's return to the village felt like a vigil in comparison to the evening excitement surrounding the bonfire.

After Roak had left, Dex and Lacy changed into outfits the Mok Tau had made for them, more fitting for a formal evening than the tatters of Earth clothes they still had and wore most days. Although Dex still kept Korr's old jacket and the clothes he'd given him on the *Silent Horizon*. They were too heavy for the Tarnok heat and humidity. The new outfits had been made at Lacy's request and Dex's chagrin. He found that their tatters were very flattering on Lacy, and quite enjoyed annoying her with his Tarzan impression.

"Just because Earth is behind us, doesn't mean we have to leave our civility, too," she jokingly scolded him. "Besides, I think you'll like what Grunna made me. Wait outside, would you?"

Dex threw her a playful grin. "Thought I wouldn't have to hear that again once I was married." He did as he was asked, though, leaving her be to change but feigning annoyance on his way out.

Waiting outside for him, before he could even sneak a peek back in through a crack in the door, a group of the Mok Tau children, led by Robbie, waited for him.

"The tails wanted to know if they could see a story now," Robbie blurted like he'd been waiting decades for Dex or Lacy to come out of the hut. Worried Dex would give an excuse as he had the previous night, and the night before, and any night Lacy didn't step in to set it up, Robbie blurted again, "I will make sure nothing breaks this time. Bup is not invited."

The other tails nodded in agreement and shuffled around, although Dex could still see a blushing child hiding in the back of the crowd.

Dex rolled his eyes. "We don't have a lot of spare sheets left, Robbie. If I do this..." He scanned the crowd, pointing at each and every one of the children, "You all sit still and *don't* attack the screen. Okay?"

All together the children answered back, "Yes, captan Dex."

"*Aaaall right.* Good. Robbie, get the projector from the ship."

The robot and his horde of children rushed down the hill to the landing pad before the final word was out of Dex's mouth. He was sure the parents would be thankful the children were occupied for the night, but... his soft Earth bedsheets.

Nothing the Mok Tau had as far as fabric went even came close to the thread count Dex and Lacy had brought with them.

Through the pattering of children's feet rushing away, Dex heard the door to the hut crack open behind him.

"Mind if I look now?" he asked.

Lacy didn't answer him, only opened the door further and stepped out.

When Dex turned, a feeling came over him that reality had somehow warped, and they had never even left Grand Central Space Station. He was back in the observatory with Lacy on their first date. She stood before him then wearing a dress of a deep green color, cut off just below the knees, and hanging lightly on the brim of her shoulders. Not an exact replica, but as close as the Mok Tau could get with the materials they had. All that was missing was the necklace she'd worn and...

Lacy pulled a bottle of wine from behind her back, standing once again as she had that night.

"I thought it was the right time to have that drink."

Dex stepped closer to her. He tried to bring his hands to her waist, but was so in awe of her beauty that he felt too weak to raise his arms.

"You are..." One hand managed to meet her side, while the other caressed her cheek. Lacy dropped her face into his hand and looked up into his eyes with a brilliance he would have faced the Emperor alone for the chance to see again. "...everything in the universe worth living for." He lowered his eyes to the bottle of wine. "So, this is it?"

"I think it can be," she breathed, waiting for his lips to meet hers.

"Wherever you're happy, that's where I want to call home." He leaned into her, guiding them both back through the doorway.

Lacy kissed him again, then laughed. "Not just yet, darling. This wine's for later." *Much later,* she told herself. "Just wanted to let you know what's waiting. And you have someone waiting for you, don't you?"

"Robbie can wait a little longer."

"I think they've waited long enough. And the others will be here soon. You and I will have plenty of time after the bonfire."

Dex breathed in a deep, strained sigh. "You just love to tease me, don't you?"

"Later," she whispered into his ear, and gently pushed Dex away.

There was something in her voice then, he realized as he left the hut again. The last word may not have been a sultry tease. It carried in it something else. Something exciting, yes, but not the promise of any very-late-honeymoon activities. He dwelt on it, arguing with himself whether he was overthinking it or not. But for the time being, his attention was needed elsewhere.

Lacy closed the door between them, and the first few steps Dex took away from the hut were backwards down the hill. Even if he could no longer see her, he didn't want to look away. Her beauty remained an imprint on his eyes like the sun after staring directly at it. But, after almost tripping, he righted himself and jogged through the village, making one quick stop before reaching his final destination.

Dex stepped uninvited into a hut that was only just starting to resemble a field hospital. It had been one of the village's first priorities to create when the lost Mok Tau warriors had returned from Torro-Kaal. And with all the supplies gathered on subsequent raids, and some elementary modern-day medical know-how from Dex and Lacy, the Mok Tau were able to certify their first doctor and nurse. Although, between Dex and Lacy, they weren't entirely confident in the doctor's ability to perform any surgeries yet. Major or minor. Hopefully, that would change before Dex turned forty.

Six hospital beds had been squeezed into the hut. Two were currently in use. Dex walked up to the nearest one where a bruised and bandaged male slept. An IV bag scavenged from the imperial base hung next to his bed, feding into his arm. Dex inspected the application of the catheter. Things seemed fine all around.

He moved onto the next occupied bed, where the clumsy soldier from the moon base assault reclined. Next to the bed stood the village doctor. It started as a joke and ended up taking off, that the doctor wore a ripped white jacket that had been found at Torro-Kaal.

"How's our brave soldier doing?" Dex asked the doctor.

The doctor replied, "Just a burn. Truppup be on feet t'marr."

"Oh, damn, we'll have to amputate you say?" Dex joked, then slapped Truppup's shoulder. "Better be more careful with your weapon, private. Don't want you out of commission. Shooting yourself in the foot doesn't get you a ticket out of my army, got it?"

Truppup only understood about a quarter of the words Dex said. But his expression said he would do better at soldiering in the future.

To the doctor, Dex asked, "What's the deal with that guy?" He jabbed his thumb in the direction of the unconscious frog.

"Bad hunt," the doctor said flatly. A year ago, a bad hunt was a surefire death sentence, yet life would go on for the rest of the village without so much as a second thought. Now, even if the doctor was still struggling to understand different blood types and how transfusion worked without the help of witchcraft, there was hope.

Off in another part of the village, a clearing underneath a thick tree just inside the wall, the Mok Tau children jittered in anticipation. In the center of all of them was Robbie, trying desperately to hold high and protect a folded-up sheet and homemade projection device Lacy had made them for nights like this.

Dex arrived shortly after his detour to the hospital and ducked down into the tree's underlair. "All right, all right, quiet down, you little brats, I'm here. Toss me the projector, Robbie, and hang up the screen. And sit down, kids!" Dex shouted over the insistent screams of excitement. "You want the movie or not?" Then to himself, he said, "Be kicked right out of the theater back on Earth, acting like this."

On the other side of the underlair, Robbie feebly attempted to hang the white sheet they used as a screen, while the children watched without offering help.

"All right, kids, what are we watching tonight? Something silly? Something exciting? Something your parents will get mad at me for showing?" *As if any of the Mok Tau would allow themselves to be mad at us.*

"Nothing too long, please. I would like to power down at a reasonable time tonight," Robbie said, looping one of the sheet's corners through a slit in the tree's roots.

"That's fine, Robbie, you don't need sleep." Dex flicked through the data tablet filled with the *Silent Horizon*'s film catalog. After only a few moments, he narrowed down his browsing to two. One he thought would melt their primitive brains in sheer amazement, and one to test the parents' patience with.

"Okay, kids, what sounds better: Metropolis or Frankenstein?"

In a way, Robbie lucked out. Neither title made any sense to the Mok Tau children, but the later sounded better. They wouldn't rush to Robbie with nightmares from the monster film, but the spectacle of a world-of-the-future that was Metropolis was sure to overstimulate them. Either way, the parents who were bold enough would be angry at Dex for either outcome, so why not go for broke and scare the daylights out of them?

Dex stayed and watched the film with them until a little more light faded from the treetops. With less of a glare, the picture became stronger, and the flash of lightning on screen and Dr. Frankenstein shouting "It's alive!" sent the children into a fear- and excitement-induced frenzy. Robbie did a fine job of holding back the kids who attempted to rush the screen and touch the people who looked similar to Dex and Lacy.

It was funny, he thought to himself, this little cinema billions of miles from Earth. When was the last time he'd been to one?

It must have been... '54. That Billy Wilder picture. Oh, what was it called? Aw, hell, Dex. It was the last time...

The last time he'd gone with his Dad.

The movie hadn't been funny for a Wilder film. It hadn't been funny at all, actually. Not when the jokes had been about the war. Not when a man missing his legs heard others laughing at what should have been a terrifying scene. Not when he gripped Dex's arm so tight it bruised because he couldn't tell if what he was seeing was from the screen or his own memory.

The cinema wasn't so fun after that Billy Wilder picture. No, they both preferred watching movies at home without the crowds, where they could flip the channel if the imagery took too much of a hold on reality. Westerns were a good balance for them. Their violence wasn't too real, and the good guy always won. Even on their last heroic stand when all seemed lost, the gunslinger would break out of the saloon with their weapon held high, never losing faith in the goodness of the town they were willing to give their lives to defend.

The westerns were good. They were never too real.

Dex shuffled backward out of the underlair. He had other places to be, or so he told himself.

* * *

Lacy waited patiently for Dex with Roak and the priestesses at the village gate. The spotters had sent word that the other tribal chiefs were approaching, only a few minutes out on foot.

Ronpup leaned into Lacy's ear, hiding her voice from Roak. "Mok Rork come, too," she said. "Does you want to stay? I can tell Roak you not feel well."

"No, that's quite all right," Lacy smiled politely, fidgeting with her dress. "No use in dwelling on the past. Has Boritt said anything though?"

"Boritt not happy Mok Rork come. But he will be at feast." Boritt hadn't expressed happiness about much of anything over the last few months. He'd made most of the journey to Torro-Kaal with Dex and Lacy's company, but lost both of his legs in a battle against a kron-kaal, a great terror that was believed to have been spawned in what was discovered to be an imperial base all along. Even though a tenuous peace was made with the Mok Rork tribe where Boritt was forced to rest and recover while the others completed the journey, his time was far from pleasant.

Lacy breathed a sigh of relief that he would still be making an effort to show face in front of those who were once his enemy. "Good. That'll be good for him. And the others?"

"I not hear from Toork or Gurg. They not seen since you come back from moon."

Lacy pursed her lips. Voices off in the distance signaled their guests' approach. "I don't blame them."

The gate opened slowly as the first of the guests arrived; the chief of the Mok Krak, a tribe from the other side of the Great Break, was leading them. He was a short frog-man, practically a child, surrounded by equally scrawny guards. It wasn't far-reaching for Dex and Lacy to guess that the guards had been some of those liberated from Torro-

Kaal. Walking next to the chief was a tall priest in gaudier attire, who looked to be the healthiest of the group.

Ronpup led Roak by the arm to meet their guests, but the Mok Krak raised their curled hands to Lacy and bowed their heads. "We thank host Roak and the Red Gods for safe journey. Glory be you."

Lacy blushed with polite discomfort at the Emperor's blessing. Word had spread across the planet of Dex and Lacy's arrival, but not enough truth to break the old doctrines the Emperor had established. It was uncomfortable knowing that thousands, maybe millions of people around the planet, were praying to her and Dex. It wasn't a far stretch of thought either to think that many were still praying to the Emperor through the bishop of their race in his court. And that thought brought the others up again, reeling in her mind one after the next like a scratched vinyl playing on a loop.

If the Emperor knew where to find them, why hadn't any warships or assassins arrived since their attack on Torro-Kaal? Why was the moon outpost deserted? The Emperor surely wouldn't have given up on his search for Earth. What was he planning?

Lacy pulled herself out of her thoughts and acknowledged the Mok Krak with a bow, not the Emperor's salute. "I'm honored that you came this evening. I hope the road wasn't too long."

The young Mok Krak chief pushed past Roak and said to Lacy, "My people blessed with strongest legs of Taranok. No road too long for us."

"That's wonderful to hear," Lacy said with a proud smile. "I hope to visit your village and meet your people someday."

At this point, Roak stepped into the conversation. "Mok T- Tau... th- thank..." He wheezed, and Ronpup put a hand on his shoulder.

"Chief Roak and Mok Tau thank you for coming," she finished for him. "Please, join in temple where we may speak for others come."

One of the other Mok Tau priestesses approached them and escorted the Mok Krak party to Roak's temple, where the incoming chiefs would gather.

The next group to arrive was a representative of the Mok Tur tribe, along with six of their people all carrying baskets of food. At first glance, Lacy registered a clear distinction between the Mok Tur tribe and all the others they had met so far. Their skin had patches of a much rougher texture, almost leathery and scarred.

"Why does their skin look like that?" Lacy asked Ronpup while the Mok Tur were still out of earshot.

"Mok Tur tribe born with red marks on skin. It is against god."

Of course, Lacy thought, her heart sinking with pain for the tribe. *The Emperor's colors.*

The Mok Tur's skin were all streaked in long lines from their scalps down to their toes with scars. Jagged rivers of generations of horrifying tradition. Lacy saw the hands of one of the basket carriers and noticed that there wasn't a single inch of smooth flesh.

Seeing the sorrow in Lacy's eyes, Ronpup took her by the hand. "It is time of change, my Lacy. Mok Tur be okay. Already there change. You will see."

Lacy wiped a tear from her eye. "You don't have to call me that. Lacy's all right. And that's not an order or anything," she rushed out before another tenet of the new Law of Dex and Lacy could be established.

Ronpup nodded, and they both turned their attention toward the guests.

The Mok Tur were escorted to the village temple, followed minutes later by the Mok Grut tribe, who wore had painted lines along their bodies as yellow as their eyes, and jawless hyper-raptor skulls as shoulder plates for either armor or shows of force, and Mok Tarp tribe representatives minutes after them. Finally, once the light of day was completely gone, the village gate opened one last time for the Mok Rork.

Leading the troop was a blue-spotted frog-man familiar to Lacy and her companions from the journey to Torro-Kaal.

What had happened in their village when they had been taken as prisoners was in the past and not the fault of the Mok Rork, but the witch who had corrupted their tribe beyond what the Emperor had already done to them.

The blue-spotted Mok Rork approached Lacy with his head bowed, fists up, but kept a few feet away from her and didn't say a word.

Lacy glanced from him to Ronpup for guidance, but she did not have any guidance. The expression on the Mok Rork's face was hard to read, but from their history, Lacy felt he was disrespecting her and the Mok Tau by not addressing her first as the other chiefs had done. Still, it wasn't in Lacy's nature to let something so trivial bother her.

"Welcome," Lacy said through a strained breath. "We're glad you could make it."

The blue-spotted Mok Rork raised his head and lowered his hands. When he spoke, his tone was cold. "There much to speak to."

Lacy nodded her agreement and extended her hand toward the temple where the others waited. She noted the subtle shift backward the chief made as he watched her arm arc outward, though she made no comment on it. "Yes, I believe there is. Please, join us."

"Comp-yons wait with others," Ronpup said, addressing the other Mok Rork. Behind them all in the village center, the Mok Tau and representatives from the other tribes were circled around the bonfire, eating, drinking, and generally engaging in merriment.

* * *

The damp, claustrophobic temple was a buzz of anxious chatter until Lacy entered the room alongside the Mok Rork chief. All eyes fell on her in wonder, but only

Roak's face had a smile on it.

"All...*wheeze*... here." Roak observed, watching Lacy and the chief take their seats. "But..." he took a deep breath in. "D- Dex... is..?"

"He will be on his way shortly. He was with the children- er, tails," Lacy said, prompting murmuring from the others in the frog language. She asked herself, *Is it below a god to play with children? Or honorable?*

Even if no one else showed it, the feeble smile on Roak's face told her he, at least, found it to be a good excuse for Dex's tardiness.

Roak opened his mouth to speak again, took another deep breath, but then stopped, and put his frail hand on Ronpup's arm next to him. Lacy noticed the strain in his chest and in his eyes.

"Mok Tau thank you for be here tonight," Ronpup said in Roak's place. "It has been long last eat as all."

An aggressive voice shot out of the circle, the Mok Tarp chief, saying something in their alien tongue.

A few of the heads nodded in agreement with whatever it was that he said, but Ronpup's eyes hardened, and she held up a hand to quiet the others. "Taranok is no home to only tribes now." Gesturing to Lacy, she said, "We have others. Do not know how to speak. How to hear. And meet tonight is for her, too."

The Mok Krak Chief then said, "Gods do not know speak of Taranok?"

Lacy and Ronpup locked cautious eyes. Touching Ronpup's hand, she read the Mok Tau woman's mind, the thought an echo of her own. *Dangerous territory already.*

Before Lacy or Ronpup could speak, though, the blue-spotted Mok Rork chief rose and addressed the room. "The two... hoomans... they called, not gods."

Uneasy stirring quickly turned to low shouting, but the Mok Rork chief didn't back down from his claim. He held his stance over the others in the room, dominating them with his energy. "It true, Mok Rork seen. Hooman not god." He glared down at Lacy. "But hooman strong in magic. Hooman show Mok Rork Red God is lie. Hooman save Mok Rork from Torro-Kaal."

The Mok Grut chief beat his chest in agreement. The hyper-raptor skull on his shoulder rattled as he threw his arm across himself. "Mok Grut come back from Torro-Kaal. Red God not save Mok Grut. They say hooman," he pointed at Lacy. "Not mean Red God is lie. My people plague with vision."

"As mine," added the Mok Krak chief.

"Night last, I have dream." The Mok Grut chief stood, signaling the Mok Rork to step down. The yellow paint along his body illuminated by the glow of the fire in a way that reminded Lacy of the humanoid alien Jaskek when his emotions ran hot, as happened with those of his species. "Red God call my name. He speak our words. Say Black Flame come. Taranok has turn on Red God, and Red God punish."

Murmurs of agreement sounded in the temple.

Lacy glanced over at Roak to catch his reaction, but the old man sat quietly, looking like he hadn't heard the eerie prophesying.

The Mok Grut continued, slowly lowering to one knee. "My people scared. Mok Grut village bad place. Torro-Kaal surv-iors... some attacked. Not know who did. But some talk. Say they should have stay in beast. Red God leave us be if they stay. If hoomans not come to Taranok."

"It do no good to say that," Ronpup cut in, and venom seethed from her words. "Human here. Humans help Taranok. Mok Grut fools to not see."

At this, Roak did perk up and tried to speak to ease the growing tensions, but his voice was stuck in his throat.

Lacy, instead, threw herself into the conversation. "I'm sorry for your village. *All* of your villages. We didn't come here to make trouble. And by no means did we intend to cause trouble between you and the Em-... your god."

The chief's expressions didn't still. The reverence

they had for her when they arrived at the village was almost entirely gone now that revelation talks had begun.

"Okay," Lacy added, "that's not entirely true, is it? This god, my husband and I have been running from him. We were trying to get home, back to our planet, but needed something to show our own people so we could prepare for him. We didn't mean to start anything here because we didn't know what was in that base. I'm sorry our actions have caused more trouble, but I promise you and your tribes that this god is something we can beat. He is strong, but he's *not* all-powerful. We've already dealt a massive blow to him here and in the sky. And now look at you. Listen to your people out there by the fire. When did you say was the last time you were all together? Think of what we could do united against this threat. Things will be hard moving forward. Some of us may have to give our lives. But this planet will finally be free of the monsters."

Very well said, came a familiar voice in her mind. *Thank God this crowd looks a little younger than Roak. Conversation would go on all night.*

I was wondering when you would show up, she shot back.

Dex snuck into the room behind her and took a seat against the wall, an easy thing to miss when everyone was so focused on Lacy.

"Mok Rork know better than fight against hoomans, and give thank for free people," said the blue-spotted frog. "But you do not know what hoomans bring to Taranok." He paused, scanning the other chiefs to see if they were aware of what he meant. "Something calls Great Break home. Animals leave, but we hear monster still."

"One of the kron-kaal," Dex offered, dismissing the danger in the frog's voice.

"This no kron-kaal. Mok Rork say a ghost make home of Great Break. Shadow walks through trees. My people, some gone. Disappear in night. One say they see in shadow burn flame, but no light shine."

"Black Flame," whispered the Mok Grut chief.

The blue-spotted frog nodded. "We fear yes."

Lacy noticed Dex stiffening, then asked, "What is this 'Black Flame' you keep mentioning?"

Ronpup answered but addressed the entire room. "Black Flame is myth, no more. As same as lie was Torro-Kaal. It is spirit of death that some say will bring end of Taranok. But if Red God is lie, so is threat he make." She turned her attention onto the Mok Rork chief. "Have you see spirit? Or is your people spread words?"

"Black Flame is why I late," the Mok Rork Chief said, with vitriol in his voice and a puffed chest.

Dex rolled his eyes toward Lacy. Of course the one guy they didn't like would have an excuse for his tardiness.

You were late to the meeting too, Lacy was quick to remind him.

The Mok Rork Chief continued, unbothered and unsurprised by Dex's dismissive gesture. "My wife brother, he go missing. She say he taken by Black Flame. I search around Great Break and find great horror. I saw with own eye, altar. On altar many body. All like old fruit. Withered, dried, rotted. And burned. Do not now look like Mok Rork. But I know it, my people the foundation. Mok Rork bodies twisted, skin pulled tight, bones tied together. And on altar, paint with blood, my people made into form of Red God."

The image sickened Lacy. Bile rose in her stomach. And the description of how the bodies were mutilated revealed an image in Lacy's mind of the Children of the Void being sacrificed to the Emperor, how their bodies, too, looked withered and dried up, mangled together in a charred, unspeakable horror, with only the look of terror in their eyes giving any indication they once had a soul.

It was Dex's turn to speak now, and he did so as if he and the Mok Rork Chief were the only ones in the room of note. Everyone else was just a part of the audience. "Given our history, yours in particular with your freaky, eyeless witch lady, how should we be expected to believe this really is some imperial doing, and not another one of your weird rituals you're trying to play us for?"

Lacy's hand jutted out and took hold of his forearm. She reminded him mentally, *they came in good faith. We can show the same courtesy.*

I'm not yet convinced they did, he replied.

The other chiefs exchanged glances and murmurs at the accusation, but particularly the use of the word "imperial," which they still did not understand.

"Blood ritual gone with going of Morgup. You woman saw to that," the Mok Rork Chief said, for once taking his attention off of Dex and nodding toward Lacy.

At this point, the chief of the Mok Krak tribe shared his thoughts. "Mok Krak close to Mok Rork tribe. We not make friend in age, but we know what of they speak not they ritual. Blood ritual evil for all tribes of Taranok."

Dex tilted up his chin and leaned back an inch, seemingly beat for that argument. But he still had another round in his chamber. "How long did it take you to get here? You rode razorbacks, yes?" He turned to Ronpup and asked, "What is that, five day ride? Four if you're in a rush to get to a meeting?"

Ronpup nodded, but the Mok Rork Chief answered. "Four day it take us."

"Awesome. It would take a few days for bodies to be rotted and dried completely in this humidity, had to have been there for a while, right?"

The chief nodded. His face strained with impatience.

"So, you say it's been up for a while. Yet, our scouts haven't reported anything of the sort."

Murmurs again from the other chiefs, and Lacy too this time. She whispered to him, "You've been sending these people out to spy on our neighbors?"

Dex whispered back, "Not all of them. Just the ones who tried to kill us."

Still, the Mok Rork Chief showed no hint of betrayal. "Mok Rork nothing to hide. My people know not hurt yours when see them."

Before it could escalate further, as Lacy sensed in Dex, she interjected, "Whatever you found, there must be a reason for it, and probably leftovers of the Red God." Then to Dex, "It's a big jungle. Even searching I'm sure it'd be easy to miss." Mentally, she added, *maybe your spies can look again and confirm it.*

Dex grunted his agreement. "It's like the lady said," he nodded toward Lacy. "It's just another game of the Emperor, or god, whatever y'all want to call him. There may be something out there, but it's there to scare you. Whatever it is, it's something that can be fought. And to be frank, I think it's a little silly acting like the end of days are coming to this planet."

"Dex!" Lacy shot him a glare. *Don't be insensitive!*
I'm not. It's fine.

"Look, people." Dex let out a breath of a laugh and stood. He looked around the room at their worried faces. Here was this man who had come from the stars and cast doubt on their entire history, and was now attempting to dismantle their perception of the future too, amidst an atrocity one of the tribes was already facing. But who was this man, making such a dire claim? The Mok Rork chief did nothing to hide his animosity toward Dex and Lacy. He may have come to the meeting in peace and cooperation with the Mok Tau, but that courtesy did not extend to the humans. And Dex, for his part, felt no particular obligation to humor the frog who had tortured them. The Mok Rork chief held no reservations on gruesome acts when it wasn't his skin in the game. So why should he expect Dex and Lacy to help them now?

Because we're better than that, Lacy told him, dropping into his head at the tail end of his thought process.

"We're here, and we're here to stay," Dex went on. "Whatever's coming, we'll face it alongside you. All of you. In fact, I'd like to check out this 'altar' you saw," he said, gesturing toward — but without making eye contact with — the Mok Rork chief, even though he dreaded the idea of going on a journey with him.

In his head he heard Lacy shout, *I said your spies, not you!*

"I'll see this thing for myself and inspect the Great Break together for evidence of this 'Black Flame,'" he continued. Then, to the rest of the gathering, he said, "But *right now*, we're the only people in the village not having a great time by that fire."

For once during the meeting, their minds were taken away from dark and gloomy dooms, and the idea of a party, the reason they'd all come, sounded very inviting.

That was, to say, everyone except for the blue-spotted Mok Rork chief. "I will take short pale man Altar of Red God. Eat well tonight. You not want eat after see what I see."

Dex's shoulders slumped and he sighed, annoyed he hadn't gotten through to the chief. "It's not that I don't believe you. I've just got a pretty good idea of the games this guy plays." He looked around the room for validation, then to Lacy, who sucked in her bottom lip and gave a tentative shake of her head at the thoughts she read from his mind. But, the offer was already made, and if they were going to help make Taranok the world the Mok Tau and all of the planet's tribes wanted it to be, he could go on one quick mission.

He announced to the room, "I will go with the Mok Rork and a small contingent of my men to inspect this altar. You have my condolences for your lost people, but I can already assure you that it is nothing more than a psychological attack, probably an officer who made it out of Torro-Kaal after the fight. But the power the Emperor holds on you now is only fear. If you continue to fear him, he continues to control your lives." His voice rising in a way that even Lacy couldn't deny its emboldening effects, he said, "I will put an end to this superstition so we can finally have a peaceful Taranok."

All of the meeting attendees wailed and beat their fists against the floor of the temple.

As everyone began to rise to close the meeting, Ronpup stood and added a final word. "Before we eat, Mok Tau ask: are we one? When the Red God return, will tribes fight together?"

They all debated in silence with themselves, but one by one, the Chiefs agreed, "My tribe stand with Mok Tau."

The chiefs, along with Dex and Lacy, then turned to Roak for his say, something to solidify the moment. The Mok Tau elder grinned and opened his mouth to speak, but before words could come out, he fell into a coughing fit and could only hold up his thumb in a gesture Lacy had taught him as a signal that the meeting was adjourned on a high note.

35. Bonfires

Dex watched Lacy as she danced with a young Mok Tau boy by the light of the bonfire. The band played something reminiscent of an Al Jolson tune, but with just enough notes out of place to be considered an "original." *Or just good old-fashioned jazz*, Dex thought.

Lacy let the boy lead their dance, him being only half her size, trying to swing her around and do dips with her as he'd (and the rest of the tribe for that matter) seen Dex do a million and a half times. Every few steps, she'd throw her head back in laughter as the Mok Tau boy would attempt another of Dex's moves.

Dex couldn't take his eyes off of her. Nights like this, when the air was filled with joy and the world was lit by Lacy's smile and cosmic eyes, how could he not feel blessed?

It's not polite to stare, her voice in his head.

How could I not?

Jealous of my new dance partner?

Dex laughed. *Only a little.*

You can have the next dance, she told him. *Pinky promise.*

He accepted the temporary rejection with grace and shuffled in his place to better watch her.

A tray of food made its way around the bonfire, eventually given to Dex by a pair of blue-spotted hands.

"Mok Rork not sorry for Morgup," the Mok Rork chief said bluntly.

Dex took a piece of fruit from the tray and passed it on. "I'm sorry to hear that. Thought y'all woulda learned your lesson."

"Why you say Morgup bad?" There was no irony in the frog's voice, only genuine interest.

"Well, ya see that girl?" Dex pointed and they both looked at Lacy who was having the time of her life. "I'm not a fan of people hurting her. Now, I like to think I'm a pretty level-headed guy, and past differences aside, I'm glad your people came tonight. Glad you came, even." Dex leaned in then and whispered, "But you so much as give her a look I don't like, and I'll make sure you get reintroduced to your witch friend real fast."

"Do hooman smoke?" The chief opened a pouch hanging from his side and pulled out, of all things, two short cigars.

A fine peace offering.

The Mok Rork Chief rose and passed through the crowd of dancers to light the cigars with the bonfire, then returned to his seat next to Dex. Dex accepted the cigar, took a puff, and thought of Korr, his first, yet short-lived, friend so far from Earth. *That damned space pirate.* He nodded his thanks to the frog.

The frog nodded and showed no sign of hostility. "Did ever hear of Morgup before hooman come to our village?"

Dex lifted his head in a display of curiosity.

"Morgup born of strange spawn," the chief began. "We born in group. Three, four tail at time. But Morgup only tail of her spawn. Tribe knew she would be great. From tail she was raised by Mok Rork spirit elder. Red God give Morgup many vision, many promises for Mok Rork tribe. Say we will be greatest among tribes of Taranok. She was prophet, unlike any other tail. And she not touchable. Then Morgup grow out of tail, and vision no longer come. But she say she still hear voice of Red God, but not able see him. Too much distraction in world around. Elder and priestess all try to help, tell her it over, but Morgup won't believe. She say the eye blinds, and without think twice, pluck both eyes from head.

"Village all horrified, but she tell them all, she say, 'I will walk among the beasts, crawling like serpent on the ground to humble myself to Red God, and in three and ten days she return unharmed.' Mok Rork all laugh, but three and ten days go by, and Morgup returns on back of kron-kaal. Elder and priestesses then cast out of village. But they not unharmed like Morgup. And They never come back."

It was at this point that Dex interrupted. "I get it. She spent her forty days in the desert and you all thought she was a messiah. One with god, right?"

"No, hooman," the chief said, blowing out the smoke from his cigar. "Morgup not say she one with Red God. She say Red God come to her, strike fear in her heart, and say she will be one to lead all of Taranok, and lead its people through stars. She say there place for her in Red God temple."

"Too bad she didn't make it to that great temple in the sky," Dex said with a puff of the cigar. "But I've got an idea of where she did end up."

"Mok Rork keep Mok Rork safe. Kron-kaal leave us be because Morgup. We survive, because Morgup. Witch, you call, Robert sister."

"Robert?" Dex almost laughed. "Who's Robert?"

"I Robert."

Dex restrained himself from mocking the frog's name, and when he saw that the frog wasn't joking, his smile faded away.

"You can be angry at Mok Rork," Robert continued. "Me too, would be, if it me. But does that make Mok Rork evil? Taranok dangerous place. Morgup and Mok Rork stay survive. We not seek out hoomans. We do not know hoomans. Hoomans find Mok Rork. And hoomans bring kron-kaal. If we evil for protec-ting Mok Rork, how evil will hooman Dex be for Lacy?"

Dex had no words. From his perspective, he saw the situations as two totally different things. But how many people had he already killed to protect her? How much in recent nights had he fantasized about hurting others who had threatened her? How far *would* he go to keep them safe? It was something Lacy had already pointed out. Morgup didn't have to die. Lacy had already won the people over. But he had wanted it. He wanted so badly to have revenge on her behalf.

"Mok Rork leave past behind. We work together now with Mok Tau and hooman."

"For now?" Dex challenged. "When we're out in the jungle, searching for your Black Fire, should I keep the eyes in the back of my head open?"

Robert took a deep puff of his cigar. "Mok Rork do not need revenge. Mok Rork not hooman." He crushed what remained of the cigar on the ground and stood, then leaned back and studied the back of Dex's head. "Do hooman have eyes in back of head?"

Dex found he could laugh again and pulled up his scraggly hair.

Robert huffed, then took his leave for the night.

The young Mok Tau, whom Lacy had been dancing with, began showing signs that he couldn't keep up with the Earth woman's moves. Even if Taranok had rugs, the boy wouldn't have been able to cut any. Lacy kicked one leg out and the boy would be a beat and a half late to kick out his own, and when he did, it dragged out. When he tried to dip her as they'd all seen Dex do, Lacy almost fell to the ground. But she laughed through it and pulled herself back up.

"Sure you haven't had enough?" she teased the boy.

The young Mok Tau searched for the proper translation of what he wanted to say through strained breaths. His eyes were wide with both elation and exhaustion, screaming *I've still got some in me!* and *Please, I need a break!*

A hand tapped his shoulder, and Dex's voice told him, "Tap out, kid. Let me show you how it's done back where we're from."

Once he'd let go of Lacy's hand, the Mok Tau boy fell on his behind, totally spent. His friends rushed in to tease and pull him away as the band transitioned from the Al Jolson tune to a lyricless rendition of Little Richie's *Tutti Frutti*.

Dex swung Lacy this way and that, singing in her ear "Tutti Frutti, oh rooty" at every instance the band missed.

"You've really kept them busy, haven't you?" Lacy jeered.

Dex smiled back, "I didn't think that tablet's speakers were loud enough." He spun her out, then down between his legs and up again into his arms. She fell, her back into his chest with his strong arms wrapped tightly around her, and they bounced from left to right and back again with the swing of the music. Together they sang, "Wop bop a loo bop! Lop bam boo!" and he spun her around again to gaze into her eyes, before locking lips in an ecstacy they refused to pull away from.

When Lacy did reluctantly break the kiss, she said, "Oh! Of all the songs. At least somewhere in the universe it'll be a hit."

"Maybe in another lifetime that Richy guy got big." With hands interlocked they danced together like they were in high school. Roak kept an eye on them like an overly strict principal, waiting to whip out the ruler. Gotta leave room for Jesus.

But no, Roak wouldn't be intervening with a ruler, and Dex wouldn't be leaving any room. He was with his girl, and nothing would ever again separate him from her.

The music faded. Lacy slowly realized the others at the bonfire had stopped dancing quite some time ago and all the instruments were being carried away while something new was brought in.

"Dex, what is this?" she asked, but Dex didn't answer. He kept his smile wide and his eyes on the big box thing a trio of Mok Tau brought into the light.

A fourth Mok Tau followed them, dressed in what looked like a cheap tuxedo jacket and carrying a stool.

He put his stool down behind the box, flipped

something up, then addressed the crown, "Lady gent-man, at rekest of hooman Dex, Mok Tau present…" he paused then and met Dex's eye.

Lacy looked from the frog to her husband, and noticed a nod of confirmation pass between them. She knew she shouldn't have, but she listened to his mind and heard, *go on, just like we practiced*.

The tuxedoed Mok Tau cleared his throat and announced with perfect pronunciation, "Clair de Lune."

From the first press of the keys, tears welled in Lacy's eyes. The jungle was consumed by the sound of gentle moonlight, a melody that no words can truly do justice, and a romance greater than the majesty of the universe that not even the most eloquent poet can describe. And for that reason, I ask that you take a pause from reading, find the one you love, and hold them tightly. Only the feel of their cheek on yours will compare to how Dex and Lacy felt every moment they were alive together.

* * *

"Have you seen the guys around at all?" Dex asked, leading Lacy around the village on a late-night stroll. The band was still playing away, having returned to something a bit more rockin' and rollin'. Lacy herself was bobbing her head from side to side with the distant melody, sipping a Mok Tau cocktail like they were vacationing on a beach, not hearing the question. "Hey, pretty lady," Dex pinched her side.

"Hey!"

"You with me?"

Her eyes beamed as she giddily nodded her head. "Always," she said with a peck on his cheek.

"Well, that's good to hear. How strong is that thing anyway?" Dex eyed the contents of her cup.

"Not. I have *yet* to find a drink on this world above point-oh-one percent alcohol." Lacy giggled as she took another sip.

"And I'm sure you've properly tested plenty of samples?"

Lacy shrugged, "Maybe not in a scientific way. Besides, I shouldn't be drinking anyway." *This is your in, Lacy. Now's the time.*

"If you were gonna drink, now's as good a time as any," Dex said before she could break the news. "But on the other hand, you're probably right. Gotta keep the mind clear in a place like this. I never really took you for a party girl, anyway."

Her shoulders slumped the littlest bit, barely perceptible if the shift wasn't being closely observed, but she laughed anyway. "Shoulda seen me in college. *Don't worry!* Don't worry, I wasn't some tramp or anything like that. But I ran with a fun gang of ladies."

"Oh yeah?" Dex teased. "Sure you got inta' all sorts of trouble."

She playfully smacked his arm. "Don't laugh. We were some seriously tough girls. How do you think I made it this far?"

"I don't know. You always made it seem like your dad raised you like one of the boys."

Lacy stopped and crossed her arms. "So *that's* what you like about me, huh? I'm just like one of the guys?"

Dex refused to give in to the obvious bait of making him look bad, even if it was in good fun. "He raised a tough girl's all I'm saying. The perfect girl." Dex fell back to where she stood her ground and wrapped his arm around her again. His voice dropped low. "No other girl I'd want to be out here with. The girl I want to spend my life with."

"And... what kind of life would that be?"

His tone shifted and became defensive. "Oh, you know, picket fence, manufactured home, 9-5, come home to a TV dinner. You know, the simple life." Dex guided her into step to continue their walk.

"Is there anyone else in this 'perfect life' of yours?" *Come on, Dex, say it.*

"Well, of course! It'd get lonely just the two of us."

This is it! she thought. *This is the time to tell him!*

"We've got our friends; Gurg, Toork, and Boritt. We'd spend time with them too."

"And little ones?" Lacy blurted out.

Without hesitation, Dex fired back, "Well, yeah, I wouldn't kick Robbie out of the house. Permanently, at least." His mind began to wander then, wondering where the robot was. The movie should have been over a while ago but he was yet to be seen.

Lacy took a deep breath. Whether he wasn't taking the hint or if he wanted to avoid it she couldn't tell, and she refused to invade his mind. There wasn't any putting it off, though. He had to know.

"Dex-"

"Have you seen them anyway? Robbie or the guys?"

"Dex!"

"What?" His arm jerked tightly around her at her shout, and a nonchalant laugh escaped him.

"There's something I have to tell you."

Dex's smile fell. They both paused, staring at each other, waiting for the other to let the news flood into reality. As long as Lacy avoided it, she didn't have to accept it. As long as the words weren't said out loud, nothing had changed.

But it had. More than when they first stumbled upon the Empire, more than when they'd been separated, more so even than when her body and mind were altered in the Emperor's court, the world had changed for them.

"Dex..." She swallowed. Her heart jumped from her chest. Her eyes went dry yet felt like they were flooded with tears. "I'm pregnant."

As soon as it was out she wanted to take it back. *No, I'm not pregnant. I made a mistake. It was just a joke.* Blood rushed to her face. She felt a cold bead of sweat run down her back. She couldn't see it in his face but didn't have to read his mind to know he was about to push back. Not now, not here of all places could they have a child. She was angry at herself. Angry she let this happen, angry it was here, angry she waited so long to tell him. And at the same time, she was ecstatic.

Finally! It's out there!

The child in her womb was finally real now to both of them. There was no turning back. It wasn't terrifying, it was beautiful! It was all she wanted! Everything was perfect now, it wasn't scary. She'd be with the man she loved, the man she trusted above all things to be there with her to care for their child. Nothing could stop them from the joy of this life they created together.

Nothing except the Empire.

Nothing except the constant fear of a sudden death sweeping down from the sky to cut all of their lives short. To take them away from their child, leaving them alone in the universe. Or worse, taking the child's life before it even had a chance to live. One thought after the next rushed into her mind, one terrible scenario after another of all the ways they'd fail the child. And with each one, a tug-of-war of arguments with herself, whether or not they could do right by their baby. If they had a chance, or if she should just...

Lacy didn't even realize Dex had put his hands on her cheeks. He had a gentle look in his eye, but the rest of his face was unreadable.

The words dribbled feebly from her tear-soaked lips, "I'm sorry." Lacy tried to turn her head away, but Dex held her firm. And of all things, he laughed.

"Lacy," he brushed away a tear from her cherry-red cheeks, "why are you sorry?"

She couldn't meet his gaze and instead stared down at his feet. "I... I know you didn't want this." Whatever there was being held back was let loose like a damn bursting. Her hands fell onto his chest, fingers tightening on his shirt.

Again he laughed, then pulled her in tight and kissed her head. "Lacy, you are a silly, silly girl."

She could have killed him. Lacy tried to hit his chest,

but her hands, arms, legs, everything, were too weak to do anything but cry in his embrace.

Dex lifted her chin to look at her face again. Lacy's eyes were bloodshot around the sparkles in her irises. Some blood vessels looked like they had popped in her cheeks, her nose ran, and she had an overall look like she might vomit.

She was still the most beautiful thing Dex had ever seen in his life. "This is everything I have ever wanted."

"But what about-"

"What about nothin'." He cut her off, rubbing her back in slow, deep circles. "We're safe here. We'll stay safe here. I won't let anything happen to us."

Lacy squeezed out a near-silent, "Okay."

"Okay?" Dex asked, lifting her chin from his chest.

"Okay," she echoed.

"Okay. Good... so the bottle earlier was just a tease, then?"

A smile, almost a laugh, broke the strain on Lacy's face. "The sentiment was there."

"Yeah, but now I have to wait nine months to have a good drink."

Lacy pulled away and led Dex by the hand to a nearby bench just barely in view of the distant bonfire. "Maybe this will be more good news, then. It won't be that long of a wait."

"What do you mean? Wait, Lacy, how long have you known?"

"Not long," she rushed out. "I... I had an idea, or... I felt off weeks ago when we found that cave with the pool. The morning after was when I first started getting morning sickness. But since then, well, it doesn't matter they don't have a drug store here so I can get a test. But I know. I feel her as clearly as I can feel your hand in mine."

"Her? Lacy, if you say you're pregnant, I believe you, but... what do you mean 'her?' The cave was less than two months ago. The baby is just-"

Slight irritation crept into her voice. "The days are

longer here. By the ship's computer, it's already been almost twelve weeks, but I don't need a doctor to tell me what I already know. I can feel her heartbeat. She doesn't have a voice yet, but I hear her sometimes, the same as I can hear your mind."

Dex nodded, trying to accept what she was saying, but all rational thought told him it was a knee-jerk, defensive reaction to life-changing news. "...And, what does she say?"

Lacy fought to keep her eyes from going wide. "I- it's hard to explain. Like trying to explain what a color sounds like."

Now what the hell is she talking about? Dex struggled to keep the annoyed confusion from showing on his face.

"It's like... oh... I don't know!" She threw up her hands and paced in front of him, with her arms wrapped around her stomach. Already she could feel her belly swell just under the skin. "Sometimes at night, or when it's quiet, it's like she's trying to talk to me, say hello, let me know she's there and doing okay. It's not words, just emotions."

It wasn't terribly hard to grasp, even if it was a little out there for Dex. After all, she could read his mind, manipulate living beings with a touch of her hand, and siphon the energy from objects around her. Why not add this super-awareness to the list of powers Lacy had gained from her time with the Emperor?

He took a deep breath. "All right. Lacy, this is all quite a bit to take in."

She shot her head in his direction. "I'm aware."

The music and shouting from the party was raging as strong as ever. Dex glanced back at the fire and, through the sliver of space between the huts, he saw the Mok Tau and their guests still enjoying the night.

"There could have been worse times to tell me this, though," he said.

Lacy looked where he did, at the joviality by the fire.

"Could be better times, too," he laughed. "Just promised the blue jerks I'd help their investigation." The look Lacy gave him told him that now was not the time to criticize her choice of timing. So, Dex added, "I think this would be a good place to raise a kid. There'll be others its age."

"Her age," Lacy corrected.

"Her," Dex agreed. "Okay, her age. It's not Earth, but it's safer than when we first got here. Yeah, yeah I think we'll be okay." He leaned against the wall behind the bench, not taking his eyes off the fire.

Lacy joined him again, resting her legs over his lap. "You don't think she'll feel a little out of place here? Won't be a lot of kids in school that look like her."

Dex laughed. "I'm not worried. If she's our kid, she'll be tough. Besides, I don't think a lot of the kids here will want to bully *our* daughter."

Lacy rested her head against her fist, watching Dex watch the party. She said nothing but considered looking into his mind to see what was really there.

"And I'm sure in all this time you've thought of plenty of names, huh?" Dex finally met her gaze.

She couldn't hide her elation. It had been another dam waiting to burst, but this one was much easier to let flow. "I've thought of a few."

"All right," he sighed. "Let's hear 'em."

Lacy straightened herself, and her tone perked up. "There are a few. I never really thought I'd have a daughter, at least as my first kid, but there were a few names I always liked. Linda?"

Dex laughed, "No. Ha, no, thank you."

Lacy pursed her lips in disappointment. "Barbara."

"Uh uh."

"Bernadette."

"That was my Grandmother's name. No way."

Lacy shot out names like a machine gun, and each of them, Dex shot down just as fast. "Mary. Janet. Dorothy. Gloria. Martha. Beverly. Bonnie. Peggy. Cheryl…"

"No. No. No. Nope. No. No way. Eh. Hard no.

Maybe. No thanks, I dated one in college. Baby, listen, none of these are good enough for our daughter."

"What do you mean? What's wrong with *any* of these names?"

He reached for her hand in a gesture of peace, but she pulled away. Lacy's eyes said she was just as playful as he was trying to be, but she was still going to play hardball.

"These names are all so plain! We're talking about the first human child born outside of the known universe. This is a kid they'll write books about for Christ's sake, and you want to name her Janet?"

"Well, I think it's a pretty name. And plenty of great women have had plain names. *For Christ's sake,* Mary is a pretty plain name, but I can think of two history holds in high regard."

"So, do you want to go with Mary, then?"

"No, I just mean- I don't think the ones I have are so 'simple,' as you say."

Dex laughed, "They are. But that's okay, I still love you."

"Yeah, yeah, yeah," Lacy rolled her eyes.

"Yeah, yeah, yeah nothin'. What else ya got?"

Lacy harrumphed. "No, you're being mean. I'm just gonna pick a name and you'll have to live with it if all you want to do is complain about my choices."

"Lacyyyyy..." Dex reached over and, with two fingers on her far cheek, turned her face back toward him. "I know you're saving the best for last."

"Mm Mm," she sounded off with her eyes shut tight, resisting him like a stubborn child.

"*Lacyyyyyyy...* what other name are you thinking? They still got dessert over there, but only if you're gonna be a good girl."

She reluctantly let out her breath but kept her face scrunched. "I do have one more."

"I thought so. Let's hear it."

She pushed his hand off of her face, trying to act

tough, but they both knew it was part of a friendly repertoire. "What's the dessert? If it's nothing good, I'm just picking a name on my own."

"It's those thin cake rolls with the hazelnutty and fruit toppings you like. Now, come on. What is it?"

I do like those cakes, she told herself. "Nova."

Dex lifted his chin and fell back an inch, letting the name settle in his mind. "Nova," he repeated as if testing it out. "No-va. Nova." He nodded and said one more time, "Nova. Now that's a good name for our daughter."

"Nova," Lacy said back to him.

"Nova."

"Noooooo-va."

They threw the name back and forth a number of times like they were calling an infant to crawl toward them. With each "Nova," they laughed louder and louder, and even threw in some middle names, figuring out what worked until the name was real. The child of Dex and Lacy Prullen had a name.

Nova Prullen. She was just about twelve Earth weeks along, two Taranok months, no bigger than a lime. And she was perfect.

"When should we tell the others, do you think?" Lacy asked, once again wrapped in Dex's arms.

He hadn't even thought of how or if they would break the news at all to anyone else, but he suddenly remembered all of their friends; Gurg, Toork, and Boritt, the ones that had been there traveling with them when the baby was first conceived. And Roak and Ronpup, they'd be the most excited to hear that Dex and Lacy were expecting. There was a massive celebration going on tonight, but, hell, if they spread the word now the party would carry on through the rest of the week!

"Come on!" Dex took Lacy by the hand and escorted her back toward the party. "Now! We tell them now!" Damn the rest of his responsibilities, this was far more important than a silly investigation alongside an untrustworthy ally.

They rushed through the village so fast Lacy's feet barely touched the ground. Dex pushed through the thickening crowds to get to the center of the party, keeping his eyes open for their closest friends. If anyone should hear the good news first, it'd be one of the boys; Toork, Gurg, Boritt, or Robbie. But Robbie was far off with the children and Dex didn't want to keep it in a moment longer.

"Toork! Have you seen Toork?" He asked someone in the crowd. "Gurg, anybody seen that damn frog? Boritt! You around yet? Jeez, where are they?" He'd been keeping an eye out for the three of them all night, and it was now truly setting on him that there was a very real chance the three Mok Tau hadn't attended the party at all. In fact, Dex considered the possibility that they were intentionally avoiding the festivities, specifically their Mok Rork guests.

Dex grabbed the attention of one frog after another, looking for a lead, each time asking more frantically than the next in a tone that was slowly shifting from excitement to militaristic command. Eventually, he wasn't looking to share the good news with his friends; he was an officer looking for his AWOL men. The little voice in the back of his head almost told him he'd smoke the hell out of them when he *did* find them, just for not reporting for duty. It would have been the one time they were allowed to drink while on the job, but now? So long parties, so long weekend passes, Toork and Gurg were going to be on KP for a month if they weren't going to share in his excitement.

"You seen my Staff Sergeant? You seen Toork?"

Big eyes and curious looks were all he got.

"You know who I mean; tall guy, green skin, big eyes, looks nothing like me."

"Dex, they're not here," Lacy rebuked.

"I know they're not, that's why I'm asking where they are. Hey!" he called to Jurrnup. "Hey, Sergeant! You seen Toork or Gurg anywhere?"

The Mok Tau let go of his dance partner and shifted his posture as if he was about to stand at attention, but caught himself halfway and stopped. It was a party after all, and neither of them cared too much for formalities past proper titles. "I not see. But I hear they with Roak."

"Roak!" Dex breathed a sigh of relief. That would knock down the number of times they'd have to re-break the news. "Great. Thank you, Sergeant. Ya'll enjoy yourself tonight, all right?" Dex patted both Jurrnup and his lady on the shoulders and once again ran off with Lacy.

"Damn, just imagine what Roak is gonna think when he hears this!" Dex gleamed at Lacy.

"Oh yeah!" She bounced out the words, half out of breath from Dex's dragging. "Might give him a heart attack!"

Roak didn't need to hear the news to have a heart attack.

When they pulled open the curtain to the temple, they saw him lying on a cot up against the side wall; Ronpup, another priestess, Toork, Gurg, and, of all people, Boritt, huddled around him. The legless frog was the only one to watch the two humans as they entered, giving them both a small nod of acknowledgment.

Lacy was quicker to process what was going on, but Dex quipped, "What's this? Party going past your bedtime, old man?"

Lacy whispered his name in warning as all the candlelit eyes in the room fell on him.

Ronpup opened her mouth to speak, but was cut off by Roak. "C... Come..." he wheezed, with what little of a smile he could still muster.

They stepped forward gingerly, hand held tightly in hand. Gurg shuffled to the side to make room for them as they both took a knee beside the old man, who reached out an arm that was now no thicker than a twig. His fingers had almost no color left in them, now looking like bones that could blow away like dust with the slightest gust of wind.

Taking Roak's hand gently into his own, Dex asked, "How ya feeling there? Too much excitement for one day?" He tried to sound more sympathetic than he had upon entering the temple, and Lacy, ever the sweetheart, chimed in to help ease the tension.

"Finally meet another chief out there who took your breath away?" She was halfway there and knew it. She also knew there was no getting around what he was about to say.

"I..." Roak took a deep breath in, and slowly let it out. "I th... think... I... took... hers."

The others in the room didn't know if it was okay to laugh or not, so Dex and Lacy took the burden on themselves with restraint.

"I'm sure you showed her a wonderful time," Lacy said, putting her hand on top of his and Dex's. She could feel the tears threatening to well in her eyes.

Ronpup leaned in toward the humans. "He not have much time. Roak glad you-"

She was interrupted by a boisterous wheeze from Roak, then, "I have..." *wheeze* "some... air... yet in... me... R- R... Ro..." The rest of her name faded out, but the message was clear.

Lacy looked around the circle of their closest Mok Tau friends. Everyone was staring them down as if there was some important ceremony they should have known about, as if Roak would suffer in his bed barely able to breathe until she or Dex said the magic word or gave the proper Mok Tau blessing to let his spirit pass on.

"Is..." Lacy leaned in and spoke softly. "Is there anything we can do for you, Roak?"

What started as a laugh quickly descended into a coughing fit. Roak's hand tightened as much as a hand without any strength left in it could.

"You... all..." Deep breath. "All red-dy... have." Roak gave Ronpup a glance, silently commanding her.

The priestess and her counterpart gently raised Roak's torso to help him get a better look at Dex and Lacy.

"Here, let me help." Lacy offered and took his hand from Dex's.

"What are you doing?" Dex asked.

Lacy didn't answer. She centered her mind, her energy, on Roak. Little by little she poured into him. Faintly, a modicum of color returned to Roak's skin. Sweat dripped from Lacy's brow, and she felt her stomach tighten.

"Lacy," Dex warned.

Lacy didn't listen. The man who had welcomed them into their village, had given them food, shelter, and protection, had given them both purpose again and a home, was suffering in his final moments and if she couldn't give him life again she could at least ease his pain. But the tightening in her stomach sharpened. A cry of pain, a plea for help rang in her mind.

"Lacy, stop!"

The other Mok Tau had perked up. Fear had overcome all of them.

Lacy pushed a little more, hoping light would come into Roak's eyes, wishing she could give him more time. But the pain inside her, the anguish, and then the Voice.

Far in the distance of her mind's eye arose a building of tainted ivory, and a thousand soft and vicious voices whispered in the back of her mind, *I see you...*

"Lacy!" Dex shouted and tore her hand away from Roak's.

She fell onto her back, utterly drenched in sweat, with a fever burning in her brain. But worst of all was the pain in her stomach.

"Lacy, what the hell is going on?" Dex cupped her tear- and sweat-soaked cheek in his hand.

She clung to her stomach with both arms. "I just wanted to help."

Dex pulled her up to his chest and kissed her forehead. "It's okay," he whispered. "It's okay."

"It is time," Roak spoke clearly.

They all turned back to the old man, who still looked very much an old man, but now a few feet away from death's door rather than on it.

Dex helped Lacy sit up again, unknowingly putting his hand on her stomach too.

Just as fast as the color had returned to Roak, it was fading again. "Dex... Lacy... I have waited... long time for you. Taranok... hard planet. Hard life for all." He took a controlled breath in but shook, letting it out. "Mok Tau, all peoples, we survive, we grateful... even with evil in world... because we know... there is... still... good. There is you. And there is... more." Roak paused, taking a few breaths. No one thought to interrupt him. "Red God. Not true. Red God... liar. Evil... But that not mean real... true... god... is not there... somewhere. Out there." Pointing to Dex, he said, "You not see now. But... you... will. I not know... who I... pray to. But I k- know... know they... listen. They..." he looked back and forth between Dex and Lacy. "They... send you." Roak coughed again. He was a few steps closer to the door now.

Roak then focused on Lacy. "You strong. And... you... good. Bu..." Roak's chest tightened with his inhale, and he coughed letting it out. "But heart... can... lie. Keep y-... your heart... safe." His hand drifted back to his body. "Th- thank... you. I... leave... now. Happy...

"People...

"Like...

He looked around the room one final time, meeting the gaze of everyone present.

"You...

"In. The... world."

Roak closed his eyes.

The Mok Tau and Dex all bowed their heads.

Not Lacy, though. Lacy leaned in and whispered through her weeping, "We wanted you to know, Dex and I, we're having a baby." She sniffed back her tears. Her voice trembled as she said, "One more little tail in the village. Isn't that great?"

Ever so softly, Roak breathed out his final words. "That... is... wonderful."

36. Altar of the Red God

The cries of merriment were solemnly replaced with cries of mourning as the news of Roak's passing spread throughout the village. A procession led by Ronpup carried the body of the deceased chief around the dying embers of the bonfire as the sun began to rise on Taranok.

In the procession behind Ronpup were four pallbearers of the decorated slab Roak lay on, for all to see. Behind them, Dex and Lacy, then the visiting tribal chiefs, and in the ever-growing rear, the rest of the tribe as the procession passed them by and led them out of the village gate to Roak's final resting place.

Lacy, to the confusion of the funeral procession, asked that a hole be dug in a nearby clearing for Roak's body to be buried in. Although the purpose of this request was not entirely understood, the Mok Tau did as they were told. Prior to the humans' arrival on Taranok, what was in the past stayed in the past. Whatever served no purpose to their survival, or the Emperor, was of no concern to the natives of the jungle planet. If someone died, they could no longer pray or live in service to their god, and memory of something deemed no longer significant should not be held higher than god. Change took time. With the return of the imprisoned warriors, the tribe had attempted to turn from these old traditions. But it was a very slow work in progress.

Very slow.

So it was that the Mok Tau and the chiefs of the other tribes could barely grasp what the purpose of Lacy's theatrics were. Even less so, what she meant by pressing two sticks tied together into the ground where Roak was buried.

Lacy didn't elaborate on the latter, nor did she justify it to Dex when he gave her a disagreeable glance over it.

The crowd began to disperse before Lacy had even pierced the freshly laid dirt with the cross. The world outside was still dangerous. With a short, wordless nod of his head, Dex tried to tell her to return to the village. But she stayed with her head low in a quiet vigil, saying a prayer under her breath.

Dex waited impatiently for her to finish, watching everyone else return to the safety of the village. Eventually, it was just the two of them left. Sounds of daily life began to creep over the village wall. The Mok Tau got on with their lives.

When she was done, Lacy took Dex's hand and let him escort her back into the village where the Mok Rork chief was waiting to get a move on for their investigation.

"Journey long," Chief Robert announced before the gates had even closed behind Dex and Lacy. He seemed to have no care for the state of the village he was a guest in. Though, in his defense, the people weren't acting as if they were in a state of anything at all.

Still, even if the Mok Tau didn't need much more time to mourn, Lacy did.

"The journey can wait a few more minutes," Dex told Chief Robert, pulling Lacy in a little closer. "There's some stuff we've got to work out first, anyway."

The Mok Rork dismissed Dex's words with a proud jerk of his head. "We leave soon. Beasts ready for road back."

Dex held up a hand. "Give me time," he demanded. "I told you I'd come along, and I will. But this tribe just lost its chief. I'll send my men to get my ride ready and meet you outside the walls in half an hour. All right?"

Robert narrowed his eyes. "How many? Mok Rork not travel with Mok Tau war party."

"Just two. My two best men. We'll bring our own supplies and animals. You won't have to take care of us if that is your concern."

The chief pulled back, contemplating his next words very carefully, and in the end decided not to say anything. Dex's terms were acceptable, and he would not be the one to instigate. The human seemed a twinge unpredictable. The resentment was still there on Dex's end, but the human was making an effort to maintain peace, and that was commendable.

When Robert didn't speak, Dex said again, this time softer, "Half an hour. I'll be ready."

* * *

"I want to come with you," Lacy told Dex as she watched him pack his rucksack. The few possessions they had in their little hut on the hill were rapidly swept away with his packing. There had not been much need for non-utilitarian items. Everything they owned served a purpose for their survival. So now, with a nearly full pack, Dex looked like he was moving them out.

Although he dreaded saying it, Dex had to argue her demand. "Maybe if this came up a week ago. But not now, baby, not while you've got one."

With arms crossed in front of her chest, she argued back, "You were fine with me coming on the last mission."

"You didn't tell me you were pregnant," he said plainly without missing a beat. Dex pulled a half dozen beetle wraps from their food store and packed them into a side pouch of the rucksack; the final items. The bugs had grown on him as a part of their diet, even though they had discovered much better options that were not meant to serve as travel foods.

Lacy continued to press, "And if I told you sooner, you wouldn't let me go on the raid? Dex, you know you needed me up there." Even as she said it, she knew he'd find a way to argue around it or otherwise nullify her argument with a quick-witted response, so before he could speak, she repositioned her defense and doubled down. "What if I had known before you wiped Earth from the ship's computer?"

"Did you?" he asked, eyebrows raised. After the battle at Torro-Kaal, it hadn't been that hard of a decision to make, cutting themselves off from Earth entirely for the rest of their lives. But at the time, he was only considering the future of two people.

"Would you have brought us back because of the baby?"

His sense of duty strained at the challenge. They'd made a commitment to the people of Taranok, but he couldn't deny that his family was more important.

But Lacy felt no such conflict. There was a path she could follow in her mind. It was narrower than she believed, but nevertheless a path they could walk, living for both their family and the fight against the Empire. "Do you think something's really out there?"

Dex almost laughed. "I think there's an angry frog that would like to stab me in the back..." Lacy rolled her eyes, and he continued, "...as well as, at most, a salty imperial who managed to escape the attack. He's trying to scare these guys, nothing more. And that's *if* our blue friend isn't lying."

Lacy stepped closer and took hold of Dex's ruck as he picked it up. "You need me out there."

He smiled back, replying casually, "I always need you."

Lacy pursed her lips. "If you're so distrustful, let me look into his mind. I'll touch his hand and know if he's lying or not."

Dex considered it, but knew it wouldn't work. "He'll never let you get that close. The whole tribe saw what you did to their witch."

Someone outside knocked on their door. Dex lifted his head to look past Lacy's shoulder, but she stole his attention back.

"One of his men, then," she offered.

"Good luck. Again, they all saw." He slung the ruck over his right shoulder and sidestepped her as their guest knocked again.

From the other side of the door came the voice of one of the First Squad privates. "Cap-tain Dex, Sar-gants ready to go for you."

Dex nodded to the door as if the private could see him, then told Lacy, "Stay here. I'll be back as soon as I can. Just about a week." If he could have loaded up the company in the *Silent Horizon*, that would have been his first choice of method of travel. But unless they sent someone ahead to the Mok Rork camp to tell the villagers there to clear a landing zone, they likely wouldn't be able to land anywhere reasonably close. Additionally, the Mok Rork had to bring their razorbacks back to their village.

To stop him from leaving, Lacy threw her arms around Dex and kept him grounded. "I don't want to be without you again. This is the worst time you could leave."

Dex squeezed her tightly and kissed her cheek. "You think I want to be without *you* again? Come on, you silly girl," he laughed. "I'm only doing this to impress you."

She pulled back with her face scrunched in confusion, cheeks a cherry red.

His face only showed humor and a charming smile. "So you think I'm some big, strong hero. Earth has Tarzan of the Apes, Taranok has Dex of the Frogs."

Lacy rolled her eyes and accepted the fact that there was no stopping him. She puffed up her cheeks and gave him a quick guppy kiss on the cheek. "Just swing back to me fast, Tarzan."

* * *

Toork and Gurg - *Sergeants* Toork and Gurg - sat mounted on their respective razorbacks, a fair distance away from the Mok Rork party, awaiting Dex. The early morning humidity had begun to dissipate, along with the yellow, low-light glow of the frog-creatures' eyes. While they were ablaze, the glow took up the entirety of their eyes, and it was difficult to perceive what exactly they were looking at. Now, though, it was hard to miss that the Mok Rork were looking at everything *but* Toork and Gurg. With the death of Morgup the Mok Rork witch through a gloriously theatrical display of Lacy's godlike powers, the tribe was briefly welcoming of the change of leadership. But it was after they had left and attacks on their village increased from their shadowy foe, many were questioning how better off they were under the protection of the witch's dark rituals.

Under his breath, and in their native language, Toork whispered to Gurg, "Bpur'ta rrtpu ta up brub," loosely translated to, *How much would you bet it's a trap?*

Gurp scoffed with a grin, "Trup'pa tab." *It definitely is.*

When Toork laughed back, the Mok Rork Chief shot him a hard glare. The wind may have carried the Mok Tau's words, but the dialects between the two tribes were different enough that he might not have understood them clearly.

As if to test their luck, Gurg added while staring Robert back down, "Pbuura t'tapa Jurrnup ah, grbutta tup ribbit rr'ub Mok Rork rutuba." *Put a tup in the Mok Rork's food store, and I'll take Jurrnup from your squad.*

Toork doubted what he'd heard. Jurrnup was a good warrior, but had a habit of questioning orders and bringing morale down. To get him off his webbed hands, hell, he'd put one of those eternally hungry critters in their own food store at Gurg's request.

The two of them shook hands, sealing the deal, as Captain Dex told them, well aware that Robert could see their scheming.

The village gate opened, and standing on the other side was Dex with his rucksack. When the humans had first come to the village, the gate would have been opened just enough for someone to get in and then closed immediately behind them. Now, though, times had changed. Whoever manned the gate took their time letting it swing shut.

Dex wiped his brow from the rapidly accumulating

sweat and threw the strap of his ruck over one of the spikes on his razorback. "We all ready to step off?" he asked his men.

"We good, frog leader," Toork answered. "I inspect Sar-gent Gurg back. He ready fight if Mok Rork play games." He made sure to say it loud enough for the other tribe to hear.

"*Staff* Sar-gent," Gurg corrected with a smirk. "Soon Sar-gant one class."

For the sake of being diplomatic and not having a *totally* uncomfortable journey, Dex chided, "I'm sure that won't be an issue." Then, to the Mok Rork chief, "Will it, Robert?"

The chief responded with something in his own tribe's dialect.

"You catch any of that?" Dex asked his men.

Both Toork and Gurg shook their heads, and Gurg mused, "Maybe he offer Mok Rork women to make good."

Toork, for his part, loved the thought. Dex laughed along with them, mounting the slick hide of the razorback, but said, "You can keep their women if you like. I'm all good with the one I've got." He glanced up the the village wall as he spun his razorback around toward the direction of the Mok Rork village, expecting to see Lacy atop it watching him leave, like a maiden in a fairy tale bidding farewell to her knight, even though he knew that wasn't where she would be. They both had jobs to do, and it wasn't the end of the world. There was no use acting like it was.

Just another mission, Dex thought to himself.

Pulling him out of his head, Gurg asked Dex, "Robbie not come?"

"No, Robbie's not coming this time," Dex replied. He flicked the reins of his razorback, kicking their convoy into motion. "We've all got our roles around here. I lead the troops, Lacy leads me and inspires the troops, and Robbie hangs out with the kids so the troops don't have to worry about them."

Seeing Dex and the two Mok Tau moving, the Mok Rork party kicked off as well, leading the party from the front, Robert at the head. Toork and Gurg rode on either side of Dex in the rear, even though it was difficult to maintain a solid line with the heavy jungle foliage getting in the way.

"Robbie useful to team," Gurg said. "Hand fire, good against jungle beast."

"Yeah, it is," Dex agreed. "But so are these." He held up his blaster, thankful that Toork and Gurg now had blasters of their own.

"Robbie not come to moon raid, too," Gurg added, with what sounded like a hint of concern in his rubbery voice.

Dex only laughed. "If I'd known you wanted him to come along so badly, I would've grabbed him. What? Toork and I aren't good enough company anymore?"

This time, Toork spoke up. "Robbie good for team. Not good not ap- apprec..." he threw Gurg a questioning look and rubbed his long fingers together, searching for the right word in Dex's language.

"Aprec-e-ate," Gurg informed incorrectly with a victorious grin.

"Yes," Toork beamed. "Dex aprec-e-ate Robbie. Not forget to aprec-e-ate Robbie."

Dex looked back and forth between the two. His face still held humor, but there was a nibble of concern that they were truly questioning him. "I do *appreciate* him. Robbie's like a son to me. If I didn't treat him like that, Lacy would kill me."

"Lacy smart hooman," Toork said, tapping his cranium.

"Yeah, she is," Dex grinned, taking the compliment of her as a compliment for himself, as he sure knew how to pick 'em.

"May be Mok Rork women smart too, like Loo-tent Lacy," Gurg thought out loud.

Happy to be off the subject of Robbie, Dex let the humor return in full to his smile. "What is it with you and these girls?"

Toork leaned forward on his razorback to hear Gurg's answer.

Gurg shrugged and said, "Some thing about they dress. Dark colors, mean look. Markings they make on skin. Morgup evil witch, but..." He shook in an over-the-top way to demonstrate his excitement, much to Dex and Toork's confusion.

"Gurg," Dex had to hold back a laugh, "She tortured you and didn't have eyes in her sockets."

The Mok Rork toward the back of the trail were beginning to pick up on the conversation and look back at them, but Gurg did not mind. In fact, he was partially saying it just to get a reaction from them. "Morgup had it where counts."

Partially to get a reaction.

Dex stammered out his words. "I... I don't even know what does 'count' to you guys. I don't know if I want to."

* * *

Lacy didn't watch Dex leave from a parapet. She didn't have a chance to watch him leave at all. While the Mok Tau were still grappling with the new mentality of allowing themselves to mourn and honor the memory of the dead, their actions showed they were more than ready to move on and find a new chief-slash-religious leader. From the moment Dex stepped out of the hut, like him, Lacy was called to duty.

Ronpup had been waiting outside the hut alongside the First Squad private, who shied away at her presence for her newly assumed role. She, more so than the rest of the tribe, felt constrained by the death of Roak. For the time being, all of his leadership and spiritual responsibilities fell to her. Many of those responsibilities currently centered around the deconstruction of the Emperor's influence. Roak had handled the transition to the best of his ability. But now he was gone, and the pieces were falling apart faster than Ronpup could put them back together.

Already, concerned villagers had gathered at the temple with offerings to whoever would take Roak's place and sacrifice them to whichever higher being would accept them. Without Roak's sturdy anti-Red God belief, those in the woodwork who still harbored comfort in the tradition of the Red God crept out and considered returning to the old ways; the irony of this new ideology of not letting the past die.

Ronpup escorted Lacy through the village, back to the temple with a rushed grace. Lacy could read in her body language, her overly stiff upper body and chin held excessively high, just how unprepared she was for that morning. Roak had looked to be inches from death since the humans had first met him, but whether it was because he constantly found reasons to keep living, or he was too physically slow to walk those few inches, the idea that he would actually die someday seemed much further away from the threshold of death.

And now, it seemed, some of the villagers may have been waiting for the old frog to croak just so fresh blood could lead them. For when Ronpup and Lacy came upon the temple, it was Lacy that the arms extended with offerings gravitated toward.

"Take food gifts to store," Ronpup commanded the gathering, throwing out her hand to send the villagers away. Her bangles and necklaces clinked with the motion. Food had been plentiful in the recent weeks, but there was still no need to waste it all on one person. Things could take a turn at any moment, and neither Ronpup nor Lacy would be the gluttons hoarding it for a false sense of status; social or divine.

But the villagers didn't heed her command. Some

waited for Lacy to tell them what to do. Others, those who still sympathized with the Red God, pushed forward through the crowd. For their entire lives and far earlier than that, the Red God resided in the dreams of the tails, and his word became law through the Elder in the temple. They would deliver their gifts there if the Red God would still have them.

"Do as she says," Lacy told the crowd. "Roak trusted her, and so do I. Take the food to the storehouse. That food is for the tribe." To quell the crowd's trepidation, she said with a soft smile, "It still doesn't sit perfectly well with me."

Those in the crowd looked to each other for approval, and one by one, a few of them separated and backed away toward the food storehouse.

Ronpup then added to appease the crowd, "All other gift leave here, then be gone. And tell others, no more. We not give to old god."

Her demand, even though it was supported by Lacy, was met with grumbling. And still, only another two or three villagers pulled away.

Seeing that there was nothing they could say other than "bring us your firstborn" that would truly satisfy the people, Ronpup and Lacy retreated into the temple, and Ronpup ordered two of Roak's assistants to stand outside and collect offerings. She told them in the Mok Tau tongue, *Remember who gives what. We will see to it that gifts are discreetly returned when things have settled.*

The temple assistants nodded and exited the temple to do as they were told.

With a moment to finally breathe, Ronpup took a seat in her usual place by the low altar, just next to where Roak used to sit.

"I did not think would be this way," Ronpup said, wiping sweat from the side of her head. "One hundred forty year, Roak lead Mok Tau. Lead Mok Tau good. I not heard his name once in that crowd."

Lacy bit her lip, then found her seat across from

Ronpup. On a now-empty cot just beside them, Roak had drawn his final breath only a few hours earlier. And Ronpup was right, the people outside were acting like he'd never been there at all. It wasn't a surprise that things would be tenuous with his passing, but neither of them had considered - or, more accurately, wanted to consider - how much change the village was facing all at once.

"One hundred and forty years is quite the accomplishment," Lacy said. "Back where Dex and I are from, we only allow our leaders to serve for four. Eight if they're good at their job."

Lacy expected a response in surprise, but Ronpup took the stark cultural divide with stride. "What if they bad at leading? Chief before Roak only lead one year. Tails dream Red God curse him and next day banished."

"Well..." she said, wondering exactly how bad the chief had to be in order to receive such a severe punishment, "At least in my part of the world, we just find someone new. Other places are a bit more uncivilized about it."

"Un-civilized? Mok Tau not know that word."

Realizing she had to explain what she meant, Lacy became embarrassed, knowing that by her Earth standards, banishing their chief to a harsh jungle death because of a dream, the Mok Tau fit the bill.

"It just means..." she began, searching for something appropriate to say, then leaned in as if they were being listened in on. "Like the Mok Rork. Just a little... rude. Not at all like this tribe."

"Ah," Ronpup exclaimed. "I see. Of lesser beliefs."

Lacy did not like the implications of where this conversation was going.

"The people won't be stilled until someone reins them in," Lacy said hesitantly. "I don't mean to be brash, but the Mok Tau have only ever known life like that. I'll accept the blame on my and my husband's end, we turned things upside down a little fast for everyone."

"It was needed change," Ronpup replied. "I not

know that when you come, but I know now, seeing tribes come together. But that change mean new strong leader too."

"I agree. The Mok Tau need someone like you to guide them. You're more than capable, and I'm sure they'll come around when-"

In a move none other in the village would dare, Ronpup raised her hand in front of her chest to politely silence Lacy. "I not the leader Mok Tau need," she said. "I not the leader Mok Tau listen to."

"I don't see why not. The people already respect you, they trust you."

"But Mok Tau not believe in Ronpup," she said. There was no sadness or defeat in her voice. It was stated very matter-of-factly. She continued, "Mok Tau need something to worship. Dex and Lacy kill Mok Tau god."

Lacy pursed her lips, almost feeling guilty for the Emperor, but quickly corrected herself.

Ronpup went on. "Red God strong. May not be real god, as you say, but even you can not say Red God not have true power."

Unfortunately, Lacy couldn't argue. Even on the furthest planet they could find from the Heart of the Void, the Emperor's grasp could still reach them. "Then it becomes your responsibility to change the way things are around here." Lacy tried to assert herself, but Ronpup was already set in her thoughts.

"I not believe Lacy and Dex gods. I know what you are. And I know what you have." Ronpup reached out and touched Lacy's hand. A shudder of energy passed between them, and if she wanted, Lacy could have seen into Ronpup's mind, or transferred life from one of them to the other. She held power over the Mok Tau woman, and Ronpup knew it. "Lacy can lead Mok Tau. Mok Tau know you have power. They not know what to do, now Roak gone, because they not know what *you* will do."

Lacy pulled away, scooting back a few inches. "I...

I can't… That's not my place in all this." She tried to laugh it off as if Ronpup was playing a joke on her. *Thanks for besting our god, would you like his throne? What about a healthy serving of our best sacrifices?*

"No, not your place. But Mok Tau have need. And Lacy have power." Ronpup then paused and concentrated hard in preparing her next words. The Emperor's language was taught to the people of Taranok through the visions he'd sent the young children, and tribal leaders. Now that it was known he was not the benevolent god he was once thought to be, the drive to perfect their understanding of his language had somewhat diminished. But, it was also the language the humans spoke. So for Lacy, she spoke slowly and intently. "These are my people. Roak trusted me to do what is best for my people. You may not want it, but you can take it." She leaned in again and whispered, "No Mok Tau, no Mok Rork or other tribe can stop power of Loo-tent Lacy."

Lacy picked herself up off the ground. Her heart raced, and a little voice somewhere in her mind shouted a warning in the quietest decibel level she could perceive. She hadn't even considered her power for something like that, or even how others in the tribe perceived it. Sure, the Mok Rork were scared of her, but she had a justifiable cause to use the power as she did on the witch. What had she done for the Mok Tau to fear her? Or was it that they didn't fear her yet, and were just waiting for her to give them a reason to?

"I can't do that," she said. "Dex and I are…" *Guests? Here to stay?* No, neither of those were true anymore.

"I not talk about Dex. Cap-tain Dex strong in own way. But he not you."

The warning persisted. It would be so easy to step in as chief. But what was the need? Things may be a bit messy now, yes, but it would stabilize. Things would work themselves out.

But will they? Another voice, one unfamiliar, but just as persistent. *The castle is crumbling. Before long, the people will lose direction. Their tenets are falling apart, their world falling apart. All they knew was a lie, and you're the reason. It's only right you tie them all back together. Lead the pack. Guide them as you see fit. Cull those who don't fall in line.*

With the voice came a soft haze over her vision. She saw Ronpup in front of her, sitting by the altar, staring up at her, but the painting on the wall was different. The images Roak had commissioned were gone, and in its place, a cloud of deep red so real, the wall was not even there anymore. She could see miles past the wall, and drawing close was a structure of brown ivory. Towers grew on the sides, doubling the building's height.

That was where the voice came from. And it was drawing ever closer.

Lacy cast the vision away, and returned her attention to Ronpup. "I can't be what you need for these people. I can help– I *will* help in any way I can. But what you're asking of me I cannot do."

Ronpup made no mention of it, but had seen Lacy's lost look. She bowed her head and said, "Then I will take all help I can get. As say, Roak trust me to do best for Mok Tau. I will lead if Roak tell me to."

* * *

Dinner on the second night of their journey was as tense as dinner on the first night of their journey. The Mok Rork kept to one side of their low-burning fire, while Dex and his Mok Tau friends kept to the other side, picking at their rations but keeping their focus on their unwanted allies. The crackling of the fire and the distant chirping of insects were the only sounds of the jungle breaking up the awkward silence between the two groups.

Lacy would have wanted Dex to be the bigger person and create either peace or at least tolerance between the two parties through his leadership. But it was Robert, the Mok Rork chief, who took the lead.

"Ibut," he said to one of his men with the lift of his chin. "Rok biddu rup." One of the other Mok Rork grabbed a spear without hesitation and leapt into the nearest tree, his glowing yellow eyes vanishing into the night.

Dex leaned in toward Toork, who sat closer to him. "What did he say?"

Toork slurped the remaining meat from the smoked beetle ration he'd been picking at. "Ibut," he pointed in the direction of the now disappeared Mok Rork, "he 'pull security' as you call it."

Dex pursed his lips. It was a smart move by the chief, and should have been ordered by himself already. But they were all still awake and alert, and the only danger Dex had been concerned with at the time was the frogs sitting opposite the fire from him. And now, even more than before, they were at the mercy of the Mok Rork.

"I want you up there, too," Dex told Toork. "You, Gurg, and I will take shifts tonight. One of us and one of them awake at all times." He then nudged Gurg. "You hear what I said?"

Gurg tossed the remains of his dinner into the fire, where it burned up as fast as it had fallen in, and there remained no evidence the bug had ever existed. "I not pay attention. Dinner too good," he said. "Torimmin make my pack special."

If he had been by Gurg's side instead of Dex, Toork would have bumped Gurg's arm in jest. All he said instead was, "You with Torimmin or get evil, tattoo women?" He spoke intentionally in what was still referred to as the Emperor's tongue so that the Mok Rork were less likely to hear talk of their own women.

"I with whoever make best meal for strong warrior like *Staff* Sar-gant Gurg," Gurg said, smacking a flexed bicep.

Toork scoffed humorously, but Dex was in no such mood. "You can think about women when we get back to the village. But for now, listen up." He then relayed his thoughts to both sets of listening ears, and Gurg, for his previous lack of awareness and misplaced priorities, took first watch.

He waited a few minutes before grabbing his spear and climbing up the nearest tree, so as not to look like he was acting in direct response to the Mok Rork.

The Mok Rork chief was the only one on his side of the party who made no attempt to hide that he was watching Gurg follow his man up into a defensive position. All of the others kept their attention on their food or areas of the jungle just outside their circle, and only briefly glanced up at Gurg.

"I'll take the next watch," Dex told Toork. "You'll relieve me four hours after that. Understood?"

Toork nodded and affirmed, "Understood."

* * *

Lacy was kept up far later than she had expected to be that same night. On the first day of Roak's passing there had been confusion among the villagers. On the second day since his death it was almost as if there were two separate clans living within the walls of the Mok Tau village. There was an unsmelled foulness in the air between neighbors, a certain knowing that invisible lines had been drawn in the sand.

On that morning, offerings to Lacy and Dex which had been left outside of the village temple had been found by Ronpup destroyed. Only a handful had been left untouched, and without any indication as to why those were spared from desecration. Lacy spent the morning picking up the debris that had been left, even though Ronpup asked her not to. "Talking to Mok Tau would do better than cleaning their mess," she told her.

"They're not my people to tell what to do," Lacy said in response. "They're scared and confused. They need time to be able to work things out for themselves." Though with each basket of squashed fruits she brought out to the livestock trough she made, she wished more and more that the people would need less and less time to figure their issues out.

By evening, things were not much better. There was no formal event or celebration being held, but Ronpup sent out word for any who wished to join together for a communal dinner with food that had been brought in offering to the temple. The meaning was not lost on Lacy once certain disgruntled faces shuffled around the outskirts of the village center, nor those who had given those particular offerings to begin with.

"I see you discovered why some of the baskets were left untouched," Lacy commented after dinner had begun.

Ronpup had a very openly displayed platter of fruit in front of her. She ate of it and shared it with those nearby with embellished courtesy. But in quiet, to Lacy she said, "What was left, left for Red God. But Red God not will receive offering. This for Mok Tau."

Lacy caught the glare of one of the villagers sitting under the awning of his hut. A red line, faint but very intentional, had been painted above his door. It hadn't registered until that moment, but that was not the first marking Lacy had seen around town. Even deep within herself, a whisper of a thought forewarned her of growing hostilities among the Mok Tau.

"Do you really think testing their patience is the best way to win them over?" Lacy asked.

Ronpup's fake smile jittered and cracked. "If you would like do otherwise, I would not stop you."

Instead of an answer, Lacy decided that she was no longer hungry. Ronpup hadn't set this all up for the sole purpose of making a statement for the tribe. She'd done it to prove a point to Lacy, to push her in the direction she thought the tribe needed from the human. For the time being, there were others she felt would better appreciate her time.

Lacy found Robbie where he'd been all day, in the underlair of the big cinema-tree. Even though the setting sun was shining through the trees just perfectly onto the makeshift screen, it was apparent that the projector wasn't at its full power. The black-and-white image of two saucermen from mars - or some other distant planet - standing by their ship in front of a platoon of soldiers, faded in and out of clarity.

"Haven't gotten tired of these old movies yet?" she asked, taking a seat next to the robot.

Robbie jumped at her voice, only just noticing the other children had left a long time ago. "I didn't hear you coming."

"That's all right." She paused to watch the action, then added, "I remember this one. Caused quite the stir when it came out." In one respect, she wasn't speaking from memory. *Visitors from the Stars* was one of those movies Dex had forced her to watch during the early days of their journey aboard the *Silent Horizon*. She never told him that she had in fact seen it with her family when it came out in the mid '30s, but she let him believe it was her first time so he could fill her in on all the trivia around the movie, such as it being the center of an apparent conspiracy in which the government had commissioned the film to be made in order to cover up an actual arrival or visitors from the stars. Once Hollywood put their mark on it and played up the fantastical elements, believers of the "cover-up" would be relegated to nut-jobs who couldn't distinguish movies from reality. It was a fascinating little history lesson, and a good laugh, but now that she was actually out here with actual aliens, the chances of visitors having actually come down to Earth years before didn't seem so outlandish.

His response came a few seconds delayed as if in contemplation. "It is fun. B-but it feels like many of the same elements as others I have watched."

For the first time that day, Lacy thought she could laugh. "Quite the critic already, aren't ya? You'll have to talk to Dex about this one when he gets back, hear his thoughts on it."

"What is a critic?"

"You, if all you do is watch these movies all day. Come on. Last one for the night or you'll drain the batt-" She cut herself short.

Robbie's turn toward her was as delayed as his prior response. And in one of those moments where his voice didn't sound quite so robotic, he asked, "But you can find new batteries for it, right?"

Lacy bit her lip, hoping Robbie hadn't learned to pick up on every nuance yet. "Of course we can," she eventually said. "As soon as humanly possible."

* * *

On the third day of their journey, Dex was jostled awake by Toork's shaking and wide eyes.

"Cap-tain Dex. Must wake. Mok Rork kill us now."

Dex threw off of himself the heavy leaf of a juwappa tree he had been using as concealment and a blanket, and came into a low crouch position with his blaster drawn. "Where are they?" he whispered. "Where's Sergeant G? Get your blaster out, come on!"

Instead of doing as his senior officer ordered, Toork raised his spear, the weapon he still preferred to use over the more advanced firearm. "Gurg with Mok Rork."

Dex jumped to his feet with his blaster held outward and took a few steps forward. "Now, why the hell would he be with them? He a prisoner?"

Toork came up close behind, but did not have his spear in a position ready to attack with. "Mok Rork say man go missing. They take off to look, and Gurg with them. But I stay back to tell you. I think they mean kill us off one at time."

"Someone's missing?" Dex paused, keeping his blaster raised but turned his head back toward Toork.

"While on guard. They say Mok Rork disappear during Gurg watch. Mok Rork blame Gurg, but Gurg deny, so he go to help."

It was entirely possible, Dex thought, that someone really was missing. If they had wanted to kill Dex and the Mok Tau, there had been plenty of opportunities over the last two days, and they were severely outnumbered. Even now, they could have killed Dex in his sleep or not let Toork get away to warn him. Toork hadn't even seemed to be in a frenzy, waking Dex up, so it was safe to assume he hadn't been chased.

Seeing the others had left their packs with the animals around their camp, Dex told Toork to "Hang back and pull security. Don't let strays get our food... or Robert's guys our gear. I don't think they set a trap for us, but just in case they come back looking a little too happy I'm not with them, be ready to run. Don't fight, just get back to the village and tell the others what happened. Understood?"

Toork nodded. "I gather Mok Tau to crush Mok Rork camp."

"That's fine with me. Do whatever you have to, but get back to the village first. Now, which way did they all take off?"

Toork pointed in the direction he had come from, where Dex could then faintly hear sounds of group movement through the jungle, then leapt to a higher vantage point among the trees. From his perch, he kept a close eye on Dex's careful movement through the canopy. The razorbacks were a fire deterrent from predators, but it would be a surprise to no one if an exceptionally hungry hyper-raptor or a pack of rabid barq cubs were looking for a meal to drag back to their nest.

Dex left without another word, taking deliberate steps, avoiding twigs and dead leaves on the ground. Unfortunately, his lack of proper training in areas of stealth made itself apparent when two Mok Rork managed to get the jump on him from higher up.

"Chief Robert waiting for you," one of the frogs said at full volume. And when Dex began to lower his blaster to his side, the frog added, "Keep ready. Something here with us."

Although the threat of a mystery antagonist was by no means resolved, Dex did feel a little more at ease now that he hadn't immediately been skewered by the Mok Rork. Yet still, he felt as if he was being watched. Not by one of the frogs, his own or the Mok Rork, but the "something" his guide was talking about. Something foreign.

Very foreign.

Not-of-this-jungle kinda' foreign, Dex thought to himself.

"Have you found anything yet?" Dex asked his new companion.

The Mok Rork only shook his head and wordlessly pushed on, being obviously careful to make as little noise as possible, and keeping low. Following his lead, Dex kept to a path that led him under overhanging leaves, and stuck close to the trees for cover. Open spaces, no matter how small, had suddenly felt extremely dangerous.

They ran into no enemies, though, as they navigated the jungle floor. Tiny alien insects skittered across Dex's feet, biting at the boots the Mok Tau had made for him from razorback hide.

A few meters ahead, yet still out of sight, he could begin to hear the low chatter of the rest of the Mok Rork and, to his relief, Gurg's familiar voice. But accompanying their voices was the smell of death.

A successful morning hunt? Dex thought to himself, although he very well knew that couldn't be further from the truth; he couldn't pick up on the pheromones a Taranok boar released upon death to warn others nearby of danger. This was an unnaturally foul stench. It invaded his nostrils and latched onto his flesh. A hundred hot showers couldn't cleanse him of the evil that was the source of this smell.

Coming into a clearing where the stench was the strongest, Dex had to hold back his horror at what he saw. The Mok Rork all kept to the rim of the clearing. There was a darkness cast over it all by a swarm of buzzing, bloated flies, and crawling all over the decaying vegetation of the jungle floor was a carpet of maggots. And in the center of it all, death itself.

The Altar of the Red God.

It was the shock of its reality that bludgeoned Dex. He had been so sure the Mok Rork chief was playing him; that with Morgup gone, nothing could be so vile. The altar was propped up just over two feet high by four legs of twisted bone wrapped in dark crimson tendons that spread like roots into and across the ground. The tabletop was rectangular, about four feet long and a little more than two feet wide. It was made of the same material as the legs, but the edges were overlaid with what looked like the native's jewelry, rusted to the same crimson as the meat dripping from the table. Two rows of ribcages, side by side and pulled open, with taut, black flesh clinging to them, stacked from the back side of the altar, over six feet high. Bundles of arm bones; humeri, radii, and ulnae were melded together to create new arms as thick as one's torso, held up toward the sky. From the shoulders was the only part of the statue not made with body parts; a flowing cape made with the same kind of leaf Dex had slept with, painted red. It hung down well past the base of the altar and trailed as far out as the edge of the clearing. Atop all of it was the most stark difference between the real man and the statue. Unlike the rest of the body, the skull was only sourced from one being. But it was stretched thin to fit the larger dimension of the rest of the corrupted body. The tension around the jaw and the eye sockets in particular resembled that of a living man's skin when he screams at a pain incomprehensible; when all the light and good of the world has been torn away, and all that is left is the horror of the emptiness, but death cannot come quick enough.

Within the clearing, there was nothing left but dread.

"Tear it down."

Everyone's eyes shot to Dex. His voice didn't sound real as it broke the silence that infested the clearing.

Without being able to look away from the warped face of the Emperor, Dex repeated himself more authoritatively. "Tear it down, now. Burn it. Do whatever needs to be done. Just destroy it."

The Mok Rork chief took a single step toward him. "These our family. We must give bodies respect. Not destroy."

Dex felt his hand tremble. He wanted to reach out, grab the Mok Rork chief, and throw him to the ground for his resistance. Letting this thing stand for another moment was nothing short of an abomination. And to not want it destroyed utterly, sin.

"Those people aren't your family anymore," Dex said, rage he couldn't justify building inside of him. "Burn it," he repeated. "Burn it, and we'll get to finding our missing man."

The Mok Rork chief and two of his men closed in on Dex, stepping between him and the altar. Gurg was quick to jump beside Dex, blaster ready to fire.

"We come to find who do this to Mok Rork people," the chief said. "And Prubba no longer missing." He pointed to the skull atop the altar. "I know my men. I know who do this. Black Fire steal Prubba in night. Defile body and make sure we see and fear." The chief's face hardened. "I see. But I not fear Black Fire. We find Black fire for Mok Rork people, and for Prubba."

"And we will," Dex replied, a little annoyed they were still talking about their mystery enemy as if they were revelation incarnate. "Whoever built this wants you to fear them, yes. They also take their job, their loyalty to the Emperor, very seriously. If we torch it, we'll get their attention." He paused and scanned the trees around them, suddenly sensing that the evil within the jungle was not just in the clearing with them. In a whisper, Dex told the chief, "We'll ambush this guy when he returns to defend his god. We'll kill him for all of this world's people."

37. Stalker

Lacy sat on the side of her bed for most of the morning, arms wrapped around her stomach. Listening. Falling asleep, even with all the troubles of her growing responsibilities around the village, was easy enough. Staying asleep posed a challenge. And waking up was the most difficult task of all. Nova didn't exactly sit well in her. But, especially with Dex gone, she didn't want to spend that morning with anyone else.

She moved her hands over her belly, feeling the semi-hardened womb. Nova was still too small to kick big enough for her mother to feel the sudden jolt, but Lacy somehow knew her baby was moving around. Blocking out all of the outside noise from the village, Lacy lay back down on the bed, pulled the covers over herself, and curled up in a ball so that she could be that much closer to Nova.

"I can't wait to meet you," she whispered. "You'll love it here. It can get a bit crazy," she laughed gently, worried that too much movement would disturb Nova, "but it's fun all the same. And there'll be lots of other kids to play with, and they have a great band here, you and your dad and I can dance to. And one day, when you're a little older, we'll make it safe enough for you to play in the jungle. Under our supervision, of course.

"I'm sure your dad will want to teach you how to swing from tree to tree as soon as you're able to walk. You don't have to if you don't want to, but..." Lacy felt a wave of warm color come over her. "Something tells me you'll be all about that life. A bold adventurer, just like your daddy."

Lacy tightened a little more, both wishing Dex

had been there and also glad that she and Nova had a few minutes to themselves. She wondered if her own mother had moments like that when she was pregnant with Lacy. The subject never came up before, and with the duration of the mission, Lacy hadn't been sure it would ever be a conversation needed having. For all she'd know, if they'd returned to Earth at all, time could have been up for her by then. It was a risk she'd accepted when preparing for the flight out from Earth. The expansion of the human race across the stars seemed grander, more important at the time, than the expansion of her family.

But now, even with all things considered, she questioned how that had ever crossed her mind. Being alone with Nova, curled up with her, was perfection. She was in a perfect paradise with her baby.

"We'll always protect you," Lacy promised Nova.

Again, a wave of warmth like an embrace flowed through her and over her.

* * *

The Taranok humidity invaded even the most well-hidden crannies of the jungle. The Mok Rork were all spread out among the trees, with the exception of two who stayed closer to the ground to keep close to Dex. The group had done such a fine job of hiding that, even though Dex knew where each of them was, he still couldn't see them. Gurg was the only member of their party not in hiding.

When all of the preparations were made, Gurg volunteered to ignite the altar. The Mok Rork chief argued that if anyone was to burn the remains of his tribe, it should be one of the Mok Rork. The only problem was, none of them actually wanted to do it. Dex had offered, but he was the slowest person in the group, and if their target were to jump in at the last minute to attempt to stop him, Dex surely wouldn't be able to get out of the way in time. That all left Gurg as the only person willing.

"Before I go," Gurg whispered to Dex in their camouflaged hasty fighting hole, "make sure Toork know I the hero. In case I die. He will be very mad if he learn I save the planet."

Dex scoffed. "That's why you're doing this? To have one up on him?"

Gurg nodded. "Good reason as any. And if not die, promotion, yes?"

"I'll put you in for an award when we get back to the village if that'll make you happy."

Gurg seemed to consider this. "Toork not have this 'award,' he does?" The two sergeants were eternally locked in a friendly competition of one-upping each other. Toork had been automatically given the rank of sergeant when Dex and Lacy first came to the planet due to his position as a supplies handler, and bumped up to staff sergeant after their reunion while crossing the Great Break. But Gurg received a promotion directly from private to staff sergeant after the battle of Torro-Kaal. Now that they were the same rank, it was a race to get to the next one, or achieve more decorations.

Growing impatient, Dex grumbled, "No one does. But you definitely won't if you don't get out there and burn that damn thing to the ground. Now move it, Sergeant, before Toork outranks you again." He gave the frog a stern shove to force him out of the hasty fighting hole.

Gurg held his torch out, but carefully so as not to accidentally light the entire jungle on fire. The flies kept their distance from the flame, but only by a few inches. The torch did nothing to save Gurg from insistent bites from the bloated insects, all the more motivation to get in and out of the clearing.

He rushed up to the altar and plunged his torch under the bundles of sticks they'd built underneath the table. The bundles were quick to catch and quicker to spread. Gurg was already out of the clearing and back in his hasty before the fire had made contact with any part of the altar, but that was no great feat. Even as the flames licked the crimson-stained bones, there was no sign that they were going to burn.

Dex mumbled encouragement, as if his words could command the fire to destroy the hellish structure. If it didn't catch, Dex had a Plan B, but that drew too much risk. He wanted a clean jump on the altar's builder, not a full-on battle.

"Need more fuel," Gurg told him.

"I can see that," Dex replied. In their rush they hadn't built any reserve bundles. If anyone left their position now to gather more firewood, they'd blow everyone's cover. Reluctantly, Dex told his sergeant, "Stand by for Plan B."

Gurg reached into the pouch that hung at his side and pulled out an amber grenade. "Standing by, cap-tain."

"Remember," Dex said, "precise toss just under the table. Don't want any of our friends catching stray debris. Those branches will be shooting out like spears."

"Yes, cap-tain." Gurg crawled up to the edge of the hasty and aligned his throw.

"On my mark," Dex whispered.

Gurg's thumb traced over the side of the grenade, rubbing back and forth.

Before Dex could give the command, there was a rustling in the trees above. "Hold!" he whispered. Dex then regretted not sharing a comms device with any of the Mok Rork. All he could do was whisper to himself in frustration, "What the hell are they doing up there?" Dex then signaled Gurg to pull back into their hole and put the grenade away.

The altar still hadn't caught, but he found a new priority. "Can you get up there, quietly, and see what's going on?" he asked Gurg.

Gurg glanced up at the source of the rustling, then down at the unburned altar, then nodded at Dex. "I be ready with gren-dade too, if need."

"That's fine. Just be careful. And *quiet.*"

Again, Gurg nodded and was then off. Except for an initial brush against the leaves and branches as he left their hasty, Dex heard no sounds throughout the whole jungle. Gurg's skills were well honed, more than Dex could match even if he spent the rest of his life living off the land on that planet.

But is it good enough for our mystery friend? Dex asked himself, again cursing the Mok Rork for their apparent inability to maintain stealth.

Up above, Gurg leapt from one tree to another, with only a barely audible *thump* as his webbed feet landed on the next branch, checking in on the Mok Rork in their perches. One after the next had nothing to report, until Gurg came to the other side of the clearing, and was pulled into an alcove of a tree by the chief.

"Haaaah," *quiet*, the Mok Rork chief whispered, patting down the air between them. He then added, *It can see us*, also in their language.

The dialect was a bit off between the Mok Tau and the Mok Rork, but Gurg understood him well enough and, matching his volume, asked, *"What can see us?"*

"The Black Fire. Its flame is weak, but the man within is strong."

"Speak clearly," Gurg insisted. *"What do you mean?"*

The chief put a finger to his lips and beckoned for Gurg to follow him back outside of their hole in the tree, and pointed down at the ground where the other Mok Rork had fallen. Gurg saw what the chief was talking about, but still could not comprehend. It was clear whose body it was from the armor and accessories he wore, but the face and body were almost unrecognizable. Although he had landed a few feet away from the still unburned fire, the corpse's flesh was blackened and warped. The blue spots and tattoos common to the Mok Rork were burned out to be almost indistinguishable from the rest of the skin.

The chief pulled Gurg back to the safety of their concealment and said, *"I saw it happen. A man came from that way. He looked weak, sickly, but when he went in for the kill, he did it faster than a hyper-raptor, and his skin began to burn a dull glow."*

Gurg's hand tightened around the pistol grip of his blaster. *"Why didn't you call for an attack?"*

"He was too fast. He sees our trap."

"Then we attack now!" Gurg's voice rose, and he inched closer to the exit.

"No! Black Fire will kill you. We must move together and regroup. We need a new plan."

Just then, another crash below. Gurg rushed to see what it was, and beneath the swaying branches below and falling leaves, another Mok Rork body had fallen into the clearing.

Gurg didn't wait for the chief to follow. With a war cry that could be heard on the other side of the Great Break, Gurg plunged into the clearing and grabbed one of the burning sticks from the base of the fire and lifted it high into the air, swinging it around his head.

From outside the perimeter of the clearing, Dex angrily called to Gurg, "Get down, you damn fool! Get the hell down!"

Gurg ignored the order. Still walloping his war cry, he removed two of the grenades from his pouch and tossed them on top of the altar. He hopped another lap around the table, screaming at the top of his lungs, then stopped a few feet away from the foot of the altar and took in a deep breath.

"Mok Tau curse the Red God!" he shouted, and threw the torch at the grenades.

In the treetops above, the Mok Rork were crawling out of their hiding spots to see what was going on. Was this a call to action? Time to attack? Some seemed to think so, others remained unsure, but all of them had weapons raised and were ready to leap if their target showed themself.

Gurg had just enough time to jump into the safety of the hasty before detonation.

Gurg found safety, but only for a few moments. The Black Fire was watching everything. It knew where he was hiding.

* * *

The desecration of the temple was so intense, Lacy's shock almost prevented her from registering it at all. It had to have been some time deep into the night before that a gang of the Red God stragglers had come through and ransacked the place. But how Ronpup hadn't noticed it happening was even more boggling than the sheer vitriol the assailants had acted with.

Red paint, still running along the sides of the hut, was splattered all over the outside. Chunks of the old wooden walls were hacked away, and, in some cases, looked like they had been ripped out with bare hands or crude tools. The curtain had been ripped off its post so that all could see the disaster that had been made of the temple's interior. The ceiling had been caved in, either by lack of remaining support or by being intentionally pulled down or bashed in, and Ronpup's cot was torn up. Even the mural on the back wall of Dex and Lacy defeating the imperials at Torro-Kaal had been ruined, painted over with a blocky outline of the Emperor reigning over cowering Mok peoples.

"Where were you when this happened?" Lacy fought hard to keep herself from stuttering when she spoke to Ronpup.

"Out," Ronpup answered, unable to pull herself away from the scene. "Could not sleep. Had to go for a walk. A long walk."

"And you didn't hear anything? Didn't see anything?"

Ronpup shook her head as if she were in a trance, only hearing every other word but still understanding enough. "The village was asleep. I heard nothing. Saw nothing. When I come back, found it like this."

"When was that?"

"Before sun up. I try to clean."

Lacy kicked a piece of debris from the ceiling out

of her way, uncovering a shattered chunk of the altar where they first formally spoke with Roak. "Hours ago? Why didn't you get me sooner?"

Ronpup waded through the rubble toward her cot and sank into it. She had said she'd been cleaning, but it didn't look like anything had been touched since the attack. "This not your res-pona-bility. Mok Tau my people, I must clean up their mess."

"They're my people, too," Lacy said with a little too much force in her voice for her liking. She immediately pulled back and tried to bring her voice to a more empathetic level. Ronpup was clearly struggling to process what had happened, and raising her voice wouldn't help anything. She thought it was probably best Dex hadn't been there to see what happened. Lacy knew he would likely jump into action and start interrogating people around the village to find the culprit. Or culprits. A witch hunt was the last thing they needed.

"*Could be* your people," Ronpup said, only now meeting Lacy's eye. "You said not want that power over Mok Tau."

"I don't want *any* power over them. I don't get why I have to have any! I just want to be a part of this village, same as anyone else living their life here."

Ronpup took a deep breath that reminded Lacy of the way Roak would prepare for a long-winded speech. Something had been brewing in her head she never wished to speak aloud. But now, it had to come out. "Lacy, you never to be part of Mok Tau. You are not one of us."

Lacy fell back a step, utterly aghast and insulted, although part of her knew it was true.

The Mok Tau priestess continued, her voice shifting from authority to a hint of consolation. "Dex, he can be part of Mok Tau. He is good man. Good leader. But just a man. You are not *just* woman. The both you destroy Red God, but only you have power to fill the hole left for these people. You are above Mok Tau people, and they, even followers of

Red God, see that. If you demand it, they will follow you. You can make example." She leaned forward and reached her long arm toward Lacy's midsection. "If child you carry anything like you, Mok Tau strength carry on under her one day."

A sudden defensiveness came over Lacy for the sake of her daughter. She wasn't even born yet, and Lacy's closest friend in the village was trying to push delusions of some grand theocratic throne upon her baby. Her arms wrapped around her stomach. "Don't bring Nova into this," Lacy said, weaker than she had intended.

Ronpup stood. "The child already in it. No matter what you do, or not do, Mok Tau have decided who you are. They know Lacy either god, or god killer. But she not no one. Any less than what they say you are, they not accept. You not have choice here anymore." She took a short step toward Lacy. "If you not take power over them, Mok Tau eat themselves." She gestured to the destruction around them. "First their own village. Then, when one side kill the other, they will destroy other tribes."

"I... can't."

"Mok Tau need something bigger than them."

"Then you lead them," Lacy said with newfound assurance. "Roak did just fine as a speaker for the Emperor, and continued to do just fine these last few weeks. Why can't you be the one to follow after him?"

Ronpup gathered herself again to make sure she spoke slowly and clearly in Lacy's language, so that there was no doubting the conviction she had in what she was saying. "Because I speak for no one now. The people stayed by Roak because they knew him. But even then, the doubts had been casted. They only knew me as Roak's second."

This, too, was undeniably true. Ronpup had been a strong presence within the village, but only because she was always at Roak's side. Even though they were friends – though it seemed as if Ronpup was the one stretching that definition now – Lacy had to put aside her bias and accept that Ronpup wasn't by any means the most popular person around. Respected, sure. But at the end of the day, a vice president of the Mok Tau. As well-liked as Roak was, no one really paid much mind to the vice president.

Seeing the strain on Lacy's face, Ronpup conceded for the time being. "Consider," she said. "But do not wait. At least give them something to believe."

* * *

The Mok Rork chief boiled with rage at the insubordination and downright carelessness of the Mok Tau who had accompanied the human. And then to draw in more attention and rile the others up with a war cry, he would see to it that the man was punished.

Or rather, he *meant* to see to it.

Before he could jump down to the clearing to join the others, a cold burn had him by the throat. His vision went dark, and for only a moment before his heart stopped, he saw a faint maroon and the oddest structure miles ahead of him, from which a voice called out in some ancient dialect of Taranok.

And when the life was gone from his body, all that remained was the torment.

* * *

One frog after another jumped down into the clearing. Some had their spears held in defensive postures. Others had them held back, ready to throw, with their free hands down by the daggers on their belts. Gurg and Dex were the only ones with blasters.

The flaming scraps of the demolished altar burned out quickly. Only two of the legs still remained embedded in the ground. But the rest of the altar was scattered in every direction, though its perverse aura lingered, and would continue to linger for millennia to come. But the evil of the clearing had become the company's lowest priority now.

"Where's the chief?" Dex demanded of the nearest Mok Rork.

The frog scanned the treetops, the tip of his spear matching his line of sight, and was soon joined in his search by everyone else. One of them shouted the chief's name in their own language.

No response.

Silence was brief, as the Mok Rork not so quietly threw distressed words at each other.

"What are they saying?" Dex asked Gurg.

Gurg spat out the words with disgust toward the men accompanying them. "They talk retreat. They want go back to Mok Rork village."

Dex responded by speaking to the whole company. "Nobody break!" he said. "We move as a team. No one goes off on their own!"

"But cap-tain," Gurg leaned in, "Toork on own. He at camp."

Dex shot his head around, as if searching the clearing, hoping Toork was with them even though he knew better. He cursed, then ordered, "Everyone back to camp. Keep a tight formation. We'll take a defensive fighting posture there."

When he took his first step toward their base camp, only Gurg stepped with him. From the corner of his eye, he saw the Mok Rork step in the opposite direction.

"What the hell are you all doing?" Dex demanded.

One of the Mok Rork spoke for their group. "Mok Rork village." He pointed away. "Go. Safe."

"All of our gear is *this* way!"

Something moved in the trees above them. Something loud. And the accompanying wind through the canopy did nothing to ease them. For all they knew, it could have just been the creaking of an old tree. But whether it was their attacker or a passing animal, one thing was for sure. It was their cue to leave.

"Black Fire can have gear," the Mok Rork said to the agreeing murmurs of the rest of his men.

"Have it now. Waiting," another said.

Then a third, "We go back-" *a word Dex did not know* - "...village."

"He say they protect-" Gurg began, but Dex cut him off.

"I got it, I got it. He said they're cowards! Abandoning us out here, huh?" In a horrible way, one in which he knew Lacy would be disappointed in, Dex actually felt satisfied that the Mok Rork were abandoning him. Even though they weren't outright killing him and his companions, they were proving that the Mok Rork were not to be trusted. That either their actions or inactions would lead to his death. At least, that seemed like their intention here. Their chief was probably watching all of this play out, Dex thought.

He's reveling in this, I bet.

Unfortunately for the Mok Rork, Dex had a wife and daughter to get back to, and he had no intention of dying.

He wanted to taunt them. Wanted to shout, curse them out, and belittle their cowardice further. Dex wanted to press their fears and make them feel small. For all the good he and Lacy had done for these people, they were still ready to abandon him. What did he care how he treated them in return now?

But Lacy wouldn't act like that. Lacy would give them grace, and probably even wish them safe travels. And Dex couldn't live with himself for doing something Lacy wouldn't approve of, especially if death was on the line.

He took a slow breath, glanced up again at the canopy, then back down to the Mok Rork who were another few inches away as if waiting on his blessing to go. "You can go back to your village," Dex said. "But... please," he forced himself to say the words, thinking of Lacy, "Just walk with us back to base camp. It'll be safer for everyone. Please."

The Mok Rork ran. All of them shot out of the clearing in the direction of their village.

All of them except one.

The remaining Mok Rork stepped forward. "I Ibribit. I go with to camp."

Dex could almost hear Lacy's voice, her little victory laugh.

"Thank you, Ibribit," he said. "We won't be long. I'm sure you can catch up to your men."

Ibribit looked back. The branches and brush still swayed from being run through, but even the sound of the fleeing Mok Rork had ceased. "May not safe try."

"Then you can come back to our village." As soon as he said it, Dex could feel a sneer of disappointment from Gurg. "And that's *fine*," he added.

Ibribit led them back through the jungle to their base camp. From the moment they were out of the clearing, the fact that Toork was alone truly began to burrow in his brain and gnaw at him. How could he have been so stupid as to leave him alone? Sure, he didn't believe in this Black Fire nonsense, but he was still surrounded by untrustworthy savages.

Dex encouraged Ibribit to move faster, but caution was paramount. They were well concealed from any elevated predators, and to move any faster risked giving away their position, granted whoever was with them was thrown off by the company's splitting. In fact, Dex had less to worry about than the others, being almost a foot shorter than both of them. But they were a team, and he moved as a team. And if the point man set the pace, he followed.

But still, each step that didn't land them back at base camp, regardless of how close they were getting, was another step adding anxiety to their situation. Perhaps the Mok Rork were right, and their attacker was waiting for them there. The others who had been killed had been done-in silently. Would Toork have had time to scream?

God, I hope so, Dex thought, almost knocking into Ibribit. *Please, at least give him time to scream for us.*

The trek was beginning to feel so much further than

it was getting from the camp to the clearing.

Is this *the trap? Was the cowardice just a feint to move around us?*

He needed Lacy. Lacy would hear his thoughts and put him straight. Lacy would tell him he's being unreasonable and paranoid.

Lacy would comfort him.

Dex was so distracted by his paranoia, he didn't even realize they had made it back to camp.

Toork jumped to his feet with his spear at the ready at the sight of the three of them.

"Did kill Black Fire?" he asked.

Dex sighed in relief, and the other two spread out to secure their position. "No," he admitted. "Whatever's out there got two of ours."

"Maybe three," Ibribit added, talking about the chief.

"Yeah," Dex agreed. "Maybe three. But here isn't the place for a debrief." He strode over to the nearest razorback, which had previously belonged to the Mok Rork chief, and unfastened the saddle and packs. "Let them go. All the ones we don't need anymore."

"Where are others?" Toork asked, confused, but already doing what he was ordered to do.

"They coward," Gurg answered. He climbed atop his steed, then said, "We should leave them. Waste time. Should go back now."

Dex moved onto the next riderless razorback. "Something tells me Lacy wouldn't want me to leave them like this. I wanna get home too, and we'll be moving double time. But, this first." His face held a calmness that any leader under pressure would want to maintain in front of his men, but the subtle shaking in his rushed movements betrayed that sense of calm. All four of them could feel their stalker lingering. Why it didn't go in for the kill, when the troop was more vulnerable now than when they were positioned around the clearing, remained unknown. But, to push their luck and see how long they could take to release the unneeded animals and check their gear before departing was something none of them had interest in.

Gurg didn't assist in the release. Toork hastily cut two of the saddle-packs off a pair of razorbacks, then mounted his own. Ibribit released none, instead opting to push them off in the direction of the Mok Rork village.

"They lose trail quick," he said. "But Mok Rork may be find them on hunt. Save some gear."

Dex heard the lack of conviction in his voice. Those particular animals would either die wandering the jungle still wearing their saddles or would be torn off by being rubbed against a tree. But the supplies left behind would never be recovered. Especially not now, when a new terror had found dominion in the jungles of Taranok.

"It's time to go," Dex announced when only their four rides remained. "We'll ride through the night, as much as we can. Stick to the dense regions. If we have any followers..."

"May can lose them," Gurg finished for him.

Dex nodded and spurred his razorback.

* * *

There had been no bonfires for a few days. There had been no community meals either.

The Mok Tau village had gone quiet.

When Lacy fetched water from the well in the morning, few people greeted her. When she went to the temple to help with the repairs, Ronpup said very little, instead communicating through grunts of acknowledgement to her questions that would go unanswered.

Fears of violence had mostly simmered out, but there was still heat from the coals. It could be felt in the wind, in the heavy morning dew like an oppressive blanket that weighed down the whole village. There had been no further action after the desecration of the temple, but Lacy thought that perhaps the perpetrators were only waiting for retaliation so that their next move had more justification.

Whatever the case was, she was grateful for at least a sense of peace. She needed all she could get outside of the Prullen hut, because inside was where the shadow of the Emperor fell on her the darkest.

In her time spent alone, Lacy focused her mind on Nova. She tried listening to the ever-strengthening heartbeat. She whispered things in hopes of hearing Nova's nonexistent voice in her own heart.

She prayed for the safety of her baby and for Dex.

But moments between prayer and too-deep meditation, her focus fell. And the Cathedral drew closer.

With each day, the distant towers became taller. There was more definition to its warped sides. At one point, she thought she could see the outline of a great set of bronze doors. The only thing that was a certainty in her vision was that there was something behind those doors. Something waiting for her. Not calling, never calling. But there was anticipation on the other side. Anticipation that perfectly matched in contrast the intensity of Lacy's wish to stay as far away from the doors as possible.

In these episodes were recollections of when the Emperor had tapped into her mind when they first arrived on Taranok. She had heard his voice as clearly as anyone else's. "There you are," he had said before she fell unconscious. But now it was no longer his voice she heard. Whose it was, she could not tell. And similar to how Nova did not speak to her mother with a solid voice, whatever it was behind the door called her with an otherworldly, inaudible cry.

Lacy was pulled from her slow fall into a trance by the sound of a horn on the other side of the village. She brought herself upright, waiting for a second blast; two being the signal for a returning party.

The second horn sounded, and Lacy was on her feet and rushing through the door before it had faded. She ran to the gate and arrived as it opened. Dex, Gurg, Toork, and one of the Mok Rork waited on the other side. Their razorbacks had already been dropped off in their pens outside the village.

None of the four men looked harmed or showed signs of battle, though they were all exhausted. Dex's hair had grown out long and was now greasy from the days of traveling without a shower or bathing. He looked, just as he always called himself, like Tarzan.

Lacy ducked under the rising gate and threw her arms around him. On their touch, she could sense a subconscious anxiety in him that was growing into a fear he did not yet recognize, and saw the image in his memory of the altar.

Dex didn't have to ask her to know what she was thinking. He kissed her cheek and said, "I'll tell you about it later. In the morning, when we can all meet."

The sun was setting somewhere far behind the trees. Darkness was falling on Taranok.

And a Darkness had followed Dex and his men home.

38. Black Fire

A dim, scarlet haze enveloped Lacy's vision. She reached out her hands into the bloody darkness and shuffled her feet forward, cautious of whatever lay unseen before her. Words refused to escape her lips, try as she might to call Dex's name.

Somewhere far behind, a familiar presence searched for her, threatening to find her in the haze. Pushing through it, away from the presence, she found her feet pressing against a surface made of many small objects that cracked like sticks. But even as she pushed on, away from this unseen pursuer, she felt it again, now in front of her.

Lacy waved her hands in front of her face as if to rid herself of the haze. It swirled like water in a shallow pool in front of her, and a faint light shone through it. She squinted her eyes and leaned forward, feeling stuck as if the ground had swallowed up her feet, and a structure came into view far beyond the haze.

Revealing itself now, closer than ever, was the Cathedral, and it rushed toward her as she rushed away from the entity lurking behind her, dispersing the haze as it grew, until she stood at its base, and she could see it was not made of bricks or wood. But what the material was, she could not say with certainty. She reached out to feel the tall - not bronze, as she thought at first, but a burnt ivory - door. Still, there was the radiance of some great being on the other side. And still it called her forward to pass through the great doors. And though her heart warned against it, her body was compelled to do as she was told.

The door cracked open at her full weight pushing

against it, and though she saw nothing, the creak of the door was electric and broke her from her trance. Lacy fell back, her heart beating at a record pace, and the door remained the slightest bit ajar.

At her retreat, the presence behind her moved so that it was breathing down her neck. Lacy spun around, her eyes wide with panic. Thousands of softly biting voices in her head called to her, "*I am coming... I have missed you... I crave your soul, and now...*" The voices leapt from the recesses of her mind where they had hidden, to torment her soul. "*I have found you!*"

A hand grabbed Lacy's shoulder, fingers digging into her flesh, and spun her around again to see that the Cathedral had been replaced by a being of black flame burning inward on itself. From miles behind the face of lightless fire, eyes penetrated deep into Lacy's soul.

She tried pulling away, but the being's hands were on the sides of her head. Heat was sucked away from her face, her blood, like air being sucked from lungs, until a new voice, one that didn't speak in words, commanded her to wake.

* * *

Lacy's eyes burst open. All was dark around her, save the small streams of moonlight coming into their hut from the windows and cracks in the roof. Dex was dead asleep next to her, snoring lightly.

She steadied her breathing, not yet having realized how fast her heart was beating or how much sweat she was drenched in. Lacy wiped her brow, a stream of perspiration rolling down her forearm, then put a hand to her chest, then her stomach.

"Thank you, Nova," she whispered through staggered breaths. Now awake and calming herself, she recognized the second voice in the dream and was grateful. "My little protector."

Lacy glanced over at Dex, who mumbled something from his own dream before turning on his side. *At least one of us will get a good night's rest*, she thought before swinging her legs around to the side of the bed. She sat there for a short while with her clammy arms wrapped around her stomach.

It was only a dream, she lied to herself. *Just a bad dream.*

But who was she kidding? This wasn't the first time something of the sort had happened, and not just to her. Dex had seen things too, though his visions more peaceful. She couldn't tell if this repeating nightmare was a vision or a warning. Regardless, she was at the foot of the Cathedral now. The next time she slept or let herself fall too deeply into a meditation, she knew she might not be able to pull away from whatever was waiting for her beyond those burnt ivory doors. Either she would have to let the vision take her where it meant to, or she would have to face it some other way. Some way that being on Taranok would not allow for. And more than that, she knew that no matter what path she stood at the beginning of, the people of Taranok would be in danger if she didn't take the first step.

Lacy sighed and whispered, "You don't know how badly we need you." Tears welled up in her eyes. "I'm so sorry, Nova. You don't deserve this life. I wish we could stay here. I wish you could meet these people. They're so wonderful. Everyone would have loved you."

She looked up and out the window. A gentle breeze blew back the curtain just enough to show her the quiet village.

I wonder if they ever knew peaceful nights like this before.

Nights of celebration and great big bonfires, even if they were becoming less common these days, surely there had been plenty over the planet's history. And there would be again in the future. Lacy knew there would be. Somehow, Ronpup would unite the village again. From the very first bonfire Dex and Lacy attended, it was clear that the Mok

Tau knew how to have fun. But nights of quiet and security, unburdened by the threat of the Emperor's beasts attacking them? Nights when the Mok Tau wives slept peacefully in their husbands' arms, or content that their sons were safe at home? Children being put to bed without tears for their missing fathers and brothers? When else had they known a night like that before the humans arrived?

If that is the smallest victory we have on this world, it will be the greatest, Lacy told herself assuredly.

She licked her lips, realizing then how dry her throat was. Her eyes, too, felt dry. She looked around their bedside. One of their canteens was there, on the small table Dex had built for her. Lacy grabbed it, but didn't have to bring it to her lips before noticing it was empty. She muttered a curse, then looked around the room again.

"Robbie?" she whispered. "Hey, Robbie, are you there?"

Silence.

"Golly, where'd you go?" Lacy pushed herself off the bed, feeling body aches obtained in her vision transferred to her reality.

"Robbie?" She stumbled to the front of the hut and peered her head out of the door, scanning the area around what they called their "porch," but still no sign of the little robot.

"Good lord," she muttered, retreating into the hut to grab a robe made by one of the villagers, before setting out to find Robbie.

The outside air carried a warm breeze through the village. The smell that had once been off-putting, smelling unnaturally, artificially sweet, had grown on her. It was the smell of a breeze that only passed through at night, and was now associated with long nights spent around the fire and being held by Dex. Now, even though there hadn't been a bonfire to celebrate the party's return from their inspection with the Mok Rork, it was still a good smell when Dex was home to lie in bed with her.

A single pair of guards patrolled the village wall. It was an optimistic downsizing from the dozen watchers in the trees the village had been used to. The vast quiet of the sleeping village made Lacy's soft footsteps all the louder on the dirt path. One of the night watchmen glanced her way, then quickly dismissed her.

She peered around every alley, in every garden, and around every corner looking for their robot friend, but found no sign of him anywhere. Eventually, she had walked a straight line to the village gate and still hadn't seen him. Lacy stopped and looked around. One of the guards on the wall was approaching. She could ask him, she considered, *but no, they'll wake up everyone and pull a full search and rescue. No need to start all that up.*

Lacy circled around the village wall, considering where Robbie could be. Where he would hide, or have wandered off to. But the answer was obvious. The theater.

She picked up her pace, lightly bounding alongside the wall to the rear of the village where Dex had set up the projector. Under the Tree had still shown signs of use, the projector was still there – thankfully turned off, of course – but still no robot.

After removing herself from the crammed space of Under the Tree, Lacy paused and put her hands on her hips. No sign of, and not a word from, Robbie by the end of the night.

Is it even strange that he didn't come back? Is he obligated to say goodnight or check in?

Like all the others in the village – though, still a bit out of place as a robot – Robbie had been showing quite a bit more complacency in their daily lives. By the day, he was showing more independence, so why *should* he have to check in with her or Dex?

Robbie's his own being, if he wants to be alone for the night, he can be alone for the night.

She turned her head in the direction of their little hut on the hill.

But it is... strange.

Lacy surveyed the area around her before deciding to climb the steps to the top of the wall. Maybe asking the guards for help wouldn't prompt them to wake the entire village. Once at the top, her plans, she realized, had gone south.

The guards were gone. There was not a soul she could see walking the village now except herself. But the kick in her stomach warned her otherwise.

A cold shiver ran down her spine. Where had they gone?

It's a change of shift, she told herself. *Any moment now someone else will climb the wall and take their place.*

Lacy waited, frozen, for her prediction to come true. She stared ahead toward the gate. A moment passed. A minute. Two. The sweetness in the air had faded and turned stale.

Someone will come. It's just a change of shift.

In the distance, a dark shape moved, pulling itself onto the walkway of the wall, then stood tall.

Lacy finally breathed a sigh of relief. The change of shift had come.

But her heart still raced, and the chill on her spine was still slowly traversing down her flesh.

Ignore it, Lacy. It's just the night.

She glanced around again. Her feeling of discomfort grew. The shape of the night watchman was off. It was only a silhouette, but even that was somehow wrong. The proportions just weren't there. And the way it moved like a wounded animal disturbed her to her core.

On second thought, she didn't need the guard's help. The man looked tired, which explained his odd walk, and she could find Robbie on her own. No big deal, he was probably just-

There, Lacy spied the *Silent Horizon*. The main cabin light was off, but through the viewport she saw the glow of a different light, possibly the hallway or the head.

She took another look at the guard who was hobbling toward her. He was shorter than the other watchmen, but still had an imposing height.

Best to leave now.

Lacy hauled herself over the outer side of the wall and climbed down. She brushed her hands of the dirt and leaves that had come loose when she climbed, then trudged over to the ship, constantly looking over her shoulder at the man on the wall. He kept his pace, clearly having seen Lacy – how could he not have? – but under the cover of the trees, she couldn't see his face.

Just keep moving.

She shuffled further from the wall, closing the distance between herself and the ship. Listing a bit to the left, she could see the airlock hatch was open, and the ramp down, but no light from the hallway. Lacy found herself in a rush, climbing up the steps and into the *Silent Horizon*, desperate to escape the cold gaze she thought she felt from the watchman on the wall. But she was in the ship now. She was secure.

"Robbie?" she whispered. "Are you there?" She walked slowly through the hall, feeling like a small child searching for something in a dark basement. She could turn the lights on and see that there was nothing to fear, but reaching for the light switch was just when whatever lurked in the dark would attack.

Lacy whispered again. "Robbie, where are you? Come on out."

The main cabin was just as empty as the rest of the ship, the rest of the village. But off to the port side shone the source of the light. As she'd thought, it came from the head.

"Robbie, if this is because you did something wrong, I promise I won't get mad." After a moment, she added, "And I promise I won't tell Dex. He's back, you know. You never even said 'hello.' I'm sure he'd be real excited to see you. You've got nothing to be worried about, just don't jump out at me."

It was really a silly thing to say.

A small robotic claw crossed the head's doorway, followed by the half-dome head of Robbie. The small creak the floor made as Robbie's weight shifted startled Lacy so, she jumped back against the wall, thrusting a hand onto her chest to keep her heart from bursting out.

"Jesus! Robbie! Don't scare me like that!" Lacy shouted.

Robbie's head twitched in a movement that resembled his version of a blink. "I am sorry. I didn't want to alarm you."

"Well... Ha! Ya did! Whatever are you doing in here?" Lacy dropped to her knees and held out her arms for him.

Robbie hesitated, holding one claw in the other, embarrassment obvious in his emotionless face. "I... I do not know."

Do not. It was a subtle thing, but it stuck out to Lacy. More and more, the robot had taken on her and Dex's speech mannerisms, sounding less... robotic. But now, reverting back to it?

"Want to tell me what's going on?" Her arms lowered the slightest bit, but remained high enough to let him know he was still welcome.

"I do not know what happened."

"You don't know how you got here?"

"I came here. I know that. I think that I felt something. That made me want to come here, and I do not know why."

Knowing Robbie was staying planted right where he was, Lacy scooted forward a few feet to meet him. "What was going on when you 'felt something?'"

"I do not say," Robbie admitted, his volume dropping lower with every word. "I think the movie I put on was too long. And now I got too sleepy. And then I think..."

Lacy waited patiently for Robbie to finish, but her thoughts lingered on his strange choice of words. Contractions had slowly become a norm for him, but his phrases always made sense grammatically. *And now I got too sleepy*. He was speaking like a child, or a drunk. But more so than that, the fact that he was feeling sleepy at all.

When Robbie didn't continue speaking, Lacy offered up, "Robbie, have you been feeling very tired lately?"

He shrugged his wiry arms. "A little bit," he whispered.

"Do robots like you usually get tired?"

"I'm not sure. I do not see it in my programming. And I do not know many other robots like me. I don't know if I know any others at all, anymore." He paused, then looked up at Lacy. "Why are you crying?"

Lacy wiped her eyes. "It's nothing, buddy. I'm just tired, too. It's been a long day, huh?"

"Yes. It has."

They sat together in silence for a full minute before Robbie spoke again. "It's my battery, isn't it? Yes, that is it. I'm beginning to run low."

"No, stop," Lacy pleaded, pulling Robbie into her chest like a stuffed animal for comfort. "You just need a nap, is all. You're just burnt out. Humans get like that, too." She tried to laugh, but it came out as a faint cough. "You should have seen Dex before we left Earth. I don't know if it was commitment to the mission or trying to impress me, but he was full speed ahead at all times. There were days he had the heaviest bags under his eyes; he hadn't slept in a week, trying to get to the top of our class. When we got our first weekend of leave, *oh!*, I don't think he left his room until Sunday night, and that was just to meet us at the bar right before closing. He said Major Haxley needed to get a message to me, but he couldn't remember what it was. Blamed it on burnout. But... I know he was just looking for an excuse to say 'hi.'"

Robbie's internal computer made a whirring noise that sounded like he was taking a deep breath. "Dex is a funny human."

"Yeah, he can be a silly guy sometimes. My silly guy."

"Hmm..." Robbie's speaker vibrated a sigh. "Maybe

you are right. I'm just burnt out. I will try taking a nap."

"That's a good idea." Lacy wiped her tears one more time. The crisis was averted for now, yet still just as pressing. In the morning, she decided, she would talk to Dex about pulling parts from the *Silent Horizon* to recharge Robbie. They would be careful not to take anything that would make the ship inoperable, just enough to get them around if they needed a quick getaway or over to one of the abandoned imperial bases to find more permanent parts. "You wanna sleep in here tonight or in the hut? I think these beds are a little more comfy, personally, and I'll stay with you if you'd like."

"Why do you sleep in the hut then?"

"It's something different, more room to breathe."

"Oh, I do not understand that either. But I will come with you to the hut." Robbie hopped off of Lacy's lap and extended a claw to hold her hand. She had to lean a little to hold it properly, but the slight discomfort in her posture was welcome in exchange for these moments with her friend.

"What happens when you sleep?" Robbie asked, seeming more like a child than ever.

Lacy looked down at him with wonder. *Such a strange little guy*, she thought.

"You dream, buddy. You see things that aren't real but feel as real as anything." They'd been feeling real now more than ever, but Lacy knew this wasn't the time to impose her own issues on the little robot, especially the idea of nightmares.

"Oh. I don't like that," he said as they turned into the hallway.

Then he froze and pointed his clawed hand.

"Is that really real?"

Lacy followed where his hand pointed and saw the black silhouette of a man, a humanoid man, standing in the airlock threshold. She threw herself between the figure and Robbie. Her first thought was to reach for a blaster or a spear, something, anything to defend herself from this thing that was clearly not Dex coming to check on her.

The pieces slowly came together as the figure stepped forward, yet even though it stepped into the light, the shadows seemed to Lacy as if they were tied to his face. The thing's chin, mouth, and the tip of its nose were lit, but just as its eyes were about to be revealed, the shadow fell again.

Lacy retreated from the thing, shoving Robbie to move with her, and eked out, "Robbie, sound the alarm."

At her words, Robbie jumped back, and rushed to the ship's computer. At the same time, the shape sped up its pace and, before Lacy knew it, the thing's fingers were wrapped around her throat and she was lifted into the air.

Her head slammed against the ceiling of the ship with a thud that sounded and felt like it cracked her skull. With all her strength, Lacy fought, kicking at the shadow man and tugging at his hand on her throat. Faintly, too faintly and growing even more faint, she heard the ship's alarm blare through the cabin, through the hall, through the village. And when she laid a flailing hand on the face of the shape she saw...

Torro-Kaal. Their assault. The man Romek strutting toward her, engulfed in flame and consuming it. She saw from his eyes the chase across the Great Break on the back of a kron-kaal. The trap they'd set and the explosion. She saw him fall down, down, down, to the depths of the planet. Saw how he drained the kron-kaal of life to survive, and all the terrible beasts that lived below the surface, how he attacked them and fed off of them, slowly climbing back to the top. Saw the Mok Rork he hunted, draining for the littlest bits of sustenance they offered. She saw the altars he built and the way he searched for her. She saw deep in his mind the awareness he temporarily gained when she'd tapped into the Emperor's power, revealing herself like a blip on a radar that he would follow until he needed to feed again. He had waited for the sibling moon's alignments to lessen the planet's gravitational pull so that he could crawl from the Great Break's abyss, almost always on the verge of death, nothing but a drained shell of what he once was, stealing life to gain an inch closer here or a foot closer there, to find them. To find her. Only Lacy was on his mind. Only she was the target. And she saw what he'd done in the village. The fire he'd started and was now spreading as he cut off her breathing. Not to kill her, though, she saw that clearly. No, she would not die. But her child. The factor he didn't know about, didn't care about, Nova wouldn't survive.

Nova then sparked something in her. A reserve she'd been too terrified to access.

Just before her vision faded, she saw something rush across the floor of the hall and leap up onto the shadow. At that moment, Lacy pulled. She pulled what she could back from Romek, his energy, his strength, just enough to cause him to drop his guard, making him vulnerable to the surprise attack from the rear.

A cry of pain rang through the hall of the *Silent Horizon* and the shadow's fingers loosened from Lacy's neck. All went dark for half a moment as blood and oxygen rushed back into her head. The world spun around her. Each desperate gulp for air sent shocks of pain through her lungs. When her vision cleared, she saw her rescuer, a Mok Tau warrior without legs.

"Go!" Boritt shouted at her. "*Go!* Lacy, go!"

Romek thrashed this way and that to get Boritt off of him, but Boritt held fast with one arm around his neck, and the other hand stabbing him repeatedly with a small stone dagger. Little, though, did it affect Romek.

Lacy scrambled to her feet and rushed past the struggle, kicking out her leg as she passed to knock Romek's knee in.

His leg buckled the littlest bit, only alerting him to Lacy's attempt to flee. In a burst of fury, Romek reached back, over his head, and dug his fingers into Boritt's shoulders, then threw him with all his might in an arch and down onto the floor.

The air in Boritt's lungs escaped him and struggled to find its way back. The thud temporarily halted Lacy, who wanted to go back and help him, but Romek's determined strides toward her made her move.

Jumping onto the dirt from the airlock, Lacy found herself no longer in the shadows of the trees but lit up by the orange glow of a terrible fire raging across the village. She looked and saw flames on the other side of the wall spreading across the tops of huts and black smoke filling the air. Sentries ran across the wall with buckets of water, shouting at each other over where to extinguish first, and dousing the flames. Only a moment ago, the night was dead silent, and now the world was ending before her eyes.

Lacy pulled herself to her feet and ran in the direction of the gate, shouting Dex's name, hoping someone along the wall would see her.

She didn't even make it twenty feet, running at full speed, before she was caught again. Something searing pierced her shoulder, shot through it. Hot blood sprayed across her face. The smell of burnt flesh hit her nose.

A blaster, she thought, collapsing again to the ground with a scream of pain. Against her better judgment, Lacy looked over her shoulder and saw Romek closing in on her with what looked like a sword in one hand, resting over the opposite forearm. A faint wisp of heat ripples hovered over the hilt of the weapon. The shot placement, she knew, was intentional. At that distance, he should have had no problem hitting her heart or head.

Too terrified to think clearly, she crawled backward and desperately searched for something on the ground; a rock, a stick, anything that could be used as a weapon.

The weapons that she found, though, didn't come from the ground, but above. Spears rained down from the wall, landing around Romek's feet. Some darted toward his head, but his reflexes were too quick. He turned, knelt, and aimed his blaster-sword. From the small crossguard, three blaster bolts shot out. With unnatural accuracy and speed,

Romek slew three Mok Tau warriors. They dropped on either side of the wall with blaster burns seared into their foreheads.

When he returned his attention to Lacy, she was gone. No longer running for the gate, she scaled the wall and screamed for help.

Another bolt shot into her shoulder, no more than a centimeter off from the first shot.

Lacy gripped the hold she had ever tighter through the pain, but Romek's hand was on her leg, and once again, she felt her life fading away, her energy being stolen from her. As Romek pulled at her leg, two sets of hands tugged at her arms.

"Come! Come Loo-tent!" Gurg commanded her.

Standing at Gurg's side, Toork pulled Lacy up with one hand, and, with the other, threw a spear at Romek.

Romek dodged out of the way of the missile, tugging hard on Lacy's leg. But Lacy, being driven purely by adrenaline pumped by a survival instinct for both herself and her baby, was stronger in her hold of Toork and Gurg.

Romek's grip on Lacy's leg was lost.

Life rushed back into her, like she'd been drowning and came back up for air. It took her a moment to realize they were on the other side of the wall, running through the burning village.

"Dex! Where's Dex?" Lacy pleaded.

"He help with fire," Gurg told her. "I take to him!"

They ran through the village square. Everyone from the village was awake and out of their homes, terrified and confused. Children's screams overpowered the cries of their mothers and fathers trying to coordinate fighting the flames.

"They be okay!" Toork pulled at Lacy's arm, catching her hesitation at the tears in the eyes of the little ones. "Come! Come!"

Following close behind them, Lacy could feel the dark energy of the Emperor's assassin growing nearer. She knew in her soul that he could be on top of them at any moment, but was holding back. He was playing with her. He was letting her take in the suffering he had cast upon the village. Further screams of agony and fear told her he was indiscriminately cutting down more of the Mok Tau as he neared. What sounded like that of a child's final cry before death took them, faltered Lacy, but Toork wouldn't let her totally collapse. He beckoned still, "Come! Must run!"

Behind them was the evil aura of the assassin, descending on them like a beast of the jungle, but the path ahead of them was no better. While groups of confused villagers rushed this way and that, attempting to fight the fire, a line of Mok Tau pushed through the crowds grabbing anyone who got in their way and threw them to the ground and kicked away their water buckets.

"This was promised!" the leader of the group shouted, and yanked a rope attached to something behind him. "Mok Tau condemned! Must let it burn so to be clean!"

Gurg pushed past Lacy and Toork to make the way clear for them. With a blowing wind, the smoke obstructing the heathen Mok Tau lightened and Lacy could see clearly who it was leading the pack, and who he was pulling by the rope like a dog.

"Jurrnup! You rat-bastard!" Gurg shouted with a leap, and brought his fist down hard into Jurrnup's face. Ronpup yanked at her bindings to keep Jurrnup from defending himself with both hands. That, in tandem with Gurg's war-cry and surprise attack, was enough to begin and end the fight without even an attempt at a counterattack.

Their leader felled, and his blood sprayed on two of their faces, the heathens scattered like cockroaches in the light, but not without causing chaos where they went.

Ronpup rushed toward Lacy. Her hands were still tied, but Toork saw to that, and cut her bonds before either of the women could speak.

"Loo-tent Lacy," Ronpup said, weeping. "They saw the flames, and it caught in them. They would let the whole jungle burn!"

First in her mind came thoughts of battle with the heathens, but Toork was tugging at her arm. They had to find Dex and get to safety. But Ronpup couldn't come with them.

"Take whoever you can to the Mok Tur village," Lacy instructed, hoping that the tribe which had been so physically disfigured by the Emperor's rule would provide them sanctuary. "Dex and I will find you again. There's no time to argue, *go!*"

Toork pulled Lacy's forward, leaving Ronpup behind to lead the tribe, and running toward them, Lacy saw Dex with his blaster bared.

Dex threw himself between Toork and Lacy and threw an arm around her, pulling her in tight, with the blaster hand extended. One eye was closed, pressed against her head, and the other remained open, looking down the sights of the blaster for their attacker - *or attackers*, he thought.

"Where did you go? What happened?" he asked.

But before Lacy could answer, Toork again intervened. "Must get to safe place. Out back of village. Into forest. We go Mok Krak tribe."

"No!" Lacy argued. "We can't lead him to another tribe. He'll kill them, too, if they're protecting us!"

"Lacy's right. We need to leave Taranok," Dex stated, taking his wife's hand.

Her eyes widened in shock. Leave Taranok? The home they'd built here? Leave all of these people defenseless? It was exactly what she knew they needed to do, but now it was spoken aloud and validated by someone else.

"They won't be defenseless," Dex told her. "They're stronger now. There's nothing more we can do for them now." Without letting her protest, he pulled her in the direction Toork led them, toward the rear gate of the village.

A million things raced through her mind; things she knew were not nearly as important as their or anyone else's immediate survival, but important nonetheless. All of their belongings were still in the hut. Much of their provisions, their clothes, the bottle of wine. All of these things, these thoughts, she knew Dex could hear. She projected them loudly enough with her distress taking over, and she could feel in the squeeze of his hand at each thought she had that he felt the same way.

Arriving at the back wall, Toork and Gurg had to work together with all of their strength to lift the gate.

"Stuck!" Gurg called, thrusting the old door against overgrown logs held together by hardened Taranok mud so strong it was like stone.

Dex looked from the gate to the burning village. Amidst the flaming buildings and terrified Mok Tau, a figure strode toward them, devouring all of the lights around him, fueling his own dark flames. Both Dex and Lacy shared the same thought, an image reminiscent of the planet's apocalyptic fears. A Black Fire blazed before them, sent from the stars to burn the planet for its actions against their god.

The Emperor's Wrath was unleashed on Taranok.

Dex tightened his grip on the blaster and steadied his hand. Though no eyes could be seen, Dex felt a pair staring him down, challenging him, knowing that the bolt was merely energy he could consume and use to strengthen himself. Fighting was useless.

"Loo-tent! Cap-tan! Go!" Gurg struggled to speak as both he and Toork's muscles strained. Only a few inches separated the ground and the bottom of the gate, it would not open any further.

Dex put himself between Lacy and their attacker, blaster still raised. "Go on, baby. I'll be right behind you! Go!"

Lacy blew a quick guppy kiss on his cheek, then dove under the gate, scrambling through it to the other side. As soon as she touched the ground, Dex was behind her, crawling so quickly he nearly pushed her across the dirt.

The assassin picked up his pace and quickly broke into a sprint.

Toork and Gurg released the gate and readied for a fight.

In the mere moments they had before the Black Fire engulfed them, both Toork and Gurg thought of something to say to the other. Some brave words for their final stand to inspire hope. Something to honor their friendship. Something that let them know they'd made the right choices even though it ultimately led them to this moment. But all they could do was give each other a smile, and give Dex and Lacy any number of seconds it would take for them to make their escape.

It was a valiant end to their time on Taranok.

But it was not an end Dex or Lacy saw, nor ever knew about, although the assumption they would not be seeing their friends again was palpable. All they had was a mere hope that Toork and Gurg had survived the night. That little hope kept their legs strong and moving fast toward the *Silent Horizon*.

As they curved around the village wall, the ship's engine whirred, and the light of the burning repulsors silhouetted the trees. Lacy glanced back for only a moment, nearly losing her footing, and saw Dex speaking into his communication device. What he said couldn't be heard over the cries from the village, but it was clear it had been a call to Robbie, telling him to start up the ship.

The ramp was still down, and the airlock still open as they came upon it. Dex guided Lacy up the ramp in front of him, then jumped up and stood in the doorway as Lacy raced to her station. Not even ten seconds after boarding, the ship was hovering, but not yet in full take-off.

"What's the hold-up?" Dex shouted to the bow.

"The engine needs a second to warm up!" Lacy called back. They were seconds she knew they didn't have. She could already feel Romek descending upon them like a bullet racing through the air.

"I *gave* us seconds! What was Robbie doing?"

Robbie shied away in the Captain's seat, hiding from Dex's admonition.

"It's not his fault," Lacy shouted in the robot's defense. "He doesn't know the proper start-up sequence!"

Dex caught himself then, realizing the mistake he was making trying to defend them on his own. This man the Emperor had sent wasn't one of the Zar-Mecks, wasn't even a real flesh-and-blood being, for all Dex knew. He walked more like a spirit, a primordial being unconcerned with the limits of the physical world. When death surrounded him in his strut through the village, it was as if he was merely breathing it in like oxygen, just as he had the flames.

Dex holstered the blaster in his gunner's strap and sealed the airlock.

The *Silent Horizon* jolted forward as Lacy gave the thrusters a nudge and tripped Dex in his rush to the front. The ship wasn't quite ready to make a break out of the atmosphere, but distance was gained between them and the ground. Hopefully, Lacy thought, enough to keep them from Romek. Though with the agility and speed he'd shown her, a great leap multiple stories high didn't seem out of the question.

She pulled up the rear camera display just as Dex took Robbie's place in the Captain's seat. "Out of the way, buddy!"

Robbie jumped down under the console and hid, unsure what was needed of him or how he could help. Neither Dex nor Lacy was paying him any mind, and interjecting himself now didn't feel like the right option.

"He's on our butt," Lacy stated as calmly as she could manage.

"I see him." Dex let her retain flight controls while he armed the rear turret, scanning the aft view through the monitor.

Dex fired two shots in quick succession, hitting just in front of and beside Romek. His attempts to launch himself into the air were marred by the shock of the heavy blasts, and when Romek lifted his head again, the ship's rear thrusters turned from a bright orange to an intense blue.

"Engine's hot. We're clear!" Lacy announced and lifted the ship into the air. The undersides of the branches were brightly lit red all the way to the tops of the trees. Smoke encircled them and spread across the canopy of the forest. The smell of it seeped into the *Silent Horizon*, a smell of charred wood and burnt meat. Lacy covered her mouth and nose to block it out, but the smell...

Dex glanced at his wife, then quickly away, and took control of the ship without a word.

The sky shifted a shade darker as the *Silent Horizon* pushed through the upper atmosphere and away from Taranok. Through the rear camera monitor, Dex watched as the two halves of the planet, along with its moons, shrank and faded into nothing among the blackness of space. All of their time with the Mok Tau was gone, all of their plans for their new home erased.

But the smell... the smell still lingered.

39. The Asteroid Field

"I hate to do this to you, baby, but we're not out of it yet." With his eyes focused on an asteroid belt ahead of them, and nearing quickly, Dex pulled up the *Silent Horizon*'s star map on the central monitor. The planets they'd visited previously - Reechi, The Heart of the Void, RVO-19, and Taranok - were all marked with red dots, while unidentified masses the ship's radar picked up during their travel through hyperspace to Taranok were marked with smaller blue dots; unknown planets or cosmic bodies. Other locations of note, such as space stations and nebulae, were marked with white dots. And now the asteroid belt was being added. But that wasn't the only use for the map Dex had at that moment.

"That empire goon is probably already on our trail," Dex said, not taking his eyes off the map. "We need a plan."

Lacy brushed a loose strand of hair out of the way of her bloodshot eyes and composed herself. It was clear what Dex was getting at; The *Silent Horizon* wasn't the only ship around the Mok Tau village. They also had a small squadron of captured Zar-Meck starfighters, and they'd had good reason to believe from months prior that Romek knew how to fly one.

"What do you need from me, Captain?" Lacy asked, clearing her throat.

Dex raised an eyebrow at her respect for rank. "Ideas," he said. "We need a course of action."

He pressed a little harder on the thrusters and sped closer toward the asteroids.

"What are you doing?" Lacy asked.

"Just want some cover. Some time to think before he catches up."

Dex slowed again when they entered the asteroid field and weaved between the floating rocks, looking for an alcove to hide in.

Lacy's heart leapt, and she bit her lip. "You sure this is such a good idea?" Asteroids drifted dangerously close to the ship. But save for a few minor dings against the hull from pebbles, Dex flew through the field as cool as if it were any other part of space.

"Pretty sure," he answered back with a slight nod of his head. "There. We can land and power down. Just don't want to be here too long."

Dex took his time navigating through the veins of the asteroid, careful to account for the rock's movement through space with the rest of the belt, as well as its own rotation. Finding the right speed to match its rotation proved challenging, but he fell into a groove, listing lazily to the left with its spin, and flew with that in mind.

"Here feels good," Dex said, thinking out loud.

Lacy prepped the landing gear and sighed in relief when she heard the hiss of the hydraulics ease their landing.

"Ain't nothin to it," Dex said with a forced grin, hoping that his calm demeanor would help her regain that light he missed seeing in her eyes that morning. The stars in her eyes seemed dull now, but they were still the brightest things in Dex's world.

Lacy smirked – tried to smirk at least – and unbuckled herself from her seat.

Dex swiveled around and followed her with his gaze. "Where are you going?"

"I just need to stand."

"Do you need anything?" Dex asked, unbuckling his own straps and beginning to rise.

But Lacy cut him off. "No, I just need-"

"How about a cup of-" He was going to say 'tea,' momentarily forgetting that they no longer had the means to make any after leaving Taranok. It didn't matter anyway, though.

"Please. I just..." She fought hard to stop herself

from shaking. Her skin went pale, and Lacy put her hand to her mouth then rushed for the head. A mix of morning sickness, Dex's flying, and the total realization of the horror they had witnessed had hit her all at once. And as salt in the wound, whether self-manifested or real, she could almost hear the spread of lips forming a maniacal grin.

This time, Dex did jump up and rushed after her. Lacy didn't even make it through the doorway before falling to her knees and throwing up, missing the toilet by only half a foot. Dex stood over her, feeling absolutely useless, with a look of unnerved shock across his face.

Robbie poked his head between them but saw nothing past Lacy's back. "Are you dying?"

Dex nudged the robot away with his foot. "Lacy, what can I do?"

"Nothing!" Lacy breathed harshly before retching again. Nothing came out, but the sense of nausea had her in a vice. "Air. I just need some air. I'm fine." If she could have sprinted out of the airlock, she would have.

Even though Dex knew she'd protest, he jumped back to the storage cabinet with their medical supplies and found a small bottle of motion sickness pills. They shouldn't have been needed with all the training they'd done to first prepare for the mission, but *thank God for small miracles.*

While he rummaged, Lacy propped herself up on the toilet. One knee sat in her bile, but she didn't care. "It's not me," she called to Dex. "It's Nova. Morning sickness." She paused to breathe, then said, "I don't think she likes all the flying either. All the..." she wiggled her hand around to communicate Dex's swerving around the asteroids.

Dex only nodded and then returned to the head with a pill and a glass of water.

Lacy saw the pill and immediately worried about choking on it. Throwing up once was enough. With a queasy grimace toward Dex, she shook her head.

"Come on, take it. Nova will thank you."

"Nova doesn't want it."

Robbie peaked his head in again. "Who's Nova?"

"What does Nova want, then?" Dex sank against the doorway to sit on his butt.

Lacy turned around but kept an arm resting on the rim of the toilet. Her head rested on her arm. As if half asleep, she said, "A hamburger."

Dex could practically smell it when she said it.

Lacy continued, "A real greasy one. Like they had at Al's Diner in Park Slope."

"Oh my God, darling," Dex laughed, his fantasy erased. "Those were the worst!"

A flame burned in his heart when he saw Lacy laugh too. "They really were. I felt sick for a week after eating it."

"I don't think that was real beef, even. One of my friends once said he saw Al trying to catch stray alley cats to use for meat."

"I'd believe it. You couldn't pay me to go back there... But Nova must really want to try that burger."

"How about a pill that tastes like a burger. And I promise it'll be better than that crappy diner food."

Lacy pursed her lips. "No more pills," she said, flopping her hand up and down. "I can't go back to those supplements."

Dex huffed. "You'll have to eat something. I think Nova would prefer those over nothing."

Lacy moaned. If she couldn't have a questionably-made, heart-attack-inducing hamburger, she wouldn't have anything.

"Come on," Dex said softly, rising, then holding out his hands for her. When she took them, he said, "Why don't you lay down. I'll figure out our next move."

Dex pulled her up from her stupor. She grabbed a towel to wipe her knee, then they slowly walked back to their bunk. Lacy lay down on top of the blanket, feet facing the command console. She watched him flip through a number of screens while he thought up a plan. Every other moment though, he was distracted by the radar screen. Nothing so far from their imperial tail.

When Lacy spoke up, it solidified something they both knew was coming. "We're not running again, are we?"

Dex sighed. "No. No, we're not. The Emperor probably could have killed everyone on Taranok when he almost found you. And I don't think the Mok Tau are a special case. One of these days the Empire is bound to find Earth. I'm not a fan of him being able to wipe out the entire human race if he's having a bad day. Or the people of Taranok for that matter."

Lacy propped herself up to lean against the bunk's headboard. "Do you really think he would? Will?"

He couldn't say it out loud for the sole purpose of not wanting her to panic in case he was wrong, but Dex wouldn't have been surprised if they were already dead. Instead, he left it at, "He already laid the groundwork for it, setting up prophecy for their apocalypse. It looks to me like that's already begun."

"But that assassin is only one man," she said, propping herself up an inch. "And if we were the target, he's probably already gone from there. The soldiers were all pulled out, anyway. They'll be fine."

Dex turned around in his seat and leaned forward. "The officers were pulled out," Dex corrected. "All the foot soldiers were still stationed on the outpost. I don't know why it was otherwise abandoned, but I know it won't stay that way for long."

"Why would they just pull out the officers, though?" Lacy found herself sitting upright again, with one leg hanging over the edge of the bed.

"Change of command? Maybe top brass got pissed that the guys stationed there failed him and wanted to see some new leadership to get the planet under control."

"Under control? Dex, you were talking about the apocalypse just a second ago. Either the planet's been abandoned or it hasn't. In all reality, all that prophesying is probably just a scare tactic to keep the people in line."

Dex rubbed his chin. "No... no that's not it. We hurt

the Emperor much more than getting a handful of stone age tribesmen to rise up against him. All anyone in the universe knows is the Emperor. For once people around here aren't living in ignorance. The Emperor isn't going to take that sitting down."

"He might," Lacy said wishfully.

Dex picked his eyes up from the floor and noted that Lacy had scooted a few inches closer.

"The moon base was abandoned, and the mountain base was downsizing. If he was going to kill everyone he'd have done it by now."

Dex still only shook his head. "There's more to this. There has to be."

And in that moment, there was. Something sounded on the radar. Dex spun around in his seat and pulled up the screen. "Our friend's here," he announced, and began flicking knobs and pressing buttons. "Powering down. Let's hope he passes right by us."

The lights of the *Silent Horizon* went dark. The engine stopped whirring. Even the life support shut off. Oxygen wouldn't flow anymore; they had to be sparse with their breathing. Dex held a finger to his mouth. Not even a word.

Not a single wasted breath.

On the wall of one of the tunnels, a light flared and intensified at a constant speed until a black shape like a blade cut across their vision, a side view of a Zar-Meck starfighter. It passed just fast enough that Dex and Lacy hoped he hadn't had time to look out the starboard side of his ship. The silver sheen of the *Silent Horizon* was a dead giveaway, especially if providence was against them and the light of a distant star reflected off their hull at just the right moment.

Dex thought to himself, *Next port we stop at, I'm installing forward lasers... if anyone's selling.*

He expected a mental response from Lacy, but she kept the lips of her mind shut. Use of the Emperor's powers would be more reliable to Romek than the most advanced radar tech. Instead, she slowly snuck up behind him and wrapped her arms around his torso. Dex kissed her forearm, keeping his eyes out on the viewport.

"Do you think he's gone?"

Both Dex and Lacy's eyes went wide in shock. Neither of them had spoken. Their electronic friend did.

As if on cue, Romek's ship appeared at the entrance of their cave. An intense spotlight shone on them, blinding the humans.

"Power up!" Dex shouted.

Lacy jumped into her seat and began the sequence, priming the engine.

The robot jumped up with claws on the command console to get a better view. "What should I-"

"Just sit down, Robbie!" Dex shouted. The cabin lights came up and Dex lifted the ship into a hover.

Blaster fire reigned down on them from the opposing starfighter with terrible accuracy. Each blast rocked the cavern of the asteroid. Bits of rock and dust rained down from the ceiling. The *Silent Horizon* had no shields, only a tough hull material that dispersed some of the energy of the impact. But it wasn't enough.

Lacy pulled in the landing gear just in time for Dex's mad dash past Romek and down one of the tunnels.

"Dex! This isn't the way we came!"

"Did you want me to ask for directions?"

"Dex!" she shouted, feeling a twinge of annoyance even from Nova.

"I know! I'm sorry!"

Romek followed closely behind in pursuit, sending another volley over them, each laser beam lighting up the path ahead up them in strobes.

"He overshot us," Lacy observed.

"Wonderful news, darling, now fire back!"

Lacy was already on it. Announcing a play-by-play, she realized, wouldn't help anyone except the assassin. "Can't get a good shot!" The targeting monitor was totally overblown by the Zar-Meck starfighter's searchlights.

Dex dove the ship down ninety degrees into a new vein of the asteroid, then banked hard to starboard at a three-way intersection of pathways. Lacy fired upward at the intersection point, hoping to knock loose some rocks. They fell as she'd intended, but it did little to slow their pursuer.

Chunks of rock slammed into the starfighter, and Romek's attempt to dodge only rammed him into the cave wall, but it was only a trifle against the starfighter's shields. He fired again, a long burst of laser fire that tore off a piece of the hull.

"Hull integrity dropping," Lacy announced.

Dex grit his teeth. "Yeah, I figured it'd do that."

Lacy fired blindly, hoping something would hit, but for all she knew, every attempt flew right past the starfighter and the intensity of the searchlights only grew until the rear monitor was completely white.

"Dex, he's on top of us!"

He white knuckled the controls, searching for a new path to pursue, then pulled up. It gave Lacy the perfect shot for only a split second before the other starfighter adjusted, as the new angle relieved the monitor of the glare before Romek could turn with them. Lacy held down the trigger like it was a machine gun, spraying and praying in Romek's direction, even when the monitor was blinded again.

"There!" Dex pointed out to a thin strip of open space. "I see a way out! Prep the ship to jump!"

Lacy spun around and picked up Robbie, who'd been hiding behind her chair, and swapped her seat with him. "Keep holding down the trigger, Robbie." With him on the gun, Lacy stepped to the side, between Dex and Robbie, and prepared the engine for a jump and quipped to Dex, "We should probably get another seat installed too while we're at it."

Dex grinned but couldn't look away from the viewport or think of anything to say.

"Where to? I need coordinates!" Lacy glanced back

and forth between Dex and the nearly barren map.

The cave exit neared, but not nearly quickly enough.

"Dex?" she shouted.

He avoided the question. "What's the hull integrity at?"

Lacy was absolutely befuddled. "Dex, I need-!"

"I know, I know, just tell me!"

Another blast struck the ship, and the sound of nails on a chalkboard tore across the port-side wing.

"Fifty-two percent."

Dex cursed, then begrudgingly said, "That'll do," and thrust the ship along the roof of the tunnel, and reached across the console to push up on the turret controls while Robbie held down the trigger. The blasterfire loosened the rest of the rest of the weak rocks from the tunnel roof, and they all fell onto Romek's starfighter until he pulled back.

Lacy watched with terror as the monitor showed their hull integrity drop from fifty, to forty-five, to forty, to thirty seven, when Dex dropped from the roof and piloted them out of the asteroid.

Romek did not come with them, but he had not given up his pursuit. There were still other pathways in the asteroid.

Once free of him, Dex and Lacy audibly sighed relief. Robbie mimicked a sigh to the best of his ability.

"I don't want to brag," Robbie said, "but I think I may have saved us just then."

Lacy sensed the thrashing Dex was about to give the robot for tipping Romek's sensors off to their location, even though it was their fault for not thinking to turn him off, so she got to him first. "You did *great*, Robbie," she said, emphasizing "great" while looking at Dex so he knew she wasn't in the mood to make Robbie feel bad. "Why don't you go take a break? Check on the plants, huh? Make sure nothing fell over or out of its pot."

She helped him up and out of her chair, and saluted him back when he saluted her.

Robbie waddled away to the greenhouse in the rear of the ship filled with Taranok plants. Lacy gave Dex a look as if to say, *At least we're still alive*, to which Dex responded with a raised brow that said, *for now*.

Just then, as the greenhouse door opened, Robbie announced, "There is a man in here with us."

Both Dex and Lacy jumped up, Dex drawing his blaster and stepping in front of Lacy.

From inside the greenhouse they heard a crash.

Dex called to the robot, "Robbie? Are you okay?" Suddenly the ship felt very small, and they were both aware of how much damage they had already taken.

Lacy sent her thoughts into Dex's mind. *Don't shoot. You might tear a hole through the ship.*

"Got a knife or something?" he whispered, and slowly stepped forward.

Had the assassin not been alone when he attacked the tribe? Or was their pursuer through the asteroid field not really him? Maybe he'd somehow snuck aboard the ship before they flew off. Lacy reached out with her mind in an attempt to sense him, but nothing came from the room. No life energies, hostile or otherwise.

Dex leaned against the wall of the corridor, just next to the greenhouse, and held out a hand for Lacy to stay back. She took it, rather than fall away, and willed strength into him like a prayer. She could feel his heart beating rapidly. Or was it her own? Or Nova's?

He mouthed, *three... two...* and on "one" spun into the doorway with the blaster dropping quickly from eye to waist level, and a moment later, dropped it back into his holster. His cheeks went red with embarrassment, and Dex couldn't help but laugh, and whispered to himself, "Jesus Christ."

Eyes wide, Lacy asked, "What is it?"

Dex shook his head and entered the greenhouse. A moment later, after a muffled grunt and Robbie saying, "he fell on me," Dex reemerged holding the body of a Zar-Meck who was missing a chunk of its face. "I forgot, we grabbed a souvenir from the outpost."

Lacy's shocked expression turned to disgust and annoyance. "Why the hell did you keep that thing?"

Dex shrugged. "I had this crazy idea that we could use 'em. Their armor at least. It'd give our boys back on the ground an upper hand if the Empire *did* come back to pick another fight."

"Did you have to take the body too?" she asked, almost disappointed, but mostly disgusted.

"Clock was ticking. Thought we'd look into it when we got back to the village, but... things got in the way." Then, half to himself, "Couldn't really rely on anyone else to be smart enough to figure out how to get this thing off the corpse without destroying the suit."

Now he expected Lacy to play the role of the bleeding heart and defend the Mok Tau's intelligence, as if many of them weren't still preferable to sticks and stones over laser weapons. But, she didn't argue.

He continued, setting the carcass back down on the floor, "And since we've got it here, one thing that's been bothering me is those guys look like us, humanoid enough, but everything about them seems mechanical."

Lacy shook her head and threw up her hands. "I... I don't know why that matters. Cyborgs, I guess. The robots around here are advanced enough, so what if they wrapped it in skin?"

Dex looked down at the hole in the Zar-Meck's face. Blood never spilled when it had been shot, but the insides looked more than likely organic. "Doesn't look like wires in there. We've seen the Empire's robots," he nodded toward Robbie. "This isn't one of those, yet they act more like a machine than he does. Maybe it's nothing, but it doesn't sit right with me."

Lacy spun around, back toward her seat at the console and rubbed a temple. "Get rid of that thing. I don't want it on the ship."

Robbie hobbled into the hallway and looked up at Dex. "I think I was scared when I saw it."

"Nothing to be scared of, buddy. Just a dead guy. We're used to 'em by now." Dex left the robot to clean up the room, and joined Lacy at the console. He could understand her discomfort of having a dead and, at this point, decomposing body on their ship, but was disappointed she didn't share the intrigue he had in them. There were so many more things about their condition that didn't make sense. In time he could drop hints here and there of where his head was at in concern to the Zar-Mecks, possibly planting seeds of interest, another mystery solved that could help them fight the Emperor. Or, at the very least, give the people of Taranok another leg up.

But, one mission at a time. Dex pressed the buttons on the command console that brought up the star map.

"You manage to get the info you were looking for on the moon outpost?" he asked, glancing up at her.

Lacy perked up, remembering something that had been buried in her mind for what she now felt was too long without a good excuse. "Oh! Golly, yes!" She jumped from her seat to grab the data tablet, then returned and scrolled through it with fervor. "Sorry, I was meaning to download it when we completed the mission but, Robbie: he wasn't here to link us up. Here, just as we thought. Look," she pointed to characters on the screen which Dex couldn't read. "The cargo ship we were on *did* come from there."

Dex's acknowledgement was setting a destination to the location she provided, knowing what she meant even though he couldn't read it.

"Sure that's the right move? Going back into enemy territory?"

Dex's lips pulled to the right, and he shook his head. "Not at all. But I'm hoping we can get some answers there." He activated the hyperdrive. Time slowed and light wrapped around the viewport before they rocketed faster than light across the stars. "At least it should put us on the right track."

40. Ghost Port

Lacy sat hunched over the command console, reading an analog re-creation of "The Wizard of Oz" off of the monitor while a fuzzy recording of Jenny Mae serenaded her with "No More Grey Skies." Unlike the version of "Oz" she'd grown up with, this one didn't have the pictures she used to love. But there was a copy of the movie - both the original Judy Garland version and the '52 version with the lost musical numbers added back in - saved onto the ship's computer, and if there was time down the road, she planned on watching it again after she finished the book. Thinking about the book prompted her to rub her stomach. "I can't wait to read this to you," she whispered.

What kind of girl would Nova be? Lacy asked herself. Nova stirred in her womb but gave no hint of an answer.

Lacy could already see Nova as a young woman, first learning how to pilot the *Silent Horizon* if they were still flying around in it by then, eager to take the controls on her own with her father's sense of confidence. But if Nova were anything like her mother, would Lacy still look forward to her teenage years? All the immature, rebel-without-a-cause attitude Lacy had thrown in her own mother's direction?

Maybe one day they could go back to the jungle planet and Nova could meet the Mok Tau who'd fought so hard to protect her parents. She'd be the prodigal daughter of Taranok.

"What are you thinking about?" Dex asked from the port side bunk.

Lacy caught herself in her daydream and looked up from her blank stare at the monitor. Robbie was next to her, his claws hovering over the captain-side controls as if he were steering the ship. She gently patted his half-dome head as she spun around to see Dex half asleep on the bunk.

"Just thinking," she said.

Dex held out a hand, beckoning her to join him in bed. "We've got hours," he said. "Come on, get some rest."

Lacy looked out the viewport. The swirling mix of stars, galaxies, and nebulae passing by at incredible speed looked like a projection of her own eyes.

"Robbie's got the controls, we're fine," Dex added.

Lacy sighed and curled up next to him in the bed.

Dex wrapped an arm around her, pulling her in close to his chest. "Gonna tell me what's going on in that brain?"

She brought his hand up to her mouth and kissed his fingers, then pulled him tightly around her torso. "Just thinking about Nova."

"Yeah? What about her?"

Lacy's eyes wandered around the cabin. "For one..." she laughed. "Not a lot of room for the nursery I'd always pictured."

Dex sat up an inch and also looked around, for the first time realizing that a baby would be crawling around the ship soon enough.

"At least we already have a bed for her when she's big enough." She pointed toward the starboard side bunk. "The Sears catalog probably doesn't ship out this far, do they?"

Dex grinned. "No, I'm sure they do. Probably just takes a little longer than usual, but I'm sure it'd make it eventually." They both laughed, and he squeezed her a bit tighter, then kissed her ear. "What about a cradle, though? I probably could have had the boys back in the jungle make us one. We could put it in the greenhouse."

Lacy nudged his side. "I'm not putting her that close to the engine. She can go right here next to us."

"Gonna be real annoying when she starts crying."

"Comes with the job."

"There isn't much room in the head for a baby changing station." Dex felt then a mild annoyance growing in her at his unnecessary – *though true*, he told himself – assessment. He added quickly, "But I'm sure we can make it work."

The annoyance began to fade.

For good measure, he added, "And I promise to change her my fair share."

"I know, dear." She kissed his hand again. "I'd kick you off this ship if you didn't."

* * *

"I've got a bad feeling about this..." Dex mused when they'd pulled out of hyperspace. They'd both changed out of their night attire and into wear better suited for this excursion; Dex in the clothes Korr the cyborg had once given him, and Lacy in an outfit that blended the greens and naturey feel of the Mok Tau's garments with something a little more modern. But over her shoulders she wore Dex's jacket, which had also once been Korr's, though she only ever knew it now as her husbands, and in turn, hers.

Lacy helped Robbie poke his head over the console. He did not share Dex's sentiment. "I have a good feeling about this," he said. They were getting deeper into the dredges of imperial territory, and that meant more imperial tech.

Lacy met them somewhere in the middle. "It gives me the creeps, but maybe it's our lucky day."

Dex slowed the *Silent Horizon* down as they approached a seemingly abandoned space station. Other than there being no apparent signs of life or activity of any kind, the station looked exactly the same as it did months ago. At the very least, there was no one to catch them at the docks and report them to the Empire.

Yet, at the same time, "Probably no one to point us in the right direction, then," Dex grumbled.

"Look on the bright side, darling," Lacy put her hand on his forearm. "No one to stop us from walking around, either."

She was right. They decided that the best course of action was to find their way over to a station control tower. The transport which had brought the kron-kaal to Taranok had stopped here, if not originated from the station. Likely, it was the very cargo ship that they had been on before they were forced to flee. It had been headed in the same direction, after all, and had similar equipment that they'd seen in Torro-Kaal. And if they could find the cargo transfer orders or another manifest, they could hopefully track the creature all the way to the source and answer the big question: Why?

Why go through all the trouble of importing predators?

"Which building do you think is the tower?" Dex asked, first to Lacy, then promptly turning to the robot. "Robbie? Any of these look familiar?"

Robbie didn't even have to look out the window to answer the question. "I worked in a kitchen when I met Lacy. I don't know what anything is supposed to look like except stoves and sinks."

"Very helpful," Dex grumbled.

They did a slow lap around the station, studying each building that looked like a possible control tower, hoping it wouldn't be too far different from ones they used to see at airports, with a thin base and a wide glass observation deck at the top.

"What about that one?" Dex jerked his head toward a tower with a halo observatory nearby the docks they recognized as being for commercial vessels. It was hard to mistake after their narrow escape on their previous visit.

"It's promising," Lacy concurred. "And plenty of space to park."

Dex pitched the *Silent Horizon* downward toward an empty plot of land near the tower. But, as they drew closer, the controls began to stiffen.

"Hold on now," Dex grunted. "Looks like we're getting some kind of interference."

A notification popped up on the central monitor as if they were being hailed. Lacy addressed it while Dex maintained the controls, gently pushing the ship further downward toward the docks.

"Not as empty as we thought?" Dex pried. "Tell me now if we have to bail."

Lacy read the words that appeared on the screen. Imperial characters. "We don't have proper clearance for this zone. It's a shield repelling us."

Dex pulled away, leveling out and flying around the docking area. Once he was no longer pushing down, the controls lost their stiffness.

"Glorious," Dex sighed, trying not to sound defeated. "All right, I'm taking us down. Looks like we're walking. Robbie, think you can help us navigate this place? Read all the signs and what not?"

Before Robbie could speak, Lacy answered, "I can do that."

It took Dex a moment to remember her strange ability to translate the alien text they'd come across. "Right. Okay, that's actually perfect. Robbie, you stay with the ship and take these." He then held up his communications device and the spare blaster. "If you see anything pop up on the radar, you call us. Okay? Robbie, hey!"

Robbie stopped his playing with the console buttons – not pressing anything, just pretending he was – and responded to Dex by asking, "When you are gone, will you still look for a new power source for me?"

Lacy put a hand on Robbie's half-dome head and mouthed to Dex with pleading eyes, *Yes!*

"Y- yeah, buddy. We'll keep an eye out."

Robbie didn't process the lack of conviction in his voice. He jumped off Lacy's lap and walked with them to the airlock. "Do not forget, it needs to be nuclear powered or else I may run slower. Oh! And I may be requiring more fuel for my torch soon if you can find that. And I may be requiring more fuel for my torch soon if you can find that."

"You don't have to tell me twice. I got it the first time," Dex said, stopping just before opening the airlock.

"I did?" Robbie raised a claw to his speaker, an attempt to mimic how he'd seen Dex when in thought. "I did. That is my mistake."

Lacy tugged at Dex's sleeve. "Come on. Let's get him a battery."

She opened the airlock, and once they stepped out of the ship and sealed it behind them, Dex said, "We'll look for one *after* we find the control tower."

"Just as long as we look for one."

Dex took her by the hand and walked her down the dock toward the empty station. "I promise we'll find one," he said, and kissed her cheek.

The air about the station tasted hollow. It wasn't as if the place had been evacuated, it was like they stood on a plane outside of time and space. There was such perfect stillness, such perfect quiet. If one closed their eyes and laid down, one felt like they could slip through reality. Not through space, or drifting on the waves on an ocean. Merely drifting.

Neither Dex nor Lacy wanted to be the one to break the silence. They cursed their own footsteps for sounding so loud against the complete emptiness of the station, and found themselves stepping very slowly and even more gently through the once busy streets of the station. Even artificial wind from the station's life support systems blowing through an awning would have been welcome. A mouse or small alien creature knocking over a loose trinket in the bazaar would have made them jump, but it'd be a welcome scare if it broke up the uneasiness of the atmosphere.

Walking through what appeared to be a shopping district, Dex leaned in to Lacy's ear and whispered, "..."

"What?" she said, slightly louder than a whisper.

Dex hadn't realized just how quiet he was being. "I

said, 'See any signs of it?'"

Lacy saw plenty of signs, including one large display stand at the intersection of two corridors, and could read them all, but understanding was totally different. Her best assumption was that they were names of stores, services, or food vendors. Some, though, were much clearer.

"Commercial docks are that way." She pointed to one of the signs, then moved her hand in the direction it presumably pointed.

"Didn't look like that far of a walk from above." He said it as he surveyed their surroundings. The layout of the the port city was not as orderly as he would have hoped. It was overly crowded with many levels of walkways and roads intersecting at odd angles. Even though it was not currently populated, it still looked like it would be easy to get lost in the labyrinth.

"I hope not." Lacy put her hands on her stomach and rubbed the small bump. "Nova's getting hungry."

Dex looked around the tight corridor of unattended vendor stands. The theme of this alley was clothing and jewelry. "Any of those signs point to food?"

Lacy led Dex to the large display and traced a finger over the alien characters. She bit her lip as she tried to read them, growing increasingly annoyed at her inability to figure out where they were. "I'm gonna go out on a limb and say there should be some restaurants in this area. And it's not too far out of the way. I don't think it's out of the way, at least. Best guess is we're right around..." She circled a wide swath of land. "This general area."

"Never let a lieutenant do land nav," Dex joked to himself.

Lacy didn't appreciate the comment and, not particularly playfully, punched his arm.

"Hey!" he laughed.

"You make that joke all the time. It's gotten old."

Dex rubbed the sore spot on his arm. "It's just a joke. Come on, you're doing great."

Lacy pursed her lips.

"You wanna get something to eat or you wanna be mad at me?"

"I am mad at you."

He took her hand again. "That's fine. You can be mad while you eat."

They wandered again in the general direction of the commercial docks, veering down the alleys Lacy felt were right to bring them closer to food.

"Still feeling that burger?" Dex asked.

"Mmm… no, Nova's in the mood for breakfast now. Preferably pancakes."

Dex scoffed. "All right, I'll see what I can cook up. This place looks good. What's that sign say?"

They both looked up at the sign on a building that looked less like letters and more like braille with some of the dots constantly moving up-and-down and side-to-side.

Lacy tried to pronounce how it translated in her mind, grunting, "Rau… ruoc… trua…frthhh… I really don't know, it doesn't make any sense."

"Well. Looks to me like it says 'diner.' Let's check it out!"

The inside of the building resembled a Greek diner, or at least a cafeteria. Dex led Lacy to a booth near what looked like the kitchen, then helped her into her seat.

"Give me just a few minutes. If anyone comes in, just scream. And fight them off. Okay?"

"Okay. Don't be back there too long. I can eat back on the ship if we have to."

"Oh, no-no-no," Dex laughed, putting a hand on her cheek. He rubbed her cheek with his thumb, loving the feel of her soft skin. "I'm gonna make you something delicious even if it gives us an alien virus."

Lacy rolled her eyes as her cheeks blushed with the trace of his thumb. "I'm not that desperate. But I am getting hungrier and Nova's getting impatient, so off with you, Captain."

He let go of her cheek and took her hand instead, kissing her fingers. "Yes, darling."

Nova leapt with joy inside of Lacy, and Lacy prayed that her baby would only ever know moments like these when she was born. Moments when they could put the troubles of the world out of their mind and be content with the love of the family they'd created. And she couldn't wait for Dex to formally meet her.

"I'll be back in a bit, okay?" Dex said softly.

"Okay."

It was then off to the kitchen to try to find something good enough for human consumption.

Dex searched each cabinet thoroughly for ingredients that resembled Earth food. There was a white powder that had the feel and smell of flour, and when he tasted a dab, it was close enough to the real thing, although a bit salty. In another cabinet he found bowls and pans, in another a whisk. The sink worked when he tested it, and the clear liquid that spouted from it was water in every way he could tell.

"Thank God for small miracles," he muttered, then searched for a refrigerator. There was nothing in the immediate vicinity or that looked like one he would find in a house. But what was he thinking? This wasn't a home kitchen, it was a diner. Odds were they would have a walk-in freezer or cooler. In the back of the kitchen there were two doors, neither with windows or handles. He took a chance with the door on the right and was disappointed to find that it led him out the back of the building to another street of vendor stands.

Just as he was about to close the door, something across the street caught his eye. A tiny object caught the light and shone for him as if it were meant to be found. Dex couldn't help himself. And he told himself that if by some cosmic chance the owner of the stand appeared, he would find a way to pay for his thievery. But, as no one was there, he didn't worry about his bill being collected any time soon.

With his new treasure secured, Dex returned to the kitchen and tried the other door. This one, another small miracle, he thought, was indeed a freezer. Tentacled beasts like giant squids with scaled hides hung along one wall. On the shelves next to the hides were cuts of alien meat, fruits, and vegetables. Probably. On the other wall, Dex guessed, dairy products. Cartons of frozen liquids of all different colors, some even multiple colors. All the colors he could imagine except two: red and yellow.

Dex reached for a carton of white liquid and took a whiff. It smelled like nothing. There was no chance in the universe it was milk from an abducted cow, but if the flour-like powder was good enough, this could be, too.

It was at this point he wished he hadn't told Lacy to wait for her meal. Boxes of other foodstuffs were actually labeled. Imitation butter may not have been a thing to the Empire, but for the time being, everything in the kitchen was imitation. The only thing that was instantly recognizable in the freezer were the eggs, and even those weren't quite right.

They were about a quarter size larger than the jumbo eggs Dex and Lacy sorely missed from Earth, and at the top was a crease like a pair of lips. The shell had a rough texture to it and off putting coloring as if someone had spilled black ink overtop of it.

Dex reached for the egg with more hesitation than any of the other ingredients. It was heavier than a typical egg, even one of unusual size. He brought the egg up to better inspect it, and as he did, the lips began to part.

He nearly dropped the egg in surprise. The egg let out a little *hiss* when it opened.

Then, being a reasonable person, Dex put the egg back where he found it. He was taking enough risks ingesting mystery foods that only nominally resembled flour, milk, butter, and water, he didn't need to feed Lacy or Nova anything creeping and or crawling.

While Dex worked in the kitchen, Lacy tried to sit patiently in the booth, waiting for her meal. But she couldn't sit still. She tapped her heel constantly and was always glancing out the front window for signs of movement, or tried blocking out the sound of Dex's cooking which rang too loudly against the utter silence of the rest of the station. Lacy felt it would be impossible for her to hear anyone sneak up on them, especially the Emperor's assassin.

"Tell me I'm overthinking this," she cooed to Nova. In response, she felt a sense of cautious ease wash over her. As far as they could tell, they were safe for the time being. They were still alone on the station. No monsters here.

Dex came out of the kitchen a few minutes later with silverware and a platter of brown – not golden brown, but flat brow – flapjacks, and placed them on the table in front of Lacy.

"They taste real enough," he said with a carefree demeanor. "Took a lot of guesswork but I think I finally brought a real, meaningful contribution to the Empire. Buttermilk pancakes. Hope you're still in the mood for them."

Lacy smiled curtly, the closest Dex got to an answer.

"Well, dig in," he said, somewhat disappointed. "You want burgers again, don't you."

Lacy sagged her shoulders and looked up at him with pouting eyes. "They sounded so good when you talked about them before."

Dex took a deep breath in and held his smile. "I don't think you'll want a burger with the stuff I found back there."

She pushed the plate away an inch.

"Those are fine," Dex laughed, and pushed them back her way. "Trust me, I tested. Not sick yet." He then pulled out a chair and took a seat across from her. "They're better than what we're used to on Taranok. I'll miss the guys but-"

"Won't miss the meals," Lacy finished for him, and cut a sliver of the pancakes. She eyed Dex one more time before taking a bite. "Any syrup back there?" she asked jokingly, then slowly brought the piece to her mouth.

Dex watched her face intently for any distaste or surprise approval. "So?"

Again, that curt smile. "I'm sure you did your best, darling."

Instead of being hurt, Dex nodded proudly. "I did. Thank you."

"Its just..." she began with a half-full mouth, "there's something I think missing."

"Eggs," Dex told her quickly. "I don't... you wouldn't even want to think about them."

Lacy needed to hear no more. "Do you want some?" she asked, pointing at the stack with her knife.

"I taste tested enough. Besides, Nova needs some, too."

Lacy took another bite, then another, and soon was scarfing them down. As she finished the last bite, Dex said, "Actually, I found something else back there you might like."

Her eyebrows raised quizzically. "Oh yeah?" she said with a full mouth, her hand only slightly covering herself.

Dex reached into his pocket and pulled something out, keeping his fist clasped, and one hand over the other. His voice began to falter, filled with fear. Not the same fear they'd felt in the presence of the Empire. No, this was a fear of which when Lacy saw it on his face, she felt like a high school classmate was about to ask her to prom.

"I uh... I just, I saw something..."

Lacy's pulse quickened. "What's wrong? Is someone out there?" Did he see someone and wait until now to tell her?

"No, no it's not like that. No, I just..." he took a deep breath. "I don't think it's wrong to say that we haven't gone about this whole... uh... uh, marriage thing-"

"Dex, you're not b-"

He forced out a laugh to stop her from saying the words "breaking up."

"No! God, no, Lacy. No, what I'm saying is, we

didn't have a wedding, or engagement party, honeymoon, or any of that. And, I was always okay with that. Frankly, I wouldn't have had it any other way. But there is one part I always regretted not doing for you. I think your parents would have killed me if they found out you were pregnant before I did this, but it's about time you had one of these." Dex pulled himself out of the booth and bent down on one knee.

Lacy quickly swallowed the last pancake bite and tried to compose herself. Her face was a bright red, and tears were building up in her eyes. Nova's excitement did nothing to subdue Lacy's anxiety. The emotions sweeping over her were so intense she felt as if was about to black out.

Dex held his hands up toward her and continued, "Lacy, I wouldn't hesitate to do this with you all over again if you asked me to. Wherever you are in this universe is where I want to be. So, formally this time," Dex revealed a thin golden ring with a small white jewel in the halo, and swirled carvings along the bridge and shoulders.

"Will you continue to be married to me?"

Lacy couldn't speak.

He leaned in and whispered, "I'm really hoping you'll say yes. The rest of this adventure would get real awkward otherwise."

She took his hand so firmly that the protruding jewel dug into her palm, but she didn't mind. Lacy nodded her head vigorously, trying to get the words out. She couldn't understand why it was so hard. They'd been married for over a year already. In recent years, she'd heard of friends of friends renewing their vows, something that made absolutely no sense to her (a vow was a vow for life, what need was there to renew it?). And when they first professed their love – knowing it could be at least a decade, if ever, before anything formal came of it – for as real as it was, it never could have prepared her for this moment. All the love stories she'd read, the romantic movies she'd seen and novels she read, witnessing the love others shared, none of it compared to this moment. Nothing in the universe was as beautiful as that small band and what it signified as Dex slid it onto her finger.

"Yes!" She finally squeaked out and embraced her husband.

Their lips met as they had that night in the observatory at the Grand Central Space Station. The way they met the first night they shared the port side bunk of the *Silent Horizon*. The way they met when they'd escaped the Empire into an uncertain future. The way Dex always wanted to kiss her so she always knew there was nothing he wouldn't do for her.

The intensity of their kiss, the strength of its passion, was so much it was as if the entire station quaked and they felt light on their feet.

No.

No, it wasn't the kiss.

"Do you feel that?" Lacy asked. Nova sensed it too, whatever it was, and Lacy felt an immediate need to seek a safe place.

Her head felt like it was about to burst, like a trillion receptors went off all at once with an incredible amount of energy signaling to her.

The station quaked again, and from the roof they heard the soft pitter-patter of rain, slowly building until it came crashing down. A flash illuminated the room, followed by a roar of thunder, and when the inside of the diner momentarily lit, it was with a bright red hue.

They turned their heads slowly toward the window. A storm it was indeed, but it was not water falling from the sky.

Dex rose and stepped cautiously toward the front of the diner. Within moments, the windows were dripping with red. He opened the door and the metallic smell he dreaded hit his nose. He reached out a hand to catch the rain, and, fingering it in his palm, he couldn't deny that blood was raining down from the heavens.

41. The Storm

"He raised his staff in the presence of Pharaoh and his officials and struck the water of the Nile, and all the water was changed into blood." Dex flicked his wet hand toward the floor of the diner. Blood splattered on the ground in a thin line of dots and dripped from his fingertips.

Lacy looked upon him as a man who had become something else entirely from only moments before. The romantic was gone and the hard face of a soldier on the defensive had returned.

"Looks like the Emperor heard the news already." He wiped his hand against his pant leg, leaving a damp crimson streak across the yellow line that ran down the seam, then inspected his palm. With his thumb pressed against his index and middle finger, it was almost like his own blood was pouring out into his hand. "Guess the assassin didn't work out and he's sending the plagues."

Lacy rose from the booth and rushed to her husband before everything in the room that wasn't bolted down was thrust toward the ceiling.

* * *

Robbie rushed to hide under the command console at the first strike of lightning. His immediate thought was bombardment. The Empire had found them, and a capital ship or frigate was now shelling them. But then the inside of the *Silent Horizon* was illuminated a dreadful crimson, and Robbie heard the rain. He peeked out from under his hiding place and climbed up onto Lacy's seat. The station was rapidly being drenched in red, pouring down from clouds that had manifested both in and out of the station's atmospheric shield. Small bursts of lightning flashed here and there, accompanied by low rumblings of thunder. He had no apocalyptic ideations, no biblical context for what he saw, but something in his programming registered the storm as "very bad."

The comm device Dex had left behind for him was on the armrest of the Captain's chair. Updating the two seemed like a good idea at the time. But when he picked up the device and called, he only received static feedback.

"Captain Prullen, this is Robbie. Over," he signaled just as Dex had taught him to. *Hey, you, this is me.*

No response.

"Saying again: Captain Prullen, this is Robbie. Do you hear me?"

Still no response. Only static.

Robbie's volume dropped low, and he held the comm close to his speaker. "Please respond, Dex. Lacy? Are you there?"

Just then, the most brutal quake hit, and the entirety of the *Silent Horizon* was cast onto its side. Robbie was thrown from Lacy's chair toward the port side of the ship and felt a pull as if the center of gravity had rotated a full ninety degrees to the left.

Robbie wouldn't be able to see until afterward just how close Dex and Lacy had come to being stranded at the port, but their ship and all the others skidded across the landing platform, crashing into each other and banging against the safety bars. One small unlucky ship crashed into the bars with such speed it was blown overboard and flew out past the spaceport shields into the starry abyss.

Amidst the chaos and constant thrashing, something else crashed just outside of the ship. Robbie jumped in shock and accidentally dropped the comm device and threw his attention to the docks, searching for an approaching ship. The *Silent Horizon* hadn't picked anything up on its radar, but looking at it now, it was possible the ship *had* but just wasn't displaying it. The entire system was on the fritz. Nothing was remotely readable.

Whatever it was that had crashed near him now dragged along the bottom of the hull. Robbie watched the area of floor where the sound rumbled from all the way from stem to stern, then crouched behind the back of Lacy's seat as the airlock shook.

He looked around for the comm device and spotted it just a few feet away on the wall-turned-floor. He knew he needed to try again to reach Dex and Lacy, but a horrible sound like nails on a chalkboard - *ssccrrREEEEEEE* - cut through the cabin.

"Dex? Is that you?" Robbie asked the source of the noise, knowing full well it was neither Dex nor Lacy, but wanting to be hopeful. If it were Dex and Lacy, maybe they were stuck and trying to get back in, and in that case, Robbie should open the airlock for them. And if it wasn't either of them, it was someone else, someone presumably hostile, then one little airlock wouldn't stop them from getting in, but a broken one would stop the ship from leaving.

Whatever it was scratched against the airlock a second time, accompanied by a low moan, as like a man without a mouth trying to scream for help.

Robbie reached out his arm as far as he could for the comms device. He could almost reach it, just a foot or two too far. Rerouting all the courage he could, Robbie jumped for the device and rushed back behind the wall of the bunk and shouted into the device, "Dex, Lacy, please tell me you're at the door!" He felt a sudden oncoming of fatigue after shouting the words.

Neither of them answered, but he heard a heavier moan of something pressing hard against and bending the metal airlock hatch. When he peeked over the top of the chair, it looked like the door was pressing inward as if about to blow.

"Lacy, I really hope that's you," he whispered. "I'm

going to open the door." If he was fast enough, he could unlock the door and make a rush for the spare blaster and a better hiding spot.

"You've got this, Robbie," he told himself, then hit the button to unlock the airlock. As soon as it hissed, Robbie pulled himself up into the bunk and rushed for the blaster, then threw himself into one of the storage containers.

There was silence for a moment, save for the rain pat-pat-pattering on the roof of the ship. No footsteps, or even the door being pushed further open. For a few seconds, there was nothing, and then the sound of something like one of the snakes on Taranok slithering through the ship.

Robbie reserved power anywhere within himself that had his fans running high and loud like a human unable to control their breathing. His claws gripped so tightly around the blaster and the comms device that they almost cracked.

Then there was silence again within the cabin.

Lightning flashed, and thunder followed immediately. The rain continued to quietly berate his audio receptors.

That was when, from somewhere in the back of the ship, he again heard movement. But this was no longer the sound of a serpent crawling on its stomach. Something shuffled around drunkenly, and to his terror, Robbie now heard footsteps. Slow, heavy, and cumbersome. A dull *thump... thump-swishhhh... thump...*

As quietly as he could, Robbie said into the comms, "I am very scared."

* * *

Dex was the first to fall back to the floor, with everything along his side of a nearly perfect invisible line cutting the diner in half. Lacy was thrust next in his direction, and only after that did her side of the diner return to normal. She rolled her body, holding her stomach tight, and tried to land on her back in the fetal position. Dex threw himself under her as a cushion. She landed, it felt to Dex, hard enough to push all of his organs out of both ends, like gravity had returned to the right orientation with a vengeance.

As soon as he could breathe again, he wheezed, "Is she..."

Lacy took a moment to listen, and felt Nova's tiny heartbeat and terrified energy. She took a few deep breaths, then answered him, "She's okay. A bit scared... but we'll make it. Thank God."

Dex restrained a groan at the comment and helped Lacy off of him. Then, still lying on the ground, he pulled out his comms device. "Robbie. Come in, Robbie. Tell me the ship's all right."

They waited a moment, and he called in a few more times while Lacy composed herself in the booth. But even with the sudden terror of the quake having ended, there was still the rain. The shock was over, but the reminder of the Emperor remained. In each drop that ran down the diner window she saw the flowing red robes, how they seemed to drip infinitely downward into the black abyss of his temple.

Lacy attempted to block out this horrible memory and focus a soothing energy on Nova. A breath in deeply to reassure Nova, and a slow breath out for Lacy to know she was still in control. Again and again until they were both calmed down.

"I can't reach him," Dex groaned, replacing the comms device on his belt. He then picked himself up off the ground. "I swear, if that kid is ignoring me..."

"Kid?" Lacy laughed at his euphemism.

Dex shrugged. "Acts like one sometimes." He then grumbled and added, "Acting like one now. Robbie, come in, Robbie."

"Maybe he's waiting for you to call the way you taught him to. Or maybe he's just scared."

"He's a robot. How can he be scared?"

Lacy rolled her eyes and held out her hand for the comms device. Dex begrudgingly gave it to her, feeling certain it wasn't his tone that Robbie didn't want to respond to. Holding down the transmit button, she called, "Robbie, this is Lacy. Please respond. Over."

They both stood intently, waiting for a response, but nothing came except static.

"We should go back to the ship," she told him earnestly.

Dex only shook his head. "No, when the rain dies down, we go to the tower."

"Dex, look outside. That's not normal. We need to get back to the ship before another quake hits."

"We're probably safer in here than we are on the ship. It's just an electrical storm. It'll die down."

"An electrical storm?" Lacy slid out of the booth, stomped over to the window, and knife-handed outward. "Dex, that's blood! That's not an electrical storm!"

"Maybe blood is as common around here as rain. Hell, maybe that's where all the people from the station went," he cast a finger upward.

Lacy's stomach churned at the thought. "Stop," she said, putting a hand to her mouth. "You're gonna make me sick."

"All right, all right. I'm sorry." Dex met her and placed his hands on her shoulders. "Bad joke. But trust me, it will be fine. It's weird. A little too biblical for my taste, but it's going to be fine. And I'm sure there's a perfectly reasonable explanation for it."

She gave him a curious look. "Reasonable?"

Dex shrugged, then looked out the window toward the rain for an answer. "Look, it's not... It's a storm. Sure, it *looks* like blood, but you know weird stuff happens." He clicked his fingers together as a memory came to mind. "In '28 and '29, there were those two anomalies a few months apart. Red electrical storms were recorded. The first just out of orbit, the second by Mars. Guarantee if they had capabilities for space travel back then, they would have found a blood-like precipitation in it."

"Okay, yes, I remember hearing about those, but," she paused. "Dex, I feel it in my bones. This *isn't* just some electrical storm." Lacy bit her lip and tried not to look out at the rain.

Seeing her distress persist, he added, hoping to lighten her mood, "Just as long as we don't see any frogs or locusts, I think we'll be in the clear."

Just under her breath, Lacy mumbled, "Frogs I can deal with. I wouldn't mind seeing the boys again."

Dex only grumbled his agreement, then shuffled into the booth next to Lacy. They sat silently for a time; Lacy trying to avoid looking at the rain, Dex watching it and trying to maintain the conviction that it was just that: Rain. When they returned to the ship with whatever information they were looking for, he would log the phenomenon into the *Silent Horizon* database, and when they returned to Earth-

No, not then. Earth's coordinates were wiped from the ship, and he still forgot he'd made that decision from time to time.

He bit the inside of his cheek in mild frustration. Had it been a rash decision? It was no good dwelling on it too much, but, *hell, a little more-evolved support would have gone a long way back in the village.*

Beside him, Lacy was slowly tapping her hands against her thighs. She looked down at the newly endowed ring on her finger. Dex caught this and took her left hand in his.

"Fits all right?" he asked, now feeling self-conscious about the gesture. He knew going into it that it was a cheesy thing to do, and knowing Lacy, she may have just acted as excited as she had more for his sake than for her actual excitement.

Lacy tightened her fingers around his hand. "When we left, I assumed I'd never get a proper proposal. When you proposed on the ship, I thought it couldn't be more perfect. I didn't mind not having a ring." She paused to admire it again. "I still don't have any regrets about the way you did it the first time. But I'd be lying if I didn't think this made it even more perfect. Thank you, Dex," she said, kissing them on his cheek.

Ain't a thing wrong in the world, he thought when her lips met his flesh.

Dex put his arm around her and pulled her close, then placed a soft kiss on her forehead. "We can show everyone your pretty ring when we get back to Taranok."

"We will go back, won't we?" she asked. "At some point. Just to make sure they're okay." As she looked up at him, Dex felt that if he did not answer her question just the right way, there would be no point in carrying on from the look she'd give him.

His initial comment was only spoken to make her feel better. Had he actually expected them to return? Likely not. Not as long as they were being followed. And if that were to last until their dying breaths, so be it. Dex wasn't going to put their friends in harm's way. But Lacy wanted to see them again, and how could he say no to those eyes? How could he say no to the most beautiful thing creation had blessed the universe with?

"We'll see them again," he managed to say, though barely as loud as a whisper. "One day."

Lacy nuzzled up against his chest. "Good."

And that was a promise, he told himself. To hell with playing it safe. Before the Empire got them, he'd take her back to Taranok. "But first, we need to do what we came here for."

Lacy's head grazed up and down in a nod against him.

"Gonna be a brave girl?"

Again, she nodded.

"Of course you are," Dex said with a gentle smile, pushing gently out of the booth and pulling her along.

"I'm sure we can find an umbrella somewhere. Or at least... something."

Within a few minutes, the intensity of the rain had downgraded from torrential downpour to heavily inconvenient. The other side of the street could at least be seen, and it felt like it was starting to ease up.

Using a plastic-like sheet for cover, Dex and Lacy huddled close and took small steps through the flooded street. The blood-rain bounced back up from the newborn river onto their pant legs and seeped down into their Mok Tau-made boots.

"M... ....ll fi.... m.... ew .loth.... ere...... ....eded." Dex said.

"What?" Lacy shouted to overpower the sound of the rain splattering against their ears.

Dex shouted back, a bit too loud, "I said, maybe we'll find some new clothes wherever we're headed!" He'd feel guilty about tossing the clothes Korr had given him, the only things he had to remember the cyborg by, but it didn't seem like they would be stopping by a laundromat before the pants were permanently ruined.

Lacy squirmed an inch away from him, her ear ringing. Even Nova was a little annoyed by the rain. "Right! Yeah, maybe. But I was hoping for a nice new dress." Her Mok Tau-made clothes were faring no better than Dex's.

With a grin that made his left dimple show, Dex joked, "What? The ring wasn't enough?"

She nudged his side, then glanced up at a sign just as it came into view. "This way, it looks like."

They both turned their heads to look down a new street, this one wider than the one they'd been walking on, with a clearer road and fewer overhangs, but a rushing ravine of blood running down the direction they looked. The walls of all the buildings had a more uniform design to them than the eccentric and, when not raining red, natural look of the shopping district.

"Imperial offices?" Dex asked.

"Sign said 'Government' offices."

Dex harrumphed. "Just as long as we don't get stuck at the Department of Terrestrial Vehicles."

"Or the Imperial Revenue Services. Not like that'd be too different from home."

Dex stopped and slowly turned his head to look into her eyes with admiration. "I love you so much for that joke."

She laughed, "Come on, Captain. We've got a mission." She paused then, looking up and down the wide river. "We should find another way around."

"No, this'll be fine. Here, look." Dex removed his arm from around her side and stepped from the cover of the makeshift poncho into the river. The current pushed hard against his shins, running up just above his knees, but save for the initial force, he found it was quite easy to maintain his stance. The rain quickly drenched his head and trailed down into his face. But with his head hung low, the rain dripped from his brow without getting into his eyes or mouth.

He waved to her and shouted, "Come on, it's safe!"

Lacy took a step back and shook her head. "I don't think so!"

Dex took another step away from her. Something small below the surface of the water, a piece of debris, probably, passed by his right foot. He barely gave it a second thought before waving her along again. "It's fine, trust me!"

Lacy put a hand out to hold onto a lightpost and extended one foot into the river. She felt the same amount of force pushing against her as Dex did, but for her, anything was too much. Suddenly then between them, a block of some kind sailed down the river with incredible speed. She looked up and saw Dex standing with a hand extended. His body wobbled the slightest bit, and he took a small step closer to her.

When he spoke, everything else seemed to quiet.

"I won't let anything happen to you."

She bit her lip and listened to Nova.

A hesitant yet trusting feeling came over her, and Lacy reached out her hand.

"Come on," Dex cooed, taking another step closer to meet her.

Lacy stepped out inch by inch, not yet ready to let go of the light post. Every step further out into the river had exponentially more power from the current pushing her down the road. But she stood firm, and Dex never took his eyes off of her.

"Barely a foot deep," he said. "No problem at all."

She was stepping into an artery, gushing blood that would sweep her and Nova back to the Heart of the Void.

Something rumbled off in the distance, unnerving her further, and Dex tried to offer her a comforting smile. "I'd really like to get out of this river, darling. You can swing like Jane, you can get your feet wet."

Ever so gently, she let her fingers unwind from the light post and stepped further toward Dex. He jutted out the last few inches to meet her and grasped her by her left hand pinky before fixing his grip and taking her whole hand then yanked her close as a noise like another roll of thunder rushed behind her.

Lacy turned her head away from him to see what the noise was, but Dex pulled her cheek back toward him, and he held a weary smile.

"All good," he breathed heavily. "Told ya, we're all good."

The less she knew about the hovercarriage that nearly ran her over, the better.

Even though she hadn't seen the thing that had almost dragged her down the river, Lacy was still too uncomfortable to move. Where they stood in the center of the river was the apex of the current's strength. Letting her footing loose the littlest bit carried the risk of being swept away, and she didn't have the safety of the light post to secure herself.

Dex pulled her head in close and shouted over the pounding of the rain, "If you don't pick up your feet now, I'm going to carry you. Which is it gonna be?" Before she could answer, Dex decided for her and hoisted Lacy into his arms.

"Don't say it," she warned as he picked up his feet and plodded to the other side of the river.

"Say what?" Dex grumbled.

"I can read your mind. I know you're not used to carrying two. I don't need the jokes."

With each step, the strength of the current's strength subsided.

"This is just like the first time I ever carried you. Feels no different at all. Excessive amounts of blood and everything," Dex laughed, plodding another step. They came upon a bench half-covered by the river and fought upwards against the current to get around it. "For a second I thought we were back home, taking our first steps into the honeymoon suite."

Although she'd said no jokes, his playful remark was enough to distract her from his brief thought about her Nova-weight. "The honeymoon suite?"

Now on the other side of the river, Dex guided them into one of the buildings, thankfully unlocked, and sat Lacy down by the window.

"Yeah, you remember, don't you? That resort we stayed at in Napoli? Bathtub the size of a bedroom. Pool the size of a house. Come on, darling, it was a really expensive trip. My dad paid good money for it."

Lacy's face burned a bright red, even when Dex wiped the blood off her cheeks and out of her eyes. She could hardly hold back her laughter. "What the hell are you talking about?"

"Anything," he said. "Anything that gets you smiling again. You okay to walk again?"

Lacy pursed her lips, but the ghost of a smile remained. She nodded. "We still have to get downriver, though. At least until we find another road to take."

Dex put a hand to her cheek. "We'll take it slow. Close to the wall."

* * *

After a few minutes of silence, Robbie pushed open the cabinet door and poked his head up. Dex and Lacy would not be happy at the mess of the ship the storm made, and he was far from being big enough to effectively clean the place up. Following his half-dome head, the blaster made an appearance. Just in case the source of the horrible scratching noise decided to show itself.

When there was still nothing, Robbie stood a little taller and got a better view of the cabin. He could hear the rain pouring clearly from the hall. The airlock was still open, and a small trail of red was leaking through the hall to the main cabin. Robbie couldn't properly identify it, but something in his programming warned him it definitely was not right, and his gamble at opening the door had not been a fruitful one. But nothing yet had come for him, and he couldn't hide forever. The ship had to be put right if he had it in him. At the angle it sat, Robbie wouldn't be able to climb up to the hallway and inspect the rear of the ship. But if he were careful, he could get back to Dex's seat and power up the engine and hopefully reangle the ship.

Robbie hoisted himself up out of the cabinet and onto the paneling just below the bunk. With one arm extended toward the hall, blaster in hand, he shuffled across the paneling toward the command console. A heavy footfall caused a creak in the material, and when the sound reverberated in the cabin, it was echoed by something down the hall. Only a few feet away but entirely unseen.

One of Robbie's claw prongs jumped onto the trigger of the blaster and almost pulled it back.

But there was silence again. And, though he never felt totally safe, when he felt safe enough, he continued his arduous journey across the paneling until it ended, and, not quite prepared for the ledge as he was still looking toward the hall, fell off and crashed into the wall.

He was quick on his feet and jumped back up with the blaster held high over the bunk wall.

Down the hall, something did move then. It sounded like Dex or Lacy, footsteps, someone picking themself up as Robbie had just done, but slower. Something moved weakly, disjointedly. There was rhythmless crashing and creasing as the source of the sound righted itself, then latched onto the doorway. But it moved without grunts or moans, and though Robbie could just barely see shadows move across the wall of the hallway, there was not yet any definitive shape, and its edges were blurred by the hallway lights.

The thing had heard Robbie's fall, and now it came for him.

Robbie's claw tightened on the trigger.

The shadows shuffled and darkened as they grew, moving in his direction. It took shape; the basic outline of a person.

Robbie wanted to call out, "Dex! Lacy! Is that you?" But his speakers faltered, and no noise came out. It was for the best, he knew, but still he wanted to shout, praying (as Lacy called the odd act of talking to someone but no one) that it *was* them and were only pulling a prank on him.

As the shadow darkened at the threshold of the cabin, it halted and didn't so much as sway. It merely froze.

The voice inside Robbie's head, which Dex had called his "conscience," told Robbie to leap up and start blasting. He would protect the *Silent Horizon* or die trying. But his gears didn't listen to his "conscience" as a stronger voice had developed, which overrode both his programming and so-called "conscience." This other voice, "reason," told him to sit this one out. Self-preservation would be more useful than a heroic death.

So he lowered the blaster and hid again behind the wall with just enough of his head popping up to keep an eye on the shadow until moments later it shrank again and the sound of footsteps traveled toward the airlock and down the steps until the rail drowned them out entirely.

When the voices told him he was safe, Robbie jumped up to the Captain's seat and powered up the ship.

* * *

Nearly a half mile down the river, Dex and Lacy had finally approached an intersection and broke away from the pull of the river down a narrow road that rose slightly upward, alleviating them from the current. The tower they were approaching was by then totally obscured by other buildings, but there wasn't much further to go.

"Through here," Lacy pointed to the swaying gate of an alley. The narrow corridor provided sufficient cover from the rain with pipes and a series of glass bridges extending from one building to the other. As they travelled underneath, Dex spotted glimpses of interior design reminiscent of the RVOs, and office spaces that Lacy saw as similar to the office of her old imperial acquaintance, Jaskek Dreed.

While they were mostly protected from the drenching, Dex still held the plastic sheet above their heads to block out the runoff from the roofs and bridges coming down on them inconsistently and somehow always unexpectedly. Each time they walked through a line of runoff, Lacy gave a little jump as the rain splashed in a loud slosh across the material.

They came to the end of the alley shortly thereafter and were finally able to look upon the control tower up close, looming over them as if a magical and malevolent Dark Tower out of a fantasy story. The halo ring floor at the very top overshadowed them, protecting them from the rain, but also blocked out the natural light from the nearest stars. The walls of the building were a dull grey, looking almost totally black in the shadow of itself, with not a single drop of blood blemishing its sleek texture.

A terrible fear came over Lacy that everything they'd seen so far at the station was a sham. The journey had been a trap. The station wasn't deserted. All of the Zar-Mecks and imperial officers were just waiting for them in the tower, and somehow the assassin had beaten them here. Romek was merely lying in wait.

"Hey." Lacy felt Dex nudge her arm. "Still with me, pretty lady?" he asked.

She swallowed hard. Nova had nothing to say. No fear, no warning. By her reading, everything was all right.

Lacy nodded, eyes locked on the tower's door. "Still here. This is it. This is the control tower."

Dex wiped the corner of his mouth of blood that had slipped through a tear in the plastic. "Good. One step closer."

One step closer, Lacy agreed. *One step closer to the Emperor.*

At that, Nova did shudder. For though she never met him, just as she was a part of her mother, so too was there a part of the Emperor buried deep in Nova's being.

42. The Dark Tower

The opening of the door marked the end of the rainfall. It switched off like a light switch with the hiss of the motion-activated slider. And with the rain, so too left any color in the world except for the red on the ground and the dripping from ledges. Darkness crept over the station and through the halls of the tower.

"So Moses stretched out his hand toward the sky, and total darkness covered all Egypt for three days," Dex bemused, looking over his shoulder at the darkening streets.

Lacy gripped his hand tight. "You need to cut that out. It's just night."

"It's space, it's always night. But it wasn't this dark before the rain."

They stepped through the doorway into the tower and the door hissed shut behind them. Now that they were out of the rain, they both realized just how soaked their clothes, their boots especially, were. Dex lifted one foot, then the other, feeling the pool of rain slosh around his boot.

"Think they'll have any spare uniforms in here?" he asked in a low voice, leading the two of them deeper into the unlit lobby of the tower. "Or power?" he added. Sure, the motion sensor door had opened for them, but nothing else had yet reacted to their presence, and so far as they could tell, there were no switches on the wall by the entryway. Just the flat black wall. Not even a picture highlighting the Zar-Meck of the Month.

The room was only faintly lit by outside sources, dull lights reflecting off of signs, puddles, and glass windows. One long desk stretched against the left side of the hallway, with four empty seats behind it and a translucent silver pane atop it. In the center of the room leading down to another set of doors were two rows of thin triangular posts that extended six feet high, bare of any markings on any side.

As they approached the posts, Lacy began to answer Dex, "I'll let you know if I see a locker room on the directory," before a loud ringing sounded throughout the room.

They had just stepped past the first set of posts, now glowing a bright yellow. At the same time, a yellow light flashed just next to them behind the desk, and a white outline of their bodies appeared on the silver pane with flashing alien text just above them. The two of them rushed around the desk in reaction to it, but Lacy was faster and read off the text while searching for a button to shut off the alarm.

"Unidentified visitor," she said, and the text flashed to something else. "One at a time." Her hands and fingers jumped from one button to another.

"Sorry, I forgot my employee ID. Anything there that can shut that off?"

Lacy bit her lip and looked back up at the pane. Their outline held there like a snapshot, two humans in the wrong part of the universe finally caught in their tracks.

"Lacy, can you clear that?"

"I'm working on it..." she said, drawing out the last letter. "Here! Let's see..." She slammed her index finger down on a button, and while the alarm ceased, the image held on the pane.

"One problem down," Lacy sighed, relieved to be free of the blaring noise.

"See a light switch on there?"

Lacy scanned the desk. "Not sure... It doesn't look like it."

Dex pursed his lips. It was annoying, but they could deal with it. "I still don't like our picture up for anyone to see. Can you take that down?"

Instead of searching for the right button, Lacy dropped her hands flat down on the board and glared over her shoulder at Dex.

"Or..." Dex began, "You've done great, and I love you, and I think we should carry on." He then took her by the back of her head, leaned in, and kissed her forehead. "Good job, baby."

Lacy's face told him that flattery and a kiss weren't enough to cool her annoyance.

Being a reasonable husband, Dex didn't press it any further.

"Let's get up the tower, huh?" he asked, stepping away from the desk and back toward the posts.

Lacy's hand shot up as his foot raised to cross between the first pair. "Wait!"

He stopped and looked at her with feigned caution.

"Stop. Don't cross that again," she said.

"You shut it off, right?"

Instead of answering him verbally, Lacy brought her hand around to gesture toward the empty strip of seating not surrounded by sensors.

Dex dropped his foot and grinned. "I really don't know what I would do without you." He walked back around the desk and, in a calculated move, wrapped his arms around Lacy. "You're so gosh darn smart sometimes."

"Sometimes?" There was no perceptible humor in her voice. Some, just the littlest bit to Dex's well attuned ear, but no one else would have thought so.

"Come on, girlie. Let's get what we came for."

Lacy rolled her eyes, then followed after Dex to the end of the hall.

"You want to press the button, or can I?" Dex asked, standing in front of what appeared to be an elevator.

Lacy reached out, then caught herself. Neither of them would hit the button. There were no buttons.

"Maybe they want us to take the stairs," he quipped, but Lacy already had an idea.

She pulled the data tablet from its latch on her belt and held it close to the elevator, searching for a marker; some hint as to where her tablet needed to be placed to connect to the building. But there were no markings to be seen. Point and click, maybe?

Lacy tapped the data pad's screen to wake it up, and the first thing it prompted her for was a button that read "Call Elevator," which Dex still could not read. The contact lenses that made the screen visible to him had been left on the ship.

When she pressed it, mechanical sounds shuddered from behind the doors.

"Glad it still works," Lacy said.

"We'll see," Dex said as a small bell rang, signaling the arrival of the elevator. The doors opened up to a new light source, one silver-white light shining from the top of the car.

Dex extended his foot past the doors and pressed down hard on the elevator floor.

"What are you doing?"

"Just making sure it's not going to give in when we get in," he told her.

"Dex, the place is deserted, not condemned."

Still, he stepped through cautiously, holding out a hand to tell her to stay back for the time being. "Nothing wrong with being careful, huh? All right, feels safe. Come on in, darling."

Lacy rolled her eyes with a grin and stepped into the elevator as if they were starting their nine-to-five at the office.

"No buttons in here, either," Dex noted.

Lacy checked the tablet again. It now presented her three options: "Lobby," "Security," "Control." She tapped "Control" and the elevator began to rise.

"Must be annoying, everyone having to carry those around for every little thing," Dex mused. "I mean... what's wrong with pressing a button? Why make things overly complicated?"

Lacy recalled the imperial establishments they'd been in: the RVOs, the base on Taranok, and now here at the station. This elevator was most like the one she'd been escorted through at the outposts. "Different levels of security," she guessed. "And I never saw the Zar-Mecks do it with the tablet. They only touched the wall and went where they wanted."

"Built into the suits, then?" Dex asked.

"I suppose."

"And the officers?"

"In their gloves, maybe? These tablets could just be a backup, but I'm sure they don't want civilians having easy access."

The elevator sputtered, and Dex jerked toward Lacy, ready to grab her.

"If you're looking to hold me, you don't need an excuse," she joked, hiding her building nerves. Nova also felt some of the jitters.

There was no indicator above the elevator door, nor where a button panel would be, to show them at which floor they were on, or how fast they were moving. The whirring of the machine was a small step up from the total quiet of the rest of the station, but still did not put them at ease. And now they felt as if they swapped out one hell for another.

The elevator jerked again, this time with a violent shudder.

Dex and Lacy took each other's hands.

The car stalled, dropped a few inches, then halted. All went quiet.

The light above them flickered, dimmed, then returned to its previous brightness, if not entirely as bright as before. But, as Lacy thought out loud, "Thank God for small miracles." Then, more overtly to Dex not really expecting an immediate or all that serious response, "Now what?"

"Wait for the repairman to come around. Or..." He stepped forward, searching with the tips of his fingers for a line in the elevator door. "Hope we stalled in front of another floor."

Dex could feel a very subtle, very small indent running down the middle of the door. He pushed his fingers into it, hoping to catch on his nail and pry it open. But the seam was too small.

"Lacy, think you can get your fingers in there?" he asked, gritting his teeth through his strained endeavor.

Lacy did not attempt to pry the door open as his attempt continued to fail. Instead, she tapped on her data tablet. Dex saw what she was doing and smirked.

"That's not a bad idea, either," he said. "Knew there was a reason I keep you around."

She grinned back at him but kept her eyes on the tablet. "Along with a few other reasons."

Her smile slowly faded as her fingers tapped away at the unresponsive tablet.

"I don't know what's happening. I can't connect." The elevator walls immediately seemed tighter around her.

"This is why we keep things simple. Actual buttons and emergency releases." He huffed, giving up on the door, then looked around the small space.

"All right, new plan." He pointed up to the ceiling, and Lacy's gaze followed where he pointed. "Got all this fancy technology, but that's a typical drop ceiling. I'll give you a boost up, and I'll bet you'll be able to push a panel out no problem." Before she could say anything, Dex was already crouched down with his hands cupped for her to step into.

"You sure that's the best idea with Nova?"

Dex shrugged, holding his position. "Gotta get out of here somehow. Come on, hop up."

This is a bad, bad idea, Lacy told herself. If the elevator kicked on again and dropped, it was better to be inside it than on top of it. But if it kicked on and continued up, all the way to the top...

"Just wait, Dex," she said, taking a step back.

"Wait for what?"

"Just *wait*. Let's think here for a second." She put her hand to her stomach. "Nova doesn't feel good about this."

"Lacy, I can pull rank if I want to, and she doesn't have any yet. So, come on. We can get this over with and get back to the ship."

She was stalling for time. Lacy had no better plans and admitted to herself that no better plans would be coming any time soon. But her Nova-feeling was still against it. Reluctantly, she stepped back up and put her foot in Dex's cupped hands.

He hoisted her up and, just as he'd guessed, the roof panels popped out easily, if a little heavily. At least the Empire still had some semblance of safety precautions.

With another heave, Dex helped her to pull herself up through the ceiling and atop of the elevator. Once in a good position on her hands and knees, she turned around and dropped a hand down into the car.

"I'm not hanging out up here alone," she told him with a mix of command and humor in her voice as a disguise for her growing distress. Sure, she was out of the claustrophobic elevator, but if the situation was already on the downturn, what could be stopping the elevator from plunging back down to ground level?

Dex smiled back up at her and took her hand. "That's my strong girl."

A ceiling panel shifted and sagged under Lacy when she took on the weight of Dex. But, once a few inches up, Dex could reach onto the ledge and pull himself the rest of the way until he sat upon the roof of the elevator with his feet hanging down into the car.

"That's my strong man," Lacy chided in response.

Dex held up one arm to flex and slapped his bicep to flaunt for her. "Big and strong just to impress you."

"I'm very impressed. And since you're so strong, you can carry me back to the ship after this. Nova's got me beat."

Dex leaned over and gently kissed her lips. "I'll carry you to the ends of the universe, darling."

Lacy blushed and was relieved of an ounce of her anxiety. No matter how many cheesy lines he threw at her, no matter what situation they were in, it hit her every time like it was the first time.

She found herself pulled out of the moment entirely, and Dex, while great with the flirty lines, still wasn't quite sure how to carry on after that. Instead of pushing on through the moment, he examined the shaft they were in.

At first, he thought nothing of it, but soon realized what was missing from their surroundings. Back on Earth and on all of their colonies, traditional cable-lift elevators were still in use. Dex realized he wouldn't have been all that surprised if they used the same system around here, and in fact, was sure they did in some parts, but he'd also noticed at the Royal Void Outposts that the elevators had an invisible lift system; magnetics, perhaps. Here, though, he saw a mix of Earth and advanced technology.

In the center of the roof was a raised circle with a glowing white center. A heat haze shimmered just above the white. *A propulsion system*, Dex realized. But what was odd was that a wire extended from the base of the engine and connected to the rail the elevator clung to, not unlike a train system.

If the tower systems went down, Dex concluded, the elevator, while having its own propulsion, would go down with the rest of the building. Possibly a security shutdown measure, or a safety one. Either way, something had happened to the tower while they were in the elevator.

Dex leaned over the edge of the elevator and looked down the shaft. There was a faint light underneath the car, the upward propulsion, but not enough light emanated to see very far down the shaft.

"What are you thinking?" Lacy asked him gently.

He swirled back around to meet her, and before answering, looked up the shaft.

"I'm thinking we almost made it to the next floor, but this elevator was a lot slower than we thought. Looks like there's still a little ways to the command deck.

Lacy looked up with him. He was right. There was a door another fifteen, maybe twenty feet up, and the top of the shaft was pitch black. Well out of view.

"You still feeling like my strong girl?"

Lacy scoffed. "Who's the one who used to go hiking all the time?" She picked herself up and steadied her balance on the roof beams. Although the wall wasn't ground, it was solid and unmoving, unlike the elevator. "I've done my fair share of rock climbing, I think I can handle this."

Dex laughed and stood with her, careful not to fall back into the car, or worse, backward down the shaft. "Says the girl who-"

"Watch it," she warned, barely able to keep a stern face.

When she turned around to find something to grip for their climb to the next door, Dex's eyes fell down her backside. "Don't worry, I'm watching."

After a few moments of prodding around, Lacy held a firm grip on one of the rails and began her journey upward. Dex stayed below for support and to catch her if she lost her hold. The journey was mostly taxing on her upper body, with very few, if any, places against the wall for Lacy to place her feet. More than once, her still-wet boots slipped on the wall of the shaft.

Dex teased her, "Guess we lucked out with all those weeks in the jungle, huh?"

"Shut up," Lacy grunted, trying to focus on the climb. Her arms burned. Sweat threatened her grip on the rail. In Lacy's mind, Nova was berating her for making such a hazardous choice while she was with child. Herself, if that made any difference.

"Almost there," Dex cheered. "Come on, baby, I'm right behind you."

Lacy paused to catch her breath. Almost a fatal

mistake when she nearly slipped. But with a convenient foot hold relieving tension on her arms, she was allowed to collect herself. Risking a quick glance, she dropped her head and saw Dex climbing right below her with minimal struggle.

Oh, I'll kill him, she thought to herself.

"See if you can get that door open," Dex called, his voice beginning to echo through the shaft. "It's just a few more feet. You've got this."

She did. She had this. *I've got this. I have got this.*

Even Nova began to tentatively cheer her on. A wave of motivation flushed through her.

With a short burst of strength, Lacy threw herself, almost recklessly, the next two feet, then grabbed the lip of the door.

"Got it!" she called triumphantly. "I made it!"

"Great!" Dex called back, strain seeping into his voice. "Now get it open!"

Lacy pulled herself up another few inches, then dug her fingers into the seam of the door. This time, the door did begin to slide, and after the first inch, it nearly flew open, allowing an alarm bell to sound through the elevator shaft, and a strobing light with it.

Dex and Lacy both nearly lost their grips at the surprise.

But standing on the finish line, Lacy was able to collect herself entirely and nearly threw herself through the doorway.

She fell onto the floor of this new level and flopped onto her back. Sweat from the anxiety she was finally allowing herself to feel drenched her. A bead that had been hanging on her eyebrow dropped into her eye and stung. She blinked to get it out, then tried to rub it out with her finger, cursing and laughing the whole time.

Lacy made it. Oh, she made it up all right. She actually did it, and Nova was still safe. Her heart beat rapidly. Too rapidly. But she didn't care. It was beating. And deeper in her, Nova's heart was still beating too. Everyone was all right.

Mostly everyone.

Dex grunted, his arms and chin hanging over the edge of the elevator shaft.

"Can I get a hand?"

"Oh!" Lacy exclaimed. "Oh, just a moment, dear."

Dex threw up two fingers, the only sign of dejection he could afford. "Take your time."

Blocking out the intense blare of the alarm, Lacy turned over and got to her knees, crawling to the elevator door to grab Dex and help him the rest of the way up.

Once he was in, it was her turn to flaunt. Mimicking Dex, Lacy flexed her arm and slapped her bicep with her other hand.

"Big and strong just to impress you," she said.

Dex laughed. "Great. You can carry *me* back to the ship then."

The brief flash of light strobed again.

"I thought you turned off the alarm," Dex said.

"I did," she told him, starting to stand and walk over toward the small flashing box on the hallway wall with her hands over her ears. Its intermittent flashes gave them brief images of the hall, looking very much like the layout of the RVOs.

The timing of Dex's assumption was off. If they hadn't disarmed the alarm when they passed through the lobby, the elevator never should have come for them or begun to bring them up the tower. And she *had* disarmed the alarm, lifting the security measures. So, she thought, "Something else must have tripped the alarm."

Dex paused while Lacy fidgeted with her data tablet to re-disable the alarm. Her fingers trembled as anxiety returned with a vengeance. She'd allowed herself a brief moment of levity with the success of their climb, but why would He ever allow that. Lacy was still in His world. The rain, His robes, drying on their skin and sticking in their hair, and she could not be allowed to forget it.

"Do you feel him here? The assassin?" he eventually asked.

"No," she shot back quickly. "It's not him."

He stepped closer. "Do you feel anything?"

She shook her head. Below the alarm box was a port for an imperial data tablet, like they'd seen in the outpost under Torro-Kaal. She slid the tablet in and was prompted to disable security systems and reactivate the lights in the tower. "Unless I screwed up downstairs, which I probably did, it was probably something too small to notice. A bug running across a keyboard. Some tiny animal."

She felt his hand on her shoulder and jerked. Dex spun her around and looked down at her with a cautious sternness in his eyes.

"I know you'd be able to sense that. Lacy, is anything here with us?"

"I would tell you if I knew, Dex. But there's nothing."

She backed away and started down the hall. It was only a few feet to the next door with a label above it Lacy could read at "Security." Dex followed close behind her.

"There *is* something. We didn't trip that alarm."

Lacy pushed the door open and they came into a small lobby with a circular console system. From the lobby stemmed three rooms. Above the leftward doorway was a sign marked "Officers." Above the rightward door, "Barracks." And in the rear of the room, the third door had no sign.

"If it's anything, maybe a robot got left behind. Just wandering about," Lacy said, just to dismiss the trepidation Dex was bringing to the atmosphere.

"Or a Zar-Meck?" Dex guessed, not letting the conversation drop. But he knew immediately that likely wasn't the case.

Lacy merely stated what he was already thinking. "I don't think the Zar-Mecks would be so careless as to let us know they were coming. Besides, they're organic. I'd pick up on them."

At this, Dex did have a rebuttal. "Organic, but

not alive. If anything, those are the most lifelike cyborgs anywhere in the universe."

Lacy looked back and forth from the doors marked "Barracks" and "Officers," not yet wanting to test their luck with anything unmarked. "I don't know what to tell you, Dex. I fumbled the alarm. What can I say?"

Her answer wasn't good enough for him. They both knew she'd done right by the alarm and that she was only taking responsibility for the sake of their sanity, but arguing wasn't getting them any closer to their goal at the top of the tower.

"Just, don't let your guard down, okay?"

"All right. I won't," she said, tapping the blaster hanging from her belt.

"Good. Let's try this way." Dex led them to the door marked "Officers," as it was the door he was already standing closest to. He heard Lacy's voice in his mind, *I was thinking the same thing*. It made him smile. "I know you so well," he said.

Lacy's expectations of a room marked "Officers" had her expecting an officer's club-type situation. A pool table, bar, fancy lounge chairs, things of that nature. What they walked into, though, was a very standard locker room similar to the one they had found over the moon outpost above Taranok.

The two of them paced down the aisles of lockers and benches, taking note of finely pressed uniforms, towels, and basic toiletries. Dex pulled one of the lockers open and reached down. He grabbed a pair of boots and lined them up with the sole of his foot.

"Perfect," he said. "Lacy, darling, see if anyone's got boots in your size."

Lacy searched the locker room, feeling more and more unlucky with every pair of boots she tried on. Two aisles down, she finally found a pair that, while not a perfect fit, were suitable enough. She grabbed a towel out of a locker and dried her feet, then her legs, then began wringing out her hair over a sink in the latrine.

The blood-colored rain squished out of her locks like an oversaturated sponge. Red droplets splashed back upward, around the edges of the sink, and onto the faucet and the bottom of the mirror. She rushed to turn the faucet on to clean the mess and attempt to wash some of the rain from her hair. But every squeeze seemed to release the same volume of red, so much so that she was scared to look up into the mirror. She knew that if she did, she'd see that her hair was stained crimson, never to be washed away.

But that was a silly thought, she tried to convince herself, though still refusing to look in the mirror. She was only washing in the sink after all and, if only they had time to shower before continuing on, then she could wash it all away.

"Would be nice," Dex said. Lacy hadn't realized she was projecting her thoughts. Dex added, "We'll shower when we get back to the ship."

Back in the lobby, wearing their new boots, Dex and Lacy decided it'd be best not to test the door marked "Barracks," which in all likelihood just meant "Zar-Mecks," the way the Empire distinguished between officers and enlisted. Their options were to either go back up the elevator shaft or through the unmarked door.

They gave each other a half-hearted shrug before Lacy stepped off in the direction of the door. Dex began to put himself in front of her, but Lacy was already at the door.

The door slid open and, to their relief, the room was empty. But even better than that, it was an empty stairwell that led both up and downwards.

Lacy continued in the lead with Dex close behind her. The door slid shut behind them.

Then again, much quieter this time, *swishhhh.*

Lacy halted, her right foot hovering above the next step up.

"Did you hear that?" she asked.

Dex glanced back, then up at Lacy. "It was the door."

"I know."

"It closed."

"I know," Lacy said again, a little more agitated. "It sounded like it closed twice."

"Not this door."

Lacy peeked her head down the stairwell. The lights were on, but through the slim crevice between railings, nothing could be seen. She waited, hoping whatever was in there with them would make a noise. A scuff of its foot against the floor, the soft press of a hand on the railing. Even deep, heavy breathing of some lumbering terror crawling toward them would have been more welcome than the total unknown.

Dex's hand fell toward his holstered blaster. "Still don't feel anything in here with us?"

Lacy bit her lip, then threw herself up the stairs with a quicker pace. "I'd tell you if I did."

The sound of their rapid climb echoed too loudly through the stairwell. With every thump bouncing off the walls, it sounded like whatever ghost was terrorizing their minds was running up behind them. Lacy felt again as if she were running up the basement stairs of her childhood home, running from whatever imaginary monster was lurking in the dark, hoping she'd trip up and fall back into the shadows.

At the thought, her pace quickened again, and Dex had to match. She began skipping steps.

The echoes sounded louder.

The tower ghost crawled down her spine in the form of a bead of sweat.

"Lacy."

She used the railing to propel herself forward and around the bend of the next flight.

"Lacy!"

Nova sent her mother waves of relief that were blocked out by a wall of fear.

It's getting closer. It's almost here!

"*Lacy!*" Dex shouted, lunging forward to grab her arm as her foot slipped at the top of the next flight.

Lacy pulled away to rotate onto her side as she fell. Her other arm cradled her stomach.

"What the hell are you doing?" Dex took a knee beside her. "You're running like a madman." He paused then, filtering the humor out of his voice. "Did you feel it?"

It, she thought. *Not, 'did you feel something?' It.*

Lacy hadn't felt it, but whether physically or not, something *was* in there with them. Some unknown *it*. And her heart raced to escape whatever *it* was.

"He's here," she breathed, barely managing to catch her breath. "He knows we're here and he's... he's playing with us."

"Who? The assassin?"

Lacy shook her head. Her mouth had gone so dry, but she had to say the words just so they would be out there and they could gawk at how ridiculous it was. But when she spoke the words, it only felt more real.

"The Emperor. He's in my mind all the time. He knows I'm here." She began to cry. Her tears flooded down her cheeks and onto her lips. "It doesn't matter who he sends after us. It doesn't matter where we go or don't go. He'll always be there!" Lacy threw her arms around Dex's neck and held onto him for dear life.

"I'll never be rid of him. I'll- I'll never be myself. I'll a-always have this piece, the bridge connecting us. I'll always hear those voices in my nightmares. They're calling to me. They're always calling!"

Dex stroked her hair and rocked her like a child. "Hey... hey, come on now. Don't talk like that. Nothing can hurt us here."

Lacy didn't hear him; couldn't through the barrier of her own fear. That fear she'd told herself she would not allow in. The shields she'd thrown up first in the Emperor's presence had been stolen and replaced.

"They hate me. I escaped and abandoned them. I

escaped when none of them could. We all saw the horror on the other side of the Void, and I alone was freed. They want me. They want me to suffer with them. I know they do. I hear their tongues crack like whips in my sleep. And he fuels it.

"Dex, he could have brought us in whenever he wanted. He sent one man so that we would suffer. He could have sent his legions and this would all be over. But we sinned. We sinned against him and this is our punishment. He's the Devil and he'll never let us go!"

Dex tightened his arms around her.

He'd said the same once. In conversation with his first friend in the greater universe, Dex had said the Emperor was more of a demon than a god. But there isn't one without the other. No good without evil, no darkness without light. If God must exist, so too must the Devil. The only way to reject the devil...

"On your feet, Lieutenant!" he said, lifting her up.

Lacy caught his eye. Something was different in the light in them. Something was missing.

She could see his heart in his eyes, and it had suddenly hardened.

"Dex..." she began, wiping the tears dripping from her nose on her shoulder.

"We're here for a reason. Every moment not on the ship is putting not just us, but our baby in harm's way. Once we're back, we can talk about this. But right now, it's best to put it from our minds. No one's going to help us or give us handouts, no one's going to go easy on us just cause we've been through some shit. We've got to tough it on our own just like everyone else does."

"Dex..." Lacy began again.

"I'll carry you up the stairs if you need me to, I just need you with me."

"Dex, we should leave!" She forced the words out.

Dex paused on the next step above her. "What?"

"This was a mistake. We should go back to the ship and just fly away somewhere."

"No way. No!" He stepped back down onto her level. "We've been handed the worst cards in the universe, but if that asshole is still in here," he pressed a finger against her temple, "we're doing this until I've personally killed that son-of-a-bitch in the worst way possible. I'll pull him apart with my bare hands and spread his remains from this side of the universe to the other. *Then* we can go run off somewhere. But not until I've found the man behind the curtain and ripped his goddamn head off!"

He backed up a step again, and Lacy insisted, "It's not like that. He's not just... we can't just..."

"Why not? Why not, Lacy? Is it possible that he's not all-powerful? Is it possible he's just some tough alien? We saw him with our own eyes. The last guy that claimed to be God died just like everyone else."

Lacy's face turned red with an anger she didn't know she could feel toward him. And the anger turned to shame. And the shame toward guilt. And the guilt and shame and anger ground her deeper to stand for herself. But she could only handle one argument at a time. "He's in my *head*, Dex. You've seen what he can do."

"Take it from me, Lacy, I know this stuff pretty well. And I'm sorry you're going through it now, but it makes sense. My father went through it. He saw some horrible things in the war. Things that you can't explain to other people. Things you wish you could forget, but every night when you fall asleep, they infect your mind, repeating on a loop until you only barely force yourself awake because you finally screamed loud enough to wake up the whole house. And I know it's terrifying when no one knows how to help you. When no one gets what you're going through until everyone just gives up on you. You start believing in things that you can't explain or can't see, like God or whatever else gives you comfort, because at least that's something. You latch on to the intangible because for some reason the things you can see and you can touch make even less sense than what you can't.

"But I *am* here, Lacy. You *can* see me and you *can* touch me. I'm real and I'll be here with you. When everything else abandons you, I'll still be here."

She only took his hand by instinct then. Nothing he'd said she believed except that he wouldn't abandon her. But in a way, he already had. In one fell swoop, Dex had attempted to destroy everything she believed, and blocked out some of his own truths.

Through their minds, she called his name, but Dex didn't answer. His face didn't twitch as if he couldn't even hear her.

Every rebuttal came to mind. Everything he'd said, she had an answer for. But she knew there was no use. Dex's heart was hardened, and his mind was clouded by hatred for their enemy.

Everything she wanted to say she summed up in one word.

"Please," she whispered.

"Let's go," was all he answered.

* * *

Faint shadows of computer terminals were cast across the floor. The control deck was dimly lit by the flickering lights of buttons and screens. Large windows wrapped around the entire room in nearly a perfect circle. From there, Dex and Lacy could see the entire space station and just how empty it really was.

Lacy stepped toward the window and scanned the area for their ship.

"There," she pointed out.

Dex joined her at her side and looked where she pointed.

It was hard to tell for certain, but it looked like the small speck of silvery-white she was pointing was tipped on its side. The whole area they were inspecting looked a mess, like a kid had thrown building blocks on the ground and walked away.

"Damn," Dex muttered, remembering his comm device.

"What is it?" Lacy asked, putting a hand on his shoulder.

"Can't believe we forgot to check on Robbie." He thumbed the call button and spoke into the receiver. "Robbie, you there? Come in, Robbie."

Lacy whispered, "He might be waiting for the right call signs."

But Robbie didn't wait. He responded promptly, beginning with a robotic sigh. "Haaa, I'm so glad you finally called. It seemed like this thing was broken."

Dex and Lacy both smiled with relief, hearing the robot's voice again.

"Just the storm, buddy," Dex told him. "It cut us off for a bit, but we're back."

"And safe?" Robbie asked.

"And safe," Lacy chimed in, standing on her toes to reach the height at which Dex held the comms.

"Yep," Dex added. "We had a tough time getting here, but we're not beaten that easily."

"That's good. So the monster didn't get you then?"

Dex's finger hovered over the call button. Lacy was staring up at him with a look of concern that was quickly morphing into distress.

Dex licked his lips, hoping Robbie was just talking out of his metal can. "Robbie," he said slowly, "What do you mean by a monster? Did anyone else land here?"

Robbie responded like it was no big deal, unable to sense the dread he'd just filled the control tower with. "No... One-one followed us here. But someone was in the ship during the storm."

Dex's fingers tightened around the comms device. He wanted to shout at Robbie for not alerting them sooner, but in the robot's defense, he'd probably tried but couldn't get through. Robbie may not have known it was the storm blocking their signal and assumed it was just broken.

Still, Robbie could have kept trying.

"Dex?" Lacy pried, seeing his face contort with controlled anger.

"Robbie, how long ago did you see this person?" Dex refused to call it a monster.

"A little while before the rain stopped." There was a brief pause, then, "Approximately twenty-three minutes ago. I did not see the monster, but I heard it break into the ship and then leave. It didn't come into the main cabin."

Lacy squeezed Dex's arm. "The alarm," she said.

Her face was deathly pale. Her eyes wide.

Dex took a deep breath in.

There was no use denying something *had* followed them to the tower. Something had tripped the alarm and *was* in the building with them.

The door closing in the stairwell; it wasn't deja vu, wasn't a trick of the ear.

In a low voice, Dex told Lacy, "Start your search. I'll check the stairs."

Lacy nodded.

"Find what we're looking for and we get the hell out of here."

He put his hand on her side and gave a gentle nudge away from himself, then jumped toward the door.

Lacy jacked the data tablet into the first port she could find. The resting screen popped to life and began loading a series of instruments and prompts. In the chaos of her mind, it took a bit longer than usual to decipher the imperial language. But it came through soon enough. Along one rail of the screen was a radar wheel, and a list of communication channels, all reading flat lines of silence. The bulk of the screen mimicked what she read on her data pad. Files upon files of flight logs and archived communications were on that computer. She just had to find one from months ago on a space station that had hundreds of flights a day, based on the last time they were there.

Dex stood up against the wall by the door, hoping he could crack it open just a little bit so he could listen for sounds in the stairwell or steal a quick look in. But it was an automatic sliding door like all the rest in the building. If he opened it, it was all or nothing. Worse even if the monster-

Person, Dex corrected himself. *It's not a monster.*

Worse even if the person was already at the door, waiting for Dex to let him in. Like a vampire needing an invitation.

He put his ear to the wall.

Silence. Beautiful silence.

Dex exhaled, feeling his heart beat hard against his chest.

But then it leapt. His heart leapt in sync with a dull thump on the other side of the wall.

Then another. Still dull but slightly louder.

In perfectly uniform time, like a soldier marching in cadence, the thumping grew louder.

Louder and closer.

Louder and closer.

Louder and Closer.

Dex drew his blaster from its holster.

Lacy shot up from her bent position in front of the computer.

"What is it?"

Dex answered with a hand held out to tell her to keep quiet. His other hand raised the blaster toward the door. He took slow steps backward and felt around for one of the terminals then knelt beside it for cover.

He whispered back to Lacy, "Tell me you've found it."

Her search hadn't been as difficult as she expected. But the ease of her accomplishment was far from happy.

The final date in the recorded flight logs was the day they had last been at the station. The last flight out was recorded as the cargo liner *Venture*.

No flights out after that point with thousands, maybe millions, of people aboard the space station, but not a shred of evidence where everybody aboard the station had gone to. It was like they thought when they arrived back here; everyone just vanished.

The space station truly was a ghost town.

But now, one of the ghosts had appeared.

"Hurry up, Lacy," Dex whisper-shouted.

The thumping grew loud enough so that even Lacy could hear it.

THUMP... THUMP... THUMP... right up to the door.

No time to search deeper into the records of the *Venture*, Lacy downloaded the whole file onto her data pad.

She still sensed nothing on the other side of the door. According to her mental powers, she and Dex were still the only two people on the station.

The door slid open before the download could be completed.

Lacy ducked down under the console, but Dex froze.

A creature of shadow stood crooked in the doorway. Its arms hung low at its side from sagging shoulders. The thing had a head, lilting forward, but no face. Not that it was a blank slab of flesh where features should be, there was nothing at all except hanging bits of grey meat dripping from the hole where a face should have been. Dex could see clearly through to the other side of the stairwell.

But the Zar-Meck in the doorway wasn't exactly the same as it had been when lying decommissioned in the *Silent Horizon*. Its armor was more leathery. It had a texture that looked more organic than flow-metal. There were curves in it that looked like muscles and tendons, and there was an oily sheen to the whole of its surface. Dex could just barely perceive tendrils of the armor seeping into the faceless head, digging itself into the exposed flesh and grey meat.

Dex's finger pressed down on the trigger. Not all

the way back on it, but any further pressure and the blaster would fire.

He didn't fire right away because the Zar-Meck didn't move any closer.

It swayed in the doorway.

Air released from its lungs, pushing through a mush of innards around its exposed upper jaw. The sound was a horrible, guttural squeal, followed by a tight inhale like too much air being sucked through a pinched straw.

The Zar-Meck's head jerked upward as a shrill sound escaped Lacy's lips.

It took one drunken step forward through the doorway, around the opposite side of the console from Dex.

Lacy glanced out from her alcove and saw the reanimated Zar-Meck sauntering around the computers just inches away from Dex. She focused on his mind and heard, *it can't see you. Move* very *quietly.*

She stole another silent look at the Zar-Meck. The inflicted spear wound had gouged out its right side completely, with just bits of jelly and bone around the upper left side of the left eye socket remaining.

Go on! I've got you covered, Dex mentally called, mouthing the words as he did.

Lacy fixed her crouch to get a better start on her escape. If she was too loud, she could switch up into a run. Her hand was at the ready to grab her blaster.

She counted down, taking a breath with each number.

Three. Breathe in.

Two. Breathe out.

One. Deep breath in…

With one hand on a leg of the console for steadiness, Lacy began to rise. Coming out from under the console, she slid her right foot into a better position underneath her. Slowly, very slowly, she extended to full height and watched the Zar-Meck.

Its body mostly faced her, just a few degrees off from

a direct face. But it showed no reaction to her movements. The thing's head turned slightly in her direction, but there was no clear indication it was a response.

Not just yet.

Lacy took a soft step to her left, moving closer toward Dex.

This time, with her movements, so too moved the Zar-Meck's head. With a craned neck it turned in sync with her general movements. It wasn't perfect tracking, but something in its senses told it to move in a near exact way.

Lacy's heart leapt. She held her mouth slightly ajar and forced her breathing to steady.

But her heart sounded like radar. She knew the monster could hear it. Or, if not hear it, the thing could sense it.

The Zar-Meck jerked forward.

Lacy jumped back, a little too heavily.

The Zar-Meck took another quick step toward her.

Dex...

She took another step back, but not fast enough to maintain distance between her and the Zar-Meck.

Its arms raised. Some remnant of the armor's programming shifted, attempting to form a weapon, but was unable to, whether from a lack of clear direction from the suit's operator or the warping of the organic substance that had overcome it. Whatever the cause, it looked as though the suit was mutating in some unnatural way. Something gone wrong on a cellular level, bubbling and bursting uncontrollably. It would morph until it expanded and threw itself on Lacy, sucking her into the oily black horror.

Lacy held her arms back to reach for something, anything, to grab hold of to prevent a fall. The blaster at her side seemed inconsequential.

Dex, though, thought otherwise.

Two blaster bolts, one right after the other, so that it looked to Lacy like one long line of deadly energy, flew past her head and seared into the neck of the Zar-Meck.

The Zar-Meck stumbled, but only in reaction to the force hitting its body. Aside from a brief sizzle, there was no evidence it had been attacked. It just kept jerking its body toward Lacy. And in the next moment, when she knew silence was now useless and turned to run, Dex darted past her and lunged into the Zar-Meck.

"Go!" he shouted, and fired again, three times into the Zar-Meck's chest. "Run, Lacy!"

At the anguished sound of the thing's lungs fighting to exhale air through the blocked and bloodied passageways, Lacy threw herself toward the door. She stopped on the other side, right at the top of the stairs, and turned to see Dex struggle with the Zar-Meck.

He had the Zar-Meck on its back, but only momentarily. The armor around its arm bubbled and expanded, and a moment later, Dex was thrown to the side.

Lacy shouted his name and jumped back to the door, blaster raised, but Dex grunted back, "Just go! I'll catch up!"

The Zar-Meck threw itself toward him, pushing both of them out of Lacy's sight, but all Dex shouted was, "Keep Nova safe!"

Nova called to her, signaling that they needed safety.

But Lacy couldn't leave Dex again. She wouldn't let them be separated. Not like last time.

She kept the blaster raised and took sturdy lunges around the consoles. The whole time her sights were set in the direction of the grunting and bashing.

Dex jumped up into view. His face illuminated red with each shot from his blaster into the Zar-Meck's hide. When the Zar-Meck rose to its feet, Lacy fired as well, but it was all for naught. Dex fired to keep the thing's attention, knowing full well it wouldn't take any damage.

"I'll be fine! Get to the ship!" he ordered. "Now, Lacy! Go!"

The Zar-Meck raised its arms and grabbed Dex's shoulders, then pushed him toward the wall. Toward the elevator.

Dex fired bolt after bolt after bolt, then punched upward, ramming the blaster into the Zar-Meck's chin. It made the Zar-Meck falter for a moment, possibly more than just a reaction to an opposing force, but in the next moment, the wall behind Dex cracked open.

In one second, his feet were on solid ground; in the next, both he and the Zar-Meck were falling into darkness.

Lacy ran to the elevator and nearly tripped when she threw herself into the shaft to watch their fall.

"Dex!" she shouted after him.

Two brief flashes of red, then a crash.

But in her mind, and more importantly, in her heart, she still sensed life around her. Dex's life.

She searched for him and heard an aching, *go, I'll be fine. Just please get Nova to the ship.*

He was right. It wasn't just Dex or herself she had to look after. Nova was there with them unwillingly.

There was a choice. Who would she fight for? Who needed her the most?

Lacy tried to answer then and there, on her own terms, but another variable entered into the mix.

She felt him before his ship even came out of hyperspace.

43. Nova

Dex's vision was a dark haze before his eyes. There was a line of coldness along the back of his head that trailed down to his neck. With a weak hand he reached back and felt something sticky and wet in his hair. In the darkness, he brought his hand back to his nose and smelled copper.

Blood, he told himself, knowing this wasn't the rain on him anymore.

Something moved beside him, and Dex's mind spurred back to complete consciousness. He'd fallen. Down the elevator shaft. With the half-alive Zar-Meck-thing.

The Zar-Meck shifted next to him and Dex forced himself to remain alert, throwing himself into a roll away from the re-animated corpse, and stopping himself just before going off the edge of the elevator car.

Heavy breathing echoed through the shaft.

Every movement of the Zar-Meck's crooked body rattled the car. Metallic clinks and groans filled the air.

In the faint, ever so faint, light of the two open doors stories above, Dex could see the head of the Zar-Meck cock in time with his own un-rhythmic exhales. Dex forced himself to steady, and his breathing to calm.

The Zar-Meck leaned briefly in his direction, searching for its prey...

But the man was of no interest, regardless of how much or how little sound he made.

With another sense; one not of hearing, sight, nor smell, fingers like crooked talons gripped the opposite side of the car, and the faceless Zar-Meck leaned over. It inhaled with its mind and caught the trail of its target.

Dex studied the Zar-Meck, watching how it scouted for its prey, and was not entirely certain it wasn't going to come back for him.

He brought his right hand down to his hip, his fingers jittering just over his blaster. Except, it wasn't there anymore. He'd been holding onto it when they fell and-

Damn! Dex gritted his teeth and searched in the darkness for the blaster. In his haste, he threw himself a little too far in one direction, and his hand hit hard against the metal roof of the elevator.

The Zar-Meck threw its hollowed-out head over its shoulder at an impossible angle. Whatever was left of bone and tendon in its neck snapped in the twist.

Dex froze with mouth dry and hung open. His blaster was still nowhere to be seen.

Air forced itself out of the Zar-Meck's lungs in that unnatural gurgle, followed by wheezing back in. The sound made the hair on Dex's arms rise. Its breath filled the shaft with a coldness like death. And in another moment, its crooked body twisted to match the direction of its crooked head. Dex had distracted the thing successfully enough. But with just an outline of a silhouette of a creature that could only be described as a twisted, insulting caricature of life, an abomination of intelligent design, Dex grieved.

His heart, his very bones, were filled with dread. Somehow, after everything they'd been through, everything they'd fought, everything they'd seen, there had still been something waiting beyond the veil of expectation to taint what hope he and Lacy had that one day they'd face a simple life, a simple world again. This image of a beast so unnatural, a blight on natural creation itself, was the final statement from the universe Dex needed to hear that told him there was no return to what once was. What was left behind on Earth, comfort in the known, an understanding of real and unreal, was totally gone. Now there was nothing. And in that nothing, everything. There was no comprehending the everything, because there were no rules anymore.

Dex's eyes were open to the crooked monster posturing itself above him. There was no fighting it. His blaster was useless because his blaster was real. It obeyed the laws of reality. This monster never would.

The monster reached out its arms toward Dex.

His mind had been open only so much before contact with the thing. He'd opened it briefly for something greater, but that only invited terror in. All that was left to do then was cast it out. Close off.

As if letting someone else guide his hand, Dex reached and grabbed the leg of the Zar-Meck, and tightening his grip, pulled. Half present in the moment, Dex heard distantly the thud of the Zar-Meck crashing onto the elevator roof, then saw from the corner of an unaware eye, himself twisting and throwing the Zar-Meck off the edge, fueled by an unknown strength.

The moment came and went in a matter of moments, and Dex returned to himself.

He knelt alone atop the car. He didn't even hear the Zar-Meck crash to the bottom of the shaft. Had it done so already and he missed it? Was he that out of mind?

Had he seen the thing that lingered in his mind at all?

Dex jumped to the open square of the elevator roof.

"Lacy?" he called into the empty car. "Lacy, you in there?"

No answer.

Dex looked down into the cart, then up at the first open door above him. His arms immediately weakened.

* * *

Every step Lacy took was one closer to doom. Sweat poured down her face and chest. Romek was an inferno drawing nearer to her with every step they both took.

Nova cried out, *Run!*, but all Lacy heard was her baby's fear intertwined with her own.

Lacy looked down the alley she and Dex had come from, then left and right toward other avenues away from the tower. She felt Romek's growing presence but knew not the direction trail from whence he came. And in her heart she knew, just as she by the Emperor's power could sense him, so too could sense her. And every moment spent deciding which direction to run was another moment he closed in on her.

The assassin could stay with the ship, their only escape, but that wasn't his way. He wanted her to run. He wanted the sport. The harder he fought for glory in the Emperor's name, the greater he would be rewarded.

And if that was the case, Lacy decided, she would cut short his glory.

Lacy bit her lip and said out loud to Nova, "Trust me. Oh, please trust me, sweetie."

She stepped into the alley that she and Dex had come from.

What had before been an uncomfortable aisle of alien uniformity was now a colossal blood stained cavern of red. Trails of blood had dried along the once grey walls of the imperial offices in impressionistic rivers. Her avenue had been transformed in the aftermath of the storm to another world reminiscent of the Emperor's temple. She could almost see the faces of the Emperor's phantasms in the walls around her.

Nova cowered in her womb at the fear Lacy suppressed.

Lacy rubbed a hand over the small bump. "I'm sorry, Nova," she cooed.

She couldn't suppress the fear, but she wouldn't allow herself to become a victim of it, either.

"It's just rain," she told herself. But while those were the words she vocalized, in her mind, the words were all too familiar. *I will not fear him.*

Lacy pushed her way through the alley. But even as the end drew near, her vision only filled with red.

Red.

Up and down the walls and on the ground.

Blood.

Dripping from the rafters into her boots.

Lacy quickened her pace, but the alley seemed to extend and the Presence strengthened.

In front and behind, she felt him.

The Emperor drew close.

His Wrath.

His Beast.

Him.

His hand.

Around her neck.

Tightening.

Lacy's eyes widened.

Crimson enclosed her vision and through pinholes, she saw a face. One of rage. A grin. Unholy purpose disguised as righteousness in the eyes.

Nova screamed.

Then his satin voice like a paper-thin blade cutting through her mind. "I do this for His glory. And I take pleasure in it."

Romek's fingers dug into Lacy's throat.

Lacy flailed, scratching at his forearms. Her nails tore at his black, sinewy skin, but were pulled back from her flesh. His skin was armor, sturdy and tough like the Zar-Mecks. No, not like; it *was*. She'd see it on Taranok, how he'd fused with his armor.

If she could have screamed at the pain of her torn nails, she would have, but the airflow was locked off from Romek's grip.

His grip. She could touch him as she'd done before and steal his energy.

But the moment her hands steadied enough to grip him in her few moments of coherent thought, Romek threw her to the ground.

Lacy's back shattered in pain against the concrete.

She sucked in a full breath to compensate for the pain.

"Heretic," Romek stated, stomping back and forth through the road at her feet.

With her airflow freed, Lacy took in where she was. Blood flowed around her head. They were in the street. She'd made it out of the alley and had run up the road in a state of panic a fair distance before Romek caught her.

"You were to be blessed," Romek went on. "You were given a gift. It was an honor what the Emperor, God himself, called you for. A Bishop for your race." He stomped up to her side and thrust his heel into her side.

Lacy's mind exploded in pain. Nova screamed in terror.

"You spat in the face of God. You ran from Him."

He kicked again, cracking a rib. Lacy attempted to curl to the side and balled herself up, but was restrained by her inability to push through the excruciating tendrils of suffering in her back. Her tears of pain mixed with the flowing river of blood.

"But that, too, is a gift," Romek breathed, pausing and looking up at the starry sky. "For your sins, I have been blessed. I have been given a gift, a piece of the Emperor's soul. He lives in me, heretic."

Romek knelt in the river and placed a hand on Lacy's shoulder, attempting to pull her back so that they could meet each other's eyes. But Lacy resisted.

"For that... I love you. When there is failure, there is grace. And for your failure, I have received that grace."

Romek dropped his right hand to his thigh, and between his appendages, something hardened. When Romek raised his hand again, he held a sword high above her. Its tip hovered just inches above the side of her head.

"I will not kill you," he said, continuing to wrestle her to face him. "But you have delayed me long enough." With another thrust, Romek pulled her onto her back. But as he did so, it was his turn to see the cursed crimson.

Romek fell backward in pain and shouted. The knife

dropped from his hand, which went to his face, covering a charred burn that streaked across his cheek.

Without a moment to waste, Lacy, blaster in hand, kicked herself up and ran upriver. Her side ached with each breath and each step of her right foot. But with Nova's pleas, she pushed on in the direction of the ship.

Behind her, Romek took only a moment to indulge in the pain. It was penance for his stalling. Deserved, he believed. But no longer.

Romek breathed in the pain of the laser burn and jumped to his feet. He saw Lacy flee around a corner, down a side road, and took off after her.

* * *

"Come in, Robbie, this is Dex!" he shouted into the comms device, rushing down the stairs.

Static sounded from the device briefly before Robbie's voice came alive. "This is Robbie. Is everything-?"

Dex turned a corner onto the next flight of stairs. "Robbie, listen to me! Get the engine running. Lacy's on her way. You *need* to get her to safety."

"What about you?"

"I'm on my way, too, but don't - I repeat, *don't* - wait for me if I'm not there when Lacy arrives! You got that?" Dex leapt over the railing, skipping a few steps for the next flight below.

Robbie didn't answer right away.

"Robbie, confirm the command!" Dex shouted into the device.

"I- I-"

"You get her and Nova out of here, or I'll decommission you! Acknowledge!"

"Acknowledged!" Robbie shouted back, terrified.

Dex clipped the device to his belt then threw himself through the door at the bottom of the stairwell and nearly tripped onto the floor of the familiar lobby. He glanced to the side, toward the elevator and saw the door had been clawed open, pushed outward toward the lobby. Dex looked toward the door, knowing he had to go after Lacy, but he was still without a weapon.

His blaster may have fallen all the way to the bottom of the shaft, and the creature wasn't likely to take it.

In his heart, Dex heard Lacy cry out for him. He told himself he wouldn't dally. He'd take one quick look in the shaft, and if he didn't immediately see a blaster, he'd be off to defend Lacy with nothing but his bare hands if it came to it.

Through the small sliver of light that crept in through the tower's front door and into the shaft, Dex saw only more darkness. He pushed his head through and scanned, but his search came up empty. Every second was another wasted moment, and before long, he knew he'd spent far too much time searching in vain.

Dex cursed himself and gave up. Lacy still had her blaster, so they weren't entirely defenseless. But coming out of the tower and facing the alley Lacy had run down, Dex spied a dumpster filled with scrap metal and trash. A bloodied metal pole with a jagged tip stuck out of it. He pried the pole out and held it in front of him like a spear.

Then, not taking a moment to listen for signs of struggle, raced in the direction of the ship, unknowingly retracing not just Lacy's steps, but the creature's as well.

* * *

Lacy ducked beneath a booth in the marketplace. Once fluffy, multicolored gowns were now soaked, slim and red. They gave her cover while she caught her breath. Her side ached like she'd been stabbed, and she struggled not to pull energy from Nova as she had done before, even if it were unconsciously.

She consoled her baby between drawn-out breaths, "Don't worry, Nova. Dooooooon't worry. We're gonna be okay. Everything's okay."

Footsteps approached. Something crashed. Lacy peered out between two of the gowns and saw Romek going from booth to booth in the congested marketplace, flipping tables. The goods and tables alike flew through windows with his incredible strength, and never slowed to check the now bare spots. His mind processed every empty space, and he was onto the next.

"I know you are here, human," he announced. "I can feel you. I have felt your heart. You will not run far without your other. You could have escaped on Taranok, but you stayed for him."

Another table flipped and glass shattered in a storefront.

Lacy pulled back and darted, crouched low for a new point of cover.

"I tell you now, the Emperor does admire that about you."

Crash!

"And after he gives you your place in his Cathedral, it will not be long until you are with your companion again."

In the middle of another crash of glass and wood, Lacy skittered under a garage door and found herself in a familiar shop; the mechanic's place they'd been in when first coming to the station months before. But what caught in her mind was the word Romek had used: Cathedral. The Emperor's temple was anything but that.

Outside, Romek's pace slowed. Lacy felt pressure on the back of her skull as if something was digging into her head.

"You've seen it, too." Romek's voice dropped low. It was a spider crawling down a small string of its web inching toward her spine.

Lacy's head turned down, and she saw shadows come to a halt on the other side of the garage door.

"The others spoke to you," he said. "The Bishops. You see them in your dreams, and the walls that enclose them. The Cathedral is where you belong. With your brothers and sisters."

Lacy found her whole body turned toward him, and she backed away slowly, not paying mind to any of the equipment behind her.

The shadow thickened on the ground as Romek crouched. His fingers wrapped around the base of the garage door.

His voice grew as the door opened, and light flooded into the garage. "I am delivering you to your new home. There is no need to run anymore."

Romek stood still when he was fully revealed to Lacy. His face remained expressionless. This was a victory, but not for him. In his mind, this was a victory for the Emperor, and he could take no credit for it.

Lacy took another step back and bumped into something fleshy. She turned and screamed as the Zar-Meck's claws gripped her arms. Its head bobbed around, back and forth in her direction as if it was trying to take a bite of her. Lacy fought and fought, thrashing around to escape its grasp, but the thing was too strong.

Romek crossed the room, ducking to the side of a raised hover car, and stood behind Lacy. He studied her for a moment, watching her struggle with the Zar-Meck.

"I pray I am as lucky as you one day," Romek sighed, then put his hand over Lacy's mouth and nose and pulled her in.

The Zar-Meck restrained her hands.

The shadows took over her again. She kicked out her legs, both in front and behind, hoping to hit someone. Hoping to get loose of either of their grips. But the darkness grew. Blood vessels popped in her eyes.

Nova screamed in pain and terror. Her own tiny heartbeat quickened with her mother's.

But then, feeling salvation before anyone else caught wind, Nova released a small piece of herself, feeding Lacy with temporary strength, and with a moment of mental clarity, Lacy felt Romek's hands falter as something knocked him to the side, and she kicked up her feet against the stomach of the Zar-Meck, freeing herself of it.

Romek fell into a metal toolbox, but was quickly on his feet again, seeing the human male standing behind him with what looked like a spear. Romek lifted his own blade and swung it at Dex, who blocked with his scrap metal pole.

Lacy seized her moment. She lunged under a raised hovercar and came up on the other side. The Zar-Meck followed, throwing itself like a rabid animal, and once under the lift, Lacy smashed the first control panel she saw with her fist and the lift descended.

One last horrible wheeze escaped the Zar-Meck's mangled lungs, but then there was no more.

But one enemy down wasn't enough. Lacy brought her attention to the fight between Dex and Romek.

Dex had held his own well enough against the horde of enemies coming down on them in the Emperor's palace, but Romek was an entirely different breed. Dex wasn't fast enough to gain any advantage. All he could do was attempt to block Romek's slashes, and was barely even succeeding in that.

With barely perceptible speed, Romek cut across once, then slashed down and back up, then kicked in Dex's right knee. Dex fell, then rolled out of the way of the stab of Romek's blade.

Lacy raised her blaster and aimed. Dex saw it from the corner of his eye and shouted, "No! Just run!"

Nova cried out, but what she was saying Lacy couldn't interpret. The only thing on her mind was the pressure her finger placed on the trigger. She pulled it back, then again, and again and again and again.

Romek was quick to react. He spun, with the first bolt hitting his shoulder, but the rest he blocked with his blade, and stomped toward her.

Dex tried to stand, but his knee gave out, exploding in pain, and he crumpled to the ground. "Lacy!" he cried.

"Stop! Please, just run!" He tried picking himself up again and threw his spear at Romek.

The jagged metal tip lodged in Romek's calf, but it did nothing to slow him.

Lacy kept firing, backing toward the wall.

Romek blocked every bolt, swinging his blade in quick cuts left to right.

He slashed down, slicing the blaster in two.

Lacy held up her hands, all she could do to stop him, slow him down, hold him back.

Romek thrust the blade forward as her fingers touched his chest.

Lacy heard, not in her heart, not in her mind, or even somewhere deep in her soul, but clear as any other sound in nature, Nova's final heartbeat, and then silence. She felt no pain at first. Just the sting of a tear on her cheek. Everything else was empty. There was no world around her, and even if there was, it didn't matter.

Her world was gone.

44. The Small Metal Box

For the first time, Romek's face shifted. There was no regret, but he saw plainly what he had done. And there was a hint of fear for the inevitable vengeance.

Lacy's fingers tightened as if she could have torn into his chest, and she released everything that was left in her. Every ounce of love and hatred she had in her heart was expelled in a flood of energy projected at her baby's murderer.

His body was thrown by an invisible force into the hovercar, crashing through it like a meteor, out the other side and onto the ground.

Lacy slid down the wall, falling to the cold floor of the garage. Her hands shook, and slowly the pain in her stomach made itself known. She couldn't scream. The sound wouldn't come out. But her lips still trembled, and her eyes were bloodshot.

Dex crawled to a nearby jack and picked himself up, only putting weight on his good leg, then hobbled over to Lacy. He too didn't know what to say. All that came out was, "Lacy... oh, God, Lacy..."

Once he was by her side, his leg gave out again, and he sat by her, placing his hands over the slit in her stomach. Blood crept through his fingers.

He wanted to tell her it would be all right. That it *was* all right. They would be okay. "We'll b- be okay," he lied.

Lacy's head nodded and shook. Her hands wouldn't steady.

Dex kept one hand on her stomach, and with the other turned her head to face the murderer on the other side of the garage. He did his best to keep his expression calm, but his own pain couldn't be stopped from breaking through. At the sight, Lacy's eyes filled with tears. Her cheeks were a bruised purple, the capillaries broken.

"Lacy, I'm going to get you to the ship," Dex told her. "Everything's going to be okay there. Okay?"

Romek groaned. The broken metal underneath him bent and creaked as he moved, slowly regaining consciousness.

Dex took Lacy's shaking hands and put them to her wound.

"Just keep pressure. Got it? We'll be okay. We'll be okay," he began, saying the words more for himself. Lacy knew better, but he could lie for her. "I'm going to pick you up now. One, two, *three*!" Dex's right knee burned as he stood. He clenched his jaw so tightly it felt like his teeth were about to shatter against each other.

Lacy didn't even seem to notice she was moving. She kept her hands on her stomach, holding them there with only a small amount of strength, but her eyes were dead. Staring forward.

Dex forced the burning of his muscles out of his mind. Every step he took down the road toward the ship was one he nearly tripped over. He was constantly shifting Lacy in his arms to keep a secure hold on her. Blood poured out of her back onto his arms, threatening him further to drop her.

Her skin began to turn from pale to a ghostly white. The stars in her eyes were dimming.

"Hold on to me," Dex pleaded. "Hold on to me, darling. We're almost there."

One weak hand gripped Dex's chest. Lacy's other could no longer keep pressure on the wound. Blood pulsated out of her and ran down her hand and arm, pooling between her and Dex.

They turned a corner and faintly heard the sound of a starship engine. The whirring rejuvenated Dex, though

Lacy could no longer hear anything except an undiscernable muffled anguish coming from his lips. Step after step was nothing but agony; he could feel tendons tearing in his knee. A bone must have been broken, and every time he came down on it, it fractured further. Dex took her hand from his chest and put it to his face.

With tears cutting through the blood splatter on his face, Dex screamed, "Stay with me! Lacy! Please, stay with me!"

Energy prickled from Lacy's fingertips. Dex felt his life force transferred from the point of contact on his cheek to her. His body weakened, but Lacy's eyes halted their dim. The light fluttered back briefly, fighting to stay alight.

"I can... save her..." Lacy breathed. Color dimmed again from her flesh. Energy funneled weakly from her to Nova.

"Just stay awake, Lacy!" He pressed his cheek to her fingers, forcing contact between them.

They came upon a short flight of wide steps, and from the top Dex could see the long silver antenna jutting forth from the bow of the *Silent Horizon.*

"Robbie!" He shouted and the robot's half-dome head poked up behind the viewport.

The robot's wiry arms rose slowly and waved.

"Turn the ship around!" Dex ordered, hobbling closer, slower than ever. Even with the ship in sight, no more than fifty feet away, his strength was only diminishing faster.

Robbie made no acknowledgement of the command so Dex shouted again, forcing his words through a choke. "Turn it around!" He circled his head to demonstrate what he wanted, and by a miracle, Robbie understood.

Robbie dropped out of sight and a moment later, the ship rose into a hover, leveled out, and began to rotate. The airlock door was open and the ramp was down. One small blessing amidst all the terror.

Lacy finally made a sound, but barely a whisper.

"I know, baby," Dex wept. "I know, we're almost there."

Twenty-five feet.

With what little strength she had, Lacy tried to pull herself closer into Dex's chest. Over his shoulder, looking down the road they came, she saw a shadow watching them. In her daze, she couldn't think of him as anything more. An unidentifiable figure. And around the figure loomed taller beings in crimson gowns. Though in her heart she knew who it was, and she knew her hatred for him. But he could catch up to her and finish the job, and Lacy would no longer fight back.

Let him come. What else was there left to lose?

Twenty feet.

Dex felt eyes on him, but he wouldn't look back.

Fifteen feet.

Robbie shuffled to the airlock. "I got the ship ready!" he called. "Did you get-"

"Find the first aid kit!" Dex shouted, cutting him off.

Ten feet.

The stars in Lacy's eyes were a dull grey. Blood was no longer seeping through her wounds.

Robbie asked again, voice low and claws interlocked, "Did you find-"

Spittle flew from Dex's mouth in anger when he shouted back, "Get the damn kit!"

Five feet.

Robbie jumped back and skittered away to the cabin.

Dex wanted to throw Lacy so that she at least made it onto the ship. But Robbie wouldn't be able to help her. She still needed him. Dex wanted to die, give into the pain all over his body, but not while Lacy could still live.

Each step up the airlock ramp was excruciating hell, but they made it, and Dex bumped the panel on the wall to close the door. Robbie waited at the end of the hallway with the first aid kit and jarrmin box.

"In the head," Dex told him, jerking his head to the ship's latrine.

Robbie followed after him and watched Dex lay Lacy down on the latrine floor. He saw the blood staining them both, but his system couldn't process what was happening. His brain kept pushing him to ask, "Did you find- Did you find any new batteries?"

Dex didn't hear the question. "Not now!" He then put his fingers on Lacy's neck and felt for her pulse. There were long pauses between each beat, but it was there. He could still save her.

"Lacy, I have to..." he put his hand over her stomach and held back a cry before being able to speak again. "I have to get Nov-" He couldn't bring himself to say her name. "I have to... to..."

"Lacy?" Robbie asked, leaning into the room.

Dex yelled with rage and pain in his eyes. "Go! Fly us out of here!"

Robbie jumped back and let the door shut between them. He stood there for a moment, listening. Things moved around on the other side of the door. Electric things turned on. But the loudest sound of all was tears.

Whatever was going on wasn't meant for the robot's ears.

Robbie chalked his slow response up to his failing batteries and trudged over to the console. With him at the helm, the *Silent Horizon* took off into the sky.

* * *

Hours later, Dex came out of the bathroom carrying Lacy, unconscious but alive, in his arms. The blood had been washed off both of them and they had bandages around their elbows over tightly wrapped gauze. Dex would sanitize the needles and tubes he'd used for a blood transfusion later, but for now they sat, sticky with bloody residue, in the sink. A soft pink had returned to Lacy's skin, but Dex looked worse off than before. Around his own leg was a poorly made splint. It still hurt to walk on, but he could manage the few steps from the head to the bunk.

Dex had dressed Lacy in her skivvies, and Robbie could see the stitches in her stomach.

"What happened?" he asked.

Dex only shook his head, then laid her down on the bunk.

Robbie didn't pry any further. He turned back toward the sky, then, feeling very tired, slid out of his seat and waddled over to the foot of the starboard side bunk.

Dex didn't notice, but he recognized that no one was piloting the ship and assumed the responsibility. He plotted a hasty jump in a random direction, in the hope that they wouldn't be tracked, and let space consume them.

* * *

Lacy drifted in and out of consciousness. When her eyes opened, it was only briefly, and the swirling colors of spacetravel overtook her. They hypnotized her back to sleep. Sometimes when she woke up, Dex would be at her bedside holding her hand. When she was out again, she still felt his lips on her fingers.

Soon enough she opened her eyes, and noted that the ship was no longer moving through hyperspace. There was only the stillness of the night sky and distant stars outside the viewport.

Lacy pushed herself to the head-end wall of the bunk for support to sit up. The cut in her stomach seared when she moved, but once she was upright, the pain, for the first time, started to dissipate. She took a slow, deep breath in, then let it out just as slowly, breathing away the pain. With the small movements she was able to make with her eyes, she took notice for the first time of the bandage around her arm where Dex had administered a blood transfusion, and, dangling from the frame of the bunk, an IV drip that came down and into the back of her left hand.

"Take your time," Dex said, taking a knee at her

side. He'd been slow to get into the position, but stayed in it even though it was wearing on his knee because he wasn't ready yet to put pressure back on his bad leg. "I did the best I could with the stitches. They should hold."

Lacy took her time, focusing on her breathing before she replied. Her hands rested on her stomach.

"Where is she?" Lacy fought the tears.

Dex bit his lip, not wanting to answer. He dropped his head, then whispered as if he was admitting guilt of a crime. "I had to remove her. I didn't know what else to do. Her heart-"

"I know," Lacy sniffled and wiped her nose. "I felt it when it happened." She took a moment to steady herself, then asked, "Where is she?"

"Lacy... I..." Dex coughed. Partially to give himself a few extra moments to think about what to say, and partially to clear his throat, which felt pinched shut. "I had to put her body in a... in a box."

Lacy shot her eyes up to the roof of the bunk. Her exhale was long and shaky. "I want to see her."

Dex bit his lip again and his eyes darted around everywhere but her direction. "There isn't... Lacy, she was only a few months."

"She was our daughter." Lacy's cheeks were bright red again, as red as they could be with her body still recovering. "She is my baby. I want to h- hold her, Dex. I want to hold my daughter in my arms. Let me be her mother, please. Just for a little while."

Dex wouldn't argue. "Okay."

He forced himself to stand and crossed the cabin into the restroom and when he reemerged, he carried a small box, only slightly bigger than his hand.

Lacy took it and removed the lid.

Dex stepped back to give her time alone with Nova.

Soon enough, Lacy put the lid back on the box and said, "We need to say goodbye to her."

Dex nodded and said, "I'll seal the box and we'll let her drift out the airlock."

There was no other option, and Lacy knew it. "I want to do it."

"Okay."

She used electrical tape to secure the box, and they helped each other walk over to the hallway. Lacy placed Nova by the airlock, then the two of them walked back to the main cabin and sealed themselves off. Dex readied the airlock and they looked at Nova's casket through a small window in the hallway door.

"Do you want to say anything?" Dex asked.

A thousand things ran through Lacy's mind. The things she should say, things people usually say at funerals, things she wished she would never have to say for her daughter. None of them felt right.

Lacy whispered to the glass so quietly Dex couldn't hear what she said. "I'm sorry I couldn't keep you safe." And then she was out of words. Her head fell against the window. She wanted to reach into the hallway and grab the box back. Force life back into her daughter. Even if it was just for another minute.

Dex saw her face. He pressed the button to open the airlock door.

Nova's casket gently rose a few inches into the air, then drifted out into space. The small box, already hard to see, faded into the rest of the dark sky. But from light years away, a sun's ray caught the metal box. And for a moment, just before it was entirely out of sight, Lacy saw her daughter shine for her.

"I love you, too."

* * *

"Will you say a prayer with me?"

Dex's hand finally dropped from the airlock panel. "What?"

Lacy wrapped her arms around him. "We should say a prayer for her."

The word twisted Dex's stomach. The notion of prayer suddenly felt revolting.

"Why?"

Lacy loosened her hold and looked up at him, a mix of confusion and offense on her face. "I just thought…"

"What good would that do?"

Her arms fell, and Dex trudged toward the ship's control console, wincing with every step taken on his bad leg.

"It'd do good for Nova," Lacy protested.

"Yeah?" Dex nearly shouted. "By who?"

She couldn't believe what she was hearing.

"Right now, Lacy, it seems like there's only one All-Powerful keeping an eye on us. There's only one guy listening in, and I guarantee you he's reveling in all of this."

"Dex, I'm not talking about the Emperor. The Emperor isn't God. He's the Devil."

"He's neither, Lacy. Neither." He stopped abruptly, even as it shot a lightning bolt of pain through his leg, and turned back to face her. "Because neither of them exists. It's a ridiculous notion for children. This guy is a man behind a curtain. He's big, and scary, and pretty goddamn powerful beyond what we may have thought possible, but he's just a man. And he's the reason we're in this situation now, and praying to him or anyone else isn't going to help anyone, especially Nova, because she is *dead!*, Lacy, she's dead."

Lacy held her tongue. She didn't know the man who stood over her. She'd never seen that face in her life.

"Nothing is going to bring her back, but we can at least do what we came out here for so that her death wasn't in vain."

"I know she's dead, Dex."

"Good. Then we carry on. We did what we could for her, and now it's time to complete our mission. So, we can either do it as you and me, or I can give the order for you to man your post."

All she wanted to do was scream. But the words that

came out were, "I'll download the manifest."

Dex nodded. "Good. Robbie? Help Lacy with the adaptor... Robbie?"

They both turned and saw Robbie slouched in the corner under the console.

Lacy pushed past Dex and knelt down, then extended a hand toward the robot. "Robbie? Are you okay?"

He didn't answer.

Lacy gave him a little shove and asked again, "Robbie? Can you hear me?"

Dex fell a step back. His skin went cold. Robbie kept trying to get his attention, to ask for something. He'd been asking for weeks.

"Did you find any new batteries?"

Lacy continued to try to shake him awake, but the robot didn't stir.

All that time lost, those opportunities missed. How many times a day did Robbie remind them that his battery was depleting? How many times did Dex brush it off or tell himself he'd take care of it later? There was no later now.

It was too much, too rapidly. Dex shut off his mind and let his body guide him to his seat at the console. Lacy kept calling Robbie's name and tampered with his internal systems. She may even have shouted at Dex for help, but he couldn't hear her. Instead, he heard Robbie's childlike voice in his mind, asking on repeat for Dex to help him.

* * *

The *Silent Horizon* dropped out of hyperspace. They'd been traveling in a random direction for about an hour when Dex pulled them out, altered course for another random direction, and flew for another hour. Now they had returned to the darkness of realspace, and when they had, if either of them bothered to look, would have seen the edge of a cosmic gathering of bright green dust mimicking the shape of a hand pass just over the top of the viewport.

An alert flashed on the center console. *"Low Fuel,"* it read.

Dex rose and walked back to the engine room to refill the tank from its interior emergency valve. Lacy didn't look up or notice him when he did. Her eyes were glued to her hands which were glued to the co-pilot controls. They hadn't moved for the past two jumps.

Nothing about her moved.

When the tank was full, Dex took inventory of their fuel supply. Two heavy, sealed Mok Tau jugs of ceremony wine, which acted as the best substitute for high-octane spacer fuel on this side of the universe. A full tank could last them three jumps but, at the rate they were going, those jugs might not last them another twenty four hours. Not if Romek showed up and they needed to throw him off their track again.

Dex did the math in his head for what was left in the jugs. Best-case scenario, they should have seven or eight jumps left in them. It sounded good at first, but that best-case scenario included finding a planet like Taranok where the stuff flowed like water *and* was compatible with the *Silent Horizon's* engine.

The engine.

He was no mechanic, but Dex could appreciate the sleek design of the hyperspace engine he'd gotten installed on Reechi, and for a bargain no less. Eighty-nine thousand credits in a loan he'd never have to pay back, and blood on his hands. The mechanic. Dead. Father of - *how many kids was it? -* nineteen.

Nineteen kids without a dad because he wasted time haggling over the price of a pretty new engine.

But I saved Lacy because of it.

Yes, Lacy was more important than nineteen other children.

She was. She is! What about my kid? What about Nova?

What about her? She's gone.

Dex's fist tightened atop the engine's glass cover.

Stop it. He pleaded with himself.

You didn't protect her. You didn't save her.

Stop it!

He thumped his fist against the glass.

You weren't thinking about her. She was your child, and you let her die.

"Stop it!"

You let her die, and you let Robbie die. You could have saved Robbie. You had the parts on the ship.

"Stop it!" Dex brought his fist down hard on the glass. Cracks spread like spider webs. The engine's whirring permeated the room.

You abandon everyone. You left them all behind. Toork and Gurg. Taranok. You abandoned them. Earth. Your father. He needed you.

"Shut! Up!"

He raised his fist high in the air to shatter the glass, just because it was something he could break. But he heard a voice as bright as the warmest sun and as soft as a cold pillow.

"Dex?"

He turned around and saw her standing in the doorway. Pain covered her face, but now it wasn't for the loss of Nova. It was the loss she was about to endure if Dex wasn't brought back down from the ledge in his own mind. He'd already crept so far toward it that he was nearly over it.

Lacy saw him struggle for balance on the ledge, and a rope was tied between them. If he fell, he'd take her with him. But what she couldn't see, focused solely on him and her own hands holding on tightly to the rope, Dex could. He saw her feet as stone, stuck firmly on the ground.

She would always hold onto him, fight to keep him from the edge, even if she thought she would get hurt too. But the rope that bound them wasn't for her safety. Lacy was strong. Stronger than she believed.

There was no running from this one either. There was no Plan B, no "what if."

There was Lacy.

When Earth became too much, there was Lacy, ready to take a leap into the greater universe with him. When the Emperor pulled them apart, there was Lacy, driving him on to face the hordes. When the people of Taranok needed heroes, there was Lacy, inspiring him to be something greater than he was. And when a real family was finally within reach, yet torn from his hands, there was still Lacy, with hope in her eyes.

There was always Lacy.

Dex's knees gave out, and he fell to the floor. Lacy rushed to her knees in front of him and held his face in her hands.

"Dex? Dex, talk to me. What's going on?"

When his father came home that day with no legs, Dex didn't cry for the memories they'd never make. When his mother didn't come home at all, Dex didn't cry because his father held it together. When they said goodbye for the last time before Dex was off for the stars, he didn't cry because he didn't want that to be the last image his father had of him. It wasn't his place to cry when Nova was lost because she was Lacy's to mourn more than his. She needed strength from him then. No matter how tough things were, Dex never allowed himself a tear.

When Lacy lifted his face to meet hers, tears ran along the back of her hands and filled her palms.

Dex finally wept for everything.

Lacy's movements were slow and careful, maneuvering around him, until he could rest his head on her chest.

"It's okay," she cooed, stroking his hair. Then, trying not to pry too deeply into his mind, she looked through a small window at his thoughts and told him, "You're allowed to feel this, too."

Everything poured out for both of them. And after a while, though the pain wasn't gone, it had subsided enough to let them get back on their feet and carry out their mission.

* * *

Dex and Lacy sat at the foldout table at the head of the portside bunk. Her data tablet lay between them with the *Venture* manifest displayed.

"One of these days I'll figure out how to program English into this," Lacy grumbled, half-joking and half-hopeful.

"I know you will. We've just been a bit busy lately." Dex's cheeks still felt hot and red. There was an immediate regret for the careless attempt to bring some levity back onboard the ship. But the comment made Lacy smirk, and that was enough for him.

"First off, I can't be completely positive, but I'm pretty sure this is what we were looking for. This manifest doesn't give specifics, but it was definitely carrying live... um... animals, it looks like. No description, though, of what they were. But the crates' dimensions match what we saw on Taranok."

"Glorious."

"Second, the kron-kaal were transfers. They were added to the manifest at the station. This ship came from a planet called Yundriir, but the crates didn't originate there."

Dex slunk his shoulders at the news. "Less... glorious."

"Don't lose faith yet, darling. I think someone's been looking out for us. Look at this." Lacy pointed to a line of alien characters at the top of the display.

"Lacy, I... I don't know what that is."

It may have been forced, but Lacy slapped her temple. "Stupid," she forced a laugh at her own expense.

"You're not stupid," he said with a grin and pulled her hand back down. "What would I be seeing if I were as cool as you?"

"Our ticket to wherever we're going. This line here..." she traced below the characters. "This is the transfer order, citing a planet called Mascoadon. And this line... they're clearance codes. The one used from the original ship's point of origin to the space station."

Dex rubbed his chin.

Lacy continued, "Unless something else comes along, these might be our best chance of getting to where we're going."

"Hm. Well, at this point, they're older codes, but I'm sure they'll check out."

Lacy beamed, but Dex, as much as he didn't want to see it, knew that it looked fake. It was forced joy. He studied her as she continued to talk.

"So..." she began, "What was the next part of this?"

Dex thought for a minute.

"We need to prove this guy is a lie. That he *is* just the man behind the curtain. This planet is going to be our proof. This alone proves what we thought about Taranok. He's shipping in a threat."

Lacy threw in, adding to the theory they developed when they'd discovered the truth of Torro-Kaal. "Creating a conflict that only he can resolve."

"These things could be native to that planet. Or at the very least, he breeds them there... then ships them to undeveloped worlds..."

"...with promises and prophecies that he will save them. Taranok wouldn't be the only planet he's done that on. It could be the foundation of his whole Empire."

Dex began tapping his foot. "We just have to find evidence of that."

"And a way to broadcast it," Lacy added. "But it can't be that simple."

Dex perked up. "Why not? We've met these people; they have free will. They can change their minds with enough evidence. Just look at your friend, the officer."

"Yes, I know. The Mok Tau, too. They're all living under the Emperor's thumb, but this isn't your everyday tyrant. He may be just a man at the end of the day, but Dex, he still has power. He created prophecy for his salvation of that planet, but he also created prophecy for their apocalypse. That was clearly just a safeguard to keep them in line. These more developed worlds, the ones that have been loyal for thousands of years, maybe millions... they won't crack as easily as our friends did. The Emperor, regardless of how he's doing it, is in their heads. Don't forget the bishops."

"The what? The- you mean those ghosts we saw?"

"The assassin called them Bishops. He said they were in the Emperor's Cathedral."

Dex thought back to the palace-city in the Heart of the Void. "Looked more like a pyramid than a cathedral."

"I think he meant something else. Not the Emperor's palace." Lacy paused in contemplation, worried that she had been holding back too much from him, or what she knew she had to say next would sound too crazy. "I've been seeing things in my dreams. I thought it was just... I don't know... the Emperor messing with my head. Taunting me. But the assassin knew about my visions and he mentioned exactly what I've been seeing. A cathedral. Some kind of temple on a barren world. The Bishops we saw in his palace, he said that's where they were, and that they were all waiting for me to join them. I haven't know what to think of it, but now..." she paused, not believing in her words with her whole heart, then offered, "what if this 'Cathedral' is his broadcast station? Maybe these Bishops are just brainwashed conduits. There's some kind of... of DNA-based connection that he utilizes."

Dex raised an eyebrow at her remark. "And how'd you come by that assumption?"

At this point, Lacy was merely spitballing. But as the words came out, she became more and more confident in her theory. "Look at me," she pointed to her eyes with both hands. "I can read you from a mile away, hear your thoughts, but for the Mok Tau and everyone else, I have to touch them. Maybe I'm just a short wave radio, when really I'm supposed to be hooked up to the tower. The Cathedral, the broadcast station."

"So, we add another stop to this journey?"

Lacy pursed her lips. "Hopefully not. Is it too far-fetched to think this Mascoadon is the Emperor's base of operations? The Heart of the Void is his Emerald City, the throne room is... well... the throne room. But the tiny little closet in the corner is Mascoadon." Almost shying away, and lowering her voice to a whisper, Lacy added, "Hidden away. Somewhere safe."

Dex sighed, then looked down at the data tablet. "If it was hidden away, why'd we find it so easily?"

"It's hidden. There are sure to be defense systems in place. Or, maybe they do know about it in some form or another. Have you been to every military base on Earth? You ever go to the lower levels of Fort Hamilton, check out what they were hiding down there?"

"Not me personally," Dex retorted. "But I'm sure some nut-jobs were curious."

Lacy sat back up straight. "You tell me, then. You said everyone has free will, but have you seen anyone act out of line?"

"Yes," Dex said flatly. "Your friend, the officer. All of the frogs."

"Mok Tau," she corrected, then, "But *why*?" A smile cracked on her face.

"Why?" Dex snorted a laugh. "Because the Emperor doesn't have the control he thinks he does."

"Wrong!" Lacy exclaimed, jumping up from the table. Her smile was wide like she'd just cracked the case of the century. "At the end of the day, Jaskek acted the way he did for the Emperor. He wanted to hand-deliver Earth to him. He wanted to learn what he could, untainted by the Empire. But in the end, use that to efficiently serve the Emperor a brand new planet on a silver platter. And the Mok Tau? Dex, come on. They thought they *were* serving the Emperor. Us!"

"Okay then, my friend. Korr. He didn't act for the Emperor. He's the reason we're alive and free."

Lacy thought for a moment. She knew she was at this point just pulling excuses out of her behind, but said with confidence, "He wouldn't have gone looking. You said so yourself, he was a hit-and-run guy, very careful not to stick his nose in too deep. And they thought he was already dead anyway. Your friend, God rest his soul, was an anomaly." Even though it was only thought of for the sake of the argument, once it was out, she believed it as God's honest truth with her whole heart.

The subtle religious phrase didn't go unnoticed by Dex, but he stifled an eye roll.

Lacy continued, "All I'm saying is, the Emperor doesn't have to bury it when he's already fostered such perfect obedience. He just..." she motioned sweeping the floor of the ship, "Brushes it off to the side. In its own tiny spot in the universe."

Dex took a deep breath in, more so studying Lacy's beauty than taking in what she was saying. But he got enough. And with everything else around them going wrong, he thought, *maybe the universe owes us one small win.*

He exhaled, then said, "All right. But this better only be one stop. We're gonna be out of fuel before we know it, and I'd rather not be marooned on the Emperor's planet version of Siberia."

Using the information from the data tablet and – uncomfortably salvaged – parts from Robbie's arm, Mascoadon was plotted into the *Silent Horizon's* navigation system, and the clearance codes were uploaded.

"What are you doing?" Dex asked before he could make the jump.

Lacy was focused on the computer. He could see was activating their radio. "I never had the chance to share the moon outposts' stolen data with the village. It's a long shot, but hopefully they'll get this little package and have a backdoor to the systems. Just in case they return."

Trying not to sound annoyed or disappointed, he asked, "Didn't have a chance after the mission?"

Lacy refrained from giving him a strained look. "Things were getting kinda hot in the village when you were gone. There. Let's pray that worked. Ready when you are, Captain."

Light wrapped around the ship, time slowed, and very faintly directly ahead of them, so small neither of them took note, was a drop of red.

45. In the Mountains of Mascoadon

The planet the *Silent Horizon*'s navigational computer was set to bring them to was not the first thing Dex and Lacy saw when they pulled out of hyperspace. Moments before what could have been a very swift end to their investigation, the proximity alarm rang throughout the starship. Thanks to quick thinking on Lacy's part, they were jerked from their faster-than-light travel and dropped into a Mascoadon's solar system, still hours away from their destination.

The planet was a tiny speck in the distance. It was imperceptible to their eyes, surrounded by a sea of electrical storms and islands of unidentifiable debris. Crimson clouds and neon white flashes of lightning struck all across the vastness of the solar system. And in passing, Dex and Lacy could see blobs of flowing oily black substance swimming in the clouds. As the *Silent Horizon* passed close by the flowing masses, the things twitched, as if shifting their forms to take note of the new arrivals in their domain.

"Try not to get too close," Lacy quietly warned.

Dex nodded, feeling no need to fall off on a tangent investigation while their main priority was already dangerous enough. They had their goal, and Dex planned on sticking to it. Besides, one look and he had a pretty good idea what they were seeing, and the red mist slowly dribbling on the viewport gave their theory more credence.

"It's the same as the storm we had at the station," Dex thought out loud.

"I suppose, too, this is good cover for the Emperor's room in the corner. I'm not seeing any actual defenses, but I wouldn't want to fly through this if I didn't have to."

Lighting flashed across the viewport. The *Silent Horizon* shook with the burst of cosmic energy, but the lack of thunder booming through the cabin was like an anticipated alarm that would never go off. It unnerved Lacy, who knew sound wouldn't travel in a vacuum, but then again, none of what they were seeing felt real or grounded in logic in any way. In her mind, it would have been more logical for the war-drum thunder to boom deafeningly through all of the void. In her mind, that was what it was, and her mind filled in the auditory emptiness.

War Drums.

With each flash of lightning, she heard the drums. Boom, boom, booming in an unnatural cadence, welcoming her to another of the Emperor's palaces. The clouds around them moved in the windless space like boney fingers curling in.

All around her, too, and with every gigameter closer they came to the planet, she felt a warmth surrounding her. Not a comfortable campfire warmth, mind you. It was an alien warmth, and the longer she dwelt on it, the more it became a heat. A blazing, dry heat of torches, burning hot enough to light a vast corridor that led to a chamber large enough for a god. Large enough for the Emperor and his court of phantasms. Every gigameter closer to the planet was that much closer to the Emperor's throne room, and its pillars and walls made of the fused-together bones of his victims and the great abyss of total blackness he hovered above.

She was returning to him now. Willingly.

Dex pitched the *Silent Horizon* gently downward and yawed starboard, nearly avoiding one of the black masses. It twitched, then lunged in the ship's direction, but missed and was thrust away by the engine.

For hours they sat at the controls, keeping careful watch of their surroundings. Dex's eyes burned from fatigue and the intense brightness of the storm, both the crimson clouds and the lightning. When Lacy offered to take control so he could rest – and so that she could take her mind off the invasive terror of the Emperor's throne room – he dismissed the offer on account of them needing two sets of eyes to spot hazards. Lacy protested no further, only fought harder to occupy her mind, but all she saw in the storms were further horrors she felt she couldn't voice.

In only one way, she then realized, she was glad Nova was gone. Dex and Lacy had a mission and were braving this evil part of the universe. This was no place for a child, and no matter how Lacy looked at it, their path would have ended up here one day. She was glad not to have had to bring Nova into this.

And at that thought, Lacy's face reddened, and she fought herself not to cry again.

She thought Dex was too preoccupied to notice, but he asked, "What's going on?"

Lacy bit her lip and fought the teardrop forming in her left eye. A traitorous tear, she thought of it as, for being on the side Dex could see.

She said nothing but shook her head, and Dex heard her voice in his mind, *not right now.*

"Okay," he said gently, then paused before adding, "Whenever you're ready."

But she wouldn't be. How could she tell him that? How could she allow some solace into her mind over the death of her baby?

Am I that evil? she asked herself, careful not to let the voice slip into Dex's mind. *Or was I that weak? Was I that uncaring? My own daughter... I put her in danger. I killed her.*

All the power of the Emperor, so much of it yet untapped, and Lacy cursed herself for not being strong enough to save one life.

A thousand thoughts ran through her mind. What if they tried again? What if they had another baby? They could run and hide somewhere off in the universe where no one, not even the Emperor with a thousand warships and a thousand assassins, could find them. And they would keep their baby safe. Lacy would never let her out of her sight, never let her trip and fall, or scratch her knee, or get sick.

Lacy realized her left hand had drifted from the console to her stomach, the stitches that held together where she'd been stabbed.

There won't be another baby, will there? she asked in silent prayer. Dex had acted fast to keep her alive, but some parts would never heal properly.

Another hand fell on her.

Lacy came out of her trance and saw Dex's hand on her thigh. Her eyes followed his long arm until she met his gaze.

"Still my girl?" he asked.

Her teeth-marked lips broke into a weary smile. "Always."

As the hours went on, the storm thickened. The controls became more unstable, to the point where Lacy had to assist with the flying, moving her controls in sync with Dex's. It had been a pre-requisite and part of their pre-mission psyche evaluation to be able to work in tandem as two-person pilots, not just pilot and navigator, should the need arise, but Lacy's heightened mental powers gave her a much greater advantage in the task.

Mascoadon eventually appeared before them like a black blight on an otherwise crimson sky. And two things immediately stuck out to Dex and Lacy which they didn't need the ship's scanner to tell them.

There was no heavy cloud coverage within the planet's atmosphere to hide the spoiled ground. The storms persisted, but through the few and far between openings, and even at their distance, Dex and Lacy could see the Mascoadon's unwelcoming texture; massive jagged black ranges cutting across the planet, with deep copper ravines coursing through the surface like a cancer in the planet's veins. And all of it flowed, the copper rivers and the direction of the mountain ranges, to the northern pole where the second anomaly arose.

Everything about the planet flowed into a funnel of crimson. It was a current of cosmic energy clear to the naked eye that the universe moved along. Even the storm was caught up in its flow. The funnel was nearly half the length of the planet itself, and extended up into space. Little neon flecks of red rose up alongside it, and there was some level of transparency to the funnel. It was imperfect, but continuous until it didn't end, but faded to imperceptibility. Yet it was undeniable that up close a trail could be followed through the stars.

"Can you figure out which direction that cloud is moving in?" Dex asked, but Lacy had been thinking the same thing and already had an answer.

"Y is thirty degrees south, X ten degrees north east, Z is eighty-six degrees north."

"Anything we know of fall along that trajectory?"

"Give you one guess."

The Heart of the Void.

"What do you think it is?" Lacy asked.

Dex took a long, long while to think, then eventually admitted, "I don't know. I really have no idea. But I'm sure it won't be long until we find out. Although we're sure to be hailed any moment now. You ready to transmit those clearance codes?"

"Ready." All she had to do was press send on the screen she had pulled up. Although her brain processed the words in English, Lacy had to be acutely aware that when the codes were sent, they were done so in their original imperial characters.

"Standby," Dex said, almost in a whisper.

They drew nearer to the planet, weaving through the openings in the solar storm. But with every moment that passed without a call from an imperial control station, they felt more disappointed than worried.

Dex leaned forward to look out the viewport as if an

imperial ship was right atop them. "Is no one at their station today? You'd expect to see some satellites or warships at the very least. Any defensive structures?"

"No need to push our luck," Lacy told him. "Perhaps the storm interferes with signals. When we get a little closer, I'm sure they'll call."

"Could be a trap."

"Could be."

"It *might* be," Dex corrected himself.

"Only if they were expecting us."

That wasn't good enough for Dex. "I'm sure everyone around these parts is keeping their eyes open for us."

"We'll just count our blessings then that no one's closing in on us. Not on the radar, at least."

Dex harumphed. "You don't think this planet's wiped too, do you?"

Lacy took a moment to search ahead with her mind. "No... No, there's life there."

"You can tell from all the way out here?"

"It's not so empty. I can't feel the life out there per se, but there isn't the cold absence I felt at the station."

Dex grimaced, then said, "As long as we can easily get close to the planet. If we can get some aerial shots of factories or that broadcast station – good shots, I mean – hopefully that'll be enough."

Lacy dropped him a disapproving look. "That's not all we came here for."

"Yeah, yeah, I know." Dex kept his hands firm on the controls. He tightened them a little.

The broadcast station, the Cathedral, was their main target. If that could be exposed for what it was, and these so-called Bishops seen, or better yet destroyed, the Emperor's hold on his people might break. Even if only temporarily, before a new station could be made operational. Without access into the minds of his people, the Emperor couldn't have eyes everywhere, and he wouldn't be able to relay visions as he did with the children of the tribes of Taranok, and likely, to the rest of the universe he commanded.

Anything could happen once that station was down. Lacy had pictured a wave across the universe. With everyone free of the Emperor, they would wake up all at once and see that they had been played. Their lives didn't have to be forfeit to the whim of one man. The masses would rise up in joy at true freedom without the watchful eyes of the Emperor.

Dex pictured things a little differently. While he was eager for the Emperor's downfall, the brunt of it came from a sense of revenge. And he was not as optimistic as Lacy was about the aftermath. When leaders fall without an established successor, and God knows the Emperor wouldn't publicly claim an heir apparent, the masses tended to fall into chaos. Violence would erupt as prospective leaders fought for the vacant title. There was a chance of complete collapse the likes of which the universe, known and unknown, had never seen.

But for the price they'd already paid, it was a fair exchange for Dex.

"Still nothing," Dex announced in regard to the lack of imperial hailing. "That's it. Lacy, find us a place to land. Any valleys near enough to the north pole?"

Lacy ran another scan of the planet's side facing them now that they were closer. "I'm sure we can fit in somewhere. Cover won't be an issue, but the whole plant is an absolute mess. It's all badlands, the entire planet. Wait a minute now..."

Dex glanced over to see what she was looking at. "What is it?"

There was one unnaturally flat area, like a landing pad, that looked as if it could fit one of the Empire's saucer-shaped transport ships. But around the flat area were formations like pillars jutted out of the analog display's rendering of the planet's surface. Still jagged and ununiform, but the shapes of the pillars stuck out from the rest of the mountains around them. The pillars, by the looks of the renderings, were all three-sided, rising up high like thin pyramids, yet spiraled.

Lacy clicked her tongue as she fell deep into thought, trying to extract a deeply buried memory. "I've seen that before. Those look like…"

Where had she seen them? Had there been drawings in the Mok Tau temple of similar structures? Had the broadcast station sent them images they were not meant to see?

Dex, no longer interested in the formation, proposed, "If they haven't called up yet to clear us, think they'd notice if we flew in a little closer to the surface?"

"At this point, I think all we can do is pray that the cloud's interfering with signals around the planet."

Dex harumphed again. "I'll take luck and be happy with that."

Mascoadon filled the viewport. Dex pitched the ship down toward the sector in which the ship had picked up the pyramidal formations. While he focused on the flight path, Lacy scanned through radio waves to double-check for any incoming communications.

Still nothing.

But the planet wasn't dead. Not entirely, anyway. And these were the right coordinates from the *Venture* manifest. Shipments had come from the planet recently, so why was there no response to their arrival?

Only a thin layer of mist hovered above the planet in place of an atmosphere. There was no other cloud coverage, but there was also no sun to block out. The only real source of light was the red of the funnel at the north pole.

Dex steered the ship through the mist and passed low over the mountain tops to be safe from watchful eyes now that they were within sight distance.

"Are you even picking up any chatter? Any imperials checking in on each other? Making sure no one's dozing off on patrol?"

Lacy continued to flip through the radio channels. "Nothing. Not a peep."

"And the place isn't-"

"There's life here," Lacy reiterated.

Dex only shrugged in acceptance.

The formations were coming closer until they could be seen with the naked eye. It was tough to make out in the darkness, but in person, they both noted that there was, in fact, some uniformity to the pillars. Or, if not perfect uniformity, there was a clear intent by whoever or whatever formed them to have a semblance of commonality.

They did one long lap around the area to check for any signs of imperials, and when nothing jumped out, Lacy told Dex that she wanted to prepare for landing.

"Here?" he asked, then looked around at the vast nothingness to emphasize his confusion.

"I want to get a look around. There's something familiar about this place, and I want to know what it is."

Dex didn't put up a fight. He oriented the *Silent Horizon* toward the flat spread of land, but dismissed Lacy's claim with, "It's probably just déjà vu." She didn't say anything back, so he added, "But for now, before we rush into enemy territory, it might not be a bad idea to take a breather if the imperials haven't spotted us. And if they have, might as well make sure we're ready for them."

Lacy tensed as the *Silent Horizon* descended. The eerie sense of familiarity gnawed at the back of her mind. If only she could pull it out of the recesses and force herself to remember.

The plain was about half a mile in width. When the ship touched down on the northern end, the sense of déjà vu extended even to Dex. It had felt like the *Silent Horizon* bounced a bit when it made contact with the ground. The feeling wasn't dissimilar from the spongy moonsand they walked on after they crashed onto the outpost at the dawn of their adventure. At least this time it was a decent landing.

At the first possible moment, Lacy unstrapped

herself from her seat and pushed herself up and out of the chair. Dex rushed to follow, limping through the pain in his leg, telling her to slow down, but she didn't have to hear his voice to listen to him. Pain erupted in her stomach.

Lacy bit her bottom lip hard to hold back the sudden burst of pain, and gripped the back of her chair for support.

"Hold on now, Lacy," Dex gently pleaded. "Take it slow."

Her immediate thought was, *Why?* Why slow? Why did she have to be cautious now? What was the pain holding her back from, anyway? Before, sudden sensations like that had been Nova warning her of oncoming danger. It served a purpose: protection. What was there to protect now?

The pain was irrelevant.

"I'm fine, Dex."

"Lacy, you just had an extremely-"

"I'm *fine*, Dex," Lacy bit back. She forced herself to take another step. The pain wasn't as bad that time; most of it had come from getting up too quickly. But there was still a little with every step she took; a little pinch in her abdomen.

"Lacy, *hold. On.*" Dex pressed, taking her hand.

She was careful not to spin too fast. As it turned out, it was for the best. Dex hadn't been trying to argue.

"We have one P.E.S.," he said, referring to the red planetary exploration suit meant for quick dressing and brief alien environment travel. "Let me just check the atmosphere first to see if it's safe.

Embarrassment filled Lacy for almost rushing out into a possibly hostile-slash-toxic environment without protection.

Dex ran a scan of their surroundings on the ship's computer, then read the results back to Lacy. "It's safe enough," he said. "Gravity is Earth norm. Oxygen, but it's low. Might be hard to breathe. And some minor toxins in the air."

"I'll take the suit and look around," Lacy was quick to say.

In another time, Dex would have taken that as Lacy's chipper sense of adventure and wonder, wanting to be the first one out to explore a strange new world. But here, all of that was gone.

She started off toward the cabinet where the suit was kept, and Dex followed behind her toward the ship's deep-space suit.

"We'll go out *together*," he insisted, opening the cabinet for the deep-space suit. "Give me a sec' to get this filter out and..." He grunted, pulling to disconnect the hose and tank from the rest of the suit.

"Dex, stop. That can't be safely reattached."

It was too late. The filter's fasteners broke off under Dex's strength, snapped clean.

"We'll survive. I'm not leaving you out there alone."

"Great," she grumbled. "Now what do we do if something happens to the ship mid-flight?"

The first thought that came to mind, Dex couldn't voice. He truly questioned how many more opportunities for deep-space flight they had left in them. Everything about the world they landed on had an overwhelming sense of finality. This was a planet where things went to be buried.

All he answered her with was, "We'll deal with that when it comes."

With Lacy dressed in the P.E.S. and Dex having fitted the filter around his jaw, they did a quick gear check – unfortunately, it only consisted of a single imperial blaster now – and made their way to the airlock.

It opened with a muffled hiss, as if the soundwaves themselves didn't even want to travel through Mascoadon's air. The atmosphere prickled Dex's skin like strands of hair caught on the back of your neck when you can't seem to get hold of them and pull them off. He found himself constantly rubbing his exposed skin to relieve himself of the annoyance.

Lacy, not feeling the toxic air on her, stepped out of the ship more freely and carelessly, but halted when her foot touched the ground. She bent over and brushed her hand across the planet's surface, taking in the texture that the P.E.S.s glove sensors communicated to her fingertips.

"It's like leather," she announced, and pressed her fingers deeper into the ground. It compressed like sinewey flesh but didn't crack. Lacy glanced back at the ship's landing gear and the airlock ramp and saw that, around those areas, too, there was no sign of displacement. Even if they had landed on rock on any other planet, there should at least have been small cracks, or pebbles brushed out of the way. But here, everything of the ground stayed exactly as it had been; its leathery surfaces with scars like waves that all seemed to flow toward the north pole.

Dex met her at the base of the ramp. "Lacy, I don't want to spend too much time here. Do what you've gotta do, and let's get to the pole, okay?"

Lacy picked herself back up wordlessly, then took a few steps away from Dex. She looked around the plain at the spiral tower formations surrounding them. She took a moment and closed her eyes, picturing Mascoadon with blue skies and clean air. Just then, the picture cleared, and she saw herself on a landing field after disembarking an imperial transport at the Heart of the Void. In this image, the formations were elegant gold and brown skyscrapers with connecting bridges and healthy and vast, but not quite overgrown, vegetation cascading down their sides.

"I have seen this before," she whispered.

"What was that?" Dex shouted.

Lacy picked her head up to speak over her shoulder and raised her voice to get through the P.E.S. helmet. "I've seen this before." She pointed at the ancient skyscrapers. "Those are buildings. I've seen their type on the Emperor's homeworld."

Dex caught up with her and tried to picture the skyscrapers restored. During his trip to the Heart of the Void, he hadn't had much time to look around the town anywhere but the Emperor's palace-city. But, with a little use of the imagination, he could still picture this ruined city as a once thriving hub.

"This must be a landing field," Lacy added, noting smaller square structures on the radius of the field, which she assumed were ancient starship hangars. She could also tell now that the field wasn't as entirely flat as they'd thought. Sharp boulders just smaller than the *Silent Horizon* jutted out of the ground. And they, too, were angled toward the north pole.

Lightning flashed in the distance south of them, illuminating a red cloud. Dex could smell the blood rain wafting toward them.

"Lacy," he said, breaking her from her state of dreaded wonder. "What's your plan?"

As an answer, she took off toward the city. Dex limped a jog to catch up and asked, "Why this way?"

"It feels right," she said, but immediately backpedaled her words. 'Right' wasn't the right way to put it. Putting it simply, she said, "This is the way we have to go."

They walked a short distance northward until they came upon the first tower.

Doors like those at the entrance of the Emperor's throne room hung from massive hinges, halfway torn off.

Lacy clicked on her flashlight and inspected the room they stepped into. It did not have the grandeur or height that Lacy had expected in her memory of the Emperor's throne room. This room, and all of the levels they could see through the open design of the tower, had high ceilings and wide open spaces. Lacy felt small in comparison to the amount of room between her head and the top of the door frame, but not quite like stepping into a giant's lair.

Dex caught the feeling too and said what was on her mind. "Looks like whoever was here first was a bit taller than humans."

Lacy turned a corner and shone her flashlight on a pillar with the ancient remnants of an unnatural design. She approached it and reached out to touch what looked like a face protruding from the architecture.

"It's them," she said to herself, and before Dex could ask her to speak up, she added, "The Children of the Void. That's what he called them."

Dex watched her fingers trace down what was quickly looking more and more like an elongated face with a stubby horn coming out of its chin.

"So it would seem," Dex bemused, recalling the purple alien, Mermorrum, whom he'd shot in the knees.

"It is," Lacy said with conviction. "They were here. For a time."

"I'm sure they were glad to pack up and move to another world. Or do you think this place was their colony?"

Lacy's hand fell from the pillar, and she backed away. "I don't know…" She turned then, back toward the door.

"Back to the ship, then?"

Lacy shook her head the littlest bit. "Not yet. I feel… there's something here for us."

"Lacy, there's nothing here. For anyone. Not even the Empire is here anymore."

Either she didn't hear him, or she chose to ignore him; Dex couldn't tell. Ever since they landed, it was like she was in a trance. And in her delicate state, Dex wasn't sure if he should break her from it just yet. Unless something bad happened, he told himself, he would keep his eyes open and make sure she was at least being safe.

He followed her out of the tower and up a pathway, not quite a road, weaving through the city. They came upon a bridge, whether man-made or natural, they couldn't tell, that crossed over one of the coppery rivers and into a small clearing with petrified, black, leathery trees. And behind the trees, wrapping around the clearing, was a wall like a war memorial.

Lacy was drawn to it by a greater compulsion than almost any she'd felt before. Images on the wall had somehow been preserved through whatever apocalypse had destroyed the planet, and the mixture of alien text and hieroglyphics imprinted itself on her brain.

Her eyes widened with understanding.

"This is it," she said. "The Emperor. This is his story."

She followed the images all the way to the start, never taking her hands off the mural.

Lightning cracked again. The smell of blood intensified. The storm drew closer.

Dex spun around and thought he saw movement. Far off, the waves seemed to crest and fall like slow-moving water.

"Lacy," Dex warned.

Ignoring him, Lacy said, almost excitedly, "This is how he came here. They have a history from billions of years ago."

Dex unholstered the blaster. "Just take a picture of it and let's go. Please."

Lacy couldn't do that.

Lacy was utterly and hopelessly enthralled by the dark past written in ancient stone before her eyes.

The waves blew closer in the northward wind. Something about them made Dex tense. The waves weren't just moving with the supernatural pull of the planet; they were moving deliberately toward him and Lacy.

"Dex, you need to hear this," Lacy said, and began to retell the story of the Emperor as recorded by the Children of the Void.

* * *

Before all things, there was the All.

Along infinitely branching realities, Gods and Abominations dwelt in a constant state of creation and destruction. For all eternity, endlessly looping and repeating, all of the cosmic beings warred with each other, twisted each other's entities into both real and unreal. It was the Chaos within the All, spanning eons within the blink of an eye, until the All spoke. And from the Voice came form.

Unreality became reality. And the All became greater, and many.

From the Voice of All came Infinity. Tangible universes with Gods to mold them as they saw fit to mold them.

The ones with names: Kismet, Azathoth, and Yahweh, along with the nameless; the Lion, the Turtle, the Old Ones.

But too from the voice of All, and the separation that was the Great Creation, came the Abominations into their own dwelling to serve as the anti-Gods.

It was at this moment of formation that one of these great beings saw the prison being placed around it, a barren realm of dread and suffering, of chaos and corruption. And through the forming barrier between worlds, he glimpsed the Ethereal Light, an energy of immense power that could keep him safe from the accursed hellscape. And seeing this salvation, he fled.

The great deity found itself floating through the newly born universe, an alien realm of which it could not truly exist in. It was one of Natural Law. There was form to everything. But he was formless, and by his un-nature did not belong. For eons, it wandered, suffering all the while. But it would not go back to the prison that was made for it. It would find the source of the Ethereal Light.

Its pain-filled wanderings continued until, for the first time, it beheld a sun and planets. From one of these planets, life called to it. It discovered a world surrounded by swirling voids of darkness, anomalies like itself that broke the laws of this realm's nature. The planetary system was taunting, but taken as a sign that this would be the place where the Abomination would declare his reign. And it was no accident that this planet was where its wandering led.

The inhabitants of the planet had been calling out into the Void for their God. The Abomination's presence was sensed at the dawn of this people's time and they named him Armourus, the Unseen God. His worshipers paved the way for his arrival, killing the unbelievers, and destroying their idols. When Armourus came to them, his throne was ready in a design in the likeness of the Ethereal Light.

But upon seeing the faces of his worshipers, Armourus was angered. These were not the people he had been promised. Though their civilization was grand, spanning the length of their solar system, the peoples did not have the Ethereal Light in them.

Yet, there were still sparks. And Armourus hungered for what scraps he could get.

He began to feed.

Taking up domicile inside his throne, he declared himself the God Emperor of the Void, and his followers rounded up the non-believers to be the first to feed him.

From his first bite, the Emperor felt himself take shape. The souls of those he consumed gave comfort to his pain. And the more he tasted solace, the more he craved it. But the population of his new empire was quickly growing scarce, and would soon be unsustainable. He had a limited number of worlds in his grip, but not all of the system, and some in his empire soon attempted to flee.

In a great exodus from the planet Gallach, unbelievers discovered a new world, and their leader, Mascoadon, claimed it for his own. A place to live free of the Emperor's insatiable hunger, in the hope that he would find the Ethereal Light in some other part of the universe.

* * *

Lacy took a step back from the mural. "This isn't an imperial world. This was an attack."

Dex still had his blaster close to his hip, but was more focused on the story Lacy was retelling. "They were probably the only people in the universe who knew the truth. And the Emperor just... decimated the place."

"So..." Lacy's mind went hazy. "So, he *is* a god."

Dex took her by the arm with a free hand to snap her

back to reality. "He's *not*," Dex insisted. "This is what they told themselves. Just like every other creation story, that's all it is. A story. They needed an explanation for something they didn't understand, and the Emperor was that. He was something bigger than them that they could put a label on. If anything, this *proves* he's not a god. Look!" He jumped over to the section of the mural where Lacy read of the exodus, but couldn't pinpoint exactly what hieroglyph or text was what he was looking for.

"They fled," Dex said. "They weren't being controlled by him. They were able to get up and walk away. This shows how possible it is! He doesn't have the grasp he thinks he does because he. Is. Not. A. God!" Dex punctuated every word at the end of the sentence, much to Lacy's annoyance at the condescending tone. "He kills anyone who says otherwise, and *that's* what gives him the illusion of some deity. I mean, look at this. How could these people have recorded things that happened before the universe began? It's insanity!"

Thunder boomed through the air. In the corner of his eye, Dex saw the waves blow closer.

"I don't know, Dex. But I think it's more insane to completely dismiss the possibility."

Dex took a slow breath, keeping his eyes on the waves. "Let's talk about this back on the ship. Okay?"

"Why? Let's talk about this now. Before we rush off toward whatever is waiting for us at the pole, shouldn't we discuss all possibilities of what we might find?"

"What we *will* find is an imperial broadcast station and a farm of unnatural monsters hoping to devour us." He closed the distance between them and took Lacy's hand. But this time it lacked any tenderness. "Now let's go, Lacy."

She pulled away and held firm in her footing. "No, Dex. I..."

Her throat tightened with heartache. Dex saw just how hard he'd pushed her when she wasn't ready yet. He wanted to apologize and sit her down by one of the petrified trees, but the pragmatic in him told him to push through and wait to talk it out until they were on the ship.

Lacy dropped to her knees anyway. Her face went cold and pale.

"Lacy, what's going on?"

She took a slow breath in. "I can't do it anymore."

Dex caressed the side of her helmet, wishing he could touch her cheek. "What are you talking about?"

"I wish I could believe you. I wish I could ignore the truth and live this fantasy that it will all be all right. But I can't. I can't do it anymore, Dex. What is there left for us? If the people who were here were right, then there is no escape. We can run forever, but eventually he *will* find either us or Earth, and it won't matter which one comes first.

"I can't fight it anymore, Dex. We've lost too much and… I just want it to be over."

Dex put his forehead against her helmet. "Lacy, stop. This isn't you. Please, don't talk like that."

"Why not?" she asked, only barely looking up at him. "What will change if we continue to live in delusion? Tell me honestly, Dex, do you think this will ever be over?"

Dex tried to hold his tongue, but he couldn't lie. "No," he admitted.

"Then why the ship? Why must we go back to the ship? What difference does it make if we lie down and die here or die at the hand of the Emperor? What difference will it make to Nova?"

Dex thought hard, weighing every option. None of them was any better than the last. But one, while still throwing in the towel, could give them some solace.

"If we go back to the ship, we can go out on our own terms, at least."

Lacy pulled away in surprise. "What do you mean?"

Dex sighed, hating himself for these thoughts, but said anyway, "Whatever happened here, by whatever means, the Emperor caused it. This planet didn't get like this from a natural disaster. You were there with the chiefs. You heard their fears of the Emperor's reckoning. And you know he has the power to harm the people of Taranok from the other side of the galaxy. It all comes from the broadcast station. Without that, all he has is the might of his army. He's still dangerous, but just maybe mass devastation like this won't be an option for him. Now, we don't have an army, but we have a few jugs of fuel and a nuclear-powered hyperdrive. I can't keep this fight up any longer, either. Nothing we do will put an end to the Emperor's reign, but we can at least hurt him, prevent Taranok from becoming like this wasteland, and..." he paused, contemplating again if he should commit to his thoughts, then said, "Go out when we say so."

"Are you saying...?"

Dex nodded. "Right into the broadcast station. We'll shake things up for him, even if only briefly, but he'll never get the satisfaction of getting us back."

"Dex, we're basing this off of so many maybes. Maybe there's a broadcast station here. *Maybe* it's connected to the Mok Tau's prophecies. *Maybe* he's not the god these people thought he was."

"He's *not* what these people thought he was, Lacy. He's not a god, but even if we can't kill him, we'll make him bleed like a man. *Maybe*," he said, putting strong emphasis on the word, "the least we can do is show the rest of his Empire that. We might not be around to see it, but no empire can reign forever. And if the last thing I do is set that spark alight, I can go out happily."

Dex paused, then added, "I just can't keep running. If there's no peace in this universe without you and Nova, I don't want to be a part of it. *Maybe* there is something after this. Maybe that's where we'll find peace. But I know damn well it's not here. Not in a world where men like the Emperor live with power like that."

"Is there really no other way?"

Dex lied to both himself and Lacy. "There's no other way."

Lacy felt too weak to argue. She was tired. So very tired.

The smell of the blood-rain wafted toward them again. The waves crawled closer and crashed upon the streets of the ruined city with a high pitched shriek masked by a clap of thunder.

Dex pulled the filter down from his face. Lacy twisted her helmet until it clicked and hissed with escaping clean air, then removed it from her head and held it under her arm. She took in a deep breath of the dead Mascoadon air. Dex put his hand on the back of her head and pulled her close so their foreheads touched.

"No matter what happens," he said, "Wherever our souls go from here, I will always be with you."

46. Ever Northward

The storm drew ever closer. And with the encroaching rain and loudening booms of thunder came a slight fluctuation in the immediate area's gravity. Dex and Lacy felt a little lighter on their feet; a brief moment of levity from their fatal decision, like a weight off their shoulders. But in order for it to matter, they still had to get back to the ship for the *Silent Horizon's* final flight.

Dex took Lacy by the hand and helped her to her feet as her gaze lingered on him placidly. She revealed almost nothing going on behind the dull stars in her eyes and, in truth, there was nothing left to share.

They moved with a deliberate but steady pace toward the landing field. The lightning strikes became more frequent and the wind tore at them, picking up with incredible bursts of speed as it blew down the long avenues between buildings. The waves continued to crawl closer to them until another flash of lightning cracked just overhead and Dex jerked his head upward and saw a beast of indescribable contortion lingering above them on the side of a nearby tower.

The creature's flesh broke apart, revealing insides as black and deep as the furthest depths of space. And along its torn flesh, tendrils hardened and became like teeth pointed in every direction. The teeth shifted in the creature's maw, churning around it and fusing and unfusing with other teeth.

Dex threw himself in front of Lacy and held his blaster high. When confronted then and there with a threat, Dex found there was still a little part of him that wanted to keep fighting. The only part left of him that adhered to reason. The part of him that wanted to keep Lacy safe.

On our terms, not his, Dex told himself.

The creature bucked from its perch, and another flash of lightning struck. The ensuing thunder clap had timed perfectly with the creature's movements to give it the illusion of a terrible and powerful roar like a rallying call.

Dex, blaster raised high, spun his head around their immediate area and saw the waves were rising in place, no longer crawling closer. They didn't have to crawl closer; they were already practically atop the two humans. And as they rose, like the creature above them, these things morphed and cracked into new things with new limbs; no two of the creatures looked identical, and never maintained the same shape for more than a moment. The one constant between all of them was the oily-black hide like the kron-kaals.

They inched slightly closer.

Dex aimed from one of the creatures to another, to another, to another. All Lacy felt she could do was hold her flashlight in an attempt to temporarily blind the creatures, but none of them had eyes to be blinded.

The first raindrop fell on the flashlight lens, turning the wave creature a deep red.

Another crack of lightning, this one brighter and with a wide streak. But unlike the rest of the strikes, a few things came with this one. The blood rain began to pour. The lightning strike descended toward the ground in a low streak, like the fabric of the world ripping apart. As it did, Dex and Lacy were pulled from each other; Dex upward toward the perched beast, and Lacy violently toward one of the ground creatures.

They reached for each other, fingertips nearly grazing, but the suddenness of it was too much. All of the other creatures were pulled too by the sudden thrashing of gravity, and buildings above them swayed and cracked. Debris flew everywhere.

The perched beast was pulled from its spot on the

wall in a stroke of bad luck toward Dex to meet him mid-air. If Dex hadn't been focused on Lacy, he might have had time to swing around and bash the creature out of his way with the side of his blaster. But he didn't see it coming, and teeth like a rusty serrated blade tore into his side.

Lacy witnessed this and let out the first gasp of a scream before crossing onto a new plane of gravity that pulled her too quickly to the ground. Her weight immediately doubled, and the suddenness of it as the back of her head smacked against the ground fractured her skull. Her scream was cut off by a brief sucking in of air as things went dark.

Dex threw his arm backward toward the creature biting onto his side. He hadn't seen Lacy's fall or that she was unconscious. He tried to angle the blaster around, but the creature constantly shifted and squirmed out of the way, taking on new shapes and avoiding the blaster's barrel. The teeth stayed in place, though, as did their free fall, moving in and out of gravitational planes until the two of them crossed through opposing lines and Dex was ripped from the creature's mouth.

The line of gravity dragged him down the steeply angled side of the pyramidal tower so strongly that even if he had gotten a handhold, he would have been too weak against the pressing gravity to keep himself from falling. His arms would sooner be ripped off. The creature, too, went careening into a pyramid, but one far across the street and with such force that it tore through the building.

And when Dex did hit the ground, saved only by another shift of gravity that lessened the blow, the final event happened.

All of these quick shifts happened in just a few seconds, just long enough for Dex to see what was on the other side of the lightning.

For the first moment of the moment, Dex thought he saw the outline of a human face. In the next moment, within that moment, it had already changed to the beak of a large bird. And when it turned its head, peaking out of the lightning, it was not a head at all, but a talon of which it used to pull the rest of its huge mass through the rift, and a new head that quickly became a tendril flailing about entered the picture from behind the rift.

"Lacy…" was all Dex could say as he scuttled backward and kicked himself to his feet, running to her.

This new monstrosity pushed itself out of the rift, landing on a mass of the wave creatures and absorbing them. It took no immediate notice of Dex or Lacy, but the way it jerked, twitching its head/tendril/talon, gave the impression it was tracking either one of them, much the same as the reanimated Zar-Meck had done.

The space around Lacy was cleared of the smaller wave creatures, but they too were coming back as the gravity planes subsided their sporadic shifts and all was returning to normal. Dex had only a moment to get her up and out of there, hoping on all hopes that the creatures would be as slow as the Zar-Meck had been.

Dex slid his hands under Lacy's backside and began to lift. The strain of the lift felt focused in one particular spot, the gash in his side where he'd been bitten. Dex pushed through it to pick Lacy up, burying the pain deep down.

Immediately, Lacy opened her eyes, fully conscious again. She felt pain strike the back of her head, only worsened by Dex's sudden lifting.

Dex raced, limping northward up the street, away from the new, and ever-growing, kron-kaal. The rain under his feet quickly grouped into puddles and threatened to slip him up.

His foot skidded once, and in reaction to the pain of her brain rubbing around in her fractured skull, Lacy threw her hand back to hold up her own head. But the pressure she applied also caused her a shocking pain, and by instinct, she brought her hand from the back of her head to Dex's cheek.

Dex's body, and particularly his wound, turned cold and, this time, with his broken leg feeling like it was fracturing further, he did trip. And Lacy flew from his arms.

Although it was unintentional, an action out of instinct, Lacy's contact with Dex's face began to drain him of his energy so that she could heal. It worked for a moment. The pain in her head subsided, but the transfer brought their enemy closer.

The kron-kaal bore around the corner. It had already grown over twice the size of what it had been when it came through the rift, and it was drawn to Lacy's power.

Dex struggled on hands and knees to pick himself up again. He felt so weak, not even the quaking of the ground with each step the kron-kaal took could push him to move. This time, Lacy had to be the one to carry him. She crawled to him, then buried her head under his arm and lifted.

Her legs burned under his weight. It felt like some of the gravitational shifting still lingered and pulled them harder toward the ground.

"Come on, Dex," she grunted through her teeth. The still fresh wound of Romek's blade seared her abdomen. "You're supposed to be the one carrying *me* everywhere."

Dex wanted to laugh. All he was able to do, though, was keep his feet steady and manage a feeble, short lived grin. He pushed off the ground as best he could, but his strength was slow to return, and each thud of the approaching kron-kaal caught them up again.

"Stop," Dex protested and pulled Lacy toward the nearest building. "Through here. This way!"

The open doorway he saw, though it was only a thin crack and the doors themselves were too large and heavy to push further open, was just the right boost he needed to give his good leg a little extra strength. Lacy still had to support him, but their pace quickened.

Yet from behind them, boom, boom, *boom*... the kron-kaal thundered closer. A hooked tendril lashed out blindly, striking the pyramid wall just above the doorway. The cracked open portal shifted, one of the panels breaking from its ancient hinges, and fell toward the other panel. Lacy dropped low to avoid her head being crushed, and nearly lost her hold of Dex's arm.

But at least they were through and in the relative safety of the pyramid.

The kron-kaal, though, did not give up its pursuit. The creature came to the door and began thrashing on it. It could sense Lacy's power and had locked onto her like a targeting computer.

On the other side of the room, they saw another doorway, and far beyond that, the silver hull of the *Silent Horizon* gleamed through the blood rain with a flash of lightning.

"Damn, I thought we were getting closer," Dex grunted and pressed his hand onto the bleeding wound on his side.

Lacy quickly realized he was right. In the panic of the storm's zenith, they'd run further northward, away from the ship. The kron-kaal was behind them, but a perceptive eye could see more waves rolling their way, more of the smaller kron-kaal between them and the *Silent Horizon*. It would be a mad dash, and nothing short of it. Except Dex could barely walk, much less run.

For a split second, he considered telling her to go on her own, but it was a voice in his mind that was not his own. It was an unfamiliar voice that spoke with a liar's tongue. For a split second, he almost fell for it, but his resolve quickly grew if for nothing more than spite for the accursed temptation.

Dex pushed on, almost out from under Lacy's arm, but she held tight around him.

"Not too fast there, Captain."

The pain was miserable, but he couldn't help but laugh a little. "Don't..." he breathed. "Don't make me laugh, *Lieutenant.*"

They hobbled across the floor of the abandoned tower. From behind, the kron-kaal thrashed against the doors. With every *boom!* the huge stones broke a little further inward.

"Almost there," Lacy tried to say encouragingly, but

it came out more as a plea, a desperate cry to convince herself of a truth, rather than something objective. And all along the walls and in the pillars of the tower, ancient stone faces of the Children of the Void looked down on her with eyes of dismay.

She tried blocking them out, but their long-dead energy penetrated her, and in her mind's eye she saw the Bishops. They, too, looked down on her from behind the Emperor with eyes of defeat and disappointment. Like these stone faces, they saw a fate of death she wasn't strong enough to overcome. No one was who fell into the Emperor's grasp.

I will not fear him, she repeated her mantra. The eyes of the Children of the Void, like the eyes of the Bishops, were liars. She was stronger than they knew. She had a cosmic power pulsing through her veins.

And she would wield it.

The door broke apart into two large boulders, each landing with a single thud, no reverberation.

Dex and Lacy spun around in shock. Dex nearly fell again from her grasp, but Lacy stood tall.

Seeing the massive beast approach, Dex shuffled backward, trying to pull Lacy with him. "Lacy," he pleaded, "let's *go!*"

Lacy stood her ground. If anything, she angled herself a little closer, stepping an inch in front of Dex.

"Lacy, what are you doing? Come on!"

The kron-kaal charged.

Lacy took off a glove and raised her hand. Her bare fingers stretched outward and up. She closed her eyes and thought of Nova. Under her breath, she whispered, "God, please give us strength."

The kron-kaal leapt and its front legs briefly morphed into thin, wing-like appendages and it glided closer to them before morphing again into a six-legged predator.

Dex tugged at the red P.E.S., but Lacy was as sturdily planted to the ground as the rest of the pillars around them.

Lacy kept repeating, "God, give us strength. God, give us strength."

The kron-kaal closed in, and tendrils flew from its mouth toward Lacy. Dex tried to pull her out of the way, and when she didn't move, he attempted to get in her way. But with unnatural strength, she kept him back, and the kron-kaal's tendrils wrapped around Lacy's hand and arm.

In that moment, Lacy let her soul flow.

A wave of energy, a wave of life, transferred from her hand to the beast. She thought of the reanimated Zar-Meck, how she couldn't sense its presence even when it was right there in the room with them. She thought of the Emperor himself, how he was feeding on life in this world to ease his suffering of not belonging.

The kron-kaal's body ceased its morphing, and Dex and Lacy saw that creases in its head took shape, cracked, and opened to reveal eyes.

Shoot it now! Lacy shouted into Dex's mind.

He didn't hesitate. Dex reached for Lacy's blaster and brought it up like a gunslinger to the kron-kaal's head. The Mok Tau could never kill the things, only incapacitate them until another poor creature of the jungle was absorbed into the once-dead body. In his heart, Dex knew this wasn't the same, and the blaster bolt between the eyes would be the end of the monster's short life.

His aim was true, and two quick successions of blaster fire tore through the kron-kaal's head.

The kron-kaal went limp and skidded across the floor toward them. Its tendrils loosened from Lacy's arm.

"What the hell did you do, Lacy?"

Her breathing felt staggered. Her throat was closing. Lacy's heart even skipped a few beats. But she was alive. They were both alive.

Slowly, very slowly, she lowered her hand and mouthed, "Thank you."

"Lacy," Dex insisted. "What was that?"

"It wasn't real," she said, letting the words flow from her lips before she even knew what they were going to be. "You can't kill what isn't alive. I had to give it life."

Dex couldn't yet comprehend what she meant, but told himself he'd ask again when they were back on the ship. "Whatever that was, do you think you can do it again to clear a way to the ship?"

Lightning streaked across the sky, illuminating his point. The waves grew ever larger. It made Lacy's stomach turn, and bile threatened to rise in her throat.

"Not unless you want to carry me back on a stretcher." Whatever it was she had done, Dex at least understood the toll it would take on her, and he was her only other source of energy, and already very weakened.

"I guess we'll stick to ol' reliable then," he said, bringing the blaster to the low ready.

Dex put his hand to the stone door, then Lacy rushed to put hers over his. "Wait!" she said.

He paused, and turned to her with a look as a mix of pained frustration and admiration. He could read in her face that it was just a few extra moments of relative peace she wanted before they were all used up for their lifetime.

"What?"

She jumped up on her heels, then puffed up her cheeks and met his lips.

"Guppy kisses," she said. "Just in case."

Adrenaline filled their veins.

At this point in the story, the reader must be reminded, in case it was forgotten, that Dex and Lacy do not live on the same timeline as us. So, their actions in the preceding moments were wholly stemming from Dex and Lacy's determination to make it back to the *Silent Horizon*. Though, if you were to witness it, having lived on this timeline, the glorious sight of the two battle-weary heroes bursting out of the pyramid to face down a swarm of monsters may be reminiscent of a classic western. That was, at least in Dex and Lacy's shared consciousness with no notion of Robert Redford, what they felt like.

Dex, the ever-brave gunslinger with the imperial army standard issue LB-77 pistol, and Lacy, channeling the memory of her legendary grandmother, a true cowgirl in the time of the old west. But her nine iron was her thumb and forefinger, and a will to fend off any monsters who came too close to herself or her man.

The rain blew in with a harsh, cold wind. It pushed against them, holding them back from the *Silent Horizon*. But Dex and Lacy pushed harder, fought harder, even as the weight of the planet bade them go north.

Blood poured from Dex's side, but he kept his weapon high. It was useless shooting at the kron-kaal waves, but he fired anyway, feeling a sense of victory just knowing he was still in the fight.

Just a little while longer, then we can rest, he told himself.

To Lacy's left, one of the kron-kaal waves blew her way and rose. The center of its mass widened and became concave, creating a mouth. As it fell, she reached out with her finger and called to Dex through their minds. On her touch, Dex swung the blaster around and fired two blaster bolts into the creature's mouth. It fell back to the ground as a solid mass to be eaten up by the other waves.

The victory came with a cost, though; one they both felt when Lacy stumbled.

"Be careful!" Dex warned.

At that point, they couldn't tell who was carrying whom. No longer was Dex hanging from Lacy's shoulder. They now grasped each other's arms. And with every hop, their grip fell further and further, until their hands were locked around each other.

The wind subsided briefly, then returned with a vengeance. The blood rain pelted their fronts like tiny needles, forcing them back.

Their hands only tightened.

Dex put himself in front of Lacy to be their eyes. If they could avoid the kron-kaal waves, all the better. But if one came too close, he called out, "At our eleven! At our two!" and Lacy would hold out her hand to imbue it with a spark of real life so Dex could take it away.

"We're almost there!" Dex shouted, not recognizing the joy in his own voice.

"We're gonna make it," Lacy weakly agreed.

From his right side, hidden behind his raised blaster, another kron-kaal wave rose and fell toward them. If he had noticed it sooner, they could have dodged the slow-moving monster, but it was too late, and Lacy had to use her power against it.

It was a close call, but on her touch, Lacy's legs gave out. She was so tired, barely able to keep her eyes open. Her hand slipped from his, but he grabbed tightly onto her pinky.

Dex heaved her arm over his shoulder to pull her along and let the rain drench his face.

"I really thought..." he grunted, "You'd finally be the one to carry me to the ship."

Lacy sounded half asleep in her reply, "Next time, baby. I promise."

The *Silent Horizon*'s airlock was still open, and the cabin light shone through it. The sight was a much-needed welcome.

From the moment Dex's foot touched the ramp, the adrenaline began to cease, and he remembered the pain in his side and leg, and how much blood he'd lost.

"Lacy," he said, voice now shaking, "I need you to wake up, baby."

She moaned, hearing his voice clearly but feeling too tired to respond.

He carried her along to the main cabin, slamming the airlock shut as they passed through the hall, and dropped Lacy on the starboard-side bunk.

Dex hobbled over to the food cabinet at the head of the port side bunk and grabbed a bottle of caffeine pills from their spot next to their supply of breakfast meal replacement pills. Those and a canteen, he tossed to the bed, where Lacy had already fallen onto her side, more than half asleep.

"Lacy!" he shouted, before hobbling to the latrine. "Take one of those and give me a hand!"

Lacy groaned, forcing herself to stay awake, and struggled to open the pill bottle.

High-pitched scratching sounds tore across the underside of the hull. Dex almost dropped the first aid kit and spilled all of its contents.

"They're trying to get in!" he shouted, and hastened his self-aid.

Lacy finally managed to get the top off the bottle and shook two pills into her hand.

The scratches tore again, and this time Lacy heard them, but without the concern Dex had. "Listen..." she moaned. "It's... it's going up... It's stern to bow."

Dex listened, confirming what she said, and jumped back to his seat at the command console. The kron-kaal weren't trying to get in the ship, but they were likely still doing damage to the hull. "All's well in the world, then. Just hurry up and give me a hand!" He fumbled around in the first aid kit and pulled out a stainless steel medical stapler, quickly made red and slippery by his hands, then added, "Please!"

It took far too much strength for Lacy to raise her hand to her mouth, but she got the pills in, then began the second part of her great mission and unscrewed the top of the canteen.

Dex brought the stapler to his side and pressed it against the first gash left by the kron-kaal's teeth. He took rapid breaths in and out, forcing himself to go through with it, then gritted his teeth and pressed the trigger.

"*Gahhh!*" He shouted as the sharp teeth of the staples bore into his side. The pain wasn't as lasting as the larger wound, but the immediateness of it made him almost drop the staple gun.

Lacy let a few drops of water dribble into her cheek. Half of it drooled out of her mouth and onto the bunk. But it was enough, and she rolled onto her back then tried to tilt her head up.

The first swallow got the pill stuck in her throat.

Dex spun around at her cough, but she quickly recovered, took another sip of water and forced the pill down. The second pill she couldn't bring herself to take, not just then, but her half-open eyes saw the pool spreading at Dex's feet. And as another scratch against the hull echoed through the cabin, she forced herself to down the second pill.

Ten seconds later, ten seconds of Dex holding the staple gun against his side searching for the courage to cause himself incredible pain again, Lacy's eyes shot open, and she bolted to her feet.

"Dex! Oh my God, I'm so sorry!" She rushed to his side and took the staple gun from his hand. Her body still felt weak, but her mind was wide-as-hell awake, and she had no hesitation shooting the staples into his side.

"*Ahh!*" Dex screamed again.

"It's not that bad," Lacy rushed out the words. "Just get the ship in the air!"

Dex bit his lip hard to stop himself from shouting at her. "As you wish, *Captain.*" His hands shook as he reached for the controls and brought the engine to life.

One after another, Lacy shot the staples into his side. With every *Cha-Chlunk!* Dex bit harder into his lip.

The *Silent Horizon* lifted off the ancient landing pad with Lacy still giving Dex care. Nearly every path they could go in was stormy. But there was one narrow path, a very narrow path, like an invisible beam cutting through the sky, that led them due north.

47. The Veil of Worlds

"Are we still going to go through with it?" Lacy asked.

All the adrenaline from their ensuing battle had worn off. Lacy balanced out, and while it still hurt like hell, Dex was no longer bleeding out and was beginning to feel better. Better enough, that is, to get them to their destination. If luck was on their side, there would be no more fighting. Just a matter of being in the right place at the right time and soon it would be finished. Someone else could take up their cause. Take up their fight.

Carry their cross.

Dex sighed, feeling lightheaded as the air exited his lungs. "Tell me there's another option, Lacy."

She couldn't think of anything. Lacy watched the storms pass on the starboard side of the ship. With g-force and air resistance being a part of the equation, moving through the planet's atmosphere was a much slower affair than moving through space, and their journey to the north pole was an arduous one. But the alternative was rushing to their demise. An hour or so longer with each other wouldn't hurt anyone.

After a moment, she laughed in a way that sounded like a cough.

"What's up?" Dex asked offhandedly.

Lacy shook her head. "I was just thinking."

"About?" Dex loosened his grip on the controls. Their speed dropped the littlest bit.

"Do you remember that video message my parents sent us? The one after we told them we got married."

Dex nodded and told her yes, but truth be told, he had no idea what she was talking about.

Lacy laughed again, this time more confidently. "My dad was furious."

"He was?"

"Oh, yes. I think he even told me to c-... to come back home."

"Huh. I didn't think I was *that* bad for you."

As if he didn't say anything, Lacy went on, now just thinking out loud. "My mom wasn't too happy, either. She said it was a mistake because we'd end up hating each other in no time, the way we're stuck in this ship. 'Five years,' she said. She said, 'It's a good thing you're turning around after five years, cause by then you'll be killing each other if you don't get a little distance.'"

Dex slowly nodded his head. "Well, I don't recall that message at all, I guess."

"Five years," Lacy said again.

"That would have been something. If we'd made it to the end of the mission with nothing to show for it and turned around."

"Is it better, then, that we ended up here?" Lacy asked, turning toward Dex with despair in her eyes.

Dex froze up. "That's not what I meant. It's just..."

"It is, though," she said, then turned back to look out the viewport. "Even now."

Dex took a moment, then admitted, "It doesn't matter anyway. The mission, I mean. Whatever happens out here – *happened*, I suppose – it doesn't matter. Either we found nothing and turned around, ten years of our lives wasted, who knows how many years wasted on Earth, relativity taken into account, or we find something," Dex gestured to the storms all around them, "and we don't come back anyway, no one on Earth the wiser."

Lacy's gaze fell to her side, in his direction. "So, you weren't just talking then. You really meant it?"

"Meant what?"

"You really have lost hope. We really are going through with it."

"Lacy... I never had hope. I thought I'd find it out here. I thought I'd find it when we escaped the Emperor. I thought I'd find it on Taranok. I thought we found it with Nova. But it was never there."

The last remaining foundations of Lacy's world began to crumble.

"And what about me?" she asked. "What was I in all of this?"

"You were... greater. Hope is something that comes and goes. That's why people are always searching for it. You finally think you've found it, and it slips away. Hope is a liar. You are not my hope. I've doubted everything else. I put my faith in nothing else. Because I don't have to. I took on this mission because I didn't want the life I had anymore. I couldn't have cared less if I never made it back to Earth and had let myself die out here. It was when I saw you in the selection hall that everything changed. It wasn't a hope that we would be assigned together. When I saw you, it was a truth. You and I were made for each other. If that lasted five years like your mom thought, if it lasted a whole lifetime, or if it only lasted for one anniversary, that's all I needed.

"I have no hope for this world. I never will. But I have you. Like I said, I have you now, and for whatever comes next."

Dex held out his hand for her. Lacy studied it, memorizing every line in his palm, the tiny details of his fingerprints, the calluses at the base of his fingers. But she hesitated. She couldn't accept that.

Instead, she rose from the chair and covered her face. "I'm sorry, Dex."

His hand dropped. He couldn't go after her; the ship's autopilot couldn't manage the path through the storm. He was stuck there, unable to make it right.

Their destination closed in on them, and Lacy couldn't talk to him.

* * *

Dex brought the ship down to a small patch of flat land within the crags of a mountain range that curved around the valley of the north pole. The entire sky was a deep red. Clouds, dust, and mist all drifted on the wind toward the pole, where a great crimson beam emerged and shot skyward. Scattered throughout the valley were buildings. Not buildings like the ancient pyramidal skyscrapers, these were more modern. The buildings in the valley looked like factories and warehouses. There was even a paved airfield with Zar-Meck starfighters and saucer-shaped imperial transport ships looking brand new.

But there was no movement across any of it. Still, Lacy thought she was beginning to pick up on stronger signs of life.

Dex and Lacy exited the *Silent Horizon* and perched on a cliffside. They only had one pair of binoculars, and Dex took the first watch. Lacy had very little interest in reconnoitering.

"Those are imperial, all right. They look hot off the line." He scanned along the buildings. The lights were on inside, but still no movement. No Zar-Mecks posted as guards on rooftops, no groundcars circling the base, not a sound except the constant hum of the beam.

"Wait a sec, I've got movement. My God... Lacy, look." Dex pushed the binoculars her way. "Right there, see?"

She did see.

Like a raging inferno of emptiness, a man burning with Black Fire stood on a dais from which the beam originated. His arms were outstretched toward the heavens as if in prayer.

"He's already here," Lacy said. "If he's already here..."

"Why isn't he coming after us? Surely he can sense you."

Although it was unintentional, his wording twisted her gut with a sense of guilt. Romek wasn't after *them*; he was after *her*. Arguably, the only reason Romek would want to get to Dex was as a means to find Lacy. Each time he attacked, Lacy had been his target.

"I don't know," was all Lacy could think to say, but then she added, "Maybe he's waiting for me."

Dex rolled onto his side to look at her. "What?"

Lacy kept the binoculars pressed close to her eyes. "If he's here now, it's because he knew we were coming. We went to the station to find this planet. He knew we weren't running from the Empire anymore. And if we're coming to this planet at all, like all things, we'd find ourselves here. Where the beam leads us."

He watched her closely, studying the way her eyelids scrunched. "Lacy, whatever you're thinking, stop it. We have a plan. Let's not mess with it."

At that, she lowered the binoculars. "What plan, Dex? Where's the Cathedral?"

Dex sputtered out sounds in protest, unsure what to make of her question. "W- I- I mean... Lacy, what cathedral? Were you really looking for a church in all of this? It's a broadcast station. Look over there. Radio antennas. That's probably what we're looking for. A military radio station. Hundred bucks says if we were to investigate that building, we'd find video playbacks of all of these things you think you've been seeing, including a church."

"It's not a church, Dex, I know what I saw." She had some bite in her words. But still, what he said made sense. What she needed now was a moment to think without him interjecting. Every part of her was fighting against the truth Dex spoke. She wanted so desperately to hold on to the visions she saw, as terrifying as they were. After everything she'd witnessed standing in the Emperor's court, and all the visions since, her connection with Nova, for it all to be built on the machinations of, not a supremely powerful, but supremely intelligent being, it was too much back-and-forth to take.

Lacy rolled onto her back and looked up at the crimson, storm-covered sky.

Lightning illuminated the planet, but they were thankfully well out of the path of the rain. Through a brief parting of clouds before the storm took over again, Lacy could see a sliver of clear night sky.

"I don't remember the last time we saw sunrise," she said. "All that time in the jungle. We still barely saw the sun."

"I remember the last time," Dex said, inching closer to Lacy's side and looking up toward the sky with her. "I could never forget it. You were wearing the green dress, picnic basket in hand." The sun's rays breaking over the rim of the Earth from the Grand Central Space Station observation deck shone so brightly in their memory, Lacy had to shield her eyes. Echoing his words then, he asked, "You don't think we wasted it, do you?"

"No time with you was ever a waste of time," Lacy said. "Especially not that night."

"Think we had a good run while it lasted?"

All in all, Lacy was glad that if she had to be assigned to this mission with anyone, regardless of the outcome, she was still glad it was with Dex. "I think it couldn't have been more of an adventure."

Dex propped himself up and looked across the valley, down toward the beam and the Emperor's assassin, still swaying in prayer. "Well then..." he said with growing bravado in his voice.

Lacy continued for him, "On to the next?"

He took her hand in his. "Whatever awaits us on the other side, just promise you'll be there with me."

She turned over and fixed herself into a kneeling position. "The Emperor couldn't keep us apart before. I'd like to see him try now."

Dex actually laughed at her remark. "I wouldn't. But, what the hell. Let's see what he's got in store as a last resort. It's time for one more adventure."

As if on cue, Romek's voice echoed through the

valley. "The God Emperor of the Void calls to you, human! There is no more running! It is time!"

Dex smirked and called back, too quiet for Romek to hear, "Yeah, yeah, keep your shirt on, we're coming." Then to Lacy, "Come here. Might as well get 'em in while I can." He pulled her face close and embraced her. The taste of her lips was still the only taste he ever needed in his life. That, as long as he could still taste her lips after their final strike, was the only heaven he thought he needed.

When she pulled away, Lacy told him, "I will meet Romek. You come in behind me with the ship, but there's something I want you to do first."

The idea of leaving the two of them alone was less than appealing, but if it was the end, it was the end. Technically, the ship was faster than Romek's sword arm.

* * *

As soon as he dropped Lacy off at the edge of the base, Dex regretted agreeing to her plan. Even before she was out of sight, he wanted to tear his heart from his chest. What if his timing wasn't perfect and he missed his window? Regardless of how long his life lasted afterward, could he live with himself?

Dex shook the thoughts from his mind and told himself it didn't matter. He *would* make the window. That's why he dropped her off so far away, so that he had time to catch up afterward.

Once Lacy was clear of the ship, Dex picked up again and flew the short distance to the airfield and came in close to one of the transports as Lacy directed. He'd seen them before in their escape from the Heart of the Void, but Lacy was the one who spent time on them. She knew exactly where to look for his objective. At least, with nothing left to lose, Dex had an assistant again.

Dex set the *Silent Horizon* to run on low power. Before leaving, he grabbed two things. The first was a data stick with certain files downloaded. This was the worst part of the mission Lacy had given him. The download speed was far too slow for comfort. But even he couldn't deny the necessity. Once that was completed, he secured that and Robbie's body from the back of the ship and took them both across the airfield and into one of the imperial transports.

Navigating the perfectly white walls of the ship was almost as much of a nightmare as the rest of the planet. Everything about the imperial military design was curated specifically for Zar-Mecks and officers with their data tablets. Although Dex had brought Lacy's imperial data tablet, Dex hadn't been able to find the contact lenses that made the screen's display visible. Without them, Dex wouldn't have been able to read the alien text or interpret their maps. He was going in blind, navigating the ship on faith alone.

Shaking the dead robot under his arm, Dex muttered, "If you've got any juice left in you, now's the time to use it."

Robbie didn't answer.

Dex pressed the tablet against any and everything that looked like a doorway. When first boarding, he kept expecting to find imperials hiding just out of view to ambush him. But the further along he went in the ship, the less it concerned him. There really was nobody on the planet except for the three of them. It came to the point where it was less eerie and more annoying. Even if there were imperials and they were blasting at him, Dex thought that there were slight odds that he could smooth-talk his way into getting directions from them.

But, as it were, luck was not on his side in the way he expected.

With his time running out to meet Lacy's rendezvous, Dex pressed the tablet against the doors harder and harder until he was practically slamming them. And on what seemed like his fifth lap around the ship, the right door finally opened. He came into a room that had the appearance of the space station diner's kitchen, though much more clean and bright white. And on the floor, frozen mid-task with a tray of food in its hand, was a robot identical to Robbie.

"Thank God," Dex muttered under his breath.

He put his own robot down on the floor, then waved his hand in front of the half-dome head of the ash black imperial service robot.

"May I help you?" the robot asked, jumping to attention so quickly the food almost fell off the tray.

Dex cursed, using a word Lacy had constantly told him not to use around Robbie, but not in surprise. He had hoped the robots were all turned off. Taking the battery from a live one would feel almost cruel.

"It's an imp," Dex told himself, and didn't speak anymore. Before the robot could fight back, Dex pulled the tray from its claws and pushed the robot on its back.

The small thing flailed its arms and called out with its speakers at full volume, "I am being attacked! Could somebody please give me assistance!"

But Dex was the only person around to hear. And the act felt cruel, so all he could offer in return was, "I'm really sorry about this! But my wife asked me to do it!" He pulled open the robot's chest-piece and saw its battery pack glowing brightly. How this tiny thing had a nuclear reactor stored in it, Dex had no idea. But there was no time to question, only time to act and get back to Lacy.

He disconnected the battery as carefully as he could with the service robot's arms flailing about.

"Excuse me! Excuse me! Excuse me!" the robot protested.

The manners made it all the worse for Dex, so that he forced himself to close himself off to the act, and yanked the battery from the robot's chest.

The service robot's arms froze in mid-air, and the room went quiet.

Dex told himself again that he was doing it all for a good reason, salvaged the other components he needed from the one robot to repair the other, then turned and reinstalled all of it in Robbie's chest. This time, he was much more delicate with all of the disconnecting of his old battery and reinstallation of the new one. Even with the ticking clock, for this one act, Dex took his time.

When it was fully in and connected, the reactor slowly illuminated, signaling a good connection.

Dex closed Robbie's chest plate and pushed himself back along the floor.

"Robbie?" he asked. "You there?"

Robbie made no sounds, but lights flashed on his half-dome head. One of his antennas twitched, and after a moment, he raised his arms high into the air like Frankenstein's monster and lifted himself up.

"I... I'm *Alive!*" Robbie screamed so loud his speakers crackled.

Dex huffed in relief. "You damn robot," he laughed. "That's it? I bring you back from the dead, and your first thought is to quote a movie?"

Robbie dropped his arms and cocked his half-dome head to the side. "I did? Oh, I did, didn't I? Did I?" His memory bank from recent days felt a bit fuzzy, but it was slowly coming back to him.

Dex ran a hand through his hair. "It doesn't matter. You will soon. Here," he pulled the data stick from his pocket and held it out to Robbie.

Robbie took it delicately in his claw and held it close to his dome. "What is it?"

"It's a data stick."

Robbie lowered his claw. "I know that. What's on it?"

Dex laughed again through a knot in his chest. Robbie was back only now, at the end. "We shouldn't have taught you attitude," he said. "What's on it, Robbie, is the *Silent Horizon*'s catalogue. All of our movies, books, and music. Movies especially. Lacy wanted you to have the music, but I made sure the movies got on there first just in case I ran out of time."

Robbie raised the data stick again. "Why? I can watch all of those on the ship."

"No, not anymore… buddy."

"Why not?" Robbie popped open his chest plate and put the data stick inside himself, then closed the plate again.

"Robbie…" Dex rubbed his chin, thinking about how best to tell the robot their plan. "I'm sorry. I wish Lacy were here now, too. But we're leaving. And where we're going, we can't take you with us."

Robbie looked around the kitchen. "Where is Lacy now? Why can't I come?" His wiry legs began to shake. "Where is Lacy? Dex… Dex, where is she?" Robbie's half-dome head shot around the room in all directions. "Why can't I come?" He stepped gingerly closer toward Dex and tapped his claw tips against each other like a nervous child. "Why are you giving me the movies?"

Dex almost fell back as Robbie pressed himself into his stomach. Robbie's half-dome head nuzzled against Dex's abdomen.

"Robbie, I don't know how else to say this. We can't always be with you; Lacy and I. We were never going to be there forever. But you can take those, everything on that data stick, listen to those songs, watch those movies, and always have a piece of us with you. Hear those songs and dance to them like Lacy's dancing with you. Watch those movies and think of those times we cheered together for Clark Gable and Errol Flynn, okay? We won't be here forever, but these songs and these movies are ways to remember each other. We remember not through memory alone, but through reminders of why we loved someone. That's what these are. Reminders."

Grease spilled from the bottom of Robbie's dome. "But I don't want reminders. I want you and Lacy."

Dex wrapped his arms around the robot. Time was running out, and he had to get back to the ship. But he knew Lacy would understand if he was just a little late. "I'm sorry, Robbie. But that's the best I can do." He tried to pull away then, but Robbie extended his arms around Dex and wouldn't let go.

"Not yet," Robbie pleaded. "If I can't say goodbye to Lacy, let me say goodbye to you twice."

Dex raised his head so Robbie wouldn't see the tears he was holding back.

"Robbie, part of this is carrying on. You don't have to let us go, but don't dwell, either. I did this so you could have a life again. Now listen, I want you to take one of these ships and go far away from here. Maybe you'll find Earth one day and you can tell them what happened. But no matter what, you are free. You can go wherever you want and you have all the movies you could ever want to watch. If I were your age, I'd call that living the dream. That would make Lacy and I happy, if you enjoyed your life. So please, can you do that for us? Just enjoy your life, Robbie."

Robbie stomped backward slowly. "If that would make Lacy happy. I do what makes me happy from now on?"

"Only that," Dex agreed. "Only what makes Robbie happy, forget what anyone else wants."

Robbie's speakers simulated a deep breath in, followed by an equally deep exhale. "Okay. I will do what makes me happy." Robbie held out his claw for a parting goodbye handshake.

"I'm proud of you, little buddy. You're not the robot I once knew." Dex laughed to himself. "If I ever had a kid, I'd... I'd want them to be just like you."

Dex reached out and took Robbie by the claw and pulled him in for one last hug. "Oh, I'll miss you, Robbie."

"I know." His voice simulated stress through the speakers as if Dex were crushing him. In fact, Dex may have actually dented parts of Robbie's shell.

Without much further damage, Dex put Robbie back down and then stood. He'd said enough goodbyes, so all he did then was give Robbie a polite nod and left the kitchen.

The door closed between them, and Robbie found himself back where he began. Like the first day he was turned on, Robbie was alone in a kitchen aboard an imperial transport ship. But unlike last time, he knew what he wanted for himself. He knew what path would make him happy.

Robbie popped open his chest plate again and plugged the data stick into his main memory bank. A whole host of media files scrolled across his vision. "Frankenstein" popped up, and he immediately cast it aside, now remembering with certainty he had watched it, and began scrolling away for more options, at the memory of how terrifying it was. But following that, another memory came to mind. He was surrounded by the other Mok Tau children and pestering Dex to let them watch something scary. The movie itself was terrifying, but there was a certain joy in Dex's face when they selected it. Dex knew what all the kids were getting into, and he let it happen. It was harmless fun, safe terror. Watching the movie, Robbie had thought about showing it to another unsuspecting Mok Tau kid and passing on the scares. It was the same as all the rest of the movies they'd watched together. When Dex let Robbie watch a movie he loved, Robbie couldn't wait to tell the other kids about it, especially if it was one Lacy didn't want them to see.

Robbie could have sat there for hours, days, years, rewatching all of his favorite movies and thinking of the good memories associated with them. But at the end of the day, that wouldn't have made him truly happy. What would, as he quickly processed, would be acting out the movies. They served their purpose to be reminders, as Dex had said, but at the end of the day, they were not the answer.

The movies picked him up when he was down and showed him the way forward. In the movies he loved watching with Dex, the heroes in them didn't sit down and watch other movies. The heroes in them acted on what they believed in, for the ones they loved.

Robbie would be the same, no matter the cost.

He closed out the screen of movie files and opened the music files.

An orchestra swelled throughout the imperial transport ship.

* * *

The sound of the *Silent Horizon* flying away from Lacy and toward the landing field was quickly muffled out by the storms and overall heaviness of the air. She only watched Dex fly away for the first few seconds before forcing herself to step off toward the beam and the Emperor's assassin.

With every step, she felt more and more hints of life. The aura Romek emanated was the strongest, but the rest of it lingered in the air as fragments, like ash floating on the breeze. Life had existed once in the small motes around her, and tiny remnants of it still remained.

What had this world looked like before the Emperor destroyed it? Had it ever been beautiful? Was this a place the ancient inhabitants had come to solely to escape the empire, or was it a world they chose to come to for its beauty and promise?

Lacy rounded a corner now, coming onto a wide road with a clear view of the beam. From her distance, Lacy thought she could see Romek kneeling. And scattered nearby him, things like worms swayed to and fro.

The connection between herself and Romek was undeniable. She felt as if she could reach out and touch his burning flesh, even though there was still a thousand feet between them.

Does he not notice me? Or does he no longer care?

The blaster was holstered at her side, but Lacy felt no need to draw it.

She began to walk again and finally, without turning around, Romek spoke again in a voice that bled humble righteousness. The Black Fire, The Emperor's Wrath, did not see himself as a hero or find glory in his victory. He was a knight serving his crown and kept none of the prize for himself. "The God Emperor of the Void has called you, human. He has waited long enough to bring you home."

Still, Lacy did not draw the blaster; she only drew closer.

Romek picked himself up from his knees and turned to face her, a haunting vision of the terror who had massacred the village on Taranok.

Romek was the Void. All of his features had been seared through his face and body, so there was nothing left except the darkness and the black flames that burned around him. He stepped down from the dais and came to a spot between two of the worms. His arms outstretched as if welcoming Lacy into an embrace, he said, "He is glad you have come here. He is glad you have seen his power with your own eyes before living as his."

Lacy came upon the first worm in her path. Up close, she could better see its texture and that it wasn't a worm at all. The creature had shallow outlines of eyes, a nose, and a mouth, pulled tightly against its face. At its side and on its chest, arms were postured in reverence, but they were so thin and withered, like its face, that they looked almost nonexistent. And below, its lower half was fused with the ground on which the creature sat. But it was the horn, a little stub of one where a chin should have been, that gave away what the creature once was. After a dreadful eternity, the remaining Children of the Void of Mascoadon had devolved and become like worms in constant prayer at the beam, an Altar to the Emperor.

The worms showed no acknowledgement of Lacy or Romek. Their praying never ceased.

"Where is your army, assassin?" Lacy demanded, courage holding strong in her voice.

"I did..." he began, pausing to listen to Lacy's mind. "...what you have been too afraid to even dream of. You have tasted the potential of the Emperor's gift, His power, but you refuse to embrace it. I did not know what it was about you that the Emperor craved so dearly. I did not know why I could not capture you. Why you were able to wield this great power all on your own.

"I wandered, human. For weeks I wandered the depths of that planet, my body weak and decaying. I fed constantly, but it was never enough sustenance to restore my body. How this power drained me. But there were moments that I looked inward and could sense that you, too, would dip your mind into the well of the God Emperor's might. In those moments, I saw through your eyes. I saw into your heart and your mind. And what I saw fueled my rage. It pushed me to climb from the bowels of that planet, to feed on greater and greater beings. I saw how you were bringing ruin to the Emperor's name, turning people away from his glory, and my mission became twofold.

"Before I captured and returned you to Him, I had to bring back his people. And there was joy in the bloodshed. Human, there is an ecstasy in this power. To enter the minds of the unworthy, to twist or consume the sinner. To strike fear at the deniers. I lust for, and revel in the opportunities to spread fear of the Emperor. And I am grateful, too, for the revelation that the non-believer is not enough. I am grateful that you and the Emperor have brought me to this world, where the dregs of His army have been in waiting for a higher purpose. You and I are that purpose. Their sacrifice has made my mission complete, now that you are here with me.

"I am grateful for the gift we share, but it burns bright, and it burns quickly. I must feed... constantly."

Lacy glanced around, still anticipating imperial forces to leap from their hiding spots and ambush her.

"They are no longer here," Romek continued. "The men stationed on this world have all served the Emperor's greater purpose. Their sacrifice at my hand, so that I may succeed in my mission, was one that was made willingly."

An entire military base, a small fleet worth of lives. How many had he consumed in waiting for her arrival,

Lacy questioned in horror. There was no sign of struggle around the base. No blood on the walls or the ground. Every operation had ceased all at once as men lined up before Romek to feed his power.

Now, Lacy did draw the blaster.

Romek sprang at her, closing twenty feet of distance in the blink of an eye, and held her gun hand. It was he who pulled the trigger, but felt no pain as the bolt cut through him.

He spoke softly, his voice coddling her like a child, "Return with me to the Emperor and be free of this tangible pain. Embrace a holy one."

Lacy began to recoil, falling back slowly. Her hand went cold in his grip as he drained the life from her.

On the brink of death, Romek let go, and Lacy fell to the ground.

"Amidst all of your fighting against Him," Romek said, "the Emperor still wants you by his side."

Lacy rolled away and began to crawl toward the Altar, feeling as lowly as one of the worms.

Romek paced alongside her. He looked up at the Altar and the beam. "It is beautiful. The weaker ones of the Empire fear this world. But they should see what you and I see now. A doorway to his world, he has told me. This is what holds the universe together." Romek raised his arms to behold the beam, then looked down again at Lacy.

She threw one arm onto the first step of the dais with her left hand clenched tightly.

A cruel laugh escaped the flames of Romek's face. "I know you wish to see it, and you will. I promise. But this is not a doorway for you or me to use. We are not worthy. Not yet." He knelt down beside her. "That is where our dreams go. Beyond the Altar is the Cathedral. I envy that you will see it before I do. But one day, when the Emperor calls me to rest, you and I will meet again. And we will worship Him together."

Lacy reached the top of the dais and ceased her

crawling. She could see at the very base of the beam, behind a raging flow of red energy, an ancient table. An altar.

"That is where the Bishops are?" Lacy asked.

"Indeed. Just beyond the Altar. Through the Veil of Worlds, you will find the Cathedral and all of the Emperor's Bishops."

Almost under her breath, Lacy asked, "That is how the Emperor will use me to control humanity?"

Romek scoffed. "That is how humanity will receive the gift that is the Emperor's control."

Now it was Lacy's turn to laugh. Lifting her left hand, she asked into her fist, "Got that, darling?"

The response was weak and slightly crackled, but Dex's voice echoed through the comms device. *"That's all the target confirmation I needed. I love you, Lacy."*

The flames dimmed around Romek, and behind them, fearful eyes widened.

Romek spun around and saw a bright silver ship careening toward them. Before he could act, Lacy's hand fell on his leg, and she pulled from him every ounce of energy she could.

Lacy called back into the comm, rapidly being filled with life, "I love you, too, Dex. From one end of the universe..."

"To the next," Dex's voice finished through the comm.

"Guppy kisses." She puffed up her cheeks and raspberried out, and heard in return the same from Dex.

But this wasn't how Romek could let it end. Although quickly draining, he continued to fight back, and the human's apparent victory was cut short. With the last of his strength, Romek came down on Lacy and lifted her up. She didn't realize what was happening until it was too late.

* * *

Dex sabotaged the engine just as Lacy had told him

to. Enough that it would still run, but broken just the right way so that it blow big enough to wipe out the entire base. For their final act, Dex was glad she took the time over their last few weeks on Taranok to get to know the hyperdrive engine Hwaq the mechanic had installed.

He powered up the ship and heard the engine rattle just right. Or just wrong. "Oh yeah," he said to himself. "That'll do nicely."

Dex took a long exhale and steadied his hands on the controls. This was it.

The *Silent Horizon* rose off the ground and held at a hover. The comm line was open to receive Lacy's signal. Every moment that passed was hell until he heard her voice again. Anything could be happening at that moment, but in his heart, he knew she was still alive, and that was good enough.

After far too long, a voice finally came through.

"I know you wish to see it, and you will. I promise..." Romek droned on. That was his cue to get in position.

Dex steered the ship away from the airfield and toward a position with a clear line of sight to the target.

"Here we go," Dex told himself.

"Here we go," Robbie echoed from the co-pilot seat.

Dex didn't believe his ears, but he jerked his head and saw the robot sitting next to him, with his claws holding onto his feet.

"Robbie?" Dex shouted. "What the hell are you doing?"

Robbie turned and looked up at him like there wasn't a thing wrong in the world. "Doing what makes me happy. I'm spending time with my family."

Dex cursed, but Lacy's voice through the comm cut him off. "That is where the Bishops are?"

"Damn!" There wouldn't be time to land and put Robbie down. "Damn it, Robbie! I wanted you to have a life!"

"But I had one," he said, not taking his eyes off of

Dex. "It was a good one."

Lacy's voice again, "That is how the Emperor will use me to control humanity?"

Dex heard Romek scoff, then say, "That is how humanity will receive the gift that is the Emperor's control."

Almost immediately, Lacy's tone changed, and she addressed him, "*Got that, darling?*"

Dex pressed the ship forward toward the beam and called back through the comms. "That's all the target confirmation I needed. I love you, Lacy." Then to Robbie, "God damn it..." He couldn't stay mad, though. "At least I've still got family with me, right?"

"Right," Robbie agreed.

Lacy sent one final message through the comms, "*I love you too, Dex. From one end of the universe...*"

"To the next," Dex finished for her.

"*Guppy kisses,*" came the last words.

Dex reciprocated it, and though she never heard it, Robbie sent her one too, to the best of his mechanical abilities.

The beam came up quickly in front of them, and the more Dex pushed the ship, the more the unstable engine rattled. The crash would destroy the Altar, as Romek had called it, and close off the cerebral connections the Emperor had throughout his Empire.

But in those terminal moments, Romek picked Lacy up off the ground, and Dex saw him rush her toward the beam.

Robbie propped himself up on the command console, and Dex shouted, "No, no, no!"

In an instant, Romek carried Lacy to the beam, and with a brilliant flash of light, they both disappeared into it.

With only a hundred feet between them and quickly closing, Dex pulled up on the controls to avoid collision. But he didn't miss the beam.

Light flashed again, and the universe ceased to exist.

48. Gods of the Void

Dex awoke in a field of brilliant green grass. All around him were the sounds of gently running water and soft, sweet-smelling wind. He opened his eyes to the world of a sky so vibrant blue, and light so bright, but there was no sun, nor clouds above him for it to hide behind. The clouds and the trees, and all the *real* color, Dex saw, were further beyond by the hills that looked miles away, but unbelievably clear. He'd never seen air so clear before.

Dex felt that the intensity of the light should have been blinding him, but if anything it was soothing; just warm enough on his skin.

He propped himself up on his forearms, taking in the soft brush of the grass on his body. It felt like running barefoot through the lawn after a summer day spent in the pool, without the annoyance of the grass sticking between your toes. He paused and looked around this odd scene. There was a sharp distinction in the saturation between the field he lay in and the hilly area beyond. The field embodied peace, but not quite as much beauty as the hills radiated. There was an emptiness where he sat. Not a lonely emptiness or a wrongness to it, just... a sense of being not quite *there* yet.

If not for the sight of the beautiful hills, Dex would not have minded the simplicity of the field. But seeing the beauty of what was just within walking distance, he craved it.

Dex rose to his feet, feeling a pull toward the hills coming from his chest, and his legs began to move of their own volition. Then, from somewhere that felt like everywhere, all around him, a familiar and kind but stern voice said, "Not quite yet, Dex Prullen."

Dex halted, turned, and saw someone nearby he had not noticed before.

An old woman sat in a lawn chair under a birch tree he had not noticed before, by a rivulet he did not notice before. The rivulet only ran for a few feet, and seemed to fade in and out of the land. In front of the woman was an easel with a canvas with the first few strokes of a painting she was working on, and with her other arm she held something close to her chest.

"I know your voice," Dex thought out loud.

"All do," she said with some humor. "And I'm glad you recognize it when you hear it. Too many hear it and ignore it, or pretend they don't hear it altogether."

Dex looked back at the hills, feeling the craving to walk toward them and see what was beyond.

"Not quite yet," the woman repeated. "Come. Sit with me."

His feet moved again, this time toward the woman, and his head slowly turned to match the direction. The hills could wait for now.

Dex sat in the grass by the woman and looked up at the canvas. In it, he saw the wood of the birch and a line of blue cutting across the lower third. Small branches began to break off of it, even when the woman's paintbrush wasn't on the canvas.

"I love painting," the woman said so casually. "Sometimes I'll start a new piece just for fun, but every time I do, I find that it quickly becomes a responsibility." She dabbed her brush on a blotch of paint in her palette that looked like it had run dry ages ago. But when the brush made contact with the canvas, color was transferred with ease, and excess paint even dribbled down along one of the blue branches. "You quickly learn that you don't have the control over the piece that you thought you did. Whatever is meant to be on the canvas will be there eventually. All you can do is guide it, and hope it comes out right."

Dex watched her paint. The first few strokes of the brush seemed random, and small drops fell from her brush onto unintended places, or excess would continue to run down the canvas, cutting new paths of the blue lines. But the woman didn't seem to mind.

"Why are you telling me this?" he asked.

Whatever it was that the woman held to her chest, moved.

The woman sighed patiently, then said, "Because I know it's been on your mind a lot."

Dex looked from her, back to the canvas. "I can't say I've ever been one for painting before."

"Yes," she laughed. "Too much freedom involved."

On the surface, her remark sounded like an insult, but he knew it was true. Much of the popular art he could remember from Earth at the time he left was becoming too "modern," all about the idea of, "well, what do *you* think it means?" Dex was fine with simple imagery and a clearly depicted scene, or at least if he could see an objective level of skill involved in the creation of it.

The woman continued, "Even the most talented painter will struggle to get their piece to turn out exactly the way they want it to. Because the artist loves their work, they know that the life they're creating is not their own. And it *is* a life, Dex."

The image on the canvas was beginning to take form. The blue lines were no longer just that, but flowing rivers around a birch tree. And all around him, Dex saw that the small rivulet had grown and cut through the grass around where they sat.

"What is this place?" he asked, his voice picking up. "I've seen it before. I've heard you before. You said my name. How do you know my name?"

Without pausing her work on the canvas, the woman said, "Of course I know your name. I know you *by* name. My eyes saw your unformed body, and all your days were written in my book before one of them came to be."

Dex knew those words. Joy and fear rose in his heart. "How is this possible?"

The woman continued, "And not just your name." She put the paintbrush down and carefully leaned in toward Dex.

Dex wept when he saw what she held.

In the woman's arms was a baby. And although she was small, looking not fully developed, a small heartbeat pressed against her thin chest, and Dex knew her face.

"Nova?"

The woman held Nova safely in her arms. "I know her name, too. And I will keep her in my arms now."

Anger began to take over the joy in him. Dex wanted to rip Nova from the woman's arms, but something held him back. "Why did you let this happen? Why didn't you save her? Lacy begged! Or was that your plan all along?"

"I did not raise the blade that pierced her," The woman admonished.

"But you could have stopped him! If you're so powerful, you could have ended all of this before anyone got hurt!" Dex's eyes darted from the woman to Nova. There was pity in the woman's eyes that Dex couldn't deny. He was angry at her, but when she spoke, he knew her words were honest. Yet that did little to quell his anger.

And in her arms, Nova had changed. She was a little bigger. Her head was a little more grown in and her flesh was less translucent. Her fingers and toes were more formed, curled tightly into balls.

"Tell me, Dex. Who were you fighting that brought you here?"

"All knowing and *you're* the one asking?" Dex began to rise but the woman held up a patient hand. He stopped and thought of Nova, then lowered again to a knee and tried to compose himself.

"Humor me, please," the woman said. "Tell me about him."

Dex spat through his teeth, "He's a cruel god, like you."

"How is he cruel?"

"He's... he's a tyrant. He has complete control over the lives of his people."

"Complete control?" the woman asked, feigning intrigue in her voice. "His people must be living in constant fear of him, then."

Dex wanted to agree for the sake of proving a point, but he couldn't. He caught himself just before he spoke and said, "No. They don't. They don't argue it."

"Really? But then, who are you to say he is cruel if his people love him? Totally, it would seem. Is there a single person who fell out of line?"

Dex knew she already knew the answer. "There was one."

"And where is he now?"

"Dead," Dex replied.

"I see," the woman said, sitting back in her chair. "So, other than the one who strayed, everything seems fine. Why fight him?"

The anger in Dex's heart turned to confusion. "What do you mean? What is it with these questions? Do you really not know the evil this man has done?"

"Man?" The woman laughed. "This Emperor is no man."

This time, Dex did rise to his feet, though he had no intention of acting in anger. "He is *just* a man."

"Dex," the woman sighed. "In this one instance, I will be forthright. The devil does hold certain power, far beyond that of man. Even as you speak to me now, you still deny our existence?"

"So, you are-"

The woman cut him off. "I am."

Again, Dex fell to his knees.

Again, Nova had grown. She almost looked like the baby Dex had imagined meeting when the time came, hopefully far away from the fighting.

"Why do you know better than all of the Emperor's people about his misdeeds?" The woman asked as if the previous exchange had never happened.

"Because my eyes are open," Dex told her. "I do not live blindly under him and have seen the truth. The lives these people think they live are a lie which can be cut short whenever the Emperor says it is so. And they cannot see it until it is too late. If he has true power, he abuses it, twisting the minds of his people to know only what he wants them to know, and do only what he wants them to do."

"And that is your definition of a cruel god?"

Dex nodded. "It is. That is not the god I would want to follow."

The woman laughed again, this time, big enough for Nova to shake. Dex almost jumped forward to hold her, but the woman said, "Don't worry, she's safe now."

"What's so funny?"

"You, Dex Prullen. It always brings me joy watching people finally understand."

"Understand what?" he asked, constantly checking on Nova. Small strands of black hair had grown from her head. Her cheeks were a healthy pink, and her tiny lips a bright red. She had a nose just like her mother's. Maybe it was because of a dream she was having, but her lips curled up the slightest bit into her first smile.

But the woman took Dex's attention back. "Does your father love you?"

His eyes shot up to hers. "What?"

"I know, it feels like a strange question, but please. I promise it matters."

Dex swallowed, then, "Of course he loved me."

"Then why are you here?"

"Be- because... I'm sorry, I don't know why that-"

The woman cut him off again. "How many times since you left Earth have you been shot at, stabbed, or broken bones? How many times were you inches away from death?"

"Too many times to count, but-"

"Your father must not have loved you then."

Dex's eyes hardened. "Who are *you* to-"

The woman's intensity became suddenly greater than Dex's, eliciting both fear and awe in him. "I Am," she said, silencing Dex's outburst.

He took a moment to compose himself, then said, "My father loved me more than anyone. He knew there was a chance I wouldn't come home, but he trusted me."

"And that is a loving parent?" The woman's voice returned to one of sympathy and understanding. "Even though he knew you would stumble and hurt, even though he knew he may never see you again or that you would be lost, he let you make your own choices?"

At her question, Dex began to doubt himself. His father had loved him, there was no doubt, and still Dex walked away from home into dangerous waters. Now he began to feel shame. Even though his father had accepted his leave, had doing so still been a form of betrayal?

"If you were never to return and fall victim to the hells of the Emperor, who then was to blame? Your father for giving you that freedom, or yourself for fleeing safety? And if you returned home again, do you think there would be a banquet or penalty for your transgressions?"

Before he could respond with a half-hearted defense for the sake of his pride, the woman said, "Let me put it another way. Lacy. You love her, yes? No, never mind you don't have to answer that," she laughed. "I can hear in your heart the way it beats when I say her name. You clearly do love her. Suppose the two of you were not assigned to be partners for your expedition, or that she did not *wish* to be your partner. Would it have been a loving thing to steal her away into your ship and fly off?"

Dex was disgusted at the thought. "Of course not!"

"Why not?"

"*Because* I love her. I was heartbroken when I first saw her because for a moment I thought, what if we don't end up together? I always thought that I would die without her next to me, and I still do every time her hand isn't in mine!" He held up his empty hand to emphasize his point. Where was Lacy, anyway? Dex quickly looked around for a sign, but assumed it was part of this woman's game. "But because I love her, I wouldn't force anything on her. It's love, and respect, and faith that she will love me back."

"And even if she hadn't wanted to join you on this ship?"

"Then I would still love her. I would be broken without her, but I would still love her."

The woman smiled. "Do you see it now, Dex?"

"See what?" Dex threw his head back in frustration, and when he came back down, Nova was no longer in the woman's arms. Panicked, he spun around, searching all over for her. "Nova? Nova!" When he turned back toward the woman, a girl in a little green dress, like one similar to the dress the Mok Tau had made for Lacy, sat on the woman's lap. She was maybe two years old and didn't show any awareness of Dex.

Still, the woman acted as if nothing had happened. "Truly loving someone is accepting risk. When you love someone, a parent, a child, or the person whose heart was made to beat alongside yours, it becomes your job to limit yourself for their betterment. You may have the power to shackle them and put them in a hole somewhere where no danger will ever find them, but that is not allowing them to live. That is not love.

"They may not give you the love in return that you had hoped for, but then there comes also humility. Always offer yourself, but do not force them into your arms."

Dex's eyes were locked on Nova's puffy cheeks. She picked up the paintbrush from the palette and laughed as she made random strokes of purple paint across the canvas. Dex wanted to be a parent and tell her not to mess up the woman's painting, but the woman only laughed.

"It's all right," she said. "These things happen. And

now all we have to do is work around it and figure out how this can all work together on the canvas. As long as you always keep an eye out for the bigger picture, even though there will be little slip ups and distractions along the way, everything may still come out the way it is intended."

Dex watched as the woman continued to let Nova spread the paint wildly across the scene.

"But what happens if the damage is too great?" he asked. "What if they... what if they slip away and I never see her again?" He wanted desperately to reach out and take Nova into his arms.

"Ha!" the woman laughed, almost teasing Dex. "I thought you said you weren't blind. Nova is here before you now, and still you worry it is the end?"

"Isn't it? Isn't this..."

"Heaven? No, not yet anyway."

"I'm not dead? But the ship crashed." For the first time, the *Silent Horizon* and Robbie came to mind. They were nowhere to be seen.

"Crashed?" the woman asked, looking all around half-heartedly. "I didn't hear a crash."

"But, I saw it."

"I can assure you, Dex, your ship and your friend are just fine. Robbie is a little confused at the moment, but he will be all right."

"So, where are we, then?"

"Almost Heaven," she said. "The Veil of Worlds is a doorway that was not supposed to be. But those who pass through go where they are meant to be, if it is their time to be there. Like you, soon enough, she will be spat back out."

"Where is Lacy, then? She came through, too."

"Yes, she passed through. But a part of her did not belong, and the greedy power of the Emperor held sway. She is in his world now, but fear not..." The woman closed her eyes and fell deep in thought. "She is on the right path. Now, I can feel in your heart that we have come to an understanding. And very soon, your wife will need a way back through the Veil." She rose, and Nova was no longer in her lap.

"Wait!" Dex jumped to his feet, searching for Nova. The area was now completely surrounded by trees of all kinds, some birch, some with purple wood or leaves, and rivulets cut through the ground everywhere. "Can't I hold her before I go?"

Still seated in her chair, the woman pursed her lips, but quickly let them fall into a grin. "In time, you will be with your daughter again. And when you find yourself in the valley beyond those hills," she pointed her paintbrush to the beautiful distance, "no evil will ever come to the three of you again. But I suppose that for now," she paused, "a few minutes won't hurt."

A hand fell on Dex's. He looked down and saw small fingers tightening around his. The most beautiful girl, maybe three years old, stared up at him with her mother's eyes. So much of her resembled Lacy, but her hair and her ears were his.

His voice caught in his throat. Dex was in complete shock and didn't know how to feel. So, Nova did what he was too stunned to do, and came around his front, throwing her arms around him.

She spoke in a voice that Dex had thought he'd never hear, and one he'd never forget. "I love you, daddy."

Dex held her so tightly he thought she might break, but Nova was strong. Just as strong as she had pictured her parents.

"I love you too, Nova," he said, kissing her forehead.

Dex couldn't tell how long they held each other for. It could have been an eternity, or only a minute. However long it was, it was as long as he needed.

When they let go of each other, Nova was a little older and had begun to look like her own person. Hints of Dex and Lacy showed on her face, but the rest of her was Nova Prullen. This time she didn't speak, and she didn't have to. Dex knew there would be all the time in the world later on to catch up.

From all around him, the voice of the woman said, "It's time to get your wife, and keep up the fight."

The light of the world intensified until everything was outshone. Everything except Nova's smile.

* * *

The world Lacy came into was less than welcoming.

Romek led the way through a canyon that dug deep into the crimson world. The leathery ground of Mascoadon had been replaced by brittle objects like sticks. Lacy had to keep her head down to avoid the gaze of great beings that protruded from the canyon walls. They were built like stone, but all turned their heads together to follow these new inhabitants of the world.

Romek's flame had burned out entirely. He once again looked like a man, though slightly emaciated, and his Zar-Meck armor, what remained of it, was fused to his body. And though he held himself in a way that exuded confidence, Lacy sensed fear in his heart.

The world was wrong. Everything about it was steeped in evil.

The faces of the canyon were like those of the Bishops; eyes of dread.

Creatures moved along the walls, crawling like a poison. Lacy turned to spy one of them. It moved like a spider on thin arms and legs, and it turned a white head with a blood red spot in place of a face toward her.

Lacy recoiled from the creature, and it scurried away into the cavern wall.

This part of the world she had never seen in her visions, and she asked Romek if he had either.

"I have seen only what the Emperor wished me to see," he said.

Lacy harrumphed. "And this doesn't make you question him? Doesn't really seem like the ideal paradise."

"It is not our place to question." Romek's voice seethed with venom, and the dark eyes he cast back at her matched his tongue's vitriol. Even as they were standing in the Emperor's realm, Romek was bitterly amazed at the Earth woman's heresy.

Something ran across the canyon floor behind them. Lacy spun around to see what it was, but just missed it as it buried itself in a hole somewhere. She could do that, too, Lacy thought. Romek was doing nothing to stop her from running away and hiding in a hole until the man withered away. But where was there for her to go except where he was heading?

To the Cathedral.

To see the Bishops.

Lacy blocked all of the monsters from her mind and focused on what was ahead. She thought of Dex and whether or not he was able to pull up in time and avoid the crash, or if he, too, were somewhere in this nightmare world. In her heart, she had faith he was all right, no matter what had happened.

Their path sloped up and eventually brought them out of the canyon to a flat plain. A little off in the distance ahead of them was a single tree. The two of them walked toward it, and Lacy had developed a hope that there would be fruit on it, only realizing when she got a glimpse of the tree how hungry she was.

But when they came up to the tree, she saw that there was – or, had been once – fruit like a fig, though it was rotten and oozed a rank blackness.

Romek plucked one of the fruits from the tree and didn't hesitate to eat of it. The fruit fell apart like sand in his mouth, and even the ooze dried up when it met his lips. But Romek forced himself to swallow what he could. And when he was finished, though his face was strained and his body tight with pain, he thanked the Emperor for the scraps that he was given.

After the tree, there was only desert for miles.

Lacy had nothing to say to Romek, and Romek seemed to have lost all interest in Lacy. In his mind, he had succeeded in his mission. It may not have been in the way he meant to, but the human woman was in the Emperor's domain. And when the Bishops had her, they could turn her into one of their own.

Throughout their journey, the sky never changed. It was a constant crimson with no sun to give her the time of day. That is, if there even was day and night in this world. If it truly were a universe of its own, it may not be a planet, and no space around it. The sky and clouds continued upward forever, and the ground below their feet descended just as eternally. And ahead of them and behind, just an endless expanse of desert, on and on for infinity.

And through it all, Lacy refused to let her legs tire. She would push on for as long as she had to. She felt a need, just as Romek did, to reach the Cathedral. Even if his body did finally give up and wither away, becoming one with the dead landscape, she would stand before the Bishops.

The Cathedral did eventually come into view. Its high towers grew out of the horizon and rose toward the sky with sharp turrets and jagged edges. As they drew closer, Lacy could make out the texture of the building, one she'd seen in her dreams far too many times before. The Cathedral, like the canyon, like the tree, like the ground under their feet, was held together with the remains of all the souls the Emperor had devoured. Bones made up the window frames and statues that decorated the Cathedral. Screaming skulls and splayed fingers lined the corners. Every inch of the building was a piece of a life stolen, and faith betrayed. Some of them moved as if with the wind, eyes and jaws widening with the air blowing through them like screams.

Romek bowed his head before the great doors and the hollow eye sockets of the long dead of his race.

Lacy looked up, trying to see and acknowledge every single face.

"It is time," Romek said, and reached out for a large knocker on the Cathedral doors.

Although the material was not metal, it rang throughout the world as if it were.

Romek stepped back, and the doors opened for them.

The sight of the room beyond sent a wave of horror through Lacy she fought hard to suppress. The Great Hall of the Cathedral was nearly identical to the Emperor's throne room, except there was no endless black pit in the ground, but an endless black void above them. And though the Emperor was not there with them, his Bishops were in all of their deathly regale.

The first glimpse of them was like staring through the window of a dream. The Bishops towered over her as they had before in the Emperor's presence, yet seeing them now, the very real memory felt like someone else's déjà vu had crept into her mind. And even with the great beings before her, her mind struggled to grapple with the reality of their existence. They were all of them warped; proportions twisted and mutilated, with exaggerated bone structure and sunken in eyes under dark lids, yet they had an air of heavenly perfection to them, aided by the scarlet robes and rust-colored jewels they wore, and the great crowns of sharp and crooked bones atop their heads. There had once been a time when Lacy had been dressed to resemble the Bishops as she was being prepared for sacrifice to the Emperor. She knew then that the ritual would force her to undergo a transformation, but seeing the horror in its own realm was of no comparison to what she could have ever believed before.

One of the Bishops came forward before all the rest. What characteristics remained of the race it had once been resembled the Children of the Void, and Lacy knew in her heart that this was the first and oldest of the Bishops.

The eyes it cast down on her were all too familiar.

"Come, woman," it said with an ancient drawl. "Let us welcome you to your place among us."

Lacy took off her helmet, holding it under her arm,

and looked down at the way she was dressed. She didn't have all the jewelry, or the crown, or the body paint the alien Rassmenda had covered her with, but she wore the right colors; the red P.E.S. suit. She looked back up and took in the faces of the other Bishops. One other she recognized. It had frog-like features in its wide face and long arms. Then, returning her attention to the Child of the Void, she said, "I did not come here to join you."

Lacy expected the court to gasp or react in shock, but they all remained neutral.

"There is no use fighting," the Bishop said. "Many of us had tried at one time or another. But in the end, the Emperor consumes all."

Romek stood to the side. His body continued to crumble in on itself, but he watched eagerly, waiting for Lacy's transformation. He knew that when it was complete, the Emperor would reward him.

"He will not consume me," Lacy said defiantly. "I am here to tell you that there is another way. You don't have to serve him. The Emperor is a false god!"

Romek almost jumped forward to strike Lacy for her blasphemy, but the power of the Bishop's voice held him still.

"Do you think we are unaware?" the Bishop bit back. "See where you stand."

Lacy looked again at the skulls that made up the walls. Even without faces, she could see the terror in their eyes. In their final moments as the Emperor consumed them, they had seen the horrible truth.

The Bishop went on. "I once led my people with the hope of finding sanctuary. We found a planet far away from the Heart of the Void, and for a time we flourished."

His words brought her back to the mural she and Dex had found, and the man it depicted. The one whom the planet was named after, Mascoadon.

"But the Emperor does not relinquish his power so easily," the Bishop, Mascoadon, went on. "He made an example of me, one that tore open the Veil of Worlds, and turned me into this, then scourged my home. Yes, I have seen it. The planet was once young and beautiful. Now it is a home for his creatures, a breeding pit he uses to collect them and spread his terror throughout the universe. And it is not the last planet this will happen to. But, for that," he pointed an ancient finger at Lacy, "you will have to take the blame."

Lacy fell a step back, "Me?"

Mascoadon moved aside so the frog-like Bishop could take his place. This one spoke with a feminine voice, but the hate was the same. "Because you have turned my people away from the Emperor, he is summoning his might again to scourge Taranok."

The Bishop cast her hand outward and down to her side, and a haze appeared in the air. Shapes took form in darkness, and Lacy could see the abandoned space station. "Already, as you have seen, beginning with those who have had contact with you, the Emperor is feeding in excess, so that through me he can release his power on the planet and wipe it from history." The image in the haze shifted to a green world: Taranok and its moons. "His forces have been withdrawn in preparation for his scourging. And after that is complete, his soulless ground forces will sweep the planet before the suits they wear fully eat away at them and become one again with the evil the Emperor has brought into your world."

The haze shifted once more, showing Lacy a vision of Taranok that looked like the corrupted landscape of Mascoadon. Zar-Mecks marched through it, killing any native who had managed to survive the Emperor's attack, and when that was completed, they morphed as the kron-kaal did, melting into the ground, leaving behind nothing but mere nothingness.

"Never will anyone remember my people," the Bishop said, holding back the clear pain in her ancient voice. "Except for me, they will never have existed."

"You... you cannot let that happen!" Lacy protested.

"There is no fighting it," Mascoadon said. "Bishop Tullup is right. Taranok will fall. So will all who turn from the Emperor. All... except yours."

Romek perked up. This was information he had never heard, and he doubted it as it did not come from the Emperor himself.

"Mine?" Lacy asked. "What is so special about Earth?"

"Nothing," Tullup said. "It is not your Earth he wants."

"It is your light," Mascodan added.

"What light?"

Mascoadon seemed to grow, filling the room, and as he did, the scene shifted. The Cathedral fell away, and Lacy saw between herself and the Bishop a vision, a brilliant ethereal light.

"The Emperor's resentment of my people came from this light. He found us, thinking that we were the source of it. But he was wrong. This light, a piece of the All, resides in another creature. One made in the All's image."

The light took form, and in it, Lacy saw every human face that had ever existed, and ever would exist.

"It's us..." she breathed.

The Cathedral returned, and the light faded.

Mascoadon went on. "The Emperor has been searching for you for his entire existence. His fleet has been amassed. From across his territory, forces are being drawn together to prepare for invasion. All he requires now is you. With you in his court, he will know where to find your planet. He will bring your race into his Empire, but not to live as the rest of his people. You will be cattle for him so that he may grow in his power and one day spread across every universe, and conquer the All."

Their theories for the retreat of Torro-Kaal that gave them an advantage on that first assault were confirmed. The cargo ship they had been on that was destined for Taranok. It was loaded with second hand equipment and delivered to the imperial base, and would be taking back the higher quality equipment. Even the fact that it was being delivered via a commercial cargo liner instead of a military vessel. She and Dex only lucked out finding and freeing Taranok because the Emperor was winding up his arm to deliver a larger blow somewhere else. How many worlds like Taranok were there that the Emperor was pulling from? How many worlds of unquestionable loyalty that he could afford to centralize his army for a single, swift blow to the human race? She and Dex had dangerously misjudged the Emperor's forces. With the element of surprise and even numbers, they had scored victories here and there. But now she could see the larger picture, a map in the warroom of intergalactic conflict. The might of a monolith of unyielding terror spanning greater space than a galaxy, against a scattering of human tribes spread across a single solar system. If Earth were to be found, there would be no war. There wouldn't even be a battle. Only immediate annihilation.

"Glory be to the Emperor," Romek stepped in with his hands clasped at his forehead.

The Bishops all turned to him with reserved anger, and he quickly shied away.

Lacy rushed to comprehend all she was hearing. "But... but you can't let that happen!"

"Why not?" Mascoadon asked, almost annoyed with her continued resistance. "He has already won. You are already here."

"But he hasn't won! Not yet!" Lacy raised her arm and scanned a finger across the host of Bishops. "All of you have been complacent. I know the power you hold, I have felt it, too! The Emperor's power runs through my veins, through his!" She jeered at Romek. "The Emperor has convinced you that he has complete control over you, but it is a lie! It's *fear* he has over you. But even that is not real."

Mascoadon protested, "As long as we hold this power, we will not die. When the Emperor eventually destroys our worlds, we shall remain."

"Can't you see that you are already dead? At the very least, this existence cannot be called life! What is the purpose of holding onto this power? All you do with it is bring pain!"

"And what have you done with yours, Earth woman?" Tullup interjected.

"Not enough, but I can do more."

Mascoadon laughed in a mocking tone. "We all have thought that, too. But by now you have surely seen that the more your power grows, the closer you are to him."

Lacy opened her mouth to argue, but she glanced over toward Romek in the corner and knew they were right. Maybe it wasn't in the same way, but like him, the brighter she burned with the Emperor's power, the closer he came to her.

"I can use it for good," Lacy said, wishing she had seen it sooner. The Mok Tau could have been united when Romek attacked their village. But instead, because she was too afraid to wield her power, the people scattered. Lives were lost because she did nothing to unite them. And now there was no changing what had happened.

Tullup jeered back at her, "Can you? The people of Taranok will never know."

Again, Mascoadon spoke. "You may intend to use the Emperor's power for good, but in the end, it is still the Emperor's power. Never can that truly be used against him." He stepped to the side, and the other Bishops behind him parted. On a mantle in the center of the Great Hall, a crown began to take shape.

"It is time," Mascoadon said. "Give up this fight."

Lacy looked from the crown, to the Bishops, and then to Romek. He was huddled in the corner. His face was so sallow he could almost blend in with the wall.

Turning back to the Bishops, she said, "If the power truly is of the Emperor, then no matter how great it is, I want none of it." She turned and walked toward Romek, then knelt in front of him.

"Without it, you will soon die, Earth woman," Mascoadon boomed. "And if it is not you holding the power, there will be another."

Her arm was extended out toward Romek, but she stopped at Mascoadon's threat and looked back over her shoulder at him. "Then let your Emperor come and find us. Earth will be ready for him." With that, she touched Romek's cheek and relinquished every trace of the Emperor from herself into him.

It was a boulder on her chest she didn't know was there, but once gone, she breathed again and already felt like she was fading from the world.

Romek breathed in new life, and he rose to his full height. His mind was fogged over, but he would quickly understand what had happened.

The Bishops, though, paid him no heed.

"You truly do have the light in you," Mascoadon said. Never before had he or any of the other Bishops witnessed such an act of merciful defiance. Countless ages had passed by them with only a signluar route for them to navigate, their vision blocked from everything not leading back to the Emperor.

Lacy got to her feet, feeling like she could fly away from all of the dread surrounding her. Death was no longer her fate.

"I have faith," she said. "Faith that the Emperor can be defeated. And I have faith that you will not let your people suffer any longer under him."

She backed away the first few steps, then turned, done with the Emperor's court, and pushed the Cathedral doors open. In her vision, the sky was already less cruel.

But from behind her, Romek shouted out, "Halt! In the name of the God Emperor of the Void, halt!"

Halfway through the doorway, Lacy stopped and turned again to see the man she had had mercy on. He burned brightly once more with the Emperor's flame and had his sword drawn.

"The Emperor *will* have his prize," he said.

Lacy turned to look beyond him at the Bishops. They were all discussing something she could not hear until Mascoadon silenced the rest and approached Lacy and Romek.

Towering high above them, Mascoadon reached out in front of Romek with fingers as long as the assassin's body, and traced them over him. It was a light touch, but the flesh slid from his bones. Romek did not scream or show any signs of pain, but his eyes rolled back and his mouth hung open. The sword dropped from his hand, and with less than a gust of wind, all that remained of Romek turned to dust and drifted away.

"You have given us much to think about, Earth woman," Mascoadon said, pulling his skeletal hand back from where Romek once stood. "Although we see your endeavor as one in vain, we wish you luck."

Lacy bowed her head in reverence. Their souls were tortured and would not easily break from their servitude. But... she had her faith in them.

The Cathedral doors shut, closing her off from the bishops. Already the memory of what was on the other side began to fade into the shape of a bad dream. It would always be remembered somewhere in the recesses of her mind, but never again could the visions haunt her. Overhead, storm clouds gathered. Lightning flashed across the sky, and down came the rain.

Lacy stood and let it fall on her. Things would only be harder now, but a voice in her heart, one far more soothing than the Emperor's, told her she'd done right. She hadn't been able to save Nova with the Emperor's power, but without it, she could save others.

The blood rain hit her face, but it wasn't warm or thick as she had anticipated.

Lacy opened her eyes and saw red above her, but looking down at her hands, she saw that the moment it touched her skin, it turned clear and was only water.

The Emperor could no longer touch her.

In front of her, the world opened up. Like a crack of lightning holding steady, the Veil waited for her, and Lacy ran to it.

49. The Return

The *Silent Horizon* careened through the Veil of Worlds. Dex found himself as if he'd woken from a dream, right back in the pilot's seat with Robbie's speakers crackling as he screamed.

Seeing Dex again, Robbie jumped from the co-pilot seat and grabbed Dex with both claws. He shouted at Dex, "Where were you?"

How to answer that one? Dex asked himself. "I, uh, I'll fill you in when we find Lacy."

Through the viewport, Dex couldn't tell if they were covering any distance, but the vibration of the ship and the pull in his stomach told him that they *were* moving. They were moving very fast.

And as he said her name, there was a loud *BANG!* in the back of the cabin as if an old fashioned propulsion-based gun had gone off, and a bright light that came and went.

Both Dex and Robbie turned around to see what it was, and Lacy stood there, soaking wet.

"Lacy!" Dex shouted.

"Robbie!" Lacy shouted back.

Dex rushed from his seat to take her in his arms, and Robbie hopped onto the controls. Just because they couldn't see anything didn't mean there wasn't anything out there to crash into.

Dex pulled her in close and said, "I have something amazing to tell you." But before he did, he could hardly restrain himself from kissing her.

Lacy could barely reciprocate. She was so overcome with joy that she couldn't help but smile as he kissed her, and his lips met her teeth.

"Dex!" she cried. "Dex, I have so much to tell you, too!"

He pulled back, her cheeks in his hands. Dex saw Nova's nose again on her face, and her eyes...

"Lacy, your eyes!"

She raised a hand to her face. "What about them?"

"They're yours."

The stars had left her eyes. Once again, as before she had encountered the Emperor, her eyes were normal and blue. Human. Although, Dex would never describe them as normal. To him, they were still the most beautiful eyes he had ever seen, save for his daughter's.

Still at the controls, Robbie called for Dex to "Please take back the controls! My system is very overstimulated right now!"

Dex and Lacy both laughed and jumped back to their seats.

"You brought him with you?" Lacy asked, a little angered, but mostly glad to see him again.

"He followed me," Dex told her. "I told him not to come, but he's very stubborn. I wonder who he gets it from." He reached out and brushed her cheek. Oh, how he loved how soft it was.

Lacy rubbed Robbie's half-dome head with a smile. "I think that could be either of us sometimes."

Ahead of them, a sliver of red appeared, and they all three knew their exit was coming up.

"Before we're out of this completely," Dex began. "Whatever happened to you, think it'll all work out?"

She reached out and took his hand. "I know it will."

"Good. Me too."

The sliver grew, and their hands tightened. They'd all been given a second chance and knew better than to waste it. Still, it was scary, and Robbie pulled himself up onto Lacy's lap for comfort, but they were all doing it together as a family.

"Wait!" Robbie shouted, reaching out to pull back on the controls.

Lacy held him back, and Dex shouted back, "What? What's wrong!"

Speaking as if it were the most critical thing in the universe, Robbie cried, "Lacy hasn't put any music on for this!"

Dex held his tongue and forced a smile from his reddening face.

Lacy could only laugh. She had just the song.

She only had seconds, but was quick to find "The Firebird Suite," skipped to the finale, and pressed play.

Only a few notes in, though, the *Silent Horizon's* computer went haywire.

"What the hell is going on?" Dex exclaimed, pressing one button after the next. Lacy pressed the command console for a diagnosis, but the closer they got to the portal, the more the ship fought back.

"It's all right, it's okay," Lacy said, trying to remain calm. "It's just interference. It'll be fine! We just have to push through!"

"Let's hope!" Dex and Robbie said in unison.

Dex charged the ship full speed ahead, and they broke through the Veil into an electrical storm.

Red light burned their vision. Blood splattered on the viewport and streamed off slowly to reveal a wall of blue and green. The *Silent Horizon's* radar hit the fritz.

"We're on top of something!" Lacy shouted, reaching for the controls to break their speed.

Dex did the same, diverting as much power as the ship would give to their forward thrusters. The unstable engine rattled like all hell in the rear. Wherever they had dropped back into the universe must have been right in front of a massive rock they couldn't even see.

"Some damn wipers on this thing would have been nice!"

"It's a planet!" Lacy exclaimed, half excited, half nervous, but totally ignoring his comment. "I'm picking up atmosphere."

"Great, but can you do something about the view?"

Lacy scanned the computer looking for options. "Here, this should do it." She pressed a button and a white light scanned across the viewport, clearing every last drop of blood and smudge of dirt so it looked fresh off the assembly line.

With a clear sight of the planet in front of them, neither spoke, only stared with wide eyes.

They knew the blue waters of the planet ahead, and the green and brown of the land, shapes that any kid in elementary school could identify. And it had never looked so clear, even when they'd last left it.

"Lacy... it's-"

"Earth."

Robbie pulled himself up onto the console to get a better view and looked out the viewport with them. "Is this home now?"

Dex huffed out a small laugh. "It looks like it, buddy."

"I can't believe it," Lacy whispered to herself.

Dex took her hand and banked to port. "You'd better, darling. We're back."

But how could they be? Just like that they were all the way on the other side of the mapped universe, passing through the entire imperial territory in the blink of an eye, without notice. It just couldn't be.

Lacy double checked, then triple checked, the navigational display. It didn't make any sense. She said, "Dex, the ship's still registering Mascoadon's coordinates."

"I don't know what to tell you, darling. That *is* Earth!" He almost shouted back, barely able to contain his excitement. And on visuals alone, it was an uncanny resemblance. At the very least, there was no way the blue waters and green valleys below could be mistaken for the scorched wasteland that was the Emperor's shadow planet.

"Where are you going?" Lacy asked, standing up from her seat to maintain a view of the planet below as Dex pitched the *Silent Horizon* into a gentle descent toward the surface.

"Docking. Grand Central must be orbiting on the other side of the planet. I'm not seeing it in the skies around here."

Lacy, leaning forward herself, looked around like the giant space station was a set of keys she'd misplaced on the kitchen counter. She then turned back to the computer, and checked the radar readings.

"Dex..." her voice threatened to shake. "Dex, I don't see the station. Or any."

"What are you talking about?" he peered down at the screen. She was right, there was only one dot on the scanner. Only Earth.

"That can't be right." His voice remained confident. But after a lap around the planet, there was still no sign of the station.

Lacy took a deep breath and slowly exhaled, "Dex, I don't like this. This isn't Earth, it can't be."

Dex only gave a slight nod, agreeing that something was wrong, though unsure if her guess was the right one, then activated their radio to call in to the station. *They've developed a cloaking device while we were away,* he told himself, knowing it was a lie.

"This is Captain Dex Prullen of the *Silent Horizon* calling Grand Central Station. Do you read me?"

They waited in unnerving silence for a response that wasn't coming.

Dex tried again. "I say again, this is Captain Dex and Lieutenant Lacy Prullen of the *Silent Horizon* calling Grand Central Station." Then to Lacy, he said, "Scan the airwaves for activity. They may be on a different frequency."

The computer scanned through open frequencies, picking up nothing but static and faint, incomprehensible signals. After another lap around the planet with no responses, Dex guided the ship deeper into the atmosphere. As they descended and flew west over the Atlantic, Lacy shot out a hand at a voice coming over the radio.

"Th-....G-..nd.....r-.....ta-.... I-...........u....."

Dex called back over the radio, "Say again. I am attempting to contact Grand Central Station. Do you read me?"

The voice came through again, a little more clearly. "T-is is....rnd...entr-l....stion. How.......you g-.....line?"

Cresting over the horizon, Dex and Lacy were able to spot the tops of buildings, though not of any familiar skyline.

Unseen by Dex, Lacy shook her head.

"We need a place to land," Dex said into the radio. "Is there a port available at the Station?"

This time when the voice on the radio came over, it was much stronger, and held much more confusion. "Port at the station? Say, who do you think you are, wise guy?"

Dex and Lacy exchanged an unnerved look as more of the skyline came into view, and a familiar green woman held a torch high to guide them in. But that was all they recognized. Lacy felt the need to ask Dex what was going on, but his face told her he had no reasonable guesses. New York City was undeniably below them, but there was no Empire State or Chrysler building, no identifiable landmarks; like they'd been plucked from the streets and vanished.

The voice on the radio again. "This is Grand Central Station. How did you get this frequency? This will have to be-" The voice was cut off and interrupted by another.

"Hey Jim, you gotta see this!"

"Not now, Tony. I ain't got time for your foolin'."

"I ain't foolin' around this time, look! It's a goddamn Martian craft!"

The line cut out, and the *Silent Horizon* filled with static.

Saying "something's wrong" wouldn't do any good now.

Dex banked the ship to port and shot for somewhere familiar and open.

"Where are you going?"

He didn't answer. The ship flew over the Brooklyn Bridge and descended onto the grass of Fort Hamilton. Down below, soldiers on foot and in vehicles rushed to surround the craft with weapons held high. But they weren't the laser rifles grunts were regularly issued, and the uniforms they wore all looked vintage, like they landed in the middle of a war reenactment. For that matter, what kind of Jeeps were these?

"These are your Earth friends?" Robbie asked, not taking in the wrongness of their situation.

"No, Robbie," Lacy said, holding him close to her chest. "We don't know these people."

"Well, we may as well introduce ourselves," Dex returned.

The *Silent Horizon* touched down, sending a wave of shudders through the crowd of soldiers. The landing gear creaked as it supported the weight of a very damaged ship. The entrance they were making was in no way a pretty one.

Dex powered down the ship, and the soldiers took a step closer, their rifles ready to fire.

"What are you doing?" Lacy held onto Dex's arm as he stood from his seat.

"Going to say hello. Come on."

"Dex, I don't think-"

"We should," he interjected. Then, pointing to Robbie, "*He* shouldn't. Not yet. But us, definitely. It's not like we have any other options."

The robot dropped off Lacy's lap and looked up at Dex. "I'll stay. Those people don't seem very friendly."

"No, they don't," Dex agreed. He pulled his arm away from Lacy's hand and took it in his own. He then said, consolation and confidence in his voice, "Come on. It'll be okay."

She was slow to get to her feet, clutching her aching abdomen and staring out the viewport as she did. One of the soldiers, an officer, Major or Colonel most likely, was standing atop one of the jeeps, shouting into a megaphone.

Dex held out a hand for her, seeing the pain in her rising. She took it and they walked toward the airlock door together.

The muffled voice of the soldier dimmed a little bit with each step they took away from it, yet its presence became more known to them. All it would take to end their "Welcome Home" party early was one scared private with an itchy trigger finger.

With a *hisssss,* the airlock opened and silenced the shouting officer. And although neither Dex nor Lacy could hear it, they felt the weight of dozens of rifles being held a little higher, gripped a little tighter. They could almost smell the lead of the bullets ready to tear through them.

Dex and Lacy's hands gripped tighter together. Who initiated it was a question for the universe. They took slow, deliberate steps down the back of the *Silent Horizon,* careful not to cause alarm among the soldiers.

Seeing human faces emerge from the spacecraft did nothing to settle the crowd. Upon the reveal of the visitors from the stars, eyes widened and murmurs grew. Dex slowly raised his hand to wave 'hello,' and from next to the officer with the megaphone, a camera snapped a photo that would promptly be developed and confiscated.

Off to the side, just outside the perimeter of the fort, civilians were rushing to the fence with more cameras. Another troop of soldiers rushed to get between them and the fence. Shouting came from both parties. Cameras flashed and cameras were smashed.

Dex and Lacy took another step closer, scanning the crowds. There was no denying that this wasn't the world they had left behind. They didn't know any of these people, these faces. That wasn't Major Haxley with the megaphone praising them for a successful mission. It was an angry man with a star on his helmet. This wasn't-

"Dex, what's wrong?" Lacy whispered as he froze, locking eyes with one of the soldiers. She caught where he was looking, and after a moment, her heart almost stopped as well.

There was one face they recognized all too well. Dex at first thought he was looking through a warped mirror. There were features similar to his, a face he knew better than any other, with his own eyes, nose, and ears, but off just slightly. And the build he knew, too, but it wasn't what it should have been. Something in the soldier's eyes recognized Dex, too.

"Identify yourselves!" The voice of the general shouted again through the megaphone. "What are your intentions with our planet? Where do you come from?"

They had answers for every question the officer continued to rattle off, but none of them were as important as the question of the Soldier standing before them.

Once the words came out, Dex and Lacy knew it was true; where they were, what had happened to Earth, to them, and who the man was. Dex recalled an offhanded comment he'd made to Lacy just before the start of their adventure with Empire; *time worked differently in space*. And passing through the Veil of Worlds, anything and everything was up for speculation.

The theory that had been growing in his mind since they touched down was confirmed as Dex breathed with fear and exhilaration, "Dad?"

Acknowledgements

This book was my hardest project to date. And except in terms of the sheer scope of story that I have planned for the further Empire books, I think this will remain the hardest story I ever write. I said in the acknowledgements of the previous book that I "enjoyed (almost) every minute" of working on it. This one had many late nights of prayer, and many tough conversations with family and friends about the events that take place in this book. It was difficult hearing their stories at times and trying to convey what they went through in a respectful way. I hope I did right by everyone with this story, and comfort was found reading it, no matter what you've been through, or where you are in life.

First and foremost, as always, I thank God for the gifts He's given me and my family. It's through His blessings, and the inspiration His Word has had on me that not just this story, but all of Valenza Publishing is possible. I often find myself straying in the types of stories I want to tell or the content involved in that, but through prayer and scripture, I am put back on the right path, and the work I do is something I can be proud to put my name on.

Thank you to the fans! The best part of this career is getting to meet you all at signing events and festivals. I love getting selfies with you all, and getting questions about the stories and where it'll go from here. The Empire Marathon is always shifting in style and tone, and you put a lot of faith in me to keep these stories unique and entertaining. I hope I do right by all of you!

Thank you to my author friends, Kiersten Marcil and Jade Nioma. If you haven't read their books, Nioma's

"Fate's Tether" and "Fate's Favor," and Marcil's "Witness to the Revolution", they better be the books you're picking up after you close this one. Jade, you came into this career at about the same time, and I'm so thankful we've stayed good friends and have been able to prop each other up. Also, I can't believe I didn't give you any creds in the last book! I'll be sure to add you in in the second edition. Kiersten, at every festival I go to, the first thing I look for is whether or not you'll be there, and then, if we're next to each other. If we are, I always know it's going to be a fantastic day. I'm so glad you don't hate me anymore, and I'll never stop thanking you for the tablecloths!

Thank you to J.T. McGee. You've been there from the beginning. This book feels especially important to thank you for, as you got me started on being passionate about reading with the Dark Tower series. The nods to that should be apparent in this book. But also, thank you for all the long car rides to signing events around the state, and the creative and emotional input that came from those conversations. To many more years of success and creativity, my friend!

Thank you to Dr. Stephen Hull, my editor. We joke that you are my "white board." After spending two hours on the phone complaining that I don't know where to go with the story or I'm not confident in my notes, you will speak for maybe 5% of that time. But you provide so much more than you give yourself credit for.

Thank you to my Aunt Patsy and Uncle Bob. It is because of their faith, and a dinner I will never forget while visiting them, that I returned to Christ. Uncle Bob, there is almost no one more vocal in their support for these books as you. At every family gathering, someone will come up to me and say, "Uncle Bob is raving about your books again to someone." You act like my team and I are celebrities and it is so incredibly validating to the work we do. Aunt Patsy, you shaped how I approached this book more than anyone else. The entire time I outlined, wrote, and edited, I felt like I was walking the thinnest tightrope over the highest heights.

I have been so terrified that there would be one sentence out of line and the entire book would therefore do a disservice to what incredible women like you have had to endure. You have reassured me every step of the way and given me the confidence I needed to put this story into words.

Thank you to my Mom, my sister, Camille, and sister-in-law, Anna. It is obvious that I am not a mother, nor will I ever be. And since Lexi and I haven't experienced the joy of parenthood yet, you were all my first resources for the happier parts of Lacy's story. I know a lot of the questions I asked and texts I sent felt very strange or random at times, but thank you so much for your candidness. Through your testimonies, I hope that Lacy's story is able to honor mothers everywhere.

To my Dad, thank you as always for the movies.

This next part, I'm so excited for.

Thank you to my **WIFE**, Lexi. That's the first time in this series I get to call her that. So much of this book was written in the months leading up to my deployment to the Middle East. Time was scarce as it was, and we had to take advantage of as much as we could. Every moment was precious. Yet, you still had patience with me, and tolerated my long, long nights and the smell of cigars. I love you THHIIIIIIIIIIIIIIIIIS much.

About the author

Andrew Valenza is an Author, veteran, and newspaper editor from upstate N.Y. He published his first novel, "Empire of the Void," in June of 2023 and soon after founded Valenza Publishing.

He is a major movie collector, much to the chagrin of his wallet. But hopefully his love of film  and storytelling made this book more enjoyable for you. Thank you for reading!

Please leave a review on Amazon or Goodreads!

Follow us on social media!

Andrew Valenza
@avcollecting - Instagram/TikTok

Valenza Publishing
www.valenzapublishing.com
@valenzapublishing - Instagram/Facebook/Threads

And support indie authors by checking out these
incredible books!

"Fate's Tether" by Jade Nioma

"The Chosen" by J.M. Gokey

"Witness to the Revolution" by Kiersten Marcil